THE WAINwRIGHT SOLUTION

Ronnie Wright
© 2023

Whilst this book is inspired by actual events, the characters, conversations and correspondence depicted are completely fictitious.

Accommodation providers on the Coast-to-Coast are excepted from the above in acknowledgement of their hospitality.

"Actions have consequences. Ignorance about the nature of those actions does not free a person from responsibility for the consequences".

Stephen Dobyns
–American author

For my wonderful and wise friends.
Sorry it took me so long . . .

Chapter	Page

Summer 2015

"Ok, Mr McKay. You are now being formally charged with the offence and a report will be sent to the Procurator Fiscal. You do not have to say anything but anything you do say may be used as evidence. Do you understand?"

I nodded, adding, "I'm sorry, I've never been in any sort of trouble like this before. Would you mind explaining what happens now?"

"Of course. So, we will shortly drive you back to your vehicle and you can be on your way. In the next few days, you will receive a notification to come back to Inverness to appear in court where they will set a date for a trial. You will need to get yourself a lawyer."

Again I nodded in acknowledgement of the explanation.

As I sat in silence, stunned with numbness, staring at the floor in front of me, I struggled to assimilate the extraordinary events of the last few hours. A joyful day was ending, so unnecessarily, in an abominable mess and I was scared by thoughts of the potential ramifications for all aspects of my life. The full far-reaching ramifications would remain hidden from me for several years.

December 2020

That sound like knocking coming from downstairs but probably just in my head.
That vibrating sound coming from the bedside table next to me, again just part of the hangover.
My head.
The pain engulfing my entire cranium.
The darkness.
Is it morning, lunchtime, afternoon, evening?
Did we actually beat Rangers last night or did I dream it?
Not sure, but I wish my head would get rid of the knocking and vibrating sounds.

That other pain is also lurking, the constant dull throbbing across the chest that refuses to go away and sends signals via my brain that I don't want to eat, sleep or concentrate on anything other than trying to avoid throwing up. The latter ailment can be temporarily dissipated with assistance from copious amounts of alcohol . . . and the vicious circle recurs.
I reach for the phone on the bedside cabinet to ascertain whether I'm in diurnal or nocturnal mode and it's vibrating with the lit-up display indicating an incoming call.
"Shit! Number One is at the door."

I donned my dressing gown whilst simultaneously trying to negotiate my descent of the stairs in a hasty but gingerly way that probably looked none too clever. I opened the front door and felt an air of frustration brush past me into the living room.
"Fuck's sake Dad!"
My 22-year-old daughter's lack of renown for swearing in front of her parent suggested an unsubtle hint of discord.
"I told you I would come over this morning, Dad. It's almost eleven. Hungover again?" she rhetorically asked with an exasperated expression.
As I glanced downward like a chastised child, she continued in a milder tone, "Dad, I know it's hard and I know you're struggling but you know you can't go on like this"

"It's ok. I'm on leave just now. I'll be fine when I go back to work," I offered in mitigation.

"You know it's not ok though Dad", came the swift reply from my fellow resident of Aberdeen, "You'll need to start living in this flat at some point whether you like it or not, preferably sooner rather than later. You need to find a strategy, a coping mechanism, something to focus on."

I entered the kitchen and flicked on the kettle.

"And I will, darlin'. Just going to get Christmas and New Year out of the way and I will sort myself out."

General conversation developed concerning that potential required strategy as I breakfasted on tea and paracetamol.

"What about that 'Coast to Coast' walk thing down in England you've talked about?", she asked and continued, "That would be a big thing to plan and focus on and there's nothing stopping you now that you're single again with the new year in front of you."

I paused and cast an inquisitive glance at the eldest of my three offspring, a glance that gently morphed into a resigned smirk, "Yeah, cheers darlin'".

Number One reciprocated with an apologetic snicker, "Sorry, Dad." Despite her inadvertent reminder of my recent and sudden change of status, the wise medical student sat opposite was correct. The shock and disbelief on just how swiftly and unexpectedly my life had changed was monopolizing my thoughts, but I would have to start looking ahead, facing up to whatever the future held. I had undertaken long-distance hikes in the past but never on my own. Perhaps a new type of challenge lay ahead, and I would investigate the possibility.

May 2021 - Day Zero – Aberdeen to St Bees

I sat on the sofa with a pre-departure cup of tea, looking out at the strong winds and heavy rain. Not the sort of weather hoped for on a late May Friday morning in Aberdeen but at least the forecasts for my weekend destinations were more favourable. Number One was dropping me off at the train station prior to commandeering my car for a fortnight. Those contemplative moments prior to departure, double checking the list, trying to ensure everything is packed but in no doubt there will be something I've forgotten.

A tingling sense of anticipation accompanied me on my way through the train station to board a train destined for London Kings Cross, albeit we would be parting company at Edinburgh Waverley. The sense of emotion and embarkation ahead of my adventure was temporarily curtailed when the conductor advised that due to flooding on the line near Stonehaven, some ballast had been displaced and the tracks would require to be checked. With the requisite checks complete, the train lurched out of the station, 35 minutes later than scheduled. We were off.

The rain rapidly assembled on the windows as the train sped through the countryside. It appeared to be that driving unforgiving type of rain, the kind that could gnaw away at even the most resilient waterproof clothing and have its persistence rewarded with infiltration onto skin, unless of course the resilient waterproof clothing was far in excess of my budget. It was hoped, but not expected, to be the last time I saw such rain over my impending two-week adventure or indeed none at all.

Wainwright's 'Coast-to-Coast' takes its name from the renowned Lake District fell-walker, writer and illustrator Alfred Wainwright. He originally described the walk in his 1973 book "A Coast-to-Coast Walk". The book has since been revised a number of times with updates to the recommended route and an up-to-date copy had been acquired together with a proper mapped guide.

The walk spans the north of England from the village of St Bees on England's north-west coast to the village of Robin Hood's Bay, 192 miles away on the east coast. En route, three national parks are traversed, The Lake District, The Yorkshire Dales and The North York Moors. I remembered seeing parts of a six-episode documentary about the route presented by Julia Bradbury back in 2009 and thinking what an adventure it would be.

On-line blogs of coast-to-coasters suggested that the 'two-week holiday' was the most common way of walking the trail. However, Wainwright explicitly stated that he did not intend people to necessarily stick to these daily stages, or even strictly to his route. My forthcoming slight deviations during my quest would therefore be a direct result of this advice from the man himself and bear no relation to my occasionally questionable sense of direction. The majority of Wainwright's stages start and end at low level with a single up-down during the day and the two-week trip should leave a little time to "stand and stare", an activity much approved of by Wainwright.

Although unofficial, the Coast-to-Coast Walk uses public rights of way, permissive paths and accessible land. It is one of the most popular of all the long-distance footpaths in the UK, despite not having National Trail status. In 2004, the walk was named as the second-best walk in the world according to a survey of experts.

Arriving in the Scottish capital some 45 minutes late, the delay resulted in failure to make my connecting train for Carlisle. The next train for Carlisle was in 30 minutes but that would have been far too convenient and easy. My tickets were for the Avanti West Coast franchise and their next train for Carlisle wasn't for almost two hours. Carrying a 70-litre rucksack as well as a large holdall, I wouldn't be venturing far. On exiting onto Princes Street, there was an open-air bar (aren't they all in a pandemic?) and I would consume my first pint of beer of the trip. It wouldn't be the last pint of beer consumed on the trip.

It was almost three o'clock when I boarded the Birmingham-bound Avanti West Coast train which would transport me to Carlisle. Although I considered myself a fairly gregarious individual, my fellow passengers on the one-hour sprint over the border reminded me of the appeal of the expected lengthy periods of solitude which lay ahead in the next fortnight. With their flagrant disregard for others, I was privy to loud argumentative telephone conversations and YouTube videos. My favourite was the young lady who was booking a hotel room and haphazardly providing the entire carriage with her name, date of birth, full address, card number and 3-digit CVV code. I resisted the temptation to arrange her purchase of pizza for some of my friends back home. Yes, I was definitely a grumpy old man . . . and proud of it. I could never show such disrespect to fellow customers . . . well, not until I got to The Lion Inn at Blakey Ridge on Day 12 . . . allegedly.

There was another one-hour enforced hiatus at Carlisle and Google Maps indicated there were several hostelries within close proximity of the station. It wouldn't be the last pint of beer consumed on the trip.

The busy Friday tea-time "Northern Rail" two-carriage train departed Carlisle for the 80-minute journey to St Bees. At Workington, the train was boarded by three middle-aged gentlemen attired in workwear. I surmised a tough week at work had culminated in a tough afternoon at the bar as they incautiously staggered onto nearby table seats whilst the remainder of the passengers purposefully avoided any eye contact. Any communication may well have proved difficult in any case, as they appeared to be conversing in a form of English only decipherable to themselves. I was still deliberating on whether they were possibly the three drunkest upright people I had ever seen when the train arrived at Whitehaven station, at which point their exchange of cryptic mutterings resulted in the tanked trio reeling onto the platform.

A much emptier train rolled into showery but sunny St Bees in the early evening, the starting point of my expedition. A pretty little coastal village founded by an Irish lass who fled here to avoid an arranged marriage to a Norwegian prince just 1,400 years ago, approximately. Folklore decrees that she asked the local lord for some land to found a convent. He agreed she could have any land that snow fell upon the following day, which happened to be midsummer's day. Lo and behold, miraculously . . . you get the gist.

A 10-minute walk along Beach Road, laden with my rucksack and dragging my courier bag along on its little wheels, I arrived at the Seacote Hotel, my Coast-to-Coast Eve accommodation by the seafront. On approaching the entrance to the establishment, it had a derelict appearance and just as I was beginning to think I had been the victim of a booking scam, I realised the hotel was in fact a going concern. A very helpful concern too, as the receptionist booked me in and arranged a table for dinner in the residents' lounge. I also arranged for the hotel to retain my couriered holdall for an extra 24 hours to allow for a potential wild camp on Day One. Fish and chip Friday ensued after a recce to the nearby official starting point of the Coast-to-Coast. It wouldn't be the last pub meal consumed on the trip.

Armed with Alfred Wainwright's book "A Coast-to-Coast Walk", I retired to the downstairs bar for a post-dinner pint and a quick refresher on some things to expect on my adventure's inaugural day. Considering the bar was fairly busy, the sound of chatter was somewhat muted and it was noticeable, just as it was on the train carriage earlier in the day, that most people were looking down at their phone. This was the life that the vast majority of society had transmogrified into, and I was just as guilty as the next person, although I could be a temporary critic as I was looking at a book . . . a book I could probably download . . . to my phone.
Of course, most things could now be done on a hand-held electronic device via the internet. The world of electronic communication was capable of shaping the direction of people's lives in various ways and I reflected that my own path over the previous eight years had very much fallen into that category, particularly social media in the initial months of those eight years.

Spring 2013

The "Making Mates" dating website had asked for a brief description of myself in categorised sections, including my likes and dislikes. I subsequently learnt that I had taken the word "brief" to entirely new levels when it came to a profile page, as clearly I was unable to see other gentlemen's profiles and would later discover that I had perhaps over-indulged. I guess I just kept typing on the premise that the more information I proffered, the more information a prospective "datee" would volunteer reciprocally. Oh well, in for a penny, in for a pound. I electronically attached a couple of pics trying to look my clean-shaven Sunday best and pressed the 'submit' button:

Who are you?

"Well, it's a bit like Day One of a course where you go round the people in the room for brief introductions.
I'm Matt, 44 years young, 6'1", medium build, originally from Paisley in Renfrewshire but been away since 1989. Fairly easy-going, broad-minded and up for a laugh, not taking myself too seriously as life's too short. Been single for a couple of years, not entirely unhappily, but perhaps time to get back on the dating scene.
Moved to Aberdeen 18 months ago to take up a job in security. Hours suit, shift pattern suits, so it will do unless something better comes along.
Prior to that, served 22 years in the Royal Air Force Police which has involved travel to different locations amid differing circumstances and situations which have broadened my mind and consequently sharpened my sense of perspective, occasionally to my detriment.

Rich in life experience but not at all fiscally so if you're a material girl looking for a rich knight in shining armour, I'm not him.
Spend time where possible with my three fabulous bambinos, daughters aged 14 and 9 and a son just shy of 8, who live with my ex-wife in Moray where cordial ties are retained.

Likes:

Walking/Hiking - Enjoy a day out on the hills but don't have the best head for heights so some summits are out of the question. Due to complete the West Highland Way this summer with my eldest daughter.
Football - avid St Mirren fan since the mid 1970s and endeavour to see them when practical.
More Football – was a referee for many years and now a development advisor, watching younger referees and offering advice to help improve their game.
Scrabble - member of an internet Scrabble club for many years.
Quizzes - both organizing and taking part.
Cinema - as the owner of one of those Cineworld Unlimited passes, can often be found sitting alone watching any standard of current release when there's nothing decent on the telly.
Music – a keen listener to BBC Radio 2 (since my early twenties!), I like a real myriad of genres from The Killers to Runrig and John Barry film scores, with lots in-between. Have been known to take a bath with Carly Simon . . . and Neil Diamond . . . though not at the same time.
Theatre - not quite so confident flying solo when it comes to the theatre which is where dating may be helpful!

Dislikes:

Mint sauce.
Things with mint sauce on them.
Pictures of mint sauce.
People who have mint sauce in their kitchen.

Ideas For First Date:

A walk along the beach carrying a dog lead, taking bets on when someone will ask if you've lost your dog or . . .
An in-depth discussion about the inside of a table tennis ball or . . .
Anything involving ice cream . . .

<u>*I Am Looking For:*</u>
(at this point, the 'profile page' presented a drop-down menu with
options ranging from 'marriage' to 'casual sex')

*I find it impossible to say exactly what I am looking for as it would
depend on the other person, the nature of any friendship and the
dynamic of any subsequent relationship.*

I guess it was my way of saying I was up for most things but leaned
more towards the 'nothing serious' end of the scale rather than the
'marriage' end.

Returning from work the following day, I logged into my profile to
discover that several members of the fairer sex had been peeking at
my profile, piquing their interest sufficiently enough to send a
message, with my inbox peaking at fourteen.
In contrast to my profile, twelve of these messages were extremely
brief along the line of "Hi there" towards which I wasn't quite pulling
out my short brown hair but there was a sense of mild
disappointment, considering my own introductory efforts. In
hindsight, those ladies were probably just wanting to instigate some
conversation, but my attention had already been drawn to "Joscot"
which I would learn was an abridgement of Joanne and Scotland.
Joanne, although based around 80 miles away in Perth, had taken
the time to construct a more unabridged reply revealing her
appreciation of my openness and concurring with my opinions on the
"I am looking for... " option.
Her own profile, whilst less busy than my own, presented a similarly
aged and easy-going individual. Her short narrative stated that she
would like to meet a "happy chappy" who didn't take himself too
seriously. She quirkily insisted that any potential date would need to
be over 5'10" tall and I smiled at her blatant "heightism". In the
accompanying photo, I saw a warm smile light up an attractive face.
Shoulder-length blonde hair covered her ears and her centrally
parted fringe extended down her entire forehead, slightly obscuring
her eyebrows whilst accentuating her piercing greenish eyes. Her
faintly freckled cheeks flanked her appealing retrousse nose.
The early electronic exchanges were cordial and light-hearted and I
felt a positive vibe towards the interesting stranger. She was fairly
quick to advise that despite her profile placing her in Perth, she

actually resided just 20 miles from the city in the 'Shire. Rather than question why she would falsify her location to a town 100 miles from her home, I viewed it as a positive that she was more local than initially indicated. The mildly flirtatious beginnings ramped up after a few minutes when Joanne teasingly enquired, "*So tell me the answer to the biggest question of all. Have you retained a set of military uniform?*"

"*Why of course!*" I typed in reply, immediately realising the answer to the question was less relevant than the fun-element. There was little doubt, based on my initial impressions of her profile and photo and the early indications of her sense of fun, that I was intrigued by Joanne from the outset.

The following evening, I found myself logging back on to the website and enjoyed some more light-hearted banter with Joscot who described me as 'newsy', a word I had hitherto never encountered. Was I beginning to really like someone I had never met? Her insistence on a particular height of partner centred around the fact that her ex-husband was slightly shorter than her and consequently she was unable to wear high-heeled shoes at functions. I considered this slightly eccentric and "heightist" and it was hard to pinpoint exactly what was going on in my mostly otherwise sensible head, but I was enjoying these brief flirtatious exchanges with someone who communicated intelligently in a similarly fun way to myself.

Such is the modern online world, it was only a matter of time before we opened up our social media profiles. I have never taken social media very seriously or indeed confused it with the real world. As the years have gone on, I have enjoyed creating posts, knowing they will reappear on future dates to initiate pleasant memories. Affording access to one's page does offer someone a glimpse into your life. However, I would realise fairly quickly that others can draw inaccurate conclusions and this would become the inaugural challenge to overcome if my friendship with Joanne was to progress.

I was preparing for nightshift the following day when I received a message on 'Making Mates' from Joanne and opened it up with a sense of anticipation. Joanne explained that, having explored my social media profile, I was "not the right fit for her".
According to Joanne, I was all "Tartan Army" and socialising and perhaps just not the right person for her. I stared at her message,

feeling a real sense of deflation. I realised I shouldn't feel this way over someone I had never met and actually struggled to comprehend why I felt such disappointment over a brief online flirtation lasting less than a week. "Better to find out now" was my consolatory theory.

The feeling of disappointment continued on my 20-minute walk to work, during which I confirmed that the impression Joanne had formed, based on my social media profile, was a fairly inaccurate representation of reality.

There are constant crossroads encountered in life at which we have to turn in a direction. Decisions on which way to turn determine the very course of that life and although hindsight is considered "a wonderful thing", there can be no hindsight without moving forward into a future we cannot predict. Something stirred inside my psyche, persuading me that there had been a potential for something special with this interesting lady and at this crossroads, I would make my turn.

Later that evening, I logged on to the dating website.

Hi Joanne,

Oh no, it's that strange bloke from the Making Mates website!

The fundamental problem with nightshifts in under-challenging employment is that active minds are prone to thinking. I sincerely hope you don't mind me doing this but please just indulge me if you will. I was thinking about your last message regarding your observations after looking at my social media profile and just wanted to clarify a few points, for what it's worth.

In my entire existence, I have attended three, yes, three Scotland matches in 1986, 1995 and 2010! The photos of me kilted and partying with friends are from our annual (yep, once a year) Jolly Boys Outing, a reunion of former RAF colleagues to the Isle of Bute Highland Games.

Yes, I'm keen on football but I've never lost perspective on where it stands in relation to more important things. In the summer of 2009, I was faced with a demanding role in the RAF, growing kids I wanted to spend more time with, and a girlfriend I also wanted to spend more time with. I also knew that I would be deploying to the Middle East (again) from that October for four months. The main problem was that a week only lasted seven days and something had to give. I knew what priority my football held and it was a no-brainer to tender my resignation from refereeing.

Football in 2013 involves advising and reporting on progressing referees, only when I've made myself available, simply putting something back in, having taken lots out of it. Facebook has been a godsend since I left the forces and moved to Aberdeen, enabling me to keep in touch with former colleagues, but I've never really taken it seriously. It will also be a handy tool for 'extortion' of money from people for my forthcoming West Highland Way adventure with my eldest daughter in aid of a local charity. Last month, my football team won only their fourth national trophy in 136 years of existence, thus it was quite a significant event for many reasons and was always going to receive a bit of coverage on my social media, particularly memorable that my daughter was able to share that joy with me but ultimately, it was only a football match! Yes, I'm keen on football but have never lost sight of where it sits in ranking of importance.

Moving on, my life underwent an untidy period between 2006 and early 2008 during which my marriage ended. Some would refer to it a mid-life crisis but there was a bit more to it than that.

"It was the best of times, it was the worst of times," only this Dickensian epic was more a 'Tale of Two Towns', namely Elgin and Nairn.

From spring 2008, there followed a very settled content period of my life which ended with heartbreak in the summer of 2011. Enough said on that. It was a difficult period emotionally in concurrence with my transition from serviceman to civilian and I was aware that only one person could pick me up . . . myself.

Believe me, that's a fairly shortened version. I feel I could write a novel about it in the anguished first-person style of Dostoevski's "Crime and Punishment"!

I'm sharing this with you because I joined Making Mates to perhaps reintroduce myself back into dating, as friends encouraging me to chat up inebriated women in a pub just doesn't do it for me.

I've never met you Joanne and do not know you, but I had no idea of the potential effect a brief flirtation with an intelligent, engaging woman would elicit. For the first time in two years, I realised that the 'moving on' process could be progressed for which I'm grateful.

Fanciful? . . maybe. Gut instinct? . .probably. Serendipity? . . definitely.

Ok, if you've got this far, thank you for your attention and I leave you secure in the knowledge that without any hope or agenda, my door will remain open.

Oh, and if that day ever comes, can you let me know what 'newsy' means?

Au revoir mais pas adieu, j'espere.

Matt x

My missive certainly provoked a positive reaction from Joanne and she replied almost immediately with a degree of empathy and was taken aback by my openness. In a way I hadn't experienced in a long time, I felt a real connection with someone and a first face-to-face meeting was inevitable.

The following afternoon, I received a message from Joanne. She enquired as to my availability to meet up as she had a window of opportunity from 4pm until an evening meeting at 7.30pm. A stroll around a city public park was hastily arranged for 5pm but a message at 4.40pm advised that she was running about half an hour late. I had no idea at this point how much of a recurring theme and standing joke a 30-minute delay would become.

The meeting was rescheduled to a local pub diner at 5.30pm. As I waited in the car park, further messages were received intimating further delays due to traffic and finally at around 6pm, amid the pervading sense of nervous excitement, her car swept into the car park. As I laid eyes on the beautiful lady in the flesh for the first time, we exchanged pleasantries and I induced a smile, suggesting that if she was any later, we could have indulged in the advertised Sunday carvery . . . it was Thursday. We entered the establishment, headed towards the bar and stood together waiting to order a drink. She unexpectedly kissed me on the cheek accompanied with her comment, "That's for waiting for me." Suddenly, all the nervousness and slight awkwardness, heightened by the way we seemed to click online, evaporated in a moment. We found a seat at a small table in a quiet alcove within the restaurant area. As I removed my jacket, Joanne did likewise before reaching into her handbag to retrieve a pocket English dictionary which she placed on the table. Of the four stools around the small table, I found myself naturally taking a stool immediately next to Joanne as I stared at the publication on the table before redirecting my puzzled enquiring gaze towards the adjacent pretty face

"I've noticed that you occasionally use some big words so I brought that along in case I need some assistance."
The resultant spontaneous giggling set the tone for an evening of enjoyable, convivial and anecdotal chat. 'Newsy' meant I liked to talk a lot and was full of news about everything. Thirty minutes in, Joanne arranged to cancel her scheduled meeting. I suspected the meeting had never existed and was a pre-planned escape mechanism, which only served to reaffirm that the evening had started well. Such was Joanne's openness and candour, that as the first hour of conversation flashed by, she uttered, "Well, isn't this going well?" I wholeheartedly concurred.

The Joanne I was meeting in the flesh was very much as I had anticipated throughout our online dalliance. Warm, friendly, engaging, witty and a little silly but in a fun, attractive way. It was patently clear in these initial face-to-face interactions that a spark had been ignited. Moreover, it's fair to say I found her physically attractive as our medium-built frames naturally edged fractionally closer together amidst our conversational exchanges.

After leaving university in the late 1980s, Joanne began a career in accounting. She worked for various companies over a period of 20 years before deciding on a change of direction, going "back to school" and requalifying as a counsellor. Now splitting her working life between private clients at home and a part-time contract with the local health board at Aberdeen Royal Infirmary, she worked with clients who were experiencing a wide range of emotional and psychological difficulties, trying to help them bring about effective change to enhance their wellbeing. As Joanne enthusiastically relayed the details of her profession, it was evident that she had gleaned much job satisfaction over the last few years.

Joanne had split up from Dave, her husband of over 20 years, the previous year, and had moved out of the matrimonial home, making temporary accommodation arrangements with a friend whilst waiting for the purchase of a new home to go through. She had a son, Scott, approaching his 21st birthday and a daughter, Angela, three years younger.

A further three hours evaporated in engaging conversation, expanding greatly on previous online discussion, and as the staff began to loiter in our vicinity in that way that suggests closing time is approaching, I sensed a mutual reluctance for the evening to end.

That instinct was revisited in the car park when, after my suggestion of a second date was readily agreed, she kissed me. This was no repeat of the earlier peck on the cheek and I zealously reciprocated, appreciating that it had been a long time since I felt such an overwhelming sense of excitement. I bade Joanne good night and returned to my car. As I pulled out of the car park, I calmly shared my thoughts with myself.
"Wow." One word uttered aloud spoke volumes.

After working through a weekend frequently punctuated with flirty text messages, we agreed to meet the following midweek on a mutual afternoon off. This would be my first introduction to Squeak, her cute little 6-year-old bichon frise. Our second meeting entailed a very enjoyable walk in an Aberdeenshire wood. The conversation flowed effortlessly and there were a few private moments for re-enacting that exciting first kiss of the previous week. During these embraces, Joanne's unanticipated declaration of "oh I'm good, by the way" in reference to her sexual adeptness was a little surprising. She knew nothing about my sexual background or experience and vice versa and I found her confidence intriguing.

Little Squeak appeared to take a shine to me which I figured wasn't going to do my chances any harm. As I drove away from our forest car park meeting point with my car radio naturally tuned into BBC Radio 2, Steve Wright's afternoon programme entered the spirit of my feelings, playing "Heartlight", a beautiful Neil Diamond ballad I was of course very familiar with. This would be the first of many musically orientated romantic moments, with a second and very significant such moment only three days thereafter.

Numbers One and Two, aware that something exciting appeared to be developing in Dad's life, were daughters keen to make me look like something from the 1980's, although many others would have argued that Dad didn't require any adoption of his fashion sense to look like he belonged in the 1980s. I headed off from Moray to our third date, looking like a cross between Simon Le Bon and Howard Jones. A friend of Joanne's was involved in organising an 80's charity disco and I was greeted in the venue's car park by Boy George herself. Once again, interaction was effortless as we chatted and danced through another successful evening, up to a point, as I had a 45-minute drive back to Aberdeen and a 4.45am alarm call for work. Before leaving, I joined Joanne in her car as we plotted a fourth meeting but, of more significance to me, she asked for the dates of that summer's West Highland Way adventure with Number One. The relevant dates were three months henceforward and as the very attractive Boy George lookalike noted them in her diary, I interpreted a healthy sign that she intended sticking around. As we headed home in convoy via the 'Shire, we reached a roundabout where our respective routes changed. Joanne pulled in and alighted from her vehicle and I did likewise. Memorable moments followed as parting kisses flourished under the clear moon's fluorescence. On driving off, my car stereo felicitously enhanced the enveloping air of excitement, playing the beautiful song "Just A Kiss", a country ballad by the band Lady Antebellum which includes the lines "Just a kiss on your lips in the moonlight" and "But we don't need to rush this. Let's just take it slow." I liked Joanne . . . a lot.

A weekend off together presented the opportunity for Joanne's inaugural visit to my humble abode to sample my culinary capabilities. Not wanting to rush things, Joanne agreed she wouldn't sleep over and would return home later in the evening. As two unattached adults in their forties who were clearly very attracted to each other, it was never really a feasible proposition. The following morning, it could be said we were in a relationship.

The next couple of weeks flew by in a whirlwind of excitement as I couldn't prevent myself steadily falling for this lovely lady. I very much sensed the feelings were mutual, particularly when Joanne's romantic communications concluded with the phrase "my heart on a plate, sweetie" on more than one occasion. A dental appointment back in Moray and Joanne's willingness to accompany me on this trip, together with an hour to kill before the appointment, was the backdrop for an unscheduled first meeting with Numbers One, Two and Three. This appeared to be successful with a mutual warming between parties, including Jennifer, my ex-wife. Joanne returned to the 'Shire unaccompanied as I was on leave and staying over in Moray, utilising the back garden to make use of the tent we acquired for the forthcoming West Highland Way adventure. The following day, as the country and my new found elation bathed in the warm late May sunshine, I received an unexpected message from Joanne requesting, with Jennifer's permission, if it were possible for her to return to Moray. It transpired that Kim, Joanne's friend and temporary landlady and co-habitee had an overnight visitor and Joanne's spontaneous idea would afford her friend some privacy.

That evening, I found myself banished to the living room to watch the Champions League Final in the company of a box of beers as Joanne and Jennifer became better acquainted over a couple of bottles of wine in the kitchen. There was a huge degree of surreality around the situation, hearing the constant chitter chatter from the kitchen and my drinks were going down well. Number One was at her boyfriend's and Numbers Two and Three had decanted to the canvas dwelling in the rear garden.

Joanne had been afforded Number One's bedroom for the night and in my inebriated state, I only vaguely recalled my 3am visit. Joanne furnished me with the details in the morning that I very briefly joined her before realising that it was neither the time nor the place, even for just a quick hug, and I had returned downstairs.

After some breakfast and a morning stroll, Joanne once more returned to the 'Shire. She stopped en route to send an impromptu text message, thanking me for a lovely weekend, complimenting my children and Jennifer on their friendliness and hospitality, and looked forward to our planned nights away at a hotel the following weekend. "*I kinda like you*" and "*your wonderful family have humbled me*", a couple of heart-warming quotes.

It was only about an hour later when she phoned . . . to end our relationship . . .

It wasn't the clearest explanation as to why or indeed what thoughts or conversation had taken place in the intervening hour since her lovely text message. It seemed to centre around my liking for football and beer, presumably based on the previous evening, a situation completely instigated by Joanne's impulsion to return to Moray and my congruence to facilitate. As she asserted her lightning decision and put the phone down with an almost flippant "Bye then", I was immediately stunned into silence and disbelief accompanied by a metaphorical painful kick in the stomach. I wanted to instinctively burst into tears but my body would take a couple of minutes to emerge from complete lockdown before allowing me to do so. Subsequently realising that Number Two was witnessing this emotional outpouring and consequently reacting with her own tears, served to increase the distress.

After a couple of years of singledom, I firmly believed I had stumbled onto something special and it would take some time to rationalise what had just happened. I suppose if parameters were set on any dating website looking for a bloke who didn't like neither beer nor football, the algorithm would narrow from potentially hundreds to a straight choice between Frankie from Fraserburgh or Barry from Banchory . . .

My instincts should perhaps have guided me towards disliking her for treating me in such a way but I remained acutely aware that deep down, I liked her way too much for that to happen.

Things were beginning to develop and suddenly they were ending. Could my conflicted feelings and emotions just let go? Was it really the end of something which was just beginning? Or was it just the end of the beginning?

Day One – St Bees to Ennerdale Water

On many occasions, I have visited the beautiful town of St Andrews in Fife, known as 'The Home of Golf'. On a summer's evening, I have strolled on the famous links, over the Swilken Bridge by the 17th 'Road Hole' and across the 18th and 1st joint fairway towards the Bruce Embankment on the seafront. For a golf enthusiast, there's a prevailing spiritual atmosphere, a feeling that one is in a special place.

The short walk from the Seacote Hotel in St Bees to the "Mile Zero" Coast-to-Coast sign on the promenade evoked a similar spiritual ambience, enriched by good luck comments from staff and residents as I exited the hotel laden with a large rucksack and walking poles. Posing for my obligatory selfie at the inaugural point of the famous walk on a still and overcast early Saturday morning, the sense of occasion was further enhanced by an elderly couple walking their dog nearby.

"Off on the Coast-to-Coast?" the gentleman shouted.

"Oh yes," my anticipatory response.

"How many days?"

"14 days. Leave some time to stand and stare," I replied in reference to advice from the walk's creator.

"I did it 25 years ago," my elderly acquaintance reminisced, "It was brilliant. Enjoy your 2021 version and good luck."

In keeping with tradition and benefitting from the high tide, I doused my boots in the shore-bound ripples of the Irish Sea and placed a small pebble, bound for the North Sea, into my rucksack.

Within moments of setting off and crossing a small bridge over Rottington Beck, I was climbing up onto the clifftops and, after a final view back over St Bees seafront to the village behind, picked up the early pace on the St Bees Head Heritage Coast, north-westwards . . . on a west to east walk. Our Alfred did have a sense of humour. This early section would also herald my first of a few encounters with cows, an animal I've always maintained a healthy wariness towards when not separated by a fence. Thankfully, their watching brief of motionless mild interest in the passing hiker was welcome. Day 5's far more entertaining encounter with cows lay ahead.

Mr Wainwright was also renowned for his traditional headwear, thus prior to the trip, I had purchased a tweed flat cap to wear in tribute.

26

Having placed the cap into the lower pocket of my hiking trousers on leaving the hotel less than an hour earlier, I reached down to retrieve the honorary attire . . . from a pocket that now contained nothing. "Oh, for f . . . "

After a steep down-and-up section skirting the isolated Fleswick Bay, the clifftop path passes the St Bees Lighthouse before curving right with a distant view to the town of Whitehaven, where at least three hangovers were being nursed. On reaching Birkham's Quarry, I joined a tarmac lane leading into the village of Sandwith. I passed a young woman pushing a baby in a buggy and juggling two dogs on leads and bade her good morning.
"Morning. Are you walking the Coast-to-Coast?" she asked and, following my affirmative response, "Good luck with it. The sun is trying to come out for you."
The response from the locals in this lovely part of Cumbria was heartening and maintained my positive attitude towards the two weeks lying ahead.

I passed uphill through the small village to a T-junction where I would cross onto a narrow path.
At this junction, the guidebooks take a warped delight in reminding hikers that they have walked over five miles, and are now two miles from St Bees by road.

The track traverses some farms before passing under a bridge carrying the railway I travelled on the previous evening. With my guidebook, my 'A to Z' map guide and sporadic makeshift signposts assisting with guidance on this unofficial route, I reached the villages of Moor Row and Cleator. A small lane on entering Cleator, signposted "Wainwright Passage" underlined the ongoing mission. It coincided with a discernible Saturday morning vibe as a couple of gentlemen were preparing the village cricket pitch whilst the sun began to breach the clouds and a few yards further on, a youth football match was in full swing. I observed that all spectators were watching the match from outside the perimeter fence of the ground, a reminder that the country was still in the process of emerging from a global pandemic lockdown. The referee appeared happier that the parents were further out of earshot too.
My pre-walk homework had strongly recommended a trip to Cleator Stores for a pie, a matter previously discussed at length with my work colleague Billy over a nightshift. The pies are so popular that a

sandwich board outside the shop advises on their availability in the style of a "vacancies / no vacancies" sign associated with a Bed and Breakfast establishment. The same board also indicated that the shop sold fruit, vegetables and potatoes, which left me pondering on how potatoes were defined in these parts. Alas, there were no vacancies at the "pie inn" and my pastry-related ambitions were thwarted as the young shop assistant advised that pies were unavailable at the weekend.

'Crustfallen' with this news, I settled for a sandwich and a chocolate bar and set off once more after pausing to text Billy with the important and devastating news.

Leaving the village on a small bridge across the River Ehen, I encountered a very friendly German Shepherd dog with his owner and stopped for a chat. I ascertained that Toby and his owner were originally from the Scottish borders but now resided in Cleator Moor, a town a mile north of Cleator, the village. I didn't enquire as to the local geographical quirkiness but making Toby's acquaintance would inadvertently set up a dog-meeting theme for the trip.

The first ascent of any note on the Coast-to-Coast is Dent Hill and after climbing a forest track through Blackhow Wood, a thick pine plantation, the path emerges onto an open climb to the summit at 1,158ft, marked by some cairns. My 'Jetboil', an innovative rapid water-boiling 21st century patented device, would receive its first outing of this 2-week exploit at this panoramic spot as I brewed up to have lunch.

With telephone reception available, I learned from a Coast-to-Coast social media page that Raymond from Hull had set off on his adventure an hour behind me. Younger, fitter and arguably more handsome than myself (for arguably, read infinitely), Raymond was tackling the route over just nine days.

Concluding my break, I followed Mr Wainwright's advice as I paused for some brief moments to 'stand and stare' at my view which encapsulated Northern Ireland, Scotland, and the Sellafield nuclear power station. Turning 180 degrees, I set off east-bound with a distant view to the east end of Ennerdale Water, today's destination. It was only 12.20pm and I was making good first-day headway as I started a gradual and boggy descent from Dent onto a track through some woods and marched on with gay abandon, completely ignoring the deer-proof ladder stile that would take me towards Raven Crag. After a few hundred yards of heading downhill in a now north-north-west direction, I began to doubt my bearings, consulted my guide and duly turned back uphill. On approaching the previously missed stile, there, of course, was Raymond from Hull, heading purposefully in the correct direction.

I didn't want to download the fancy GPS (Global Positional System) stuff that shows one exactly where to go. The thought actually sounded quite boring. A guidebook, a map and a compass would be of ample assistance but wouldn't completely negate the possibility of meandering astray, a distinct possibility in my case. To me, that was all part of the fun. Everyone is of course entitled to their own preferences and Raymond was being directed by his GPS waypoints as I joined him on the albeit brief but very steep 10-minute descent from Raven Crag down to Nannycatch Beck. With the sun now fully out and serving to highlight this charming stream, the path trailed alongside pleasantly. Before progressing onto a minor road, I stopped for a drink and replenished my water as the temperature picked up. Raymond, an architect who could only procure one week's annual leave and therefore had to design his Saturday to Sunday 9-day itinerary, was heading for Borrowdale on a longer day and pushed on.
The remainder of the route into the village of Ennerdale Bridge is on a well-designed safety-conscious roadside path.

On entering the small and quintessentially Lakeland village of Ennerdale Bridge, there is a recently renovated café and shop, The Gather, and with the mid-afternoon sunshine illuminating the village, a seat outside with an ice-cream was in order. Only 100 yards on from The Gather is one of the two village pubs, The Fox and Hounds. Prior to the trip, I had booked a table for tea at 5pm but was now two hours ahead of schedule. Fortunately, with some picnic tables available in the garden area, staff were able to accommodate an amendment to my booking and I was soon enjoying their signature burger washed down with my first pint of beer on the trail.

A heavy-looking rucksack and some walking poles accompanying a tired-looking hiker is frequently the prompt for conversation with complete strangers. The lady and gent at the adjacent table duly struck up some chat, establishing the nature of my mission and allowing me the opportunity to invite an online donation to my charity cause. As I utilised the pub's wi-fi to ascertain the latest score in the ongoing Scottish Cup Final, related conversation discovered that my latest friend from the local area had a ticket for the delayed Euro 2020 finals match between England and Scotland at Wembley Stadium three weeks hence. Noting my own national persuasion, I obviously wished his country the best of luck on finishing as runners-up in that particular contest and referenced the previous encounter in that competition at Wembley in 1996 when I was based with the RAF in Norfolk. It transpired that his female companion was also serving with the RAF just across the county border in Lincolnshire on that sunny June afternoon 25 years earlier. Just how small the world is would truly hit home on Day 8 in Reeth.

Speaking of the task in hand, I mentioned that I was carrying a voice recorder and taking notes about my adventure and my fellow football fan asked for my e-mail address. He cryptically explained that he had contacts in the "blogging" sector and would be interested in seeing my observations. I didn't foresee any harm in providing the requisite details.

Coast-to-Coast hikers were permitted to camp in the Fox and Hounds garden for a nominal fee but from 11pm until 7am, there were no toilet facilities which was unfortunately not the most conducive arrangement for someone with the incurable disease, ulcerative colitis. No, I hadn't heard of it either until diagnosis in 2010. Prepare to be educated later.

Notwithstanding my medical condition, I felt there were a few miles left in my relatively fresh legs, which were further freshened by the addition of another pint as I utilised the pub wi-fi to watch the latter stages of the aforementioned Scottish Cup Final, St Johnstone triumphing over Hibernian at a spectator-less Hampden.

I loaded up and set off around 5pm and headed a mile to the source of the River Ehen at the west end of Ennerdale Water, the most westerly lake in the Lake District National Park. Whilst the river transfers contents of the lake downstream to the Irish Sea at Sellafield, I would be heading upstream along the south shore of the lake for two and a half miles to its east end. At times, progress was hindered by some light scrambling along this uneven shoreline. It was very reminiscent of the thrice-tackled east shore of Loch Lomond on the West Highland Way, which has on more than one occasion been described outside of guidebooks as "a bit of a ball-ache."

Arriving at the east end of Ennerdale Water, my previous research on Google Maps indicated that there were good potential camping spots on the north shore of the lake. I traversed to the north side and detoured back for around half a mile to locate a fine pitch by the lake. After quickly erecting my faithful 2-person tunnel tent, I enjoyed a fresh brew on the waterfront, admiring the shimmering water under a pleasant evening sun setting on a cloudless blue sky. A tranquil end to the first day of my adventure, and with no possible communication with the world in this remote spot, I completed the day listening to the opening chapters of Richard Osman's previously downloaded "Thursday Murder Club", read by the beautiful Lesley Manville. The ambience belied the poor weather forecast for Day Two.

Akin to those early stages of my relationship with Joanne, my adventure had reached the end of the beginning.

Summer 2013

Having lodged with her friend Kim since her marital breakdown the previous year, Joanne was preparing to move into her new home nearby where she would be joined by her daughter Angela. It was most probably an ill-advised pipedream that someday in the future, I may actually live there too but there was no harm in having a fanciful notion. Besides, no-one could possibly know what the future held. Following a week of introspection, the hurt and confusion over our relationship's sudden ending persuaded me to put pen to paper in an attempt to garner some closure or even convince Joanne that there was still possibly some mileage left in our fledgeling dalliance, even just as friends for now.

"Hi Joanne,

Empty and stunned doesn't begin to cover it.

I never thought I'd meet and feel for someone like this and I miss you terribly. I must confess my heart's on/off switch is not so readily accessible.

Some people believe I should be angry and feel bitterness towards you but I think you already know me better than that. Life is too short and you had your own opinions and thoughts to deal with, which you acted upon.

So please indulge me and I'll sign off this dramatic brief chapter in writing with some positivity, hopefully gaining a friend rather than losing a love! We cannot change the past but we can always be civil in this God-forsaken world and who knows, maybe shape the future because, let's face it, no-one knows what that holds.

Perhaps a time of reflection on the past wee while.

Wow! If I had known what would happen when I put a profile on Making Mates. After two years of singledom, I was looking to meet someone nice to date, and boy did I get that in spades! You have mentioned being swept away and believe me, Joanne, you were not the only one being swept away in a whirlwind of excitement, passion and feelings.

You clearly have your own thoughts and feelings about that evening at Jennifer's and I would ask you to approach the same evening from my perspective. Banished to the sitting room to watch the football at your behest so that "you and Jennifer can have a drink" was extremely surreal but I accepted it in the knowledge that was I was beginning to feel secure with you. If my very brief visit upstairs to see you during the night was a factor, albeit a fleeting moment, then I can only apologise, but I know you'll be fully aware that we are all susceptible to having silly moments when under the influence. All unchangeable history now but little did I know how pivotal those circumstances would prove as I was simply going with the flow.

I appreciate that, just like everyone else, you have issues, Joanne and with my seldom seen 'common sense' head on, I would reluctantly admit that someone who, at the present time, is capable of a change of heart so devastatingly instantly, without any form of discussion on the matter, is probably not the ideal woman for me, romantically speaking (or my scarred ticker for that matter!). I think you've got to know me well enough not to disagree.

So, life goes on. It has to. I will move forward; I know I have to. A busy summer period coming up at work and a fitness level to be maintained in preparation for our forthcoming August stroll on the West Highland Way.

But crucially, that moving-on process would be more easily facilitated and handled positively by not losing my newest pal. I introduced you to my life, my home, my family, their home, my favourite dog-walks and even my bloody dentist! I know you would cede that you do not have that to consider as I never saw any of your life, save for the gorgeous Squeak.

Regardless of what the future holds, it would be great to stay in touch with my friend. As luck would have it, there is a natural and easy way of achieving that and I see no reason not to share my un-colourful life with you on social media as a friend, no different to any other friend.

I suppose all I'm asking you is just to care, Joanne, as the mere thought of someone I respect and care for, disliking me over a football-watching misunderstanding would be very difficult to stomach and something I wouldn't want to dwell on. It would be a nice thought that my West Highland Way progress (or lack of!) was being seen by 'all' of my friends, not that I would know you were even looking, so you wouldn't even have to! Like I said, a nice 'thought'.

Further down the road, if a new love appears on the horizon for either of us, then great. If either or both of us find happiness, surely that's paramount and one day this eternal optimist will find his utopia!

Notwithstanding all that, thanks to the wonders of modern technology, I am left with some nice photos, lovely texts and Facebook messages as well as some unforgettably romantic moments and memories of a brief happy crazy exciting time which no-one can take away from me.

Some positives in this short life are worth fighting for and I hope you can feel my determination not to make it a waste of time, but rather an episode to learn from and take some crumbs of comfort from. Anyway, I'll leave that with you and will cross everything in the sincere hope to be reinstated as your wee Paisley pal on social media, affording me positive rather than negative thoughts on my frequent through-journeys in the 'Shire. One small click of a mouse for a woman, one positive leap forward for a man. A nice analogy.

I guess you've had a busy time this week juggling work and preparation for the big move. I'll forward this to your new address tomorrow and hope and pray that it is received positively and in the spirit of friendship in which it's intended.

All that remains is to wish you, Angela and Squeak the very best of luck and health and happiness in your new home and I hope the initial moving-in process proves as glitch-free as possible and you can get settled in quickly.

Kind Regards

Matt x

P.S. Hi to Squeak!"

The following evening, I was relieved to note that Joanne had
grasped the spirit and sentiment in my letter and reconnected with
my social media page. On retiring to bed, I uploaded a photograph
taken with my children during my latest visit, a somewhat
insignificant and regular occurrence on social media. However,
when next online the following morning, I had been "un-friended"
once more by Joanne.
Her latest U-turn was accompanied by a message explaining that the
photo with the kids had "stopped her in her tracks" and that she
couldn't be my friend as she has feelings for me and finds it very
hard to say no to me. Amidst the confusion and contradiction on
reading this, my reactionary sigh of exasperation reflected the irony
that it clearly wasn't too hard for her to say no.
I had known Joanne for over two months and it was apparent that
she may have had some issues with her feelings. I began to
question why she would sign up to a dating website with these
issues or perhaps she was looking for something more casual and
hadn't been expecting to feel intensely with someone. I completely
understood that but despite my concerns over her evident
unpredictability, I had allowed myself to become invested and I
couldn't deny the potency of my feelings for her. I would leave the
ball in Joanne's court and step back.

More than a week elapsed and there was no denying I missed her
infectious sense of fun and personality and thought of her often.

It was a Friday nightshift and I was on foot patrol around the
company campus. I had recalled that this was the night of her son
Scott's birthday celebrations at a venue in the 'Shire and she would
be out enjoying the party with family and friends. I was very
surprised and admittedly a little elated when I received a text
message after 1am.
"Hi. How you doin. Great parrty but home niw"
The spelling and grammar, or lack thereof, suggested her
attentiveness may have been slightly diminished by alcohol, but
there was no denying my heart skipped a beat whilst trying to
maintain a cautious actuality.
"Glad it went well"

"Yeh it wad great" she replied, *"Scott had a ball and Dave made a arss of himself chating up my daughters mates. Hes nearly fuckin fifty and thinks hes a teenager fir fucks sake,"* she continued, adding several random emoticons.

Having never met Dave and considering Joanne's evidently inebriated state, I retained a circumspect view of her comments.

"Not really my business, sweetheart. Good you're home safe. I'm on nightshift. Just as well really" I replied, adding a smiley face to ensure she knew I wasn't overly bothered by the lateness of her message.

Around ten minutes elapsed and having assumed she had retired to bed, a further message indicated otherwise.

"I know u are. Cant u see what Im doing Matt. I'm shariong with u, making contact with u. Your the person I wanted to Speke to when I got home"

"Ok, that's nice" I replied, unbeknown of her geographical knowledge and thus resisting what would have been pointless teasing that her predictive text had placed her at an airport in Liverpool.

"Though about u a lot this week and just leting u know."

"Thank you x", I concluded.

Conscious that Joanne had evidently consumed a few fermented grapes throughout the evening, it was nevertheless exhilarating to receive communication from her. Her intoxicated inferences generated an extra spring in my step for the remainder of the shift.

Early the following evening, I was once more on a foot patrol when the presumably sobered-up lovely lady again put finger to phone screen.

"Oh my God! I've just saw these messages from last night. Can't even remember sending them. I'm so sorry Matt."

I continued on my patrol, inwardly concurring with myself that I had much preferred receiving drunken text messages from Joanne than not receiving any messages, and then the appropriate reply occurred to me.

"Don't worry about it Joanne. We are all susceptible to having silly moments when under the influence."

"Aye, very good" was her somewhat delayed penny-dropping retort.

A few minutes later, there followed an additional message, *"I'm free from 3 o'clock tomorrow if you fancy meeting up after for a coffee."*

I stared at the message with a conserved thrill, feeling like my patient approach had elicited a potential opportunity to rekindle something and one I wasn't about to pass up.
"I'm between nightshifts tomorrow but could meet up for an hour."

The following afternoon, we were sat opposite one another, sipping latte in a city mall. To the background hum of Sunday shoppers shuffling by, the general discourse was convivial as Joanne described the initial stages of settling into her new home but inevitably, the conversation would return to recent events between us. Joanne alluded to her transitional home life as being a distraction to the initial stages of our relationship. She questioned whether she should be in a relationship at the current time but that conflicted with her instinct that she really liked me and wanted to be with me. It felt great to be back in her company and I really liked her instinct.

At work in the evening, the periodic text messages illustrated that Joanne's head seemed to be back in a better place and the hoped-for romantic rekindling appeared an unequivocal possibility. The depth of feeling I'd retained for my captivating companion naturally elicited a rejuvenated air of excitement and anticipation. However, that air of unbridled optimism could never have prepared me for the unpredictable and eventful roller-coaster of a week which lay ahead.

On Monday evening, my last nightshift before a few days off, the flirty texts continued to bounce to and fro and things were bowling along nicely. Angela had been dwelling with her father since the marital split the previous year and it had been agreed that she would see out her late adolescence in co-habitation with her mother. Angela was aware of Joanne's brief relationship with someone in the recent past but was unaware of any contact after her mother had ended it. Like myself, Angela was also unaware that Joanne had set up her phone that very afternoon to display a photo of me when a text message was received and in a fleeting moment, the teenager's gaze was drawn to my mugshot on the unattended vibrating handset on their new home's kitchen table.
I obviously wasn't there to witness the resultant outburst but was assured the young woman's vehement tantrum would require some lengthy placation and the evening's typed exchanges were suspended forthwith. A couple of hours elapsed and my increasing anxiousness led to thoughts on the possibility of another "bye then"

telephone call, evoking memories of my springtime disappointment. Mercifully, Joanne eventually messaged to state that everything was ok although her daughter would take some convincing to accept that things were being rekindled. It had been less than a year since the parents Angela had spent all her young life with had separated, and the prospect of her mum entering another relationship with an unknown third party, just as they were setting up home together, would appear to have prompted her impassioned reaction.

Sleeping off nightshift until lunchtime the following day, Joanne had invited me to drive out to the 'Shire and meet her for a walk with the adorable Squeak. A pleasant riverside walk of some three and a half miles ensued in the late June sunshine before the invitation was further extended to an opening visit to Joanne's new home for tea and a biscuit.

Since I'd met Joanne, chatting with her had been effortless and our compatible humour ranged from the quick-witted to the inane dad-joke. We had found common grounds in music, TV and film. Being "newsy" was unavoidable in such engaging company and I was taken in by many aspects of her being. Just like every human on planet Earth, she was not perfect. Her occasional evident tendencies towards impulsiveness and unpredictability were a negotiable imperfection and I hoped she reciprocally felt similarly regarding imperfections she saw in me.

The track of time was lost in repartee, refills and rich tea biscuits. Sat at the same kitchen table upon which my photo on Joanne's phone had caused such consternation the previous evening, our discourse was interrupted by the sound of the front door being entered. Joanne glanced up at the wall clock with a slightly concerned expression and made for the hallway.
From the kitchen, I heard, "Oh, hi Angela. Em, just to let you know, my friend is here."
"You what!" came a reply with a distinct intonation of disapproval followed by the equally disapproving sound of stomping feet ascending the stairs.
Joanne's concerned expression reappeared at the kitchen door. "Give me a minute. I need to speak to her."
From my auditory range, I was unable to determine the vast majority of the vociferous and impassioned exchanges which filled the air on the floor above for the next few minutes.

"You're meant to be spending time with me! That's why I've moved in!" was how I deciphered one fierce shriek from the younger voice. As I felt the uneasy sense of insecurity return once more, the upstairs uproar reached its conclusion followed by a couple of minutes of silence before Joanne returned to the kitchen.
"Maybe best if you head off, Matt," she suggested as my heart sank, but only briefly, as she countered, "but I'd like to see you tomorrow. Finishing at three again. Ok if I pop over?"
I instantly replied in the affirmative, reaching for my car keys as Joanne approached and kissed me.
"You know what? I'm fed up being told what to do," she asserted, "I'll see you tomorrow."

Wednesday afternoon's meet-up inevitably would revisit the incident with Angela, Joanne explaining that after a calmer and lengthier chat, things were much improved. As a consequence, Joanne had arranged to go out for tea with her daughter that evening, which understandably curtailed her visit to mine.

Nothing was scheduled for Thursday, but as evening fell, text messages soon escalated to meeting up for an ice-cream at a MacDonalds restaurant just outside the city. Having reconnected on social media and with Joanne's blessing, I was encouraged to post online that I was her in what I perceived to be acknowledgement that things were very much back on. I would be working 12-hour shifts on Friday and Saturday and Joanne agreed to come over to my flat on the Saturday evening where I would be afforded another opportunity to display my culinary prowess.

Saturday evening's rendezvous was cast into some doubt in the afternoon when Joanne advised that ex-husband Dave, aware that her friendship with myself was once more gathering traction, had visited her new home and was trying to persuade his estranged wife not to pursue any such relationship. It appeared that Dave felt there was still a chance of reviving their marriage. As far as I had been made aware, Joanne had decisively felt the opposite way and I had a degree of empathy for Dave's predilection towards his wife of over twenty years. Nevertheless, not for the first time that week, some butterflies fluttered within me until, much to my relief, my beautiful friend arrived at my humble abode.

After some dinner, notwithstanding previous conversation regarding our pasts, a natural opportunity arose to discuss our respective journeys to this point in much greater depth.

In the year after the birth of Number Three in 2005, Jennifer and I sustained a functional and active life centred around our three young children. Jennifer maintained her social circle around her membership of a local brass band and I maintained my football refereeing career. One evening, a fellow referee picked me up from our home. It wasn't our first football appointment together during that week and as Jennifer stood in the doorway, my colleague jokingly shouted, "Hey Jennifer, he's spending more time with me these days than you."
His perfectly innocent banter was an unwitting metaphor for the approaching dissolution of our 13-year relationship.
As life was consumed by our children, jobs and extra-curricular activities, we simply forgot to make time for each other and, consciously or subconsciously, allowed our personal relationship to wane. I don't recall the term "date night" existing back then but it may have helped. Eventually realising and acknowledging what was happening, attempts were made to rekindle things over a lengthy period of time but something had been lost and it appeared the damage had been done. With three young kids, we remained committed parents and that commitment would not be allowed to falter to their detriment. Almost inevitably, during this period of uncertainty, close relationships within my working life would lead to colleagues' observations that my normally outgoing personality was proving somewhat diminished and Jennifer would astutely observe that when conversation turned to my place of employment, I rarely mentioned my colleague, Siobhan.
I had enjoyed a warm working relationship with Siobhan over the previous three years and her awareness that things weren't firing on all cylinders at home eventually led to a candid openness which revealed that both our respective home lives weren't ideal. My gradually increasing feelings for my colleague inevitably enhanced that candour and I eventually plucked up the courage to share them with her. Within a week, I was taken aback when Siobhan shared her mutual feelings for me and more life history was about to be created.
Over the following years, my relationship with Siobhan was very much kept separate from that with my kids, whose lives I naturally maintained a very active role in. When it came to family holidays

with three children, it was practical to have both parents in attendance for logistical reasons, notwithstanding the benefit to the children themselves of enjoying time with both parents.

Siobhan acknowledged this practicality and graciously accepted these arrangements for over three years, however when her mother fell seriously ill and I was unable to return from a family holiday in Wales, she didn't react well. It wasn't lost on me that Siobhan had a very poor relationship with her mother, and it was a source of great disappointment that this event would be the catalyst for her decision to end the relationship.

The demise of that relationship with Siobhan in 2011 coincided with the completion of my 22-year engagement in the military and my transition from serviceman to civilian. Admittedly, I didn't deal with the break-up very well and, recognizing the need to sort myself out and with the lack of suitable employment opportunities within the more rural Moray area, I was fortunate to procure appropriate employment towards the end of that year in Aberdeen. This would necessitate a move to the city, a new home, new work, new friends and it would provide an opportunity to get my life and my head back on the straight and narrow. Still only 90 minutes from my children, the 4-days-on, 4-days-off shift system would allow me to maintain frequent visits.

Joanne had listened attentively to my elaboration on previously outlined details of the years prior to my current two-year residence in Aberdeen. With her counselling head on, she suggested that perhaps I had endured a period of depression following the break-up of my relationship with Siobhan, concluding dreamily that fate had led me to this juncture and meeting her.

As conversation turned to her own relationship with Dave and events earlier in the day, discourse naturally developed into a detailed reciprocal account from Joanne on several years of her life. For almost an hour, I remained transfixed on my narrator as she emotionally recounted some events from her unsettled past. Openly admitting that she only married Dave "because he asked", she asserted that despite her marriage lasting over twenty years, she had never loved him. Consequently, her marriage had suffered, and over two separate periods, she had embarked on an on/off affair with an old schoolfriend, the most recent being two years prior. On discovering the affair, her husband's somewhat disconcerting reaction was to insist that she continue with the affair as long as she was still maintaining a physical relationship within their marriage. More recently, attempts to live separate lives at home had proved troublesome for similar reasons, culminating in Joanne's aforementioned lodging with Kim whilst seeking a new home. It was evident that it had been difficult for Joanne to open up in such a way and I was moved by her honesty and felt an even closer connection with her, assisted by my burgeoning emotional attachment. It would be many years in the future when my less emotionally-attached and wiser self would see the bigger and more pragmatic picture.

The option to stay over at the flat with me was available but as we hadn't slept together since getting back in touch, it seemed prudent in the circumstances for Joanne to return home. As I accompanied her back to her car, her parting kiss was accompanied by a look of certitude.
"I love you, Matt. Please don't let me down."
It felt natural and easy to offer my reassuring reply, "I love you too, Joanne. I've no intention of letting you down."

My transition onto nightshift the following day required a lie-in, easily achieved feeling at peace once more under the enchantment of my gorgeous girl. With the radio tuned to its obligatory Radio 2 setting, and most probably to the chagrin of my immediate neighbours, I vocally accompanied the last few minutes of the Sunday Love Songs programme whilst fixing some brunch. Once satiated, my short walk to the corner shop to pick up a Sunday paper would set me up for a restful afternoon before work. After a scan of the headlines and before going in-depth on the Sunday supplements, I couldn't resist checking in with my bonnie lassie and reached for my phone.
"*Good morning, gorgeous lady,*" I texted.
Some ten minutes elapsed with no reply and, having surmised that Joanne obviously wasn't by her phone, my eyes lit up when the device indicated an incoming call from the lady herself. "Ooh, a voice call", I thought to myself and touched the green option.
"Hi sweetheart, how you doing?" I cheerfully opened.
"Hi," came the short reply followed by a brief silence. It was the very definition of the term 'pregnant pause' and my heart skipped an enquiring beat.
"Everything ok?"
"Yeh I'm fine Matt, just heading to the DIY store to pick up some paint."
"Ok," I replied, with a feeling it was not the reason she had phoned.

"Been thinking a lot this morning, Matt, and I think I'm going to back-pedal. I'm going to leave you be."

"What?" my somewhat sheepish and delayed reply, notwithstanding that inquisitive corner of my mind that was questioning her prioritisation of the DIY visit over the 'back-pedalling'.

"You don't need me Matt."

"I think I'll be the judge of that," I interjected.

"Nope," she countered, "I'm back-pedalling, Matt. Just leave me be. I'm sorry. See you around."

I sat slumped in the armchair, bewildered, turning my catatonic gaze from the 'call ended' on my screen to the coffee table in front of me where it would remain for several minutes. What had just happened? She had instigated her way back into my life for a week and suddenly it appeared to be all over once more. There were no tears on this occasion, replaced by mixed feelings of exasperation and frustration. I was struggling to remove the image of her beautiful emotional face just over twelve hours earlier, "Please don't let me down, Matt."

My analytical mind went into overdrive during the afternoon, recalling our conversations the previous evening in an attempt to see a trigger point, or wondering what had happened in that short interim period as perhaps Dave had got himself involved.

Ultimately, maybe I had just fallen for someone who was mentally unstable. I realised I had no right to think of anyone as mentally unstable because despite her fairly abysmal behaviour towards me . . . I knew I would struggle to shake off my strong feelings for her.

Mercifully I had four consecutive nightshifts to try to occupy my mind in a week where there was no contact from Joanne, nor was any expected. As usual, I thought of her often and missed her company. I guess she didn't want to commit to a relationship but I knew that she really liked me and my love-blindness refused to believe things were completely over as I scrabbled for crumbs of comfort. As I approached the following weekend, my strength of feeling for Joanne ensured I wasn't about to beat about the bush and wanted to make a final pitch. Consequently and inevitably, my concerningly familiar penchant for putting fingers to keyboard would resurface, blissfully ignorant of the retrospective cringing it would induce in years ahead.

Hi Joanne,

Not like me to forward something in writing, I grant you.

I did hope to meet you in person and share my thoughts with you, but not sure on the possibility of that happening. In fact, I don't actually know what the current situation is as I'm not sure if 'back-pedalling' translates as 'dumped' as your most surreal telephone call on Sunday didn't make much sense.

What a week though! Thoroughly enjoyed being back in your company. On Sunday when you phoned to deliver the latest devastation, despite having a bit of previous, your timing was still amazingly unpredictable! You never know, we might even look back one day and see the funny side of your constant U-turns and my constant worrying about them.

On the previous Sunday night, everything was perfect again in Joanne-world. Reading through your texts is a journey on its own. When Angela kicked off on Monday night about my photo on your phone, I doubted I would get to the morning, but heh I got to visit your lovely new home on Tuesday. That evening though, sitting in your kitchen listening to Angela and you exchanging views upstairs, I wondered if I'd get to Wednesday! Wednesday, you were delayed at work and it got to half three, brief doubts but no real panic. Thursday night, milkshake at MacDonalds and tagging on social media, daring to think this might actually be for real! Saturday afternoon problems with Dave was another heart-stopper but still managed to get through to Saturday evening. Enjoyed cooking for you (don't get the chance very often) and then when we opened up in depth about our pasts, I felt so connected with you.

So, of all the potential occasions during the week when I reckoned getting the elbow was possible, the phone ringing on Sunday was certainly not one of them! Felt a bit low for a while, mainly because one of the last apparently heartfelt sentences uttered on Saturday evening through your emotional eyes was, "Don't let me down, Matt" before doing just that to me less than 12 hours later.

You've let me down twice now, but I understand you have your issues. If I thought you were stringing me along and playing with my head deliberately, I wouldn't be typing this now. You do appear determined to look for my possible fallibilities and I can guarantee you WILL find some. We all have issues and fallibilities, Joanne, it's the routine journey through human life. If we look hard enough and really want to find the 'cracks', we will. That's very easy and anyone can do it. You've already displayed some potential chinks in your armour which shows you're human and I can comfortably see through to the beautiful, funny and caring woman behind them.

As you know, I'm no rich handsome knight in shining armour or Prince Charming (not sure those people exist, sweetie!) and just like every other human being on this mortal sphere, yourself included, I am not perfect. But what the hell, I'm genuine, caring, honest, kind and open and I'm a good man with a big heart who can give you an inexhaustible supply of love, friendship, laughter, loyalty and no shortage of occasional stupidity for your amusement! Hopefully in the times ahead, when you inevitably start dating other men, you will realise that maybe I'm not the guy your head appears to be so desperately trying to convince your heart I am.

You also appear to have an issue dating someone with younger kids. My kids will always be foremost in my heart, Joanne, as you will be well aware of, being a fellow parent, but there's always room in a good heart for other loves and my children will not always be of 'dependent' age.

Joanne, I love you. Before I even met you, I knew I had fortuitously stumbled upon something special. Meeting you confirmed my gut instinct that you really were something special. I'll never forget that Tuesday afternoon driving back to Moray with such passionate feelings. I was floating, hardly concentrating on the driving, and just wanted to turn around, find you and hold you in my arms.

No-one has ever induced the excited preoccupation when you were en route to see me, looking out of the window in anticipation, watching you alight from your car and pinching myself that you were actually coming to see me.

So please retain this letter indefinitely, Joanne, and if you're ever feeling a bit low, take it out and remind yourself of how special you are to someone. Remember that someone will be thinking of you and wishing you the best of everything.

All I ask is that you leave it be until one day you perhaps decide to take a chance on me. You know where I am.

Best Regards

Matt x

After the bizarreness of that topsy-turvy fortnight, I expected a potential backlash to the strange loved-up man's subsequent uninhibited declaration of undying devotion. Joanne surprisingly did not 'unfriend' me on social media, perhaps electing not to take the online world too seriously. I had never, by tradition, 'unfriended' anyone on social media as I felt that doing so would suggest that I was taking it seriously. I'd always tried not to take life too seriously and was hardly about to do so online, usually steering well clear of entering into threads and posts leaning towards controversial or emotive subjects.

Things bowled along routinely for a couple of weeks, appending the odd friendly comment on posts and I continued to keep my fingers crossed. On a solo trip to the cinema, I was attracted to a trailer for a live concert featuring a Dutch violinist called Andre Rieu and his 'Johan Strauss Orchestra'. Whilst I essentially didn't mind attending on my own, I posted on social media, seeking friends' opinions on whether it was acceptable to attend the cinematic concert alone. It was an orchestrated attempt, pun intended, to entice Joanne to offer to join me. My endeavour failed miserably but the concert was a tremendously entertaining, colourful musical jamboree from Vrijthof Square in the Dutch city of Maastricht and I was stupefied by how much I enjoyed it, becoming an instant new fan of the long-haired sexagenarian band leader.

I was about to complete my final nightshift before going on a two-week summer leave when I noticed that my friend Joanne had disappeared from my friend list. I had indeed been 'unfriended' and having not actually seen Joanne for a couple of weeks, there wasn't much I could do about it. The fact she had gone out of her way to "unfriend" me was significant as I tried to positively reflect that if she didn't care, why would she bother drawing attention to herself? Acutely aware that my forthcoming leave was important for the family and in aid of a wonderful cause, I had to let go with that illustrious little Spanish phrase "que sera sera" tucked away in my subconscious.

That final week in July arrived and 14-year-old Number One and I, supported by Jennifer and Numbers Two and Three, set off on a very wet Sunday morning from Milngavie (pronounced Mull-guy) on the outskirts of Glasgow to begin our 6-stage West Highland Way adventure. The West Highland Way is a linear long-distance route running 96 miles from Milngavie north of Glasgow to Fort William in the Highlands. The trail, opened in 1980, was Scotland's first officially designated Long Distance Route and is now renowned as one of the world's great trails.

New Year Resolutions came up with the idea that we would undertake such an adventure in 2013 in aid of charity. Deciding upon a charity was straightforward as family friends had tragically lost their young daughter in September 2012 to acute myeloid leukaemia and had consequently set up a foundation in her memory to fund research. An astounding amount of kind donations, including two from Joanne, exceeded our aims and expectations and raised in excess of £2000 for the worthy cause. A couple of training sessions in the weeks leading up to the walk were deemed sufficient preparation, although an education on foot care on long distance hikes would ensue as we resolved to complete the task.

Having apparently established a family reputation for planning events to the nth degree, I issued Jennifer and the younger ones with written instructions and directions for campsites, which included 'things to do' and local tourist attractions whilst Number One and I were hiking before they reached those pre-arranged campsites to set up our tent pending our daily weary arrival.

After only a couple of miles on the 'Way', the Craigallian Fire Memorial is reached, a small circular monument. It was erected to commemorate the spirit of the young and jobless Glasgow folk of the post-depression 1930's who would sit around the fire sharing tales of their adventures, viewing the flickering light as a beacon of hope for future generations. As we stood in this peaceful setting on the west bank of tranquil Craigallian Loch, I was moved to share my own fanciful aspiration with my daughter.
"If we're allowed to make a wish at this beacon of hope, may I dream that one day I will be back at this spot sharing a moment with Joanne?"
With a hint of trepidation in her voice that Joanne had entered into my thoughts at such an early juncture in our adventure, Number One muttered, "Yeah, dream away Dad," to accompany the slight rolling of her eyes.

It was the catalyst for her to endure, at various points in the week, many musings about getting back into the life of the woman who had entered my heart during the previous three months.

Despite the often dreary weather, it was a gratifying week in the company of my young friend, and with excellent support from the rest of the family, we trundled into Fort William town centre on a busy Friday afternoon. After six days of walking in very rural surroundings, the urban nature of the final few hundred yards felt akin to marathon runners entering the stadium for the final lap to accept the congratulations of the massed crowd. The massed crowd in this scenario were either tourists browsing shops or locals all too familiar with the sight of weary walkers crossing the finishing line. We were greeted by the statue simply known as 'Man with Sore Feet' sat upon the inviting wooden benches by the official 'finish' sign. After the obligatory social media posts affirming the successful completion of our challenge for our kind contributors, I euphorically climbed into my hotly anticipated bath in a local hotel room. That euphoria was somewhat enhanced when I received a text message from Joanne congratulating us on our achievement. I acknowledged her message and sank back into the excessive bubbles. There was surely a chance.

Another couple of weeks elapsed incommunicado, punctuated with regular thoughts of Joanne, unaware that another musically-orientated intervention lay on the horizon. Some friends on Facebook were looking for suggestions on which track to have as their first dance at their forthcoming nuptials. I suggested "A Thousand Years" by Christina Perri in a post that was 'public' and thereby viewable to anyone. This ostensibly insignificant detail would ultimately prove to be of huge significance.

The following day, I received a text from Joanne, the first since her West Highland Way congratulations, which simply read *"That's not fair."*
I retorted with a question mark, unaware of the meaning behind her message but subconsciously hoping it was in some way related to Miss Perri's beautiful ballad.
"Making me cry isn't fair. I saw the song you posted. It's beautiful and made me cry. I hadn't heard of it."

49

"Yeah, it is beautiful and very romantic. Appropriate for a wedding I thought."

Unable to resist the temptation, I further replied, *"Being messed about over the past few months by someone I could love for a thousand years hasn't been too fair either."*

Joanne reacted, *"That's harsh. I can understand why my behaviour can be seen as mental cos it can hurt folk. And I am sincerely sorry for that, truly. If I become overwhelmed by my feelings, making me behave mentally, then that means I felt intensely with you. It was real, Matt, I know cos I couldn't handle it. Sorry for the intrusion."*

Deciphering and interpreting the paragraph she sent would take some analysis. The simplified version would suggest she couldn't be with me because she liked me too much, not a particularly ideal blueprint for getting through life. Notwithstanding that, my attention was drawn to the irksome opening two words of her message.

"If you want harsh, Joanne, think about the last four months and look at it from my perspective and current predicament. How I 'feel', not 'felt', how I 'feel' about you. How I miss your face, your smile, your laugh, your kiss, your voice . . .need I go on? Think I could write the book on harsh. "

"Ok I understand and I'm sorry again for the intrusion. Impulsive when low. Just keeping it together but it's not easy. Take care x"

I would sign off with a closing gambit.

"Life goes on and no alternative to getting on with single life. 'When you're lying on your back in the gutter, you look up and see the stars.' Think that was Oscar Wilde or something like that! Down to Glasgow tomorrow night for the Jolly Boys Outing, looking forward to catching up with some very close pals whom I'm sure will offer me their trusted guidance. Just trying to be positive, sweetheart, but like you say, it's not easy. All the best."

The following afternoon as I was preparing for the weekend shenanigans ahead, Joanne again got in touch by text.

"How are you getting to the train station. I'm in Aberdeen. Would you like a lift?"

A shiver of controlled excitement flashed over me as I looked at the message, the first suggestion of seeing Joanne face to face in almost two months.

A further more intense shiver of excitement followed an hour later as she walked into my flat but I had to try to play it cool. I had only known Joanne for four months and in that time, she had evoked overwhelming feelings and caused no little hurt. Was I doing the right thing? She looked as lovely as ever as I tried to control my inevitable and unpreventable descent into helplessness as my heart insisted on reminding my brain how much I felt for this bothered but bewitching beautiful woman.

My brain was just as quick, however to remind my heart to be wary of being hurt yet again.

A cup of tea was on the menu before my transportation and a routine catch-up on life in general. Joanne explained that she had been doing a lot of self-analysis over the past while and had come to the conclusion that she couldn't and probably shouldn't resist her feelings for me. A part of me wanted to punch the air with delight but I knew a grounded rationale needed to be maintained. That rationale was maintained when, after revealing I had been for a beer with some refereeing friends two nights earlier, Joanne inadvertently revealed in turn that whilst out, I had left my living room light on.

"I was parked outside and I wanted to come up and see you but I chickened out."

The 47-year-old woman had driven for half an hour to sit in her parked vehicle, looking up at my first floor flat. With no phone call and no attempted knock at the door, I considered it a slightly disconcerting episode.

En route to the train station, Joanne enquired about my post-weekend train and suggested she could pick me up from the train station. My brain was gaining the upper hand over my excitable heart on this occasion and I told her I was planning on the walk home but if she were there, it would be appreciated.

"You don't trust me, Matt. You're wary?"

"A wee bit, darlin'. I'm sure you understand."

"Yes I do, and I'll just have to prove to you that you can trust me," she asserted.

Joanne had no idea how much that sentence resonated with me as I floated on my journey to Glasgow amidst a colourful cocktail of buoyancy, anticipation and a sense of renewed optimism. My annual catch-up with former RAF friends was always an auspicious occasion but this year's event had already become a very special weekend.

Two inebriated sleeps later and recovering from the latest annual Jolly Boys hangover, I alighted from the train in Aberdeen to find Joanne waiting for me. We returned to my flat and I debriefed her on the weekend shenanigans as Joanne reciprocated with details of her visit to a Highland Games. A second cup of coffee ensued and as we channelled the calmness within these relaxed moments, I recalled that the comedian Jason Manford was appearing in the city later that week if Joanne was free and wanted to accompany me. She responded favourably and my excitable suggestion that it was a 'date' was somewhat stifled with an unforeseen inauspicious disclosure.

"Matt. Yes, it's a date, but if we're going to get off on the right foot, I need to tell you something."

"Go on," I urged.

"I slept with Dave a couple of weeks ago. It was stupid and I shouldn't have."

I paused to take in this information. Joanne wasn't with me thus I was reminding myself that she hadn't been unfaithful. With what I now knew about Dave and their tempestuous and physical altercations of the past and her previous narrative of countering his unwanted sexual advances, it appeared this one wasn't unwanted. To quote her own words, she had jumped into bed with the "arse that chats up my daughter's mates and he's nearly fifty, for fucks sake." As they lived in separate houses, I had no desire to know where it happened.

"I suppose you weren't with me Joanne and I appreciate you telling me. How do I know it won't happen again?"

"It was a one-off and it was stupid. It definitely won't happen again. I want to be with you Matt."

There was an air of sincerity in her voice and I knew, deep down, that I was about to let another red flag ascend the flagpole unchallenged. Striking while the iron remained hot and with my tongue in my cheek, I asked, "So, is there anything else you want to share?"

I certainly didn't expect the ensuing pause nor the reply.

"Em, well, Limpy was one of the guys on the Making Mates site I dated before you. I went out on another date with him as I was so taken aback by how I fell for you, I wanted to make sure I had no feelings for him like I had for you."

I had previously been made aware of "Limpy", her 55-year-old date with the referenced hobble and I thought better of the natural reaction, which was to question her baffling conjecture by asking if her date with Limpy to decide if she'd really fallen for me had occurred before or after she fucked her estranged husband.

With yet another red flag hoisted up the mast, Joanne was evidently going through a troublesome and perhaps transitional period and my gut was reminding me not to judge her because, after all, here she was, sitting in my kitchen, telling me that she wanted to be my girlfriend.

And I liked her so much.

The end of the week arrived and, standing outside the venue waiting for my date to arrive, I felt a palpable sense of potential for Joanne and I to metamorphosize from our unpredictable and problematic beginnings into a more solid foundation for a relationship. I was certainly willing to give things every chance. Time would tell.

Day Two – Ennerdale Water to Borrowdale

The sound of a waterfall in full spate would describe the 6.20am alarm clock. Here we were in late May and the canvas was being battered by hailstones, creating a racket I wasn't going to sleep through. It had been a disruptive night as my ultralight all-singing all-dancing inflatable sleeping mattress had lost its voice and choreography and I awoke at 3.30am feeling somewhat . . . well . . . deflated. Nightly replenishment from my lungs into my bed in the wee small hours was about to become an unforeseen ritual of the trip.

Adding boiling water to my freeze-dried 'morning oats with raspberry', I enjoyed a leisurely and nutritional breakfast, hoping for some abatement of the ongoing conditions ahead of a 9-mile day, shortened by yesterday's extra stretch. As per my standard procedure, particularly in inclement weather, I had everything packed into my rucksack and myself suited, booted and ready to rock, just leaving the tent to disassemble and attach to the front of the rucksack under the latter's protective rain cover.

With a short break in the weather just after 9am, I grasped the opportunity to make headway. On regaining the Coast-to-Coast, signposts indicated that walking on the main forest track was currently forbidden due to forestry operations. Adhering to the small detour, I crossed onto the south side of the River Liza which was then tracked eastwards on a very wet and boggy path. The trees did afford some respite as I occasionally stopped to shelter from the passing heavy hail showers. Eventually a bridge was reached on this riverside "ball-ache" where it was permissible to cross back over onto the wide forest track on the north side of the river. With the strengthening wind exacerbating the periodic hail showers, it felt more like November than May as I pressed on, with gloves and beanie complimenting my waterproof jacket, emerging from the forest onto open ground towards the Black Sail Youth Hostel. Billing itself as England's most remote Youth Hostel (Scotland has a more remote establishment at Altbeithe on the Affric Kintail Way), the attractive former bothy, dwarfed by large hills on three sides, was completely closed due to the gradual emergence from the pandemic. A few hundred yards on from the hostel and after passing some small hillocks, the thin path veers left and begins a steep relentless ascent of Loft Beck. The path is not clearly defined at the beginning and I would overtake two ladies consulting their guidebook. I offered up in passing that my research suggested the path was on the right-hand side of the falling beck and pushed on as the ongoing pluvial conditions were not conducive to stopping for a chat. The problem with overtaking fellow hikers on an ascent is that I felt I had to get far enough ahead of them to warrant stopping for a break without them catching me up. With a steely resolve and lots of exhalation from my posterior, this was achieved some 15 minutes later, looking down to see the two ladies some distance below. As is the nature of long-distance hikes, I would have no idea at this stage of the small part these two ladies would play in the first week of my journey.

On reaching the summit of Loft Beck, there was an impressive, albeit distant view north-west to Buttermere, one of the smaller lakes in the region, but with the unpleasant overhead conditions, there wasn't much time to stand and stare and I pushed on across a ridge passing Grey Knotts towards Hopper Quarry. On reaching the quarry, the path becomes a disused tramway with an increasingly gnarly descent towards the Honister Slate Mine, the last working slate mine in England and a popular tourist attraction. Most importantly, this tourist attraction involved a cafe and after a persistent soaking since the Black Sail Youth Hostel, the bowl of tomato soup, sausage roll and mug of tea was at that moment considered the highlight of the trip.

I was just finishing my lunch when 'two ladies' entered and occupied an adjacent table. Now in a more meteorologically-friendly environment, I was able to ascertain that these two friends, one from London and one from the south of Scotland, had walked the second half of the Coast-to-Coast the previous summer from Kirkby Stephen to Robin Hood's Bay and were now undertaking the first half. They were booked into a hotel in Rosthwaite, just further on from my booked camping pitch at Borrowdale Youth Hostel and, acknowledging that our paths would no doubt cross at a future point, I bade them 'bon appetit' and began the 3-mile gradual descent to the youth hostel at Borrowdale.

After passing through the small settlement of Seatoller, the trail approached my overnight stop through Johnny Wood, not the long-lost brother of Ronnie, but some forest alongside the River Derwent where the non-rolling stones gathered moss and required the assistance of chains for safe passage.

Arriving at the youth hostel at around 3pm, I was unable to gain access. Fortunately, a resident allowed me entry from within through the simplex-locked door, explaining that reception didn't open until 5pm. With no sign of the weather improving, I took the opportunity to pitch my tent in the requisite area ahead of check-in and was reunited with my transit holdall in the reception lobby.

At 5pm, I reported to reception to join the queue for check-in, a rather convoluted process, particularly with only one member of staff on reception duties.

I was able to arrange a two-course evening meal for £10 and was asked if I would require use of a shower which were booked into half hour slots. With others in the queue behind me clearly within earshot, it would take a brave hiker to turn down that offer of a shower. Subsequently, my 6pm shower room would be vacated by 6.10, changed, showered, dried and freshly clothed. Who takes half an hour for a shower? In a previous life in southern Iraq, specific shower instructions were "get wet, soap on, wash soap off" all in 30 seconds!

When it comes to value for money and a spirit of camaraderie, there isn't much that could outdo a Youth Hostel. Reporting to the small dining room to be shown to my pre-booked table, I enjoyed my very reasonably priced evening meal of home-cooked pasta Bolognese followed by some "school-dinner" reminiscence of delicious stodgy sponge and custard. Enquiring with staff as to the availability of a table in the adjacent bar for a post-dinner pint, I was shown through to a table for what I thought would be a pint and then retirement to my tent for the evening. The "bar" consisted of eight 4-seater tables, all now occupied to various extents, symmetrically positioned around a focal-point small bar in the corner.

With wi-fi available in the bar area, I managed to register for an account and availed myself of a quick catch-up on the electronic world before taking the opportunity to post some photos on social media of my opening two contrasting days. Sat alone at one of those 4-seat tables, deliberating on which of my photos to share with the outside world, my attention was distracted by a soft female voice. "Excuse me. Is anyone sitting here?"

I looked up to meet the gaze of a lady attired in standard hill-walking gear, and I instinctively replied, "No, not at all," and extending my arm towards one of the vacant seats opposite, invited her to join me.

Returning my focus to the in-progress social media post on my phone, I couldn't resist a furtive look across the table, just to confirm my instant impression that the random blonde 40-something woman who had requested the seat opposite was very pretty.

My new table-sharer appeared somewhat troubled with events unfolding on the mobile phone she was staring at.

"Everything ok?", I opened.

"Oh, this place won't let me log onto the wi-fi and I need to download routes for my walk tomorrow. The on-screen message is denying me access and says I have to be over 13 years old. I think I qualify."

"Can I help?" I offered.

"You could confirm that it's not just me doing something wrong, if you like," she replied, handing me her phone.

Now holding the stranger's phone and looking at a log-in screen, she would only be a stranger for the briefest of moments.

"My first name is Natasha, surname Buckley," she began as I populated the fields on the log-in page accordingly.

"Home town?" I read.

"Norwich."

Glancing up, I commented, "I used to be based just up the road at RAF Marham back in the 90s."

"Yeh, I'm Norwich originally then I lived in London for many years but I'm now based in Cambridge."

"It's asking for your date of birth," I continued.

"24th of April, 1965."

As I entered those details, I paused, glanced across once more and with a slight intonation, "You're 56?"

"Yes," she replied with a bashful simper and I surmised it wasn't the first time she had encountered such a reaction as it was fair to say she did not look her age.

"So, tell me. How often do you supply all your personal details to random strange men you've just met?" I joked.

"Yeh, I know. I must stop doing that," she countered with an impish smile.

As had happened inexplicably to Natasha, access to wi-fi was denied with the same on-screen message indicating that users had to be over 13 years of age.

I quickly came up with a proposed solution.

"Tell you what, I got access ok so why don't I log you in with my details?" and, entering my details and password onto her phone, access was duly granted before returning her phone.

My new acquaintance was most appreciative of my assistance. "That's so good of you and so helpful. Thank you. Can I buy you a drink?"

"That's ok, I'll get the drinks," I reacted, "you can sort out your download. What you having?"

"Oh, I'll have a Prosecco, please."

I made for the bar and duly ordered a pint for myself and a prosecco for Natasha.

"A small or a large prosecco?" the young lady on the other side of the bar asked.

I had never purchased a Prosecco in my life and, assuming she was referring to the size of the glass, I opted for the large.

"No problem, I'll bring your drinks over to your table."

I returned to the table where my newest companion was sorting out her walk for the following day and conversation began on our respective reasons for being at a Cumbrian youth hostel on a very wet Sunday evening.

Our initial dialogue was interrupted by the bartender placing a tray on the table, upon which was my pint of beer, two glasses . . . and a bottle of Prosecco. Natasha and I stared at the tray before turning to each other.

"Em," I commenced in slight confusion, "She asked if I wanted a large Prosecco. I didn't know that meant a bottle."

The attractive lady chuckled, "Well, you'll just have to help me drink it."

Our unplanned consumption of additional sparkling Italian wine developed into a most serendipitous occurrence as the next couple of hours were spent in interesting conversation, opening up our respective lives. Each of us were parents to two elder daughters with a younger brother, we had a penchant for a wee stroll into the hills and we were both romantically unattached. The latter fact inevitably led to my sharing of reflections on the past few months and my newest friend's standpoint on the advantages of singledom would help to positivise my own outlook, moving forward. Like Joanne, Natasha was also a counsellor and could have been charging me a fee for listening to my gibberish. She was a regular visitor to the Lake District where she enjoyed bagging 'Wainwrights', a list of 214 fells described by and named after the great man himself.

We were clearly not on a date, not just on account of the fact that Natasha was Premier League to my Vauxhall Conference (for non-football fans, that is a 5th tier football league, not a car) but it did feel similar to that very first evening with Joanne eight years previously. At one point, Natasha, by this stage confirmed as a brave showerless hiker, sought out my social media page and "friended" me, resulting in a quick glance at her own page where photos complemented her previously described foreign adventures. A most pleasant evening reached closing time and much later than scheduled and, parting with agreement to keep in touch with each other's adventures, I headed outside into the rainy chilly darkness and accessed my tent, quickly ensconcing myself in the warmth of my sleeping bag. A couple of days down, a dozen to go.

Summer 2014

"It was erected to remember the young and jobless Glaswegians of the post-depression 1930's. Apparently, they would sit around the fire sharing stories, viewing the flickering light as a beacon of hope for future generations. You should make a wish."
Immersed in the pleasant Saturday morning sunshine, Joanne and I stood on that peaceful west shore of Craigallian Loch reading the inscriptions on the memorial.
"Actually, Joanne, standing here, I need to share something with you," I began, pausing to transfix my sentimental gaze on her beautiful freckled face, "this is a very special moment for me. I stood in this very spot last summer with Number One and wished that one day in the future I would stand here with you. I wouldn't have dared believe that wish would come true within a year. Thank you."
Joanne's requited gaze met mine and a passionate clinch ensued. It was an endearing moment early on the first day of our scheduled 7-day adventure which set the tone for a brilliant week.

Our relationship had blossomed since the previous autumn, with those early hiccups consigned to the past. Friendship and fun came to the fore when Joanne volunteered to join me on the 26-mile 'kiltwalk', a new concept that had been initiated in Scotland to support various charities. A memorable September day ensued, bedecked in tartan as required, completing the marathon walk in around eight hours. Those eight hours spent in Joanne's exclusive company were simply wonderful with a mix of anecdotes, singing and general silliness carrying us along and assisting our tiring limbs into the latter stages.

Introductions and initial relationships had been constituted with our families over the following months, comfortably establishing a rapport with Scott and Angela as Joanne effortlessly did likewise with Numbers One, Two and Three.

One minor red flag had appeared in mid-November as Joanne attended the graduation of Angela with Scott and Dave in the city. After attending a celebratory lunch, Joanne left to call on me at my flat. On arrival, Joanne zealously relayed that Dave was absolutely furious that she hadn't spent the entire day with her daughter, electing to leave after lunch to visit "the boy" as he apparently referred to me. It would take a long time before I fully appreciated the zeal Joanne enjoyed when telling stories about other people's reactions to her. By this stage, a couple of steady months into our new relationship, Dave's comments were of no concern to me but Joanne's countering statement was rather confounding.

"I went to the graduation and I went to the lunch. I love my kids very much and I always will, but I love you more, Matt."

I was slightly taken aback by her declaration and felt compelled to clarify my own standpoint.

"I love you very much too Joanne, but I have to tell you. You will always be fourth in line where my children are concerned."

I reckoned Dave's behaviour had prompted her to find justification for her visit, a justification I didn't consider necessary, but neither was her misguided proclamation.

A stand-out moment of epiphany had occurred in December. In my role as a Development Advisor for football referees, Joanne had accompanied me to a match in the city. She had little interest in football but attended some matches with me, declaring a liking for having me "in her lug", expounding on the intricacies of the arbiter's decision-making and general game management. As the match concluded, Joanne headed back to the 'Shire and I headed for home. Due to respective work and family commitments in the week ahead, we were not scheduled to be back in each other's company for five days. Just five days. On the journey home, my feelings of abject disappointment concerning our impending brief hiatus felt incommensurate with the situation. We would be in touch throughout those five days so what was the big deal? It was a cognizant moment for me, an affirmation of the veracity of my love for Joanne. I consoled myself in my belief that I was an extremely lucky man.

A month later and a post-New Year short break away in Fort William involved a drive to the village of Kinlochleven, commonly the final overnight stop on the West Highland Way. The breath-taking vista from the head of the loch across to the snow-capped Glencoe mountains evoked reminiscence of my West Highland Way adventure with Number One and inspired conversation about the beauty of the famous trail. Within a few weeks, we were booking our very own summer adventure.

Inspired by our tartan-clad traipse on the 'kiltwalk', I decided to walk the entire West Highland Way in a kilt, obviously a cheap 'non-formal-use' plaid previously used on the Jolly Boys Outing. It certainly afforded a photo opportunity for a group of enthusiastic Icelandic hikers towards the end of our opening day's less than demanding drudge to Drymen. Having camped every night of the previous year's charity challenge, this year's 'holiday' would involve the booking of accommodation each evening to expel the need for any tent-erecting.

Our ramble to Rowardennan Youth Hostel on Day Two involved climbing Conic Hill with its extensive views of Loch Lomond and beyond. It was also on this stretch that we first encountered Hans, a solo walker from Germany. Our new 'freund' joined us for a couple of miles, entertaining us with his rather eccentric use of broken English. He was quite taken with the subtle difference between his own country's 'banane' and our English 'banana' . . . and he reminded us . . . frequently. I did possess enough conversational German to reciprocate in his native tongue where feasible. When we stopped for a brew, Hans stopped with us and it became apparent that he was tagging along for the day and hadn't received the memo detailing the general rules of solo hiking.

It was during Day Three's bound to Beinglas when fellow hikers we had met advised that Hans was looking for us. Our continental chum seemed a nice chap, however we had planned to walk The Way as a duo and thus began a daily game of "Hide from Hans".

24 hours later, deep in Strathfillan Forest, two grown adults were silently concealed behind a couple of Scots pines as our Bavarian banana buddy came into view and strolled past, never to be seen again.

Before setting off on Day Five's gambol to Glencoe, I was preparing our packed lunch in our Tyndrum 'hobbit house' accommodation when Joanne observed she was fairly positive that having a man dressed in a kilt prepare her lunch was a lifetime first. Her innate sense of fun provided another memorable moment later in the day. As we approached the aforementioned group of Icelandic tourists, they were sat in line across the entire parapet of a small bridge. My cute companion broke into an impromptu jog across the bridge, extending an open-handed arm to receive over a dozen 'high-fives' from the sedentary, surprised but receptive tourists. Her witty tomfoolery elicited much hilarity from all concerned. Funny as it was, there remained the afterthought that if our Scandinavian sidekicks had been nonplussed and not entered into the spirit of her spontaneity, leaving Joanne to run across the bridge with an untouched extended arm, I may well have caused myself an injury from laughing.

Our Day Six ascent over the Devil's Staircase and long drop down into Kinlochleven placed us back in the pretty village where our adventure had been conceived back in January and allowed wider reflection on the intervening happy months with Joanne.

Obviously unknown at this point, another heartfelt, poignant but ultimately bittersweet moment lay years ahead in Kinlochleven.

Back in the present, Joanne entered into the tartan theme for the final day's foray from Kinlochleven to Fort William, donning her 'Kiltwalk' apparel and, complimented with our kiltwalk tee-shirts, we rekindled the spirit of that previous September day. A mid-afternoon triumphant tartan finale flowed through Fort William town centre and some reacquaintance with "Man with Sore Feet" preceded the obligatory photo opportunities. This was my second completion of Scotland's most famous walk and although there's a pleasant sense of achievement, it is invariably accompanied by a reticent disappointment that it's over. Before checking in to our accommodation adjacent to the finish line, Joanne suggested a celebratory dram in a nearby hostelry. Neither of us were remotely keen on whisky but it was an auspicious occasion and a large 12-year-old malt recommended by staff was the salute to our completion of The Way. As we glowed in the warmth of the "Water of Life", I could never have anticipated how a future similar celebration would play such a significant role in my life.

A successful family holiday followed in July with all our kids and some partners joining us at a lodge in the Cairngorms at various junctures throughout an enjoyable week.

With sleepovers in Aberdeen on proverbial school-nights, my early start would regularly require that Joanne was left to her own devices in my flat until later in the morning. One particular such morning in late summer resulted in yet another beautifully romantic moment. Returning from work in the late afternoon, my general habit would routinely involve a cup of tea. As I filled the kettle and returned it to its docking station, my attention was drawn to a note, quite purposefully left alongside, unmissable to my line of sight. A small torn-off piece of paper, the size of a standard playing card, upon which Joanne had written in her own distinctive hand-writing. "How do I love thee? Let me count the ways. 1-10." A love heart had been appended to the bottom of the piece of paper and the '1-10' element of her note suggested a romantic solo treasure hunt was about to ensue around my flat. Over the following fifteen to twenty minutes, I trawled my flat, eventually locating eleven of those similarly sized pieces of paper, yes, eleven. Sitting down with my little bundle of unbridled written love, I was not only moved by the comments therein, but the romantic creativeness of her sentiment and the tangible declaration of love. Each little affectionate epistle was numbered and duly appended with a love heart.

1. *You make me laugh.*
2. *That you are a good cook (especially in a kilt)*
3. *You think of others.*
4. *You're just lovely (and a great pal!)*
5. *The way you look forward, always planning (our future!)*
6. *The way you have a bath. (dead cute). I like to sit and yap to you.*
7. *The many different ways I feel when we're in bed . . . sexy, passionate, moving, touching, caring, fun, thoughtful, together xxx*
8. *I love your independence.*
9. *Your life experience . . . you're inspiring!*
10. *Your sense of family x*
10. *When you sing x*

The quirky duplication of number 10 served to enhance her delightfully romantic gesture as I carefully assembled her notes.

Having been together more than a year, chatter would regularly turn to taking the next step in our relationship and co-habiting. Joanne had often referred to preparing her home for us to live there together and Angela had already given her blessing to what appeared to be a forthcoming inevitability.

Amidst the beautiful autumnal shades of early October, a Saturday referee development appointment was completed in the 'Shire before returning to Joanne's for tea and sleepover prior to a run of nightshifts commencing on the Sunday.

Joanne had kindly planned a hearty cooked brunch on the Sunday morning which we enjoyed together and I was concluding our repast with a cup of tea when our routine discourse took a sudden and definitively eerie turn and ultimately led my lovely lady to new levels of unpredictability.

"At the wedding, did you tell Damian that you were moving in with me?" she enquired.

A fortnight earlier, Joanne and I had attended the wedding reception of my friend Damian and his lovely new wife.

"Yeh, pretty sure I mentioned it but didn't mention any specific date," I replied enquiringly.

"It's just that I've been doing a bit of thinking, Matt, and I'm not sure I want you to move in."

Slightly taken aback by the randomness and suddenness of the direction of the conversation and not really knowing how to reply, I placed my half-full cup on the table and responded with a surprised tone

"Oh . . . right . . . ok," and after a pause, "Well let's just leave it for now then."

It had been a very long time since I felt the sense of foreboding initiated by Joanne's long pause in conversation. I felt a knot beginning to form in my full stomach and some concern as to where the conversation was going, but the question required asking.

"Are you ok, Joanne?"

"Not really Matt. I think you should go."

With feelings of instantaneous bewilderment, I stood up, "Em . . .ok," I uttered in a way which probably sounded more like a question.

"I think you should go Matt . . . permanently," Joanne announced.

My confused face met the solemn face in front of me and I struggled to utter a single word.

"What?" I instinctively muttered in complete befuddlement.

"Yes, sorry Matt. It's over."

Such was my instantly overwhelming internal turbulence that I bizarrely found myself not questioning her reasons and motives as, moments later, I stumbled towards her front door clutching my overnight bag.

"Can I have my key back?" she asked, in a manner suggesting it was more out of practicality than callousness.

I removed my copy of her front door key from my bunch and handed it over.

To this day, I have no idea why I then hugged her. I was numb, in shock and due to the astonishing swiftness of what had just transpired, it was almost like an out-of-body experience. Minutes earlier, I was enjoying brunch with my partner of over a year and looking to the future, and then . . . nothing.

And there I was, driving back to the city in a stupefied state. Over the course of that 30-minute drive, I gradually tried to piece together any potential reasons for another sudden dumping, admittedly her first in over a year. Other than her new-found reluctance to co-habitation, nothing sprang to mind. As I arrived back at my flat and the magnitude of the day's events became reality, a horrible cloud descended, necessitating a hasty retreat to the toilet where my lovely brunch was involuntarily disgorged.

My kids had built a relationship with Joanne and I knew it was going to upset them that she had ended things once again. It's a parental facet that you don't want your offspring to see you as a failure and I suppose the overriding disappointment was having to tell them that I had failed. That uncomfortable call took place via Jennifer later in the afternoon.

With an uncanny resemblance to Joanne's previous sudden let-downs, her latest unexpected disaffection would herald the beginning of a run of four nightshifts and, harder as it was after over a year together, the game-face would have to be duly displayed. Some respite arrived on the second of those nightshifts when Number Two, a keen figure skater, had just attained the level to skate competitively. Her accompanying music would be the score for the film "Forest Gump", a tremendously poignant and powerful piece of music I would attempt to use to placate my disappointment, notwithstanding its famed "box of chocolates" analogy.

That allegorical box of chocolates would be opened whilst I was on patrol on the third nightshift as I received a very unexpected message on my phone. Joanne had inexplicably forwarded a photograph of her and I dancing at the recent aforementioned wedding of my friend Damian and his new wife. It was a glorious photo of us, smiling and looking deliriously happy in each other's company. Her accompanying message simply said, "*I look so happy.*"

I stared at the message, dazed by incredulity, blissfully unaware of the numerous similar moments which still lay ahead in life.

"*Not quite sure why you're sending that, sweetie,*" was my confounded reply.

"Just saw it on Damian's wedding album and we look great, so thought I would forward it."

Once more, astonished by her palpably flagrant lack of awareness, I replied, *"Not really what I want to see right now, Joanne, under the circumstances."*

"I understand," her dilatory reply retrospectively confirming quite the opposite.

But of course, I struggled to escape my foolish love for this woman, something I believed Joanne was well aware of. Her communication suggested to me that perhaps she had suffered a blip and would once more come to her senses, and I tried to remain wary of becoming too hopeful. Always mindful that perhaps this wasn't the best disposition for my mental wellbeing, I carried on regardless.

Rested from the fourth nightshift, Friday afternoon took an interesting turn of events when I received a call from Jennifer. She explained that Joanne had telephoned her that morning asking her random questions about me. Without divulging all the details, Jennifer was rather perplexed that Joanne asked if anything had been going on between Jennifer and myself. Having been apart from Jennifer for over seven years, we both found her enquiry very bizarre but Jennifer, aware of my inescapable feelings for Joanne, did conclude the call by suggesting that if I was interested in potentially saving things, I should contact Joanne. Jennifer's tone certainly suggested that if I wanted things to revert back with Joanne, I should make that call expeditiously.

Love is blind, as the saying goes, and my excitement at the possibility that I was indeed just the victim of a temporary blip, galvanised renewed optimism that things weren't necessarily over. My heartbeat gathered pace as her phone rang and skipped a beat as I heard her voice on the other end.

"Hi Matt. How you doing?" she opened softly.

It had been five difficult days as I nervously replied.

"Hi Joanne. I've been on the phone to Jennifer and she suggested I give you a call?"

"Yes Matt. Would you like to talk?"

As a coincidence, I had previously booked tickets for a mobile cinema showing in the 'Shire that evening and had suggested that Angela and her partner could attend in our place to avoid the tickets going to waste.

"I could bring the tickets over for Angela?" I suggested.

"Why don't you bring the tickets over and you and I will attend instead?"

A shiver of excitement instantaneously ran through me.

"Ok, I'll leave shortly," I intimated, trying to sound collected.

"Bring stuff if you want to stay over," Joanne suggested.

"See you soon," I blurted in excited conclusion.

That overwhelming excitement and emotion consumed me as I hurriedly put together an overnight bag and tried to make myself presentable.

On the drive, riddled with anticipation, any doubts about Joanne's treatment of me and inevitable issues of trust were cast aside as mere vagaries and I wasn't going to allow anything to spoil the present. Life is punctuated with special moments and I hoped one such moment was imminent.

As I pulled the car onto Joanne's driveway, the lady I had inexplicably hugged five days earlier, was stood on the same threshold awaiting my return. She was already approaching the car as I alighted. No words were exchanged as she draped her outstretched arms around my neck, cradled her head into my neck and squeezed me very tightly. I couldn't help but passionately reciprocate and our tight embrace ensued for some time.

"I'm so, so sorry Matt," Joanne muttered emotionally at several points during our intense clinch. "I got scared. I now know I shouldn't have."

Once settled on the sofa, Joanne explained that she had doubts about taking the next step, became impulsive and had panicked. She explained that through research over a period of time, she reckoned she had a form of Borderline Personality Disorder (BPD), a condition that can affect how she thinks, feels and interacts with other people. Symptoms of BPD include being emotionally unstable, having upsetting thoughts and acting without thinking. She undertook to make an appointment with a view to getting therapy as well as obtaining curative literature.

Confiding in her friends during our brief hiatus, she said it had become clear that she was in love with me and should let nature take its course. Several more heartfelt apologies followed for putting me through more heartache which I readily accepted, ecstatic to be back in the company of my captivatingly beautiful friend. The aforementioned course of nature would involve our co-habitation as Joanne formally asked me to move in with her within the forthcoming weeks. I can't deny it was a special moment and underlying concerns about her impulsive unpredictability were put to one side as this wasn't going to be an opportunity I wouldn't grasp. Love is not rational and my feelings for Joanne felt beyond my control. Impulsion and potential BPD were just a part of the personality of the woman I was in love with. She wasn't perfect, of course, and neither was I, but to my mind, being perfect for each other was more important.

A week that had started disastrously with a devastating move backwards, leaving me in the doldrums, was concluding in the most breathtakingly exciting way with a huge step forward. My thoughts turned to the well-known quote about an arrow. "An arrow can only be shot by pulling it backward. When life is dragging you back with difficulties, just imagine that it's going to launch you into something great."

We didn't get round to making our trip to the mobile cinema that evening.

Day Three – Borrowdale to Grasmere

Light rain continued through the night and had mercifully paused by dawn allowing some less constrictive breaking of camp at Borrowdale Youth Hostel. A bacon roll was purchased from the hostel and with a relatively shorter day, I would rely on snacks as required on my trek to Grasmere.

The Monday morning sun was beginning to make a welcome appearance as I headed south-east on a path alongside Stonethwaite Beck and began the gradual ascent to Greenup Gill. As a result of the recent precipitation, waters were in vigorous spate and walking poles were of great assistance when fording streams and waterfalls on boulders.

High up to my right in the distance, I could see diminutive figures on the summit ridge of Eagle Crag which, from last night's encounter with Natasha, I knew to be her first port of call in a 12-peak circular hike she had planned for the day.

After Greenup Gill, there was a steep and stepped climb onto the summit of Lining Crag, where I now looked down on the aforementioned Eagle Crag. Stopping to rehydrate after the climb, I retrieved the selfie-stick from my rucksack for some obligatory photos and thanks to the now clear weather, Scafell Pike, England's highest peak was also clearly visible to the south-west.

My view of Scafell Pike would be inadvertently extended as I bounded on southwards through the boggy ground, thinking I was heading for Greenup Edge Pass, when in fact I was heading for the summit of High Raise. Realising the error of my ways, I estimated I had added at least a mile after redirecting north-eastwards to reach the pass and descend Wythburn Valley, thankfully on a much more defined path. Having overtaken a group of hikers before my involuntary detour, I found myself overtaking them once more. They didn't say anything . . . but they were thinking it.

On reaching Far Easedale, hikers are faced with a choice of route. The valley route tracks Easedale Beck on a gentle descent down to Grasmere Common and on into the village, but with the favourable weather, I elected to tackle the tougher high route along a ridge which included three Wainwrights.

The alternative higher route resulted in a fairly strenuous afternoon, commencing with the boggy ascent to the summit of Calf Crag, the most elevated point of the day at 1,762 feet. Pausing to take in the view down the valley towards Grasmere, I had my second canine introduction of the trip as Molly the bonny beagle from Sunderland and her owner were also enjoying the vista. Progressing along the ridge, the next summit was the non-Wainwright Moment Crag and from here, the impressive view expanded to include a distant Windermere, the largest lake in England. The second Wainwright, Gibson's Knott, enabled an additional view over the adjacent ridge down into Easedale Tarn, looking similar to tomorrow night's proposed camping location, Angle Tarn. After some descent, I was faced with the final ascent of the day, Helm Crag. It looked a stiff climb as I scanned my surroundings, somewhat forlornly, wondering if finding an alternative path off the ridge was cheating. I gritted my teeth and soon enough found myself atop Helm Crag, well not quite on the top, as the true summit, a cannon shaped barrel of rock known as The Howitzer involving a 25ft scramble, was beyond my energy levels and tolerance for heights. I settled for a photo of another hiker on The Howitzer and advanced across the summit ridge to meet the onset of the very steep and sharp descent towards Grasmere, "the loveliest spot that man hath ever found" according to the original romanticist William Wordsworth.

With my knees pleading for mercy, the path eventually descends through some trees to reach some flatter ground, traversing a field to re-join the Easedale Beck route. Before crossing a small wooden bridge to meet Easedale Road leading into the centre of the village, I caught up with 'two ladies' who were not complete strangers to me. My London and Scotland based acquaintances had booked into a local bed and breakfast and we walked together for some minutes, reflecting on our respective days until I had to detach myself at the entrance drive leading up to the Grasmere Butharlyp Howe Youth Hostel.

Consistent with Borrowdale, the youth hostel again didn't open until 5pm. Armed with this information and aware that I may arrive earlier than this, I had once again attached my tent to my rucksack rather than my couriered holdall. Consequently, with an hour to spare, I took the liberty of pitching my accommodation on Pitch One in the impressive garden area to the front of the imposing Victorian mansion, built in 1865 as a private home but under the proprietorship of the Youth Hostel Association since 1958. Utilising an adjacent picnic table, I brewed up and enjoyed a mug of tea in the pleasant late afternoon sunshine, a welcome contrast from the previous evening.

Reporting to reception for the 5pm check-in would be laboured as I joined the queue and once again wasn't brave enough to turn down the offer of a shower but did procure a table for another 2-course £10 dinner. When they allocated Pitch Four for my tent, I advised them that I had already set up at Pitch One. My 'inquisitive' Scottish stare to accompany this information appeared to convey the intended message that tent allocations could be re-jigged without bloodshed. I would be remaining on Pitch One.

Hoping to acquire some provisions for tomorrow's lunch and overnight remote wild camp, I enquired, "Sorry, just one more thing. How far is it to the coapy?"

The gentleman on reception paused before replying, "The what?"

Somewhat bizarrely, pointing my extended index finger in a random direction, I repeated, "The coapy?"

My host again paused in confusion, "Are you needing some photocopying?"

My pre-hike research had indicated that there was a nearby 'Co-Op' food store and I suddenly realised the error of my ways.

"I'm so sorry. The Co-op food store in the village? I was referring to it by its nickname back home," I explained with an apologetic smile.

Less than a 10-minute pre-dinner stroll away, I obtained some pork pies, sandwiches and chocolate as the next shop wouldn't be for 48 hours, notwithstanding I was carrying some freeze-dried rations. Tonight's rations would be provided by the excellent youth hostel catering services with spaghetti meatballs and fruit cocktail on the menu.

After organising some logistics for the two days ahead, my courier holdall would be staying in Grasmere for an additional night before reuniting with me in the village of Shap on Wednesday. Returning to the 'big house', a centre for evacuees during the Second World War, I purchased a couple of beers from reception and retired to the provided sitting room, taking the opportunity to charge my phone and chargebank. With wi-fi available, I also caught the closing stages of the Scottish Premier League play-off match as victorious Dundee replaced their opponents Kilmarnock in Scotland's top football division. A chat on the telephone with Number One completed my third day of what was already becoming a fabulous adventure.

Returning to the tent to settle down for the evening, the sight of a distant emergency vehicle's flashing blue lights in the gloaming felt out-of-place for this Lakeland postcard village. Hiking combined with emergency blue lights evoked memories, transporting me back six years.

Summer 2015

"Right. Taxi is on its way. Quick check to make sure we have everything?" I suggested
"I think we're good, Matt. I've checked the car," Joanne replied.

It took two and half hours to drive from the 'Shire to Inverness. A pleasant trip in the late July sunshine in the congenial company of my partner . . . and co-habitee of the past eight months. The drive afforded the opportunity for general reflection on that period and my thorough contentment with life, but I had no idea how significantly our impending 4-day adventure would affect the rest of my life.

Sharing a home with Joanne had been bliss and, regularly reminding myself just how lucky I was, we settled in together. As we did so, a few idiosyncrasies would joyfully become a progressive part of our relationship.
Thus far in our co-habitation, and in years that lay ahead, those little habits would develop seamlessly. Joanne ensured that she told me she loved me on a daily basis, more often than not using the phrase, "Have I told you today?" As we became more comfortable and secure in our relationship, I would often jokingly reply with reference to her unpredictability, "Yes, today", to which Joanne would counter, "Well, this hour anyway."
A special peculiarity would occur at midnight on the last day of the month. We would vie to be first in a race to send emoticons consisting of a pinching hand and a punching fist to indicate "pinch, punch, first of the month." Little things that became an endearing part of our consanguinity.
With myself on the sofa and Joanne on the adjacent armchair, any late-night tv-watching would be interspersed with the joining of our outstretched hands in what had become known as 'hand-hugs'.
Joanne's surprise acquisition of a karaoke machine would periodically subject the poor woman to my Neil Diamond repertoire. As a daily listener to the radio situated within the kitchen, our days off together were often punctuated with dances around the kitchen table, accompanied by my notably average singing, akin to my Neil Diamond karaoke standard.

Nightshifts at work became routinely and consistently punctuated with calls at 11pm. Even with little to discuss, the tradition of the call became sacrosanct and by 11.10pm, one had instigated a call to the other.

"I like having you in my lug," had become one of her established customary phone phrases together with, "I hate not having you in my bed." At least once a week, Joanne would remind me that she won the lottery the day she met me.

I was smitten with her, and I bought it all.

Today in Inverness, there was a pronounced air of anticipation as we were about to commence another little adventure. My old Peugeot, a trusted friend over the past five years would be left here in a corner of the Premier Lodge Hotel car park on the outskirts of the city. It would remain here for the next five nights, the last of which would be spent at this hotel. Heading to Fort William in the evening and starting tomorrow, there would be four daily stages of a 79-mile long walk back north to Inverness.

The Great Glen Way, a long-distance footpath straddling the Great Glen fault line through the heart of Scotland, was officially opened in 2002 and mainly follows the fault-line of the Great Glen from Fort William for those 79 miles due north-east to Inverness. Our research told us that the terrain varied from remote country roads and canal towpaths to woodland bridleways and paths. The planning had been undertaken months in advance, with accommodation in two budget hotels, two youth hostels and a bed and breakfast.

On the previous summer's West Highland Way adventure, we had utilized one of the many bag-carrying services to transport the bulk of our kit from stage to stage. A similar courier service wasn't available to coincide with our dates on the Great Glen Way, therefore the 4-day challenge would involve carrying our kit for the entire distance, although several practice days traipsing kit around the rolling hills of Aberdeenshire had us well prepared . . . we believed.

The taxi from the hotel ferried us and our laden rucksacks to the main bus station in the heart of the highland capital. Another taxi was planned, hopefully after successful completion of our challenge, to return us to the hotel on the Monday evening from a suitable hostelry after a customary celebratory dram.

A check of the departure information board revealed our coach for Fort William would be leaving at 4.45pm as scheduled on the two-hour trip south. As our transport pulled into its stance, I observed an important omission and stressful source of potential embarrassment.

Where was the toilet on the bus? Where was the toilet, regarding which I had specifically phoned the bus company a few days before to confirm it would be available on board? I would never contemplate travelling any distance on public transport that didn't provide toilet facilities. There was no railway line direct from Inverness to Fort William. Connection was available at great expense via an 8-hour round trip changing at Glasgow thus the bus was the only rational alternative . . . and this one would have a toilet . . . because I checked in advance . . . because the helpful lady on the phone confirmed it would have a toilet . . . because, for me, toilets on public transport are essential . . .

ULCERATIVE COLITIS

I was diagnosed with ulcerative colitis in late 2010 at the age of 41. During that final summer of my military career, I was becoming aware of and mildly concerned about the frequency and urgency of 'visits' although at this point, I could control things. When blood began appearing, it was time to look into the . . . matter. Initial medical assistance and routine testing of samples were unable to clarify the problem, and eventually an inside broadcast unit embarked on a 'fantastic voyage', more commonly known as a colonoscopy, resulting in a same-day diagnosis of ulcerative colitis. It had been a possibility and at least I had confirmation. Medical science can't offer specific reasons why people contract the disease and, sadly, has yet to discover a cure.

Ulcerative colitis is a condition that affects a person's large bowel and rectum, the linings of which become inflamed with ulcers developing. It is the most common type of inflammatory bowel disease – about 150,000 people in the UK have it.   One will usually have the disease for the rest of their life and as I would discover, there would be periods without symptoms, known as remission, and sustained periods with symptoms, known as flare-ups. During flare-ups, the main symptom is bloody diarrhoea, double entendre intended. The most disturbing aspect for a sufferer in flare-up is the inability to control things. When the need arises, there will, at best, be a few minutes to get to a toilet or an accident will unavoidably occur. Being helpless and powerless to prevent an accident in these circumstances when you regard yourself a young physically fit adult can be depressive to deal with. Fellow sufferers appreciate this and online forums can be therapeutic in reminding us that we're not alone. Losing blood through bowel movements causes anaemia which leads to fatigue and regular exercise is recommended to combat this, although the condition wasn't always conducive to my regular exercise. Any resumption of my football refereeing career would have been impossible due to the potential for a rather farcical and embarrassing situation during a match and obviously the respectful spectators and players would have understood and showed empathy . . .

Surprising and somewhat inspirational was the discovery that one of my sporting heroes, 5-time Olympic rowing gold medallist Steven Redgrave was diagnosed with ulcerative colitis in 1992, the same year he took gold in the coxless pairs in Barcelona. He followed that up with a gold in the same event four years later in Atlanta, famously inviting anyone who saw him near a boat again to shoot him, a bold statement in a country renowned for its controversial second amendment.
Despite adding diabetes to his medical record in 1997, the awesome oarsman amassed a fifth consecutive Olympic rowing gold in the coxless fours at Sydney 2000, becoming Great Britain's greatest Olympian.
The disease gained much publicity across the sports pages when, in December 2011, footballer Darren Fletcher, the Manchester United and Scotland midfield player revealed he was taking a sabbatical from the game due to his condition. The internationalist underwent surgery to remove part of his colon and resumed his playing career.
Another Olympian, English swimmer Siobhan-Marie O'Connor, helped raise awareness of the condition, taking a silver medal in the 200 metres medley at the 2016 Rio Olympics to add to her gold in the Glasgow Commonwealth Games two years earlier.
In response to these three examples of fellow sufferers, I have of course pointed out to nurses and other medical staff in the course of routine appointments and colonoscopies that the disease clearly only affects elite athletes competing at the upper echelons of their particular sport.

These appointments usually happen on a 6-monthly basis consisting of a short interview and examination with a gastroenterologist, with any remedial action taken as required.

Large one-gram tablets named Pentasa, containing the drug mesalamine had provided twice-daily assistance over the previous four years, interspersed on three occasions with an 8-week course of Prednisolone, a steroid used to combat inflammation when things became unmanageable. Due to the probability of side-effects, Prednisolone couldn't be prescribed more than once in a calendar year. A constantly adapting live mental roadmap of the location of the nearest convenience and route thereto becomes second nature to a sufferer. A local authority-issued Radar key affording 24-hour entry to accessible toilets (often mistakenly referred to as 'disabled toilets' but that's another story) is always carried and appropriate discretely-worn products are readily available from most chemists, reminding me of particular observations on life by the comedian Billy Connolly.

An ability to find a humorous angle in the most trying of situations had helped me cope in the past and would undoubtedly assist in the future. Memories of these trying situations sharpened my sense of perspective as I undertook to live a full and normal life around my medical restrictions.
A simple sentence uttered by a most courageous friend, riddled with cancer and struggling for speech just weeks before her passing at the age of just 44 would always resonate with me. In reference to another patient on her ward, she whispered, "There's always someone worse off than yourself."

Walking in the wilds of my beautiful country did afford the opportunity to enjoy the great outdoors with its naturally abundant toilet facilities, used of course in strict accordance with the countryside code. After the West Highland Way adventures of 2013 and 2014, The Great Glen Way adventure of 2015 had stumbled upon an early glitch.

As the smartly uniformed clean-shaven 40-something driver alighted from the cab of the single deck 52-seat coach to assist passengers packing the side-loading storage compartment, I approached him.

"Hi there. There appears to be no toilet on the bus?" I enquired with an intonation suggesting this was clearly a question as opposed to a statement.

"Nah, there isn't, mate."

"It's just that I have a medical condition and I phoned the company in advance to confirm there would be a toilet on board," I explained to my apparent new friend.

I had been an ex-smoker since 2008 and my increased olfactory sensitivity confirmed our chauffeur was very much still in the habit. Perhaps he was comparing his inability to have a puff en route with my inability to use the toilet en route which seemed to draw a degree of empathy as he explained apologetically that journeys in excess of three hours would have a toilet on board. Only occasionally would sub-3-hour trips have the facility. He added that he would be stopping half-way for 10 minutes at Fort Augustus and there were toilet facilities adjacent to this stop. Determined that this wouldn't be a show-stopper, I furtively disappeared briefly into the bus station toilet, re-emerging moments later with a bulkier backside than before and we were on our uneasy way.

My new friend and guide wasn't hanging around as we sped down the west shore of spectacular Loch Ness through the evening sunshine. The slightly open windows allowed a cool breeze to pervade and combat the stuffiness within the coach. I was reminded of one of the final scenes from the film "Shawshank Redemption" when Morgan Freeman's character, a 'free man', was heading to Mexico to team up once more with Tim Robbins' character, although the reminiscence was somewhat tempered as Frank Darabont's superb film failed to include half of the commuting passengers disembarking in Drumnadrochit.

We continued south from this 'Loch Ness Monster' tourism town which would be our last overnight stop on the walk back. After passing through the small lochside village of Invermoriston, another return stopover, we reached the half-way point at Fort Augustus where our host kindly invited all passengers to use the facilities or alternatively use the shop at the adjacent petrol station while he himself had a fresh-air break. I had survived to the half-way point and went about ensuring I gave myself every chance of completing the second leg unscathed.

Our heavily-laden rucksacks, given final preparation in our bed and breakfast accommodation, were going to enable steady but less than speedy progress as we set off from Fort William the following morning. Small blue posts with an embossed thistle would be our guiding lights over the next four days, with an official map and guidebook to assist in any . . . geographical misunderstandings. These strategically-placed stakes set us off on the first few miles through a couple of housing estates either side of the old castle at Inverlochy. The physically challenging Scottish sport of shinty, also sometimes referred to as 'murder-death-samurai-ball' features in these early stages, skirting the grounds of both Fort William and Kilmallie shinty clubs before joining the southern entrance to the Caledonian Canal at Corpach.

The canal was a huge Government-backed construction project undertaken by engineer Thomas Telford in the early 19th century to connect the west coast at Corpach and the east coast at Inverness, connecting Loch Lochy, Loch Oich and Loch Ness on the route. Tow paths aside this well-used waterway would form the route of the Great Glen Way to the approximately half-way village of Fort Augustus.

There are 29 locks on the canal, water-controlling gates for raising and lowering vessels. Eight of these are encountered just after Corpach at the Devil's Staircase, Britain's largest staircase lock, elevating craft up or down 64 feet as required. A north-bound old sailing ship, a twin-masted ketch was approaching the first lock and attracting spectators, including ourselves.

We continued for a few miles along the tow path to Gairlochy before beginning to skirt the lengthy west bank of Loch Lochy, stopping for lunch in the small hamlet of Clunes. At the end of the loch are "Laggan Locks" and after a strenuous 23-mile day, we encountered a canal barge converted into a small pub/restaurant, The Eagle Inn. This delightful floating establishment provided a most welcome and appreciated pint of morale to set us on our final mile to the Great Glen Hostel, our accommodation for the evening. A large bowl of self-cooked pasta Bolognese in the TV room tried to re-energise our weary limbs whilst on the TV, the legendary American golfer Tom Watson, having failed to make the half-way cut, was emotionally acknowledging the acclaim and adulation of the vast St Andrews crowds as he walked up the 18th fairway in the Friday evening twilight for the final time in a British Open Golf Championship.

Those first day exertions left my back feeling stiff as I climbed down from the top bunk to prepare kit for the second day's 18-mile trek to Invermoriston via Fort Augustus. Joanne recommended some particular stretching exercises and, fully-laden once more, we set off through the Great Glen Water Park and along the entire length of the east shore of Loch Oich before reconnecting with the canal at Aberchalder. Following the canal towpath, this was a beautiful section of our adventure, visiting the picturesque Cullochy and Kytra Locks en route to our lunchtime destination.

Fort Augustus is on the main A82 trunk road and consequently very popular with passing tourists due to its five dramatic locks cutting steeply down through the centre of the village from the Caledonian Canal to the southern entrance to vast Loch Ness. The less than imaginatively named Lock Inn (unless referring to its after-hours habits) provided welcome sustenance, not for the first time as Joanne and I had previously visited the village as 'passing tourists'. On leaving the village, visiting busloads of tourists had created a lengthy queue for the public toilets and I was extremely grateful for my Radar key, although its use was met by the usual glowers from that section of society who ignorantly cannot differentiate between 'accessible' and 'disabled' and believe I'm some sort of cheat.

Our afternoon excursion would introduce us to an entirely different terrain as the Great Glen Way rose out of the village and climbed above the west shore of Loch Ness. With the weight being carried, lunch was worked off fairly quickly but tougher sections lay ahead in the days to come. Views up Loch Ness were impressive as the Way levelled out at a reasonable height before meandering down into the village of Invermoriston, our next overnight stop. Our bed and breakfast accommodation was most pleasant and only a short walk, thankfully, from the local hotel providing dinner.

With no 'civilization' due to be encountered during the third day's 15-mile stretch to Drumnadrochit, our landlady's full Scottish breakfast and pre-arranged pack lunches tucked into our rucksacks would see us through. The day began with a long and gradual climb out of Invermoriston and when confronted with a signposted choice of 'high route' or the original 'low route', we decided to brave the higher path. The steady climb continued with some open views until, after entering forestry, the signs directed us onto a sharp steep climb, eventually rising above the forest and reaching a pinnacle where a curved stone shelter had been erected at a viewpoint. The views, assisted by clear weather, were breathtaking and for myself, the undoubted highlight of the Great Glen Way. The entire loch could be seen with the sprawling panorama of the Cairngorms beyond the hills on the opposite shore and the Nevis range to the south. It had been an energy-sapping but ultimately very rewarding climb to this point. After descending and re-joining the original route, the Way turns away from the loch and follows a tarmac road before a steep descent through a forest into Drumnadrochit. As previously mentioned, the village is the self-appointed capital of Loch Ness Monster tourism with several attractions connected to the 'allegedly' mythical beast.

We had booked a room in a backpackers' hostel which turned out to have five beds to choose from but more fortunately was very close to the toilet facilities. Determined not to let my ulcerative colitis interfere with our trip, I had been fortunate on the trip that despite being on a bit of a flare-up and prepared for possible eventualities, there had been no embarrassing episodes.

Keeping the theme of imaginatively named hostelries, the Loch Ness Inn (with the word 'Inn' designed to look like the aforementioned aquatic beast) provided fine fare and refreshments. Due to very adverse weather on the Fife coast, the golf at St Andrews had been put back a day and it was strange to be watching the third round and not the closing stages of The Open on a Sunday tea-time. We didn't stay too long before returning with our aching legs to our multi-bed accommodation to rest ahead of what our Great Glen Way guidebook promised would be the toughest day.

There are days in one's life that will always be remembered for various reasons. As stated, our guidebook indicated that the final day of the Great Glen Way would be a tough one but I could never have anticipated the significance of just how tough the day would ultimately become, one of the longest and most stressful days of my life. Stopping for some duty photographs at the Drumnadrochit signposts and food supplies at a local grocery store, we set off through the village on this last day, blissfully unaware that it was also the first day of a very different and most unexpected adventure, an adventure that would have far-reaching consequences for years to come.

The Way sets off on the lochside main road, the A82, out of the village for a short distance before we were directed away from the road and into a forest. Now on our fourth day of carrying large rucksacks, a long and steady energy-sapping ascent through the forestry with several short breaks to enjoy the view (catch our breath) between the trees onto Loch Ness would pass the first couple of hours. Eventually, the terrain evened out and we were following a wide forest track, passing a signpost indicating the highest point of the entire way. This track continued for a couple of miles until we happened upon the impressive Abriachan Forest Trust. Purchased by the local community almost twenty years before as a social enterprise, the Trust manages over 500 hectares of forest to create local employment, improve the environment and encourage visitors through a network of spectacular paths and mountain bike trails. Moreover, there was also an educational centre which included immaculately clean toilet facilities and I was grateful for permission from a member of staff to make use of these, rather than the public facility I had ascertained from signage was some distance away.

Walking on for around ten minutes, we were invited via several hand-painted amusing signposts to visit another enterprise, the Abriachan Eco-Campsite and Café. This quirky little establishment, directly on the Way and the "highest inhabited croft in Scotland", provided a pot of tea (even the teapots are quirkily hand-painted) and a biscuit. Adding to the experience, our refreshments were served on the veranda of a hand-built wooden shack by a welcoming head-scarfed, aproned landlady, and enjoyed in the company of some swans, ducks and a black pot-bellied pig named Bubble.

Leaving our interesting hosts behind, we set off on the final stretch of the Great Glen Way which developed into a slog, firstly on a tarmac road for a few miles before dropping into a forest track. The forest seemed endless on our tiring limbs with only fleeting glimpses through the trees to the Beauly Firth disrupting the monotony. Our sense of humour and spirit of adventure had kept us motivated throughout a tough walk.

Inverness eventually came into view as we exited the forest aside a small lochan above the Craig Dunain area. The view lifted those spirits although they were instantly tempered by the small signpost indicating that there were still four long miles to trudge.

Passing through a couple of small housing estates, we skirted the Torvean Golf Course to briefly reunite with the Caledonian Canal we had left in Fort Augustus two days earlier.

The fast-flowing River Ness was traversed via the pleasant Ness Islands and our exhausted bodies gratefully ascended a small hill to the grounds of Inverness Castle where a stone obelisk marked the official end of our journey.

It was around 7pm and physically and mentally drained, Joanne and I wearily and warmly embraced at our journey's end, savouring our shared sense of achievement and euphoria.

The Castle Inn, a hostelry just across the road, was metaphorically beckoning us with open arms to provide sustenance and a celebratory aperitif.

As we left the grounds of Inverness Castle, overlooking the city and River Ness, I could never have envisaged the role this impressive red sandstone structure was about to play in the next few years of my life.

A large 12-year-old malt whisky was the invited recommendation of the bar staff as we toasted our achievement in our own traditional Scottish fashion before settling down at the only available table to choose some very welcome warm pub grub from the menu.

The closing stages of the delayed British Open golf championship were being broadcast on the variously located televisions and had attracted the attention of most patrons. The United States' Zach Johnson, Australian Marc Leishman and Louis Oosthuizen of South Africa had finished level at the end of the competition and were now embroiled in a 4-hole play-off around those famous links of St Andrews. Joanne and I were also drawn to the unfolding sporting drama as the American golfer triumphed whilst we simultaneously triumphed over a large home-made burger served with chunky chips and salad, washed down with two pints of beer for myself and a couple of pints of cider for Joanne.

Following conclusion of the golf, televisual sporting attention turned to the sport of darts as two players vied on stage whilst the cameras also focused on the large vociferous crowd spurring them on. This very minor detail regarding sports coverage would provide a pivotal juncture in the evening's proceedings and bizarrely prove the catalyst for future life-affecting events.

Joanne observed, "Now. Darts. There's a daft sport and the crowd worship them like they're heroes."

I interjected, "Depends on the definition of heroes I suppose. The guys just stand there and throw three little arrows at a dartboard. It's a very basic thing to do and millions of people around the world do it.

Now these guys are the best of all those millions so I suppose they have a pretty special talent'"

"Yeh but they're not heroes," she replied, "nurses, doctors, emergency services, *they're* heroes"

"I totally agree and all those worshipping fans and the players themselves would agree with you too," I replied.

Joanne continued, "You're saying they *are* heroes for throwing darts?"

"I didn't say they were heroes," I reiterated, "I said they have a special talent for what they do and make a living from it due to sponsorship and TV coverage and fans, much like any other sport."

"Bloody sports fans. All the same," came a derogatory response from Joanne, who emitted some bemusement as she took a sip from her glass.

The hitherto mood of elation regarding the previous four days' achievement had evidently dissipated on what I regarded as conversation of a very frivolous nature.

"Ok, let's not get into a trivial conversation over a sport," I suggested with a smile of surprise.

"Whatever," came the blunt reply.

I was taken aback at such an unexpectedly sudden mood swing and reacted to what I perceived as unnecessary petulance.

"Joanne, please don't tell me that after the wonderful experience we've enjoyed over the past four days, we're going to spoil it by getting into a disagreement over a game of darts."

Joanne ignored my comment in a manner which made it clear the conversation was over. After 15 minutes of the silent treatment and my astonishment at Joanne's breathtakingly sudden mood swing in the midst of celebrating our achievement, she announced that she was getting a taxi back to the hotel, bizarrely indicating that I could stay if I wanted.

"What?" my bewildered reply, "I'll obviously come back with you."

"Suit yourself," she nonchalantly replied.

Ater bundling our rucksacks into the boot of the taxi, Joanne then joined the driver in the front, an impetuously clear show of her sudden antipathy for me. The dialogue blackout continued back to the hotel and into our room. In an attempt to break the apprehension, I sat next to Joanne on the bed.

"Joanne, are you ok? You want to speak about it?"

"I'm ok" came the curt reply in a way which clearly indicated she wasn't. "I'm going to reception to see if I can get another room."

Exasperated and realising it was pointless to try to persuade her otherwise, I advised her that I would take a bath and leave her to her own devices. The relaxing celebratory bath I had been anticipating for four days hadn't quite materialised as I lay there utterly perplexed on Joanne's extraordinary behaviour. It had been a very long day and we were fairly exhausted at the finish and perhaps that may have played a part. It felt impossible to find any rational reason for why such a trivial conversation on a trivial subject had led to this astonishing impasse, moreover and bizarrely, a conversation we had actually agreed with each other on.

Hoping that the hour of solitude would help Joanne return to her senses, I re-entered the room to be met with a statement so completely preposterous and unfathomable that I began having serious concerns for Joanne's state of mind.

"I'm getting a taxi home."

A few seconds in suspended disbelief ensued, thinking I had perhaps misheard her.

"You're what?" I enquired, with no little incredulity.

"I'm getting a taxi home. I've sorted it with the girl in reception."

"Joanne, we live over a hundred miles away. Why would you do that? Will they take you? That'll cost a packet."

I instinctively found myself pleading for sanity amidst the absurdity of Joanne taking a taxi at a cost of almost £200 when we had a room booked and a car outside. As she began gathering her things, I felt a real concern for her mental state.

"Joanne, this is totally crazy. Please don't do this. I can't possibly stay here on my own and watch you do this. You're clearly not ok. Let's talk about it."

Ignoring my pleas, Joanne made her way to reception with myself in pursuit.

"Joanne, I'm not going to watch you do this. I'll follow in the car."

"You've been drinking. You can't drive."

Although I had two pints of lager to accompany our celebratory dram, I did feel with the time that had elapsed since, I would not be over the drink-drive limit. Moreover, I believed that if Joanne thought there was that possibility, it would perhaps help her to see sense and abandon her severely irrational action. Joanne was speaking with the taxi company on the phone, passing her bank card details, as it appeared they couldn't quite believe the situation either, a sudden request for a 100-mile-plus taxi on a Monday night. To my disbelief, it appeared that the proposed madness was about to happen.

"Sorry, Joanne, I can't just watch you do this. I'll follow you in the car."

"I'll phone the police," came the chilling reply, "I don't want you to follow me."

"Why would you do that? I'm worried about you, Joanne. This is not normal behaviour."

Joanne's withdrawn manner appeared concerningly unyielding.

I quickly returned to the room, gathered my belongings, and returned the room key to reception, indicating that it may not be required. From a meaningless conversation concerning a darts match a couple of hours earlier, an evening planned to celebrate the completion of our 79-mile hike had taken an unprecedented and sinister path and was rapidly turning into one of the most disturbing nights of my life. Sadly, the night was far from over.

I placed my kit into my car and positioned myself near reception in the hotel car park, still hoping that Joanne would somehow see the derangement of her intentions and snap out of her daunting esoterism. The taxi duly arrived and I watched with a sense of dread and disenchantment as the beautiful lady, with whom I had enjoyed a wonderful four days on the trail, was boarding a taxi to make an incredibly unnecessary and expensive 100-mile-plus journey home . . . due to a non-disagreement about a game of darts. A scenario that couldn't be made up. I followed the taxi out onto the main trunk route eastwards, hoping I was just having a very bad dream and would wake up soon. A few miles into the journey, I was a couple of hundred yards behind the taxi, desperately hoping that Joanne, aware that I was behind her, would see common sense.

A couple of miles shy of the town of Nairn, my attention would be swept in a very different direction and the bad dream began turning into a horrible nightmare as bright oscillating blue lights appeared from nowhere in my rear-view mirror. I pulled into a convenient layby ahead and sat for what seemed like a couple of minutes, stunned, as the blue flashes continued to light up the mid-summer nightfall. With each passing moment, I thought of the taxi getting further away and alighted from my vehicle to be met by a police officer.

"I'm assuming you want to speak to me, guys?" I enquired.

"Yes sir," he replied, and extending an arm towards his own vehicle, "please get into the rear of our vehicle."

Once inside, another officer sat in the driver's seat asked, "Evening sir, do you know why we have pulled you over?"

"Well, I'm having a bit of an evening, gents. I am following my partner who is in a taxi ahead going to Aberdeenshire would you believe. We had a room at the Premier Lodge but we had a minor altercation and I said I would follow her and she said if I did, she would phone the police. Looks like she did."

"All I can say is that we have received specific information about your vehicle. We haven't stopped you because of your driving. Where have you been this evening?" continued the driver.

"We finished walking the Great Glen Way today from Drumnadrochit to Inverness, had tea and a couple of drinks and returned to our hotel."

"Having volunteered that information, sir, we will need to take a sample of your breath. Do you have your driving licence to hand?"

Almost in unison with handing over the document, a female voice on the vehicle radio confirmed my details and legality with regard to my vehicle.

"What did you have to drink this evening, Mr McKay?" enquired the driver.

"Well, it was much earlier this evening," I began, trying to emphasize that I felt I was fine to drive and certainly didn't feel 'under the influence'.

"I had two pints of beer with a meal and a whisky on completion of the walk."

"What kind of whisky?" the driver continued like he was some sort of connoisseur.

"Sorry, no idea. It was recommended by staff at the Castle Inn."

The officer on the passenger seat produced a hand-held alcometer and as per his simultaneous instructions, I produced a long continuous blow into the attached mouthpiece.

A few nervous seconds elapsed before the same officer uttered those shattering words.

"I'm sorry to say it's came up as a fail, Mr McKay."

My heart skipped more than a few beats and with all sorts of potential ramifications running around my mind, I simply blurted, "Em . . . ok," as the nearside officer alighted from the vehicle and joined me in the back seat.

"Ok, Mr McKay, what's going to happen is that we need to return to the police HQ in Inverness. Your vehicle will be left here. You'll be given another test at the station. I'm arresting you on suspicion of drink-driving. You are not obliged to say anything but anything you do say will be noted down and may be used in evidence. Do you understand?"

In my service career, I had arrested many individuals but it had taken 46 years to be under arrest myself.

My partner going through some form of episode, my arrest for drink-driving, my underlying exhaustion, and now arriving around midnight at a police HQ building to provide a pivotal breath specimen. It was certainly a night not to be forgotten. After passing through an electronic gate into a secure car park, my back-seat companion, who had engaged in small talk during the short journey, explained that he would need to place handcuffs on me for arrival at the desk but they would be removed as soon as I was 'processed'. My body was reminding me that my ulcerative colitis hadn't been great on the hike and I was allowed to use toilet facilities before going through the 'booking in' process and guided to a little room to be acquainted with a larger calibrated alcometer.

Jonathan Holmes, the sergeant on duty and a friend from my football days appeared in the doorway.

"Thought I recognised the name. How you doing Matt?"

"To be honest Jonathan, I've had better nights."

After some procedural explanations, I once again provided a specimen of breath into the larger machine which in turn provided a print-out of a very crucial piece of paper.

It was my back-seat friend who would once again despondently deliver the mortifying news

"Mr McKay. I'm sorry to say that the drink-drive laws in Scotland changed a few months ago and your reading of 31 is over the new lower prosecution limit of 26. Anywhere else in the UK, you're well below the prosecution limit of 40."

Aghast and confounded, how I wished in that life-changing moment that I had been in Carlisle, Cardiff or Carrickfergus.

I was officially charged with the offence and advised that a report would be sent to the procurator fiscal, together with an explanation of the court procedure which would follow, including a date around a fortnight later for an initial hearing, known as a "pleading diet."

My back-seat buddy genuinely appeared to care, explaining, "My advice to you, Mr McKay, is to find a good defence solicitor for your court appearance. This is marginal stuff and seven months ago, you wouldn't have been sitting here. I've been here with some pissed-up arseholes who deserve everything that's coming to them. You're not one of them."

I was then asked to wait around for a few minutes and offered a cup of tea before they would take me back to my car. Approximately half an hour later, I was again providing a sample of breath which was negative and subsequently conveyed back to my car near Nairn. During the journey, that familiar female voice was heard once more transmitting on the vehicle intercom, "Guys, we've had a call from Mr McKay's partner. She's quite distressed and wants to know if he's ok."

From the back of the vehicle, I muttered, "A wee bit late now," before advising the officers that my phone had ran out of charge, information which was duly relayed back to the control room.

"Look after yourself," were the officer's parting words as I alighted from their vehicle.

The biggest irony of the night was that now I was even more exhausted, stressed and distracted in the wee small hours. All those potential ramifications of a drink-drive conviction whirling round in my head whilst being left to drive back to the 'Shire, legally, which I felt was far more dangerous to myself and other road users than my illegal tailing of Joanne's taxi earlier. As I entered Moray, it was clear with an hour and a half's drive ahead that my concentration was debilitating and in the interest of safety, I would divert to Jennifer's, albeit unable to give advance warning as my phone was dead.

An awakened and confused Jennifer opened the door.

"What the hell?"

"So sorry to wake you Jen, I've having a nightmare. I'm in the shit, big time, and I'm too shattered to drive home. Can I get some sleep here?"

"Yeah, but," she paused, "Wait. What? Where's Joanne?"

"You better sit down."

On recharging my phone, I had several missed calls and messages from Joanne, with voicemails and texts imploring me to let her know I was ok. She knew I had been charged with drink-driving, insisted she had not been the one who called the police and asked if I was coming home. I replied that it had been a fairly horrendous night and I was going to try to get some sleep at Jennifer's. After managing to get around four hours sleep, I phoned Joanne who, it appeared, had mercifully returned to being Joanne again, albeit both of us were still in a state of shock. Still insistent that she had not been the one to call the police, she asked me to come home. Number Two and

Number Three were due to visit for a few days and we agreed to continue with those plans as my two younger children accompanied me home later in the morning.

As Joanne was enthusiastically greeting the children, I was aware that the corner of her enquiring eye was ascertaining my demeanour. After the trauma of the previous evening, it was heartening to see the reappearance of the more accustomed friendliness of the lovely lady whose company I had enjoyed on four challenging but wonderful days on the Great Glen Way. A subsequent impassioned private hug alone in the hallway would solidify those feelings that all was ok.

"Oh, Matt, I'm so sorry. So sorry for what you went through last night. You know I love you."

On actions taken that morning which I was obviously unaware of, Joanne continued, "I managed to make an appointment at the medical centre this morning. I already had an appointment later in the week and I'll still go to that too. The doctor said the medication I'm on, together with all the other circumstances, could easily have caused my behaviour last night."

"It's ok Joanne," I instinctively replied with a strange sense of relief that our relationship wasn't over.

"Whatever it takes, Matt, we will face this and get through it. Whatever the future holds, we will get through it together," she attested in a most assuaging manner, "and if we need to get a lawyer, I will cover that. Whatever it takes."

The consolidating intensity of our subsequent emotional embrace served to highlight that the previous night's events were an extremely rare occurrence and my psyche was reminding me that I loved this woman very much. As had been ascertained previously, she was not perfect and neither was I, but my heart was way too invested to walk away and I didn't want to believe Joanne had called the police. To this day, people in my inner circle would insist I had been naïve and gullible, but I believed her. I believed that we are all susceptible to our human frailties from time to time and of course there would be bumps in the road but I also believed in our love for each other and was prepared to work through whatever lay ahead. I believed that she had perhaps undergone an episode related to her self-diagnosed BPD condition together with symptoms of her ongoing menopausal transition for which she was under prescribed medication. And if love is blind, so be it, as I saw through her temporary irrationality to the beautiful, thoughtful, sexy, funny, caring woman I believed I was with for the overwhelming majority of our relationship.

Putting on my "game face" for the sake of the children's visit, it would be later in the day before I could conduct my initial online research into a subject I knew little about nor thought I would ever have to. The Citizens Advice Bureau website stated that if my alcometer reading was below 50, I should have been offered the "statutory option" to provide an alternative sample, i.e. a blood test. This had clearly not happened and allowed myself a little piece of hope as I anxiously contacted a company providing defence solicitors in Inverness.

After explaining my situation, I was transferred to a defence solicitor.
"Good morning. Mr Cameron here."
"Good morning, Mr Cameron, my name's Matt McKay," I began, and instinctively tried to establish a quick rapport, "What's your first name?"
"Mr Cameron."
"Oh right, ok," I replied with an intonation of acknowledgement and tried to mitigate my obvious lack of awareness on protocol, continuing, "I was charged last night with drink-driving near Inverness and have been advised to get a lawyer. I'm in my forties and have never been in any trouble with the law in my life."
"Ok I see. Can I ask what your reading was on the alcometer?"
"31."
"So you were given the option of providing an alternative sample?"
My heart skipped a hopeful beat, "I certainly wasn't, Mr Cameron."
"Oh right, no problem. I actually represented a lady in a similar situation the other day and had the case thrown out," the legal expert explained.
Completing the conversation with the arrangement of a face-to-face meeting, the call ended with tempered excitement as I sought out my partner.
"Joanne, there's a chance we might be ok."

Day Four – Grasmere to Angle Tarn

Light rain fell sporadically throughout the night, although there is something quite cosy and comforting when tucked inside a sleeping bag listening to the gentle pitter patter on the canvas. In no real rush today, I waited for an expected break in the light rain which allowed me to pack up my rucksack and the tent and I was heading back down the hostel approach road by 10am. I retraced yesterday's steps back up Easedale Road until a right turn into Helm Close, a picturesque country lane in the shadow of yesterday's final climb, Helm Crag. The trail follows this pleasant lane for just under a mile, flanked by a combination of trees, fencing and dry-stone walls, past some aesthetically pleasing rustic cottages and farm buildings. Crossing the busy A591, a wooden sign indicates the start of a public bridleway to Patterdale and after passing some buildings, the gradual ascent of Great Tongue begins alongside the fast-flowing Tongue Gill. The route is slabbed in places in an attempt to protect the landscape from erosion with signage reminding walkers to stick to the path. Under the frequent watchful eyes of several Herdwick sheep, native to these parts, with their distinctive dark coats and white heads, I reached a crossing of Tongue Gill just below an impressive waterfall in spate and traversed over the top towards Grisedale Tarn via a particularly rocky section. Amidst this rocky section, I encountered Alfie, a black lab from Manchester, replete with his little hiking rucksack attached to his back. Together with his owners, he was tackling the Coast-to-Coast in the opposite direction from Robin Hood's Bay which put them at approximately the 150-mile mark. They were heading for overnight accommodation in Grasmere with three days to go until St Bees. A brief chat ensued before I continued towards Grisedale Tarn, at the far end of which were some large boulders offering seating and protection from the elements. With other hikers availing themselves of the shelter for a break, I also took the opportunity for a pork pie and a cup of tea. Timing of my lunchtime recess was fortuitous as just after setting off, the hitherto passing showers had become more persistent as I headed down the valley towards Patterdale.

Whilst taking a bit of shelter in the doorway of the locked Ruthwaite Lodge, I was passed by three fell runners, one of which, thanks to regular updates on Coast-to-Coast social media pages, I knew to be

Damian Hall who was 46 miles en route to breaking the Wainwright's Coast-to-Coast record. His completion time would be 39 hours and 18 minutes, surpassing the previous record held by Mike Hartley since 1991 by 18 minutes.

With the rain easing off, I continued my descent on the Grisedale Valley route and shortly after the path levelled off onto a tarred track, I stopped for a chat with Bill and Gudrun who were out on a walk from their holiday home in Patterdale. Bill had completed the Coast to Coast three years earlier and was enthusiastically reminiscing whilst Gudrun looked like she'd heard his musings before . . . a couple of times.

As I continued past the Crossing Plantation on approach to Patterdale, I was greeted by withered trees with very dark brown oddly-shaped branches akin to the talking and grumpy trees in the classic MGM movie, "Wizard of Oz." Before they could start throwing apples at me, I skipped on by, as I was off to see the pub, the wonderful pub of Patterdale. The White Lion, to be precise, and nothing cowardly about it. The wonderful 19th century whitewashed 3-storey building, focal point of the south end of the village, was a welcome sight and once inside the cosy and atmospheric bar, I procured a seat near the bar and ordered some late afternoon lunch.

My pre-walk research on this establishment had inadvertently unearthed some TripAdvisor reviews. One particularly disgruntled reviewer had taken umbrage that some of the flowers in the external hanging baskets were dead and felt the need to share his disgust on the aforementioned forum.   Somewhat surprisingly, despite this vital piece of heinous and damning information, mass boycotts had been avoided and customers were still frequenting the premises. The troubling floral fatalities outside didn't seem to affect neither the deliciousness of my chicken curry-filled baked potato nor indeed my cold and welcome pint of Birra Moretti. Not wanting to commence my ascent towards Angle Tarn too early, I would enjoy a second pint just as "two ladies" entered the bar. With their day's walking complete and accommodation booked at this hostelry, they were rewarding themselves with a glass of wine as we shared our reflections on the crossover from Grasmere, perhaps spending too much time discussing that creepy copse on the approach to the village.

As the day reached 4pm, it was time to push on and begin the ascent out of the village towards Angle Tarn. Just outside the village on Patterdale Common, it was evident by some approaching ominous clouds that a burst of rain was imminent and I took the opportunity to pre-empt the precipitation, taking shelter under a line of trees. A particularly heavy shower ensued for around quarter of an hour before I continued with the ascent. Alas, some 20 minutes later, more heavy rain followed and with no available shelter, I pressed on, getting wetter and wetter.

The BBC website had earlier forecasted light rain showers with sunny spells for Patterdale and that guesswork would become a source of some frustration as the weather persisted with no sign of easing off. After traversing Angle Tarn pike, the path descends to the Angle Tarn itself. By this stage, the weather had closed in completely with heavy rain and mist turning conditions quite filthy.

Angle Tarn, measuring approximately 400m by 250m at an altitude of just under 1,600ft, is one of the Lake District's most popular wild camping spots and there were three tents pitched on the small peninsula jutting into the Tarn. I pushed on to search for a pitch higher on the south end, passing some hikers whose comment on passing, "Nice to see someone else as crazy as us out in this," summed up the ongoing conditions. With no time to waste, I decided on a pitch next to a small hillock overlooking the Tarn about 20 yards from the water and rapidly assembled the tent, quickly clambering inside to get out of the rain.

Despite the rain cover on the rucksack and clothes within in a dry sack, I had concerns that the persistent rain would eventually break through. Thankfully, on taking stock, I was glad I would have dry underwear, a t-shirt and fleece for sleeping in. My boots and socks were absolutely drenched but there was no point in taking them off as I would require water from the tarn. My rain jacket and hiking trousers would hopefully dry off somewhat during the night. On emptying the lower echelons of my rucksack, my sleeping mat was slightly damp but thankfully my sleeping bag was completely dry.

I took a moment to compose myself after what had been a slightly stressful period, thankful that I was in my tent, out of the rain and able to rub myself down with my microfibre towel. The previous hour had certainly been the most testing of the trip so far with my sense of positivity and humour facing its sternest test.

Within half an hour, the pitter-patter of rain drops began to dissipate and I took the opportunity to open the tent to reveal a wonderful view overlooking the tarn and the mountains beyond. Morale was further enhanced as the rain stopped completely and some sunshine began to infiltrate the skies. I clambered down through the sodden mountain grass to collect some water from the tarn and after boiling some of that retrieval, was enjoying the view with some pasta carbonara followed by some rice pudding. I had anticipated that a wild camp at Angle Tarn could be a highlight of the adventure and after the weather-induced teething trouble, this was coming to fruition. With some evening mist rolling in to create a blanket over the tarn, my attention was drawn to the dusky silhouettes of three deer on the ridge above. Concluding my evening meal with a mug of tea, I felt a warm appreciation of my beautiful surroundings with the misty tarn below, the inquisitive ungulates above, and the lack of any connection with the outside world. The splendid isolation ensured morale was back on track.

As darkness fell, I read up on tomorrow's estimated 14 miles to the village of Shap which was scheduled to include Kidsty Pike, the highest point of the entire Coast-to-Coast . . . or would I inadvertently find a higher point?

Summer 2015 – continued

With a distinctive hope that all was not lost, a face-to-face meeting with Mr Cameron was hastily arranged and at the end of an exigent week, we were driving back together to the Highland Capital amidst a far less anticipatory atmosphere than on the same trip just a few days before. Mr Cameron was of a similar age and build to myself and came across as an affable man with a soft but authoritative voice. He certainly didn't hide his indifference towards the Scottish Court Service, describing the Scots legal system as an "absolute shambles." My immediate concern was dealing with my employer in the event of losing my driving licence but he explained to us that the entire process would take some months and involve three stages. The first was the Pleading Diet, an initial preliminary hearing, followed by an Intermediate Diet to ensure everything was in place for the final stage, the Trial Diet. Feeling initiated that the word 'diet' appeared more in court proceedings than at a Weight Watchers meeting, I was encouraged when Mr Cameron reckoned things would not reach the Trial Diet as discussed in our inaugural telephone conversation. Mr Cameron reiterated that Drink-Driving was regarded as a serious offence despite my low reading of breath then seemed to contradict that when he explained that I was being tried at the lesser court, the Justice of the Peace court. This meant my case would not be heard by a legal expert but rather a Justice of the Peace (JP), his example being a retired shopkeeper of good standing. My subsequent research would indeed clarify that a JP had no legal qualification and judged upon less serious offences. Mr Cameron requested that Joanne and myself furnish him with a full written account of our respective events on the night in question ahead of the following week's 'Pleading Diet.' Joanne had of course verbally updated me on events on the night in question but now provided the requested written account for Mr Cameron.

"After the meal I had a cider and we were watching a darts game on the television. We then got into a debate regarding the rewards for this type of sport and the adulation displayed by the supporters/fans. To support my argument, I used nursing as an example of a poorly appreciated and rewarded profession. At this point I began to

perceive Mr McKay as being agitated and strongly defending the sport, however despite that I insisted on trying to make my point. This then changed tone to being more personal in relation to Mr McKay's passion for sport and the difference between me and him as regards that. I ordered a taxi to take us to the Premier Lodge Hotel, leaving our drinks unfinished. I was aware that I had become very withdrawn and quiet by this time and sat in the front of the taxi when it arrived and not in the back with Mr McKay.

I do not recall what time we got to the hotel, however I was the one into reception first to check in and get the swipe card/key. We got the rucksacks into the room and settled for a while. I was still in a withdrawn and quiet state, feeling extremely uncomfortable and uneasy at the atmosphere. Mr McKay quietly came over to speak with me on the bed and pacify me. I know I refused to make eye contact but told him I was putting on dry socks to go to reception to try to book another room. This provoked a withdrawal from Mr McKay, and I tried to catch his shirt, but he pulled away and went into the bathroom for a bath. At this point I gathered my things, went down to reception and asked if they had a spare room for me to rent. Unfortunately, they did not and I returned to the room. When Mr McKay came out of the bath, I told him I was getting a taxi home to Aberdeenshire and headed for reception. I would have seemed distressed and emotional when speaking with the female receptionist and told her I was upset with my partner. I asked for a taxi number to order a taxi. Whilst ordering the taxi, Mr McKay appeared and implored me to cancel what I was doing and to stop. The only thing I could think of was getting away and getting home. He kept repeating he would follow me home, but my response to deter that was that I would call the police if he did. I waited in the reception for my taxi and Mr McKay appeared with his belongings and handed the key into reception before heading out to the car park. The taxi arrived and the driver helped me with my bag and I left.

The taxi driver was concerned for me as I appeared upset and spoke with me at length about marital issues, telling me more about his own than about the events at Inverness. This had a calming effect on me and I was able to interact with him, but I was still very ill at ease and in a state of confusion.

By the time we reached Forres I received a phone call from an unknown number and a female spoke to me. She asked where I was, (I said in a taxi on the A96 beside the Forres football stadium), and if I could wait until police came. I can't recall if she said who she was and didn't ask who it was and I was given no indication as to what was going on. *My first thought was that something had happened to Mr McKay.*

After what seemed like a considerable wait, a police car drew up and a policeman came to the driver's side window. He asked me to confirm my name and advised me he was responding to my phone call. I told him I hadn't called them, and he reiterated "you didn't call us?" and I said no. At that point he turned to his colleague and said something I couldn't hear, and his colleague then came around the passenger side window and asked me my details. At this point I was more concerned about Mr McKay and asked if he was ok. I was told they were responding to an incident in Inverness but couldn't tell me any more than that. I expressed my concern for Mr McKay again and he responded that "well let's just say he's having a bad night." They advised me to go to home where some local police would be in touch.

After that I became even more upset, confused and distressed and the taxi driver tried to pacify me. I asked him to turn around and take me back to Inverness which he did for a couple of miles, however he changed my mind as he felt I should go home as the police advised. I called the local police to advise I had arrived home at 1.40am. They telephoned back after about half an hour and I spoke with a WPC called Elaine. She asked the same details as the roadside policeman did and asked if I was alright. I expressed my concern again about Mr McKay and she said she didn't have all the information about the incident in Inverness but wanted to check in with me. She was satisfied at this point that I was ok and was going to go without seeing me but I expressed that I wanted to see them in person.

Two WPCs came to my house at around 2.40am and again took my details and seemed unable to advise what was happening with Mr McKay. I expressed how concerned I was about his physical condition after walking over 20 miles that day and the fact his ulcerative colitis was displaying symptoms and had been all week. I asked if they could find out if he was ok and the WPC reiterated that "he was fine and as far as they were concerned, he had been taken back to the Premier Lodge Hotel and had done nothing wrong." At my insistence the more senior WPC contacted a colleague via radio and asked them if they had had any more information and the reply through the radio sounded like "he's too drunk to say". At this point she looked at me and turned to the young WPC and they both laughed as if embarrassed. I asked for them to confirm what it was he was saying and she dismissed this and assured me there was nothing to worry about but couldn't actually confirm that. She encouraged me to call Mr McKay directly (though there was no response and went to voicemail) or to contact the hotel, however I did not have that number and could not find it. The two WPCs left at this point.

At 3.10am I received a call from a police constable from Inverness. He advised me that they had responded to my earlier call that evening. I re-affirmed that I had not made such a call and asked if they knew who had? He seemed ill-informed as to who had made the original telephone call related to the reported incident. The constable informed me that Mr. McKay had been stopped driving by police in response to the phone call and during questioning been asked to take a breathalyser test and had marginally failed it. He advised me he had been deemed fit to drive and taken back to his vehicle a short while later. He was unable to advise or reassure me of his physical condition after I expressed my concerns. I reinforced that after the exhausting walk and how symptomatic he'd been recently with his ulcerative colitis that his physical condition was precarious and thought maybe the police had taken him to a medical centre. He seemed unaware of these facts. He did say however that Mr McKay's mobile phone was out of charge and that was probably why I could not contact him. I advised him that I had contacted my local police and had seen them earlier and that they did not seem aware as to what was going on.

At around 4am, I contacted Mr McKay by text asking if he was ok and how he was feeling. He replied he was ok. I further texted that I wasn't the one to call the police and asked if he was coming home. He advised me he was at his kids' home in Moray and had had "a horrendous, stressful night".

Just after 7am, Mr McKay called to update me. He advised that he had assumed I had been the person to call the police and he had been charged with a drink driving offence, still in a dazed, confused and shocked state, as was I. We agreed to continue with plans as arranged. (i.e. bringing his two younger children down to our home)

I arranged an urgent medical appointment that morning. I already had a review appointment arranged for later that week to review my prescription medication but felt my irrational behaviour the previous night required immediate attention. The doctor was able to assure me that the circumstances and my condition was enough to cause my irrational state. Recognising the combination of exhaustion due to the 20-plus-mile walk, the diarrhoea/dehydration symptoms, the emotional state on ending, the whisky on an empty stomach, my various prescription medications for anxiety, menopausal symptoms, nerve pain and rosacea, together with anti-inflammatory drugs would all have contributed to my irrational mental state that evening. She commented that both mine and Mr. McKay's bodies would have been low defensively given our physical exertion that day. She found me to be extremely stressed and emotional when trying to relay the information from the evening. She advised me to continue with the medication in the meantime as this seemed to have been effective prior to this incident and to still attend my review appointment later in the week.

At the follow-up appointment, I was able to relay rationally how I had felt confused, withdrawn, and dissociated after having the whisky and meal and completely detached and unapproachable on the night in question. I reported that I was in one frame of mind and could not be undeterred and the doctor agreed that my behaviour would have seemed to be extremely irrational. She added that the incident had unfortunately been due to a combination of extenuating circumstances. As the medication had been effective up to the incident, she advised me to continue in the meantime."

I was on nightshift a couple of days before the initial hearing and educating myself with more online research on the Road Traffic Act and drink-driving. To my serious concern, it appeared that the "statutory option" had been removed from the law earlier in 2015. On 11th April 2015, three months prior to the incident, the "Statutory Option" was removed by the UK Government. In contrast to the Scottish Government, the UK Government had refused to lower the drink driving limit but agreed with the North Report's recommendation that the option be removed. The resultant amendments to the Road Traffic Act covered the whole of the UK and thus further changed the drink driving laws of Scotland, sadly creating a potentially life-changing quirk of devolved government, creating further disparity to the affected less than 10% of the UK population in their place of residence.

My new-found knowledge on this aspect of the Road Traffic Act set up an underlying air of apprehension as we headed westwards once more for the 'Pleading Diet'.

It was a galling irony that the court in the city was set inside the aforementioned Inverness Castle, the exact location of the Great Glen Way finishing post. As we ascended the pedestrian approach to the impressive city centre sandstone structure, we could see across the way to the Castle Inn, the trigger point to that ignominious evening, now standing as a stark reminder of how the course of life can change in an instant.

Inside the main building, we were directed by staff to take a seat in the waiting area, seats which were spaced over a sizeable area at the bottom of a grandiose staircase befitting of such an historic building. As we sat nervously awaiting the arrival of Mr Cameron, a set of nearby double doors emblazoned with the words 'Court One' suddenly burst open and we were confronted by a tall 20-something male, dragging along two security officers, one handcuffed to each hand.

"Two minutes," he shouted aggressively, "two fucking minutes. A four fucking hour roon trip for two minutes. That's a fucking joke man." He continued towards the exit at pace, his detainers in tow, and left the building. His demeanour and observations certainly suggested that he concurred with Mr Cameron's earlier assessment of the Scots legal system.

Feeling a resultant increase in the already tense atmosphere, I turned to Joanne in quiet observation. "I guess we're not in Kansas anymore."

A few minutes elapsed and Mr Cameron duly appeared, holding some files and looking rather resplendent with his solicitor's robe over his suit. He explained that the procedure would be fairly straightforward and he would keep me right once inside. I brought up the results of my research into the recent change in the drink-driving laws which he brushed aside, commenting, "Don't worry about that."

Joanne remained in the waiting area as Mr Cameron led me through a corridor and outside across a small car park before entering another slightly smaller building. The signage at the entrance advised this building to be the Justice of the Peace Court. We climbed a set of stairs and quietly entered a room behind where some proceedings were ongoing. Mr Cameron beckoned me to take a seat on a row of seats toward the rear of the room, whispering instructions that when my name is called, I should move into the dock, indicating that to be the small enclosed seating area directly in front of me. He continued to take a position at a large square desk in the middle of the chamber.

Unfamiliar and inexperienced when it came to courtrooms, I suppose JP Court 2 in the Justice of the Peace Court was certainly smaller than I had expected. The room wasn't much bigger than a squash court. To the front was a raised desk behind a small glass screen, the reason for which wasn't clear as due to its height, it afforded no protection for the rather gaunt and stern-looking grey-haired gentlemen, the Justice of the Peace, who sat behind it. Any 'accused' who took physical exception to the JP's findings would stand a decent chance of landing a missile on their target Perhaps the screen prevented coffee being spilt on the bespectacled chap who sat directly in front of and below the JP, the Clerk of the Court or "the guy who calls my name" as I would later refer to him. Directly in front of the Clerk was the aforementioned table where 2 of the 4 chairs were occupied by Mr Cameron, now pouring over some notes, and a younger gentleman whom I would learn to be the Advocate Depute representing the Procurator Fiscal, the Crown Prosecution. On the left-hand side adjacent to the table was the slightly raised Witness Box, stood next to which was a cheerful looking short and rotund gentleman who appeared to be in his early 60s, the Court Officer. Finally, seated to the side of the Witness Box nearest to myself was a police officer whose slumped body language and facial expression indicated he would much rather be somewhere else.

I'm aware that there must be larger and more salubrious courtrooms around the country but this, this was a room in an old castle. The Clerk was involved in a conversation with Mr Cameron regarding a client paying off a fine at £5 a week which seemed apt for the surroundings, more apt than Jack Nicholson confronting Tom Cruise shouting, "You can't handle the truth!"

"Matthew McKay" came the announcement from the Clerk and I stood up and tried to enter the dock from the right-hand side only to discover no entrance. Mr Cameron quickly re-directed me to the other side where I nervously took up my position. If there was any doubt over whether I was a first-timer, this momentary lapse in basic orienteering skills confirmed completely that this amateur, now standing rigidly, was definitely a bona fide virgin when it came to court appearances.

Mr Cameron took the floor and spoke in his quiet but confident voice, "Yes your honour. My client is charged with driving with excess alcohol contrary to the Road Traffic Act. My client pleads 'not guilty' to the charge and we seek dates for Intermediate Diet and Trial Diet." A flurry of silent activity ensued amongst those present with mumblings of various dates before the black-haired bespectacled Clerk looked up at me, "Matthew McKay."

"Yes sir," were the first words and would be the only words my very dry mouth uttered twice during the very brief proceedings.

"You are summoned to appear at this court for Intermediate Diet on 23rd September and Trial Diet is set for 17th November."

"Yes Sir."

Mr Cameron then approached me and advised that I may leave the room and should wait for him outside.

My first-ever court appearance was over in a flash during which I got to stand, look smart, say 'yes sir' twice, and demonstrate my inability to correctly find my way around a castle drawing room disguised as a courtroom.

Mr Cameron emerged from the courtroom only seconds after myself and explained, "Ok Mr McKay. We should be ok for having the case dismissed at Intermediate Diet. I may even be able to have a chat with the Fiscal's office before then and get it thrown out. I'll obviously let you know if that happens, otherwise we'll see you back here in September. You may actually be excused attending the Intermediate Diet but, if necessary, we'll sort that out nearer the time."

We shook hands and I returned to the other building, reuniting with Joanne and relaying the details of my brief appearance before leaving the castle to make our way back to the 'Shire.

Joanne and I persisted in thinking positive and trying to maintain "service as usual" in the interim period and indeed enjoyed a short caravan break in the far north which involved a transit through Inverness. Having served much of my service career in Moray and with lots of football referee involvement in Inverness, I had always been openly enamoured with the Highland Capital and was determined that the ongoing predicament wouldn't affect that sentiment.

On the day of the Intermediate Diet at the end of September, I was working a dayshift and duly absolved from attending the hearing. It would be one of the longest days as I endured an anxious wait for Mr Cameron's call whilst trying to concentrate on work, my colleagues unaware of my situation. It was Joanne who called early in the afternoon.

"Oh Matt, they're not throwing it out," she advised in a most concerned tone.

My whole body tensed up and, clutching at straws, I replied, "What? What do you mean? How do you know?"

"Sorry Matt, it was becoming unbearable so I phoned Mr Cameron on the off chance and he wasn't long out of court. He wants you to give him a ring. He mentioned something called 'special reasons' which might avoid you getting a driving ban."

Almost immediately, I telephoned our legal representative who corroborated Joanne's distressing disclosure and proffered his own interpretation.

"It was such a recent change that up until now, they have been using some discretion, particularly because of the double whammy caused by the UK change to the Road Traffic Act. It appears they've decided it's time to tighten up and you've been very unfortunate. I have to say Mr McKay, under the circumstances of the case and as you were only marginally over the limit, you did seem to have special reasons."

Mr Cameron went on to explain that there were some defences to drink-driving, one of which was driving in emergency circumstances. A 'special reasons' plea would inevitably involve a 'guilty' verdict but could avoid a driving ban. As Joanne's behaviour had been extremely irrational on the night in question, my observation of her state of mind would have led me to follow her in concern for her own safety.

With my job potentially on the line as a result of losing my driving licence, it made sense to pursue Mr Cameron's hypothesis. Mr Cameron did also explain that at the Trial Diet in November, he would continue to press for a dismissal and therefore we would maintain the "not guilty" plea for the time being.

Joanne and I now had to concede that a driving ban was an impending possibility and consequently thrashed out a potential survival plan for fulfilling the 40-mile round trip to work for dayshifts and nightshifts over a prolonged period. This was of course an essential undertaking in lieu of acknowledging that the time had come to approach my own management team to appraise them of my situation. Whilst driving was an occasional requirement on the job, there were always at least two people on duty and therefore it wasn't necessarily a show-stopper. Regardless, the following day, with an acute sense of trepidation, I found myself in a small meeting room with Don Charles, my senior supervisor and Mark Alford, the regional security manager. Both men had known me a few years and had been very accommodating when I had contacted them 24 hours earlier to request an urgent meeting.

"Gents, appreciate you taking the time to see me this afternoon. I've been keeping my own counsel on a personal issue for a couple of months which I hoped would resolve itself. However, after events yesterday, it may not resolve itself. I've inadvertently got myself into a bit of trouble and need to advise you of all the circumstances which could affect my position on the team."

I furnished them with a full account of events on the night in question and the subsequent increase in the possibility of a driving ban and pledged that Joanne and myself had formulated a very workable plan of action in the event of that worst-case scenario. To my relief, the reaction of my superiors suggested that, providing my plan proved as workable in practice as in theory, my position was ok. I was grateful for their understanding and inwardly vowed that in the event of that worst-case scenario materializing, I wouldn't let them down.

Another six weeks flew by and we were once again heading to picturesque Inverness Castle. This time, proceedings would take place in a different room within the smaller building.

Mr Cameron had once again retrieved us from the main waiting room and led us into the other building to take a seat outside JP Court 3. He apologetically explained that once again, he had tried to get the case dismissed to no avail and consequently had entered a 'guilty' plea, pending a future 'Special Reasons' hearing.

The 'Trial Diet' was similar to the initial 'Pleading Diet' although in a smaller courtroom, thus my orientation was less complicated and I found my way to the dock first time. After confirming my name, Mr Cameron took over, entering a 'guilty' plea and requesting said 'Special Reasons' hearing which was set for early January 2016.

Joanne and I were determined that despite the ongoing stressful backdrop to our lives, we would see out the festive period as normally as possible. There were visits to Moray where Number One had a lead role in pantomime and Number Two had her annual figure skating gala. Joanne was also "rocking all over the world" as she headed "down down" to Glasgow with her close friend Laura to attend a Status Quo concert. Whilst there, Joanne texted to advise that Laura and her husband Gary, whose hospitality we had always enjoyed despite the guaranteed hangover, were hosting some friends at their rural home in the 'Shire to see in the New Year and we were cordially invited.
"Whatever you want," could and should have been my reply.

As we reached that last evening of 2015, replete in our onesies as everyone entered into the suggested spirit, we looked forward with optimism to 2016. As the clock struck midnight, it was a memorable kiss and embrace of hope for the year ahead.
"I love you Matt. I'm sorry."
"Don't be, darling. What's gone has gone. We'll be ok."

Early 2016

2016 was only three days old when Mr Cameron got in touch to advise that due to representing another client in a protracted high-profile case, he would be unable to represent me on the set date and consequently requested a postponement, a request which was duly granted with an alternative date set for 29th February. Whilst obviously a set-back, it did mean I could continue my 40-mile return commute during wintry weather. As a fairly regular cyclist, I had previously completed several 20-mile commutes by bicycle and was now building up the legs in anticipation of potentially more frequent 20-mile gallops as part of our ban-plan.
Despite maintaining my fitness, the stress of the previous six months was beginning to register in my bowel and the beginnings of an ulcerative colitis flare-up were evident. As was permitted, I doubled my dose of Pentasa in an attempt to combat any worsening of the situation.

The rearranged hearing would coincide with the weekend of Joanne's 50th birthday and I was determined that neither the proceedings nor my colitis would be an impediment to marking such an auspicious occasion. With little sign of my condition improving at the beginning of February, I was started on a new immuno-suppressant drug, Azathioprine. As the description suggests, it slows down the immune system but carries higher risk to the kidneys and liver and therefore I was required to have bloods taken on a weekly basis. The initial weekly tests were producing no adverse results and with an improvement in the condition, it was hoped this would have minimal impact on Joanne's 50th birthday weekend. We had planned a trip to Glasgow, continuing to Inverness with Sunday evening tickets to see comedian Ed Byrne on the eve of my definitive trip to the castle. At this stage I was unaware of how much of a milestone the birthday weekend would become.

Plans were knocked slightly askew on the Wednesday prior to the planned celebratory weekend when Mr Cameron contacted me to advise that the hearing again wouldn't be going ahead. He had been notified by the court that there were simply too many cases on the day and my hearing didn't make the cut. The problem was that Pleading, Intermediate and Trial Diets took precedence over a "Special Reasons" hearing and he guaranteed that when it did happen, it would certainly be in an afternoon session. The rearranged date would be in April and again whilst it meant I would be able to continue driving in the meantime, there remained a cloud of uncertainty. With hotel accommodation and tickets to the theatre already booked in Inverness, we decided that we would still visit as planned after Glasgow.

The weekend to mark Joanne's half-century began on the Thursday evening with a family meal before heading south to Glasgow on the Friday, the actual day of her birthday, following the obligatory dedication on Ken Bruce's 'Love Song' slot on his BBC Radio 2 morning programme. Stopping for lunch at a well-known roadside restaurant at Stracathro, I'm not sure my gorgeous girlfriend shared my levels of enthusiasm when I produced a flamboyant and oversized badge and insisted it was conspicuously worn to advertise her half-century of existence to all and sundry. Her uproarious laughter did attract some attention and some birthday wishes from complete strangers.

Arriving at our hotel in Glasgow city centre, the celebrations got into full swing when I produced champagne with a personalised 50th birthday label accompanied with a flute to which I had attached a 50th birthday wine glass charm. Simple little touches which Joanne visibly cherished, much to my delight.
Dinner was booked at a nearby Spanish tapas restaurant and my playful insistence on the ridiculous badge elicited free drinks from the very pleasant and chatty proprietor. Post-dinner liqueurs preceded our short walk to the King's Theatre to take in a production of "West Side Story," an excellent evening amongst the Jets and the Sharks. Still feeling in celebratory mood, post-theatre libations were taken round the corner in Sauchiehall Street at O'Neills Irish Bar. I had previously attended this bar as part of the Jolly Boys weekend and knew it to be a popular place on a Friday evening. With our respective gregarious dispositions, we drew conversation with several other patrons within the establishment. I was fortunate to witness an incredibly heartening moment when Joanne, deep in conversation with another lady, retrieved her phone from her

handbag to show her something. As her new acquaintance scanned the screen, my curiousness drew me closer.

"How could I not fall in love with him?" I heard her comment as it transpired Joanne had saved my original entry on the "Making Mates" website from three years prior, an epistle she was now sharing with her newest friend. Celebrations were capped off with some food from the Three-in-One take-away in Elmbank Street. Having worked in an estate agent's office just along the road in my late teens before joining the RAF, this take-away had existed back in those days and here I was, some thirty years later with my fetching and fabulously foxy 50-year-old favourite female.

Joanne and I had attended the wedding of my dear friend and former RAF colleague James Lamb to his lovely wife Deborah the previous year. With James and Deborah domiciled in the Glasgow area, we met up on Saturday afternoon at a city centre bar for a catch-up and to take in the Scotland rugby team's 6-Nations win over Italy in Rome. Joanne enjoyed watching rugby and getting audibly excited when either team neared the try line. She openly quite enjoyed the sight of "30 men's bums in tight shorts" as well. In the evening, my older sisters, still domiciled in Paisley, travelled into the city centre and all six of us enjoyed dinner and drinks at a Chinese restaurant. Not as late a night as the Friday, we returned to our hotel ahead of the journey north in the morning.

A Sunday morning lie-in was savoured before a late-morning departure heading northwards. As we had all day, we would take a longer and more scenic route, cutting through The Trossachs to join the A82 northbound at Crianlarich. Over the course of two adventures, we had walked an entire route from Glasgow to Inverness and reminiscence was inevitable, although markedly more concentrated on the West Highland Way than the Great Glen Way for ongoing reasons. After an almost obligatory stop-off in Fort William to say hello to the "Man with Sore Feet", we continued north, arriving at our city centre hotel on the banks of the River Ness in time for dinner and our date with the aforementioned funny Irishman. Due to the temporary suspension of the court hearing, I felt it enhanced our enjoyment of Mr Byrne's observations on life without the looming spectre in the background. As we were strolling back to our hotel in what was a pleasant evening for the end of February, our ears were drawn to the sound of singing from a nearby bar. A crooner, sat playing a grand piano, was impressively covering some

Billy Joel classics and a nightcap was enjoyed, a brilliant ending to a brilliant weekend.

We surfaced around 9am on the final day of February and with no court appearance to fulfil, the plan we determined prior to our trip was to relax in the morning, have some lunch and head home. I caught up on the news on breakfast TV while Joanne showered and as she was subsequently dressing and busying herself on her phone, she appeared a little preoccupied, prompting me to ask if everything was ok. She assured me all was fine without elaborating as I went for my shower. Emerging from the bathroom a few minutes later, Joanne was organising a bag and putting on her jacket.

"I'm just popping into town, Matt. I have some shopping to do."

"No problem, give me a minute and I'll join you," my instinctive reply.

"No, it's ok Matt. I'd rather just go on my own."

Taken aback, I had to ask again, "Is everything ok, darling?"

Joanne smiled, "Yeah, it's fine Matt. Just want some time on my own. Tell you what, why don't we meet for lunch up by the castle. The Castle Inn even?"

"Sure. No problem. What time?"

"If you head up there for noon and I'll see you around then?" she suggested and made her way out of the room into the corridor.

I was trying to reassure myself that it was indeed probably nothing but my conscience now had a long hour and a half to ponder if anything was wrong. We had enjoyed an incredible weekend together, just as we had enjoyed a brilliant time on the Great Glen Way the previous summer. The doubts began to creep in. Was it as brilliant a weekend as I thought? Was Joanne enjoying it as much as I believed? Despite my overriding impression that our relationship had been solid since the drink-drive incident, I began to relive every aspect of our weekend celebrations trying to ascertain if I had said or done something at any point during the weekend that could have been subsequently misconstrued.

I came up with nothing and knew that my fear of upsetting her wasn't a healthy condition, but having been suddenly and unexpectedly dumped by her on three previous occasions (four if counting the online one at the very start), her impulsive unpredictability had become part of the territory if you loved this woman.

I sorted my things, checked out of the hotel and made my way to the Castle Inn. It was the first time since that fateful night seven months earlier that I had set foot in this establishment. I thought it was a strange choice for Joanne to suggest for lunch, which added to my unsettling sense of foreboding as I ordered a coffee and perused my newspaper. Regular furtive looks at my watch ensued and as the time reached 12.25pm, I received an incoming call from Joanne.

"Hi darling. Everything ok?" I tentatively queried.

"Hi Matt. I'm at the castle. Can you come over?"

"You what? I'm at the pub as agreed," was another instinctive response.

"I know, but can you come outside and meet me up at the castle?"

"Em, yeah, sure," I responded while simultaneously gathering my jacket and moved outside.

Sure enough, I could see my gorgeous girlfriend standing by a bench on the south-facing façade of the building and I ascended the road approaching the castle, skirting the prominent statue of Flora Macdonald. Nearing the bench, Joanne beckoned me. "Come and sit down, Matt."

I couldn't help but notice that a gentleman I had never seen before was taking a close interest in proceedings and appeared to be holding Joanne's phone, distinctive in its pink polka-dot designed case. Feeling a little discombobulated, I took a seat on the bench and could never have anticipated what was coming next as Joanne got down on one knee, simultaneously placing her hand onto my knee as the stranger began taking pictures with her phone. Aware that her actions were drawing attention from onlookers, my spontaneous reaction was to enquire what she was doing but then, to my outright wonderment, from her other hand, she produced a small opened ring box containing a silver Celtic ring. I would subsequently learn that the small silver band had the words "anam charaid" inscribed on the inside, Scots Gaelic for "soul mate." Joanne began paraphrasing from a favourite scene in the movie "Braveheart."

"Matt. I love you. Always have. Always will. I want to marry you. Will you marry me?"

I stared at the beautiful woman in front of me whilst her unknown conspirator repeatedly clicked on her phone and I felt compelled to answer within a couple of seconds, "Of course I'll marry you."

My life had flashed before me in a quintessential 'Sliding Doors' moment, as I crammed a few thoughts into that couple of seconds.

Has she been planning this for a while or is it on a whim?
With her periodic unpredictability, is she sure?
If I say "no" or even "can I think about it", is our relationship over?

We kissed and hugged in consolation of my reply as I recalled that it was in fact the 29th of February, the traditional date for a lady to propose.
I never had any intention of marrying again and although I had been completely ambushed, my immediate acceptance of the proposal certainly felt like the right thing to do and I just had to hope and trust that her proposal was unequivocal. Besides, in terms of risk management, I wasn't prepared to potentially jeopardise our relationship and therefore I realistically had no choice.
As I looked out towards the aforementioned immortalised heroine Flora Macdonald on her large plinth, even she with her well-documented historical deeds couldn't have assisted with an escape from this conundrum.

The combination of shock and euphoria eventually began to suppress and Joanne suggested trying somewhere different for lunch, pointing out an attractive little white building across the way advertising as Las Cuevas, a Spanish tapas restaurant.
As we entered the establishment, we were immediately approached by a gentleman who appeared to be the proprietor. "Well?" he eagerly enquired.
"He said yes," Joanne excitedly replied, a reply that immediately initiated a round of applause from the diners sat at the four or five occupied tables.
Our host kindly proffered his congratulations before leading us to a charming and ambient little alcove towards the back of the restaurant where a table had been set for two with a lit candle and champagne flutes. Goodness me I was glad I said yes.
The irony of the champagne flutes wasn't lost on me as I certainly wouldn't be partaking due to the forthcoming drive home.
Following lunch, Joanne led me to a local brewery shop where she had procured bottles of a local beer called "Happy Chappy" together with an accompanying "Happy Chappy" glass. It was a very thoughtful touch referencing our original online contact. In a nearby art shop, she had purchased a framed pencil drawing of Inverness Castle to further commemorate the special occasion. She really did have some shopping to do that morning. Goodness me I was glad I said yes.

Amidst the ongoing excitement, my thoughtful lady had even managed to present me with a small thank you card with a heartfelt handwritten message within.

"To my darling man. Thank you for all of your lovely gifts. My 50th weekend was fantastic, thanks to you. Love you. Always. Joanne x"

We set off back to Moray and the 'Shire to share our 'engagement story' with our family and friends.

My gorgeous girlfriend had suddenly become my fair fiancée.

Day 5 – Angle Tarn to Shap

My 'old man' trip outside at 2.30am under the starry spectacular moonlight was memorable, but in a similar situation to Day Two at Ennerdale, I was awoken just over three hours later by heavy rain dancing noisily on the canvas. The forecast from the previous day had suggested there would be some morning rain with the temperature rising from five degrees to eight degrees but with no connectivity, I was unable to obtain an updated outlook. By 7am, the rain was persisting and I hoped things would ease off enough to allow an 'escape window'. Alas, by 8am, having had some porridge and tea, the pluvial conditions continued unabated and I began organising things from within for a potential damp departure. My interesting toileting procedure involved putting my bare feet into my soaking wet boots and venturing outside after donning my wet waterproof jacket.

Listening back to my notes from that morning, they included, "This is an adventure but fun is not the word at the present time. I'm stuck in a wee green nylon thing up a mountain overlooking a tarn with no phone, no internet, no facilities and the rain is relentless."

By 9am, as it became clear that the rain wasn't going to stop, everything was packed away in the rucksack, just leaving the tent itself to be attached.

I would be putting my feet, complete with dry socks, into the aforementioned soggy boots. Leaving my walking poles and map case by an adjacent boulder, my damp hiking trousers and jacket over my almost dry wicking t-shirt would complete my apparel for the day.

Within minutes, I had a very wet tent packed away and attached to my covered rucksack which now felt heavier. I was off and hiking. The earliest check-in time for the next campsite at New Ing Lodge in Shap was 3.30pm so there was no real rush to get away but similarly, I couldn't stay in situ all morning as the weather looked unlikely to improve. I reminded myself that I was taking part in something challenging and, thinking positively, I would be reunited with my courier holdall at Shap, thus a chance for a proper sort out.

The path rises away from Angle Tarn and climbs steadily over a peak called 'The Knott'. The guidebook assured that there were extensive views out over the Hayeswater Reservoir and I had to take their word for it as visibility in the clag was down to around 20ft. Hearing voices ahead, I caught up with a group of four fellow male hikers. In the conditions, it actually looked like one of them was wearing a kilt but as I passed, I realised it was poncho which extended over his shorts.

"Thought you were wearing a kilt there for a moment," I commented on passing, much to their amusement.

I had no idea at this point that I was passing poncho-wearing George and his friend Ryan, both from London, who in turn were passing Paul and Matthew from Northallerton, a town close to a later stage of the trail.

A small cairn with "C2C" painted thereon indicated a sharp left turn on to the path towards Kidsty Pike, the highest point of the Coast to Coast at 2,560 ft. Soon afterwards on the gently ascending path, a further cairn would indicate a half-right turn onto another path for the summit. As I continued at a good pace, I was unaware that I had glided past this second marker and a short time later, I came across a larger summit cairn which I erroneously assumed to be the summit of Kidsty Pike. I made a short video to mark the reaching of the highest point, mocking the fact that the views were superb beyond the 20ft of visibility. I really should have been mocking myself, as I was filming my video at the summit of Rampsgill Head, some 38ft higher than Kidsty Pike.

As I continued along the ridge, the mist began to clear and the views opened up to reveal Haweswater Reservoir below in the distance. In the sadistic style of the old tv quiz programme, "Bullseye", it was a "look at what you could've won" moment as the clearance allowed me to confirm that I was on the wrong ridge.

It wasn't really ideal with my heavier load but there was no point getting upset about it as I began a descent followed by an ascent, diagonally traversing the intervening dale to re-join the route at the head of Kidsty Howes. At this point, the biggest descent of the entire walk begins, down to the south shore of Haweswater Reservoir, steep enough in places to involve the use of my hands. Paul and Matthew, still unknown to me, had stopped for a breather on their descent as I cascaded past and, not for the first time on my adventure, I could sense fellow hikers were thinking I bore an uncanny resemblance to someone who had passed them earlier. Eventually the waterside was reached where the path proceeds northwards along the west shore of the reservoir for three miles. Any thoughts that this would be a flat shoreline amble were fanciful as the path undulated continuously until eventually reaching the dam at the north end. Fair warning was adeptly offered by my guidebook: "A lakeside amble while spinning your dainty parasol is sadly not on the cards. Instead, you are soon panting like a hippo on a treadmill high above the shore." (Coast to Coast Path – Trailblazer 8th Edition)

Some natural respite was supplied by day-walkers going in the opposite direction as I stopped for some chats in the steadily improving weather conditions. Bertie and Opie, crossbreeds from Exeter with their owners afforded today's canine encounter.
Past the dam, the trail follows the edge of a large wood before reaching the small and very pretty village of Burnbanks. With sunshine beginning to dominate, the inviting bench carved out of a tree trunk on the village green would provide the ideal stop for lunch, albeit it had now gone 2pm. Having pushed on further than intended, my shoulders were grateful of the recess as I unloaded my cargo and took some time to brew up and enjoy some salmon and broccoli pasta with my mug of tea.
Burnbanks was a most tranquil place, the aesthetic ambience only punctuated by the pleasant tunefulness of birdsong. I was surrounded on the green by half a dozen identical houses forming the original part of the village with larger houses erected around the periphery. This idyllic location obligated one of my lengthiest recesses of the entire walk and it was after 3pm when I packed up and set off for the final four miles to Shap which would consist mainly of farmland.

After passing through some woods, a minor road and wooden footbridge were crossed before the route tracked the bank of a small watercourse called Gills Dub. The path was routine enough until I had to negotiate a section occupied by several cows who didn't really look in the mood to cede passage to the lone hiker. What to do?
I raised one of my walking poles into a horizontal position and tried to confidently approach my bovine buddies, hoping they would get the message that I was coming through.
They didn't.
I stopped.
Their looks suggested they knew the human wasn't as confident as he appeared and I had been made to feel a bit silly by some Dexters, the smallest breed in the country. The only option was to divert off

117

the path and warily stick to the water's edge. Although only a couple of yards from my newly-christened nemeses, I had a potential escape route if required, albeit into the burn.

Relieved to re-join the path further along the bank, my pace picked up amidst furtive looks behind to see if I was being followed, and of course the cows were totally disinterested. My inclination towards bovinophobia would need to be addressed at some point.

After traversing over some more fields including a particularly boggy section amongst gorse, the trail descends to Shap Abbey, a church built in the late 12th century but disestablished in the 16th century. My tiring limbs were disinclined to hang around this ruin and a quick scan of the information board revealed that several Baron Cliffords were buried in the grounds. My childish thought that several "big red dogs" may be interred in the vicinity suggested it was time to get the final mile and a half out of the way.

It was around 5.30pm when I trundled into the village of Shap to be gratefully repatriated with my holdall at New Ing Lodge at the north end of the village. After pitching my wet tent on grassy grounds behind this attractive 3-storey Grade 2 listed 18th century farmhouse, I availed myself of a much-needed shower and was pleased to note a drying room was also available. Leaving my tent to dry out in the pleasant early evening sunshine, dinner would be provided by the nearby and recommended Shap Chippy which didn't disappoint. Whilst demolishing my traditional British take-away at a picnic table behind the lodge, I ascertained that one of the two single-man tents pitched on the grounds belonged to the younger gentleman I thought was wearing a kilt on this morning's misty ascent towards Kidsty Pike. Conversation was struck up with Londoners George and his friend Ryan who were tackling the Coast-to-Coast in one day less than myself.

In the football world, tonight was the Europa League Final between Manchester United and Spanish team, Villareal and enquiries with staff at the lodge revealed that the further away of the village's two pubs was the one that would be showing the match.

Shap is a linear village, which means it is formed in a long line, a line I dragged myself half a mile along southwards to the Kings Arms pub, passing the more convenient Crown Inn

I entered a small bar with limited seating only minutes before the match was due to kick off. Eyeing a raised table surrounded by four bar stools, two of which were occupied, I enquired to the older gentlemen, "Evening guys, are these seats free?"

The gentleman to my left chuckled, "Only if you're going to support Man United."

"If I must," I jokingly replied, taking a vacant seat.

I placed my jacket over the stool in the stereotypical style of a German tourist placing a towel over a deck chair on a Mediterranean beach and ventured to the bar, returning with a pint to settle down to watch the match. I had no idea at this point how secondary the match would become compared to the conversation about to unfold with the gentleman to my left who had insisted I support the British team. I was also unaware of the privilege it would be, to spend time in his company.

"Walking the Coast to Coast?" he enquired.

"Yes I am," I keenly replied, "I'm on Day 5. Came in from a wild camp up beside Angle Tarn near Patterdale last night and I have a bag being couriered so it was nice to get a shower and some fresh clothes on."

I noticed that at a table in a corner by the window sat George and Ryan, my fellow Coast to Coasters, who were also watching the match.

"Yes, it's quite a challenge. It's good to see all you guys and gals coming through," my bald on top, newest acquaintance observed, who looked like he was in his late 60s, "and it's obviously good for the village commercially with accommodation, food and of course the pubs. I think those two chaps in the corner are also walking the trail"

"Yeh, they're camping alongside me up at New Ing. The chippy was recommended for tea tonight and it was excellent," my complimentary retort.

"Aye, it's a popular place with the locals too. I usually treat myself once a week," the local man declared, before continuing, "I'm John, by the way."

"I'm Matt. Nice to meet you, John."

John raised an open palm towards the other occupant of the table, "And this is Terry," before continuing to his colleague, "Terry, this is Matt. He's hiking the Coast to Coast."

"Nice to meet you Matt," Terry replied, although it was clear that Terry was engrossed in the early stages of the Europa League Final on the two wall-mounted televisions and John and myself began watching too.

The match was a cagey affair with little to get overly excited about, resulting in the resumption of our verbal exchange a short time later.

"Safe to assume with that accent, you're from north of the border, Matt?" John enquired.

"Yes, fairly safe, John," I smirked, "I live in Aberdeen but originally from Paisley near Glasgow."

"Well, I've been up to Murrayfield many times as I'm more a fan of the other shaped ball," he replied, referring to his evidently greater passion for rugby union.

General conversation developed with my latest acquaintance and I ascertained that my inability to predict age was consistent when John revealed that he was in fact 75 years old. With his friendly, unassuming and engaging manner, discourse was effortless as we slowly began to share details of our lives with the occasional glance up at the televisions. I recounted my military background and John in turn revealed that he had served over 30 years in Cumbria Police, reaching the rank of Detective Inspector. When it came to the odd-shaped ball, he had played for both Kendal and Penrith rugby clubs in the 1960s and 1970s and had captained the Cumbrian Police rugby team for six years. After playing, he was involved in management and administration of the game for many years.

As a barmaid passed, John ordered beers for the table and I accepted his kindness on the proviso that I could reciprocate in due course. Moments later, slight commotion ensued around us as the Spanish team Villareal took the lead against Manchester United just before the half hour.

John had three children of his own during the 1970's prior to fostering children with his wife Joan. He explained that their fostering began in 1980 when a pair of siblings came to stay for the summer holiday period . . . and left 18 years later. Over the course of the following 30 years, they remarkably fostered over 50 children. Discussion around family and my ongoing hike, spending time away from home on my own, inevitably led to sharing that I had very unexpectedly became single towards the end of the previous year. I openly admitted that I hadn't coped with it very well but it did create this opportunity to take on a challenge, take stock of things and try to create new memories. My older new friend sensed my disappointment in relaying this chapter of recent history and placed a metaphorical arm around my shoulder:

"I lost my lovely wife last year after more than 50 years together," an appreciable sense of sadness in his voice, "but what can you do? You have to get on with it. She wouldn't want me to be moping around so I've got myself involved again with Penrith Rugby Club

120

and the village football team. You will usually find me in here a couple of nights a week too. Life goes on, young Matt, and you're getting out and creating new experiences. Just like your Coast to Coast, you have to keep putting one foot in front of the other."
"Thanks John. Appreciate that."

Into the second half of the Europa League Final, things brightened up for the predominantly Manchester United favouring audience in the pub when Uruguayan striker Cavani equalised for the English side. John and I concurred that there was a fair chance the match could now go to extra time and I joked that would necessitate more beers to affect my 20-mile hike across the Westmoreland plateau tomorrow.
We acknowledged that in rugby, matches ending in a tie were a much rarer occurrence and this prompted John to recall one of his visits to Murrayfield.
"I remember when England drew 15-all with the Scots up at Murrayfield in 2010. I was watching the game with Her Royal Highness Princess Anne and her husband Tim Laurence. She loves her rugby and is a huge Scotland fan."
I processed the sentence and clarified, "You were watching the game . . . with Princess Anne?"
"Yes, I was actually President of the RFU (Rugby Football Union) at the time."
"You were President of English rugby?"
"Yes, and then I was Chairman of the RFU Injured Players Foundation. In fact, we also supported the charity 'Help for Heroes' and always invited some of your injured fellow veterans to matches."
John's self-effacing demeanour belied the fact that I had been enjoying the convivial company of a local celebrity.
As he excused himself to pay a visit to the Gents, I reached for my phone to conduct a quick internet search and Terry, across the table watching the match but aware of exactly what I was doing, commented, "Yep, that's our John."
My online enquiry immediately yielded pictures of my newest drinking buddy in conversation with Prince Harry at Twickenham, England's national rugby stadium, a few years prior.

Minutes later, we were joined at the table by Avril, another local lady and friend of John and Terry. She had been at a meeting elsewhere but joined us for the latter stages of the football. I was duly introduced to her as though I was an old friend of John's, such was the warmth of the man's nature and I certainly felt amongst friends as I ordered the next round.

Whilst at the bar, "two ladies" entered from a different door and it transpired that they were residing here at the King's Arms before their final day to Kirkby Stephen. They ordered drinks to take to their room and I hoped to see them on their final day. I noted that they waved across to George and Ryan on departing the bar and it helped me feel part of a little Coast-to-Coast mini-society.

As predicted, the match finished all square and a further 30 minutes of extra time failed to find a winner and thus the taking of penalties would decide the destination of the trophy.

The shoot-out went on and on with the Spanish team eventually triumphing 11-10 on kicks at goal from 12 yards. This was conducive to prolonging a most enjoyable evening to beyond last orders and, not for the first time on the trip, led to a later night than anticipated. George and Ryan acknowledged me with a wave as they retired for the night but I had some drinking up time before doing likewise. I thanked my newest friends for a most enjoyable evening and their welcoming hospitality. Hitting the fresh air and feeling slightly inebriated, I retraced that half-mile straight line back north to my dry canvas dwelling, reflecting on what a wonderful experience this adventure had already been . . . and I was still two days from reaching the half-way point. It was imperative to appreciate and enjoy these memorable times, as life had supplied less memorable times, particularly just five years earlier.

Spring 2016

Despite being separated from Jennifer for almost 10 years, there had been no requirement to organize a divorce on account of the fact that neither of us had any notion of remarrying. Joanne's surprise proposal had obviously moved those particular goalposts and, having organized her own divorce from Dave the previous year, she was keen to regularly remind me of my need to do likewise. With the pervading uncertainty regarding the ongoing court proceedings, a date for our espousal would be placed on the back burner for the time being and my divorce proceedings were initiated accordingly.

My ulcerative colitis appeared to be under control with the new medication but it would be a nightshift in early April when stomach and chest pains became unbearably uncomfortable and I left work to attend the local casualty department. After supplying a blood sample, I was given something to relieve the pain and a short while later, the chatty young doctor returned.
"Mr McKay. I have to ask. Have you been seeing prostitutes lately?"
"You what?" I replied, my wide eyes suggesting she was winding me up.
"Do you drink to excess?" she continued.
"No more than anyone else," my plea of mitigation.
"Well," she explained, "Your liver function tests are deranged. Very deranged. You may have hepatitis. Put it this way, we're organising a bed on the ward and you'll be staying with us a couple of days at least for investigation."

I would be a guest for a worrisome four days, during which I underwent various tests and, having been taken off the new medication, my liver function tests had gradually dropped to a more settled level, enabling me to be discharged. It was concluded that the azathioprine had caused elevated liver enzymes and I would be returning to the Pentasa drugs.

Stress would have almost inevitably played its part and stress levels weren't helped when another journey back to the scene of that memorable day in February was in vain as yet again the 'special reasons hearing' would be deferred until the end of May. Mr Cameron did advise that on speaking with the relevant personnel, he was pretty sure it would go ahead next time. My fiancée and I were firmly at the stage where we just wanted a result either way.

Another fraught month elapsed and the day arrived to make yet another foray westwards to the highland capital. As with previous visits, we took our seats in the 'waiting area'. Nearby, a young well-dressed man appeared to be holding court, pun intended, with several slightly less well-dressed acquaintances, ahead of his apparent audience with a sheriff. He didn't appear to mind being easily overheard by others outwith his captive audience as he proffered a somewhat blunt assessment of his legal representative. "That fucker's fuckin' fit for fuck all. Fuckin' fanny".
I couldn't be sure if he knew what an alliteration was, and with other things on our respective minds, it seemed wholly inappropriate to point it out. Nonetheless, his noxious notions necessitated a noteworthy nod.

Mr Cameron appeared shortly after 10am and gave the familiar brief. On his re-appearance twenty minutes later, he confirmed what had been suspected on the previous sojourn in April. Things looked promising and it appeared that today would be the day, notwithstanding that it wouldn't happen until around 2.30pm. It was going to be a long four hours.

A drive out into the pleasant Inverness-shire sunshine was the preferred choice of tension alleviation and we headed west along the Beauly Firth and south as the road tracked the River Beauly and River Glass down to the village of Cannich. With our occasional penchant for long-distance paths and our hopeful attitude that life will go on as normal after the court outcome, there was in fact a reason for visiting this attractive settlement at the southern end of Strathglass.

The Affric Kintail Way, stretching 44 miles from Drumnadrochit through its spectacular eponymous glen to Morvich in Wester Ross, is Scotland's newest long-distance trail. We defiantly planned to complete the Way over four days whilst on leave in late August regardless of the outcome of the hearing. The first night stopover would be the campsite in Cannich which our recce showed to be ample with good facilities. This trip would however necessitate carrying our food and accommodation for two nights of wild camping. There were no hostelries or campsites at the Glen Affric Car Park (2nd night) and the Glen Affric Youth Hostel at Alltbeithe, Britain's most remote youth hostel (3rd night), was unable to accommodate our pampered pooch, Squeak. We had concerns on the logistics involved in this project and a practice run would require to be organized in due course.

Lunch was purchased in the local well-stocked grocery store and eaten a few miles south at the Dog Falls Car Park where the Way crosses the River Affric on a recently constructed wooden bridge. This was indeed the location where the excellent Scottish outdoors enthusiast and author Cameron McNeish had officially opened the Glen Affric Way in April 2015. Our lunch spot was also a welcome distraction from the grim matter in hand and a reminder that we lived in a most beautiful country.

To complete a looped return to Inverness, I drove back via Drumnadrochit, ironically the last village where I woke up without this dark cloud hanging over me some ten months earlier. It reminded me that I was nearing the conclusion of a long stressful journey and, whatever the outcome, the beginning of a new journey.

Mr Cameron appeared in the waiting area and confirmed it was happening. It was actually happening. He led me outside and across to the Justice of the Peace Court and upstairs to Court 2 where I took a seat in the small public gallery, a seat I had previously occupied at the Pleading Diet a summer ago. A familiar scene lay in front of me featuring my stern-faced shop-keeper and disinterested policeman. Joanne was scheduled to appear in the witness box after myself and in the meantime, she was taken to a separate room.

A short time later, the bespectacled administrator announced a special hearing regarding Matthew McKay and I was instructed to walk forward and step up into the witness box. Mr Cameron and the young prosecutor both glanced down at paperwork on the central table as I took a firm grip of the wooden edges of the pulpit-like vestibule, an attempt to steady my nerves, breathing and posture.

Mr Cameron stood and explained to the court that due to a medical condition, his client may require an instant short break during the proceedings. The Court Officer then offered me a glass of water before I whispered, "No thanks. I have ulcerative colitis," which induced a perplexed expression on the older gent's face.

Mr Cameron guided me through that fateful July evening in a chronological sequence, all fairly straightforward as the events were firmly etched in the memory. Emphasis was of course placed on my concerns for Joanne's safety following her irrational behaviour. The Advocate Depute then took to his feet.

"Yes Mr McKay, a very detailed description of the night in question but just a couple of questions if I may. Did you consider contacting the Police?"

"I think calling the police may have made the situation worse, sir. I was having difficulty with Joanne and I thought an authoritative stranger in uniform would have very possibly made the situation and possibly Joanne worse."

"Did you consider asking for help from the receptionist?"

"In the stressful circumstances, it never occurred me that the young girl in her late teens dealing with reception duties would also be experienced in dealing with domestic disputes amongst middle-aged adults," I replied, trying to be as respectful as possible and hide my disdain for what I believed to be a frankly silly question.

I didn't know his piece de resistance was still to come.

"Did you consider getting a taxi yourself?"

In that very brief moment while the question sank in, I was taken aback and began wondering if the young man had in fact been listening to any of the proceedings.

"Why would I have considered doing that?" I retorted, slightly irked.

"Well, it would have prevented the offence being committed."

"Sir, as per the events of the night in question, I absolutely believed that no offence would be committed by driving as I didn't believe I was over the limit, which, but for a change in the law a few months earlier affecting only people in Scotland, I wasn't."

I paused and took a breath, my nerves having temporarily disappeared, disappointed by the sudden decrease in the credibility of my fresh-faced inquisitor.

He advised the shop-keeper that he had no further questions and took his seat as my potential water-provider indicated that I may return to the small gallery.

Mr Cameron again took centre stage, announcing that witness, Ms Joanne Buchan was taking the stand. Joanne took her place in the witness box and again Mr Cameron guided her through her account of the night in question. On completion, the Advocate Depute declined the opportunity to ask questions, commenting, "No questions from me, your honour. Both credible witnesses."

Mr Cameron then summed up proceedings, stating that here were two decent and respectable citizens who had clearly just had a bad night. He reminded the court of my clean record, clean driving licence and my 22 years of exemplary service in the Royal Air Force. He also reiterated the "double-whammy" of the statutory alternative being removed by the UK Government three months before the offence, affecting the UK-wide Road Traffic Act.

The shop-keeper peered over his spectacles and the protective screen, "Yes, thank you Mr Cameron. I'm going to call a short recess at this point as I need to seek legal advice before passing judgement."

Mr Cameron offered some encouragement as he cast a hopeful glance in our direction with a shrug of his shoulders.

Seven minutes passed. Seven short fateful minutes.

On instruction from the clerk, I dragged my anxious body, replete with rapidly drying throat and churning stomach, the long five yards into the dock to await the imminent arrival of the retired retailer. There was surely a chance. "Mr Pleasant" ordered the courtroom to stand as the stern-faced Justice of the Peace re-entered the courtroom.

This was it.

I stood in the dock feeling very open and vulnerable with no control over what was about to happen. With that in mind, for a brief moment, I was bizarrely transported back to the autumn of 2007 and the Contingency Operating Base near Basra in southern Iraq. One afternoon, I was walking from my sandbag-laden portakabin accommodation to the air terminal across a sizeable and open unprotected area when the all-too-familiar air raid siren activated. As per my training, I instantly went to ground, tucking my hands under my face and helmet. I remember thinking in that moment that if one of the incoming salvo of mortars were to land within any reasonable distance, I wouldn't have stood a chance as I lay fearfully in the lap of the Gods.

The man in charge looked out towards me and began, "Mr McKay, thank you for your comprehensive testimony this afternoon. As Mr Cameron has alluded to, you had a bad night on the night in question and have never been in trouble before. However, no matter how recent the changes to the law and your marginal failure on the breath test, it is the law and it is considered that your special reasons just aren't strong enough to defend the drink-driving. You are found guilty of driving with an alcohol level above the limit. You will be fined £400 and banned from driving for a period of 12 months. I am offering you the opportunity to attend a drink-drive rehabilitation course which will reduce your driving ban to nine months."

Breathing had momentarily become difficult, shock, numbness, profound disappointment, helplessness . . . the list went on. Thoughts turned to the previous stressful ten months, the sleepless nights, the flare-ups of ulcerative colitis and the realisation that all our hopes had come down to an apparently very brief chat between a former newsagent and a faceless "legal advisor".

So many things were whirling round in my head. Having a driving licence removed would certainly affect my independence and make for a difficult nine months for me and those closest to me. My research had shown that I would have a criminal record for twenty years. It also showed that despite trying to sound considerate, the Justice of the Peace had handed down the maximum sentence and fine he possibly could. The endorsement would remain on my driving licence for 11 years. I was banned from driving in England, Wales and Northern Ireland but had not breached any of their driving laws. The irony that if the law had changed in England but not in Scotland, Scottish people being banned from driving in Scotland for an offence committed in England would have provoked complete uproar from the Scottish Government. Composure was required as my thoughts took a brief and sinister turn towards my wife-to-be. That non-conversation over a darts match, her ridiculous behaviour affecting the rest of my life. Would I ever be able to deal with her having a go at me or judging me about anything after what she'd put me through?
A few deep breaths of de-escalation were required as I quickly reminded myself that we had come too far together and I reminded

myself how much I loved her. The 99% of good far outweighed the 1% of, well, not so good.

On leaving the court and moving outside, despite the verdict, there was a definitive air of an ending and with that came a sense of relief. Joanne and I hugged, an emotional moment and a release of tension, recognizing the end of this challenging period and the start of a new one.
"It's done now Matt. We will move on and deal with this."
"I know, sweetheart. We will," I whispered in her ear as we remained in our embrace for a few moments more.
I retrieved the car key from my pocket and held it out towards Joanne.
"So, who's driving?"

Day 6 – Shap to Kirkby Stephen

After a long day and my impromptu night out in Shap, it was little surprise to enjoy my best sleep of the journey so far, not even wakening for the nightly inflate caused by the slow puncture to my bed. It was only around 7.30am and, aware of the favourable weather forecast, there was already a heat and brightness within the tent. Indeed, unzipping the external entrance to the tent revealed a clear blue sky gleaming in the early morning sunshine.
I set up the Jetboil and prepared a morning brew to accompany my paracetamol for my slightly tender head resulting from last night's flowing refreshments. 21 warm miles with a slight hangover lay ahead but I would be carrying less weight and tonight was one of my two scheduled nights to sleep in a proper bed.
It certainly felt advantageous to be packing away a dry tent which wouldn't be used this evening.

Leaving New Ing Lodge shortly after 9am with an acknowledging wave to George and Ryan, I headed back through the village, stopping off at the Lakes & Dales "Coapy" to acquire some lunch before continuing to the scene of last night's indulgence. Opposite the Kings Arms, signposts direct hikers over the railway tracks of the West Coast Main Line and over some fields towards the M6 motorway.

On approach to the rumbling of moving transport, my guidebook reminded me to look back towards the wedge of Kidsty Pike, the Coast-to-Coast highest point where I thought I was standing yesterday. The expansive blue skies enabled a clear view to the summit which was seven miles away, yet yesterday I struggled to see seven metres on the same ridge. Them's the breaks.
After five days of hiking in mostly remote areas, the pedestrian footbridge crossing above the thunderous din of six busy lanes on the UK's longest motorway was a bit of a culture shock. The bridge also felt like a definitive point on the journey, leaving the Lake District National Park behind and crossing onto the limestone bedrock and more gentle undulations of the Westmoreland Plateau.

After passing the scarred landscape of Hardendale Quarry, the trail skirts around the walled hamlet of Oddendale. Today's canine encounter would take place at the entrance to this hidden settlement where I was introduced to Daisy, a diminutive and excitable Pomchi, a cross between a Pomeranian and a Chihuahua. The energetic little lady enjoyed my attention and would possibly have joined me on today's hike, given the opportunity.

Some pleasant walking ensued across the moor, enhanced by a flypast from an F15 fighter jet, briefly reminding me of a previous life. Further enhancement was provided by the company of Stuart from Hebden Bridge in West Yorkshire, who was tacking the Coast-to-Coast in stages over a couple of years, utilising his campervan.

Bidding farewell to my latest companion, I stopped for a snack and a brew next to a large cairn named Robin Hood's Grave. My guidebook reassured that this was not the final resting place of the man who gave his name to my final destination on the North Yorkshire coast, which was now just over 120 miles away.

As I sat in the sunshine enjoying my sandwich and cup of tea in the pleasant quietness of the open moorland, save for the birdsong on the gentle breeze, my inner child failed to stifle my immature laugh as I learned that interrupting the sentiment of this tranquil moment with the release of a louder-than-anticipated fart, was actually rather funny.

Before completing my break, I was passed by London 20-somethings George and Ryan who stopped for a brief chat. Bare-chested George was clearly enjoying what the Scots vernacular would refer to as "taps aff" weather.

I had hoped that my faithful walking boots, now six years old, would accompany me across the entire adventure. Disappointingly, it was becoming clear that this was a journey too far and I conceded that replacements would be required in Kirkby Stephen before venturing across the more remote and less facilitating Yorkshire Dales National Park.

Shortly after my break, the route joined a tarmac lane which climbed to briefly meet the B6260 for a brief stretch before I was back on grass, descending to join country lanes around some local farms. The last of these was Scarside Farm where campervan Stuart was in conversation with the farmer. This was where Stuart detoured back off the trail to rejoin his mobile accommodation in the village of Orton and afforded me the opportunity to wish him well on his piecemeal adventure.

Keeping the exposed limestone cliffs of Orton Scar on the left, the path traversed some fields and sheepfolds via several stone stiles before joining a tarmac road. There was an inevitable added spring in my step as this road approached Sunbiggin Farm where a "refreshment stall" was pledged in the guidebook.

Just off the road on the left-hand side stood a raised garden area with seating and a sizeable green garden shed. The very colourful sign outside advertised "a wide choice of drinks, snacks and homemade goodies" and once inside this oasis, I helped myself to some cake, a chocolate bar, some ginger beer and some bottled water to top up supplies. Rounding up prices and depositing the requisite fee into the honesty box, I took a welcome seat in the sun and enjoyed some rest in the serenity of my surroundings.

Continuing eastwards, the route crosses the heather of Tarn Moor to reach a road opposite Sunbiggin Tarn, a circular lake with its abundant birdlife. Following the road south for a short while, a signposted byway directs hikers onto and over the exposed Ravenstonedale Moor. With temperatures now in excess of 20 degrees Celsius, it was a perspiring trudge but still preferred to alternative conditions where the lack of any protective surroundings could have made things very unpleasant.

The grassy wide walkways and the encircling sound of lapwings (either that or a bunch of nearby invisible toddlers playing with their squeaky toys) made for pleasant walking. Crossing another road and tracking walls of sheepfolds, I eventually descended steeply through a field, passing a boarded-up railway cottage and a dismantled railway line, down to Smardale Bridge. This attractive stone arched bridge over Scandal Beck offered another short break and water replenishment in what was becoming another long day.

During this brief stop, two males approached from the hill, becoming recognisable as George and Ryan who had passed me hours before at Robin Hood's Grave. Assuming they hadn't utilised the invisibility cloak of those toddlers and their squeaky toys back on Ravenstonedale Moor, and with memories of my own previous "double-overtakes" on the trip, the hiking boot was now on the other foot.

"Afternoon guys, been taking a wee detour?" I teasingly enquired.

"Yeah, we've been taking a few stops," a smiling Ryan replied as both men also stopped for a break and to replenish their water, insisting that I must have passed them whilst they were having one of their stops, probably just off the path. Our chat revealed that they were also having a break from camping tonight and had booked a room at the Black Bull Hotel and as I was staying in a nearby hostel, they kindly invited me to join them for a pint.

Leaving my Coast-to-Coast colleagues to their break, the final stretch to Kirkby Stephen began with a steep climb up a grassy path, affording views northwards to the nearby Smardale Gill Viaduct, part of the aforementioned dismantled railway. This impressive structure consists of 14 stone arches which carried trains across the Scandal Beck valley 90 feet below. Out of use since 1962, it didn't become a permissive footpath until 1992, perhaps the reason why Mr Wainwright's route didn't incorporate an inclusive detour.
Crossing the hilltop, the descent included a first glimpse of today's destination less than two miles ahead and in its background, The Nine Standards Rigg. The latter would keep for tomorrow morning's initial stages. Also on this short descent, I drew alongside a blonde-haired chap, slightly younger than myself, laden with a rucksack.
"Hi there. Doing the Coast-to-Coast?" I asked on passing, the fairly standard conversational prompt.
My fellow walker simply looked at me with a slightly awkward smile.
"Walking the Coast-to-Coast?" I repeated with an intonation to suggest he hadn't quite picked up the initial query.
"Yes," the one-word reply followed by a further smile.
"Heading for Kirkby Stephen?" I attempted to engage my fellow Coast-to-Coaster.
This time there was a short pause followed by an identical one-word retort accompanied with a nod.
It was now my turn to offer a slightly awkward smile and scurry on as it became clear that the hind legs of any nearby donkeys were in no danger from 'Blondie'.
There was, of course, absolutely nothing wrong with someone not keen to engage in conversation but in my hiking experience, it was somewhat unusual.

After a brief road section, a signpost indicated a stile into a large field which inclined downhill towards a small tunnel under the Carlisle to Settle railway line. I could see the tunnel about 400 yards ahead. I could also see the dozens of cows directly on my path towards the tunnel, staring at me menacingly . . . disgruntled that I was about to interfere with their Thursday evening grazing. Yes, it was fair to say my slight bovinophobia led to a rather creative imagination.

800 yards of perimeter walking later, I passed through the tunnel and continued across a couple of thankfully uninhabited fields to pass through a gully towards a farmyard.
One of the more inventive signposts sat at the end of the track through the farmyard. A large green oil barrel with an arrow of bright yellow paint pointing to the right, with bright yellow words below advising that Kirkby Stephen was half a mile ahead. I surmised that the additional smaller arrow below, pointing to the right to "drum" home the point, was a consequence of exasperated farm staff regularly redirecting ramblers.

The tarmac of Croglam Lane meandered into the backstreets of my Day Six terminus and I was soon on Market Street, the aptly-named main thoroughfare of this attractive Upper Eden Valley market town. My attention was drawn to the imposing façade of a building emblazoned in large ornate lettering with the words "Temperance Hall" and the number "1856", presumably its year of construction. Subsequent enquiries would indeed reveal that in the same year the Treaty of Paris was signed to end the Crimean War, this Grade 2 listed building was built to meet the needs of those who had taken "the pledge". Not an effortless pledge either, as I also discovered that at one point, there were no fewer than 17 pubs and inns in Kirkby Stephen. After 21 miles in today's sunshine, I would be undertaking no such "pledge" and hoped to make use of one of those hostelries remaining in existence.

Kirkby Stephen Hostel is a converted Methodist church on Market Street. It retains many of the old church's features and a staircase leading up to several rooms of varied capacity. On collecting my hold-all from a dedicated area at the bottom of the staircase, I was given directions to a door which accessed a small corridor with twin rooms at either end and a shared shower and toilet in-between. There was certainly a tinge of excitement about sleeping in a bed for the first time since the eve of the walk. Officially 78 miles into my adventure, it was probably over 80 miles when my involuntary minor diversions were added and I did feel quite tired. On returning from a welcome shower and relaxing for a while on my real bed, I discovered that, having detached the removeable legs from my hiking trousers that morning, the exposed skin on my legs had taken on a particularly red colour. Sun tan lotion would be added to the shopping list.

With full cutlery and crockery available within the 'body of the kirk', I opted to use the Chinese take-away on Market Square. When advised that there would be a wait of approximately 20 minutes for my curry, I took the opportunity to nip across the road to the Black Bull Hotel where George and Ryan were on dessert.
Joining them for a pint, I explained that after last night's extra-curricular exertions and a long warm day, I would be taking advantage of a real bed and having an early night.
As fitting occurrences go, I was leaving shortly thereafter when "two ladies" entered the bar, having completed their half-walk and, accumulatively, the entire Coast-to-Coast. I was delighted to be able to offer my congratulations and we bade each other farewell.

I collected my food and stopped off at the mini-mart opposite the hostel to acquire tomorrow's lunch, some juice and the all-important Factor 30. I noted "Eden Outdoors", a local outdoors shop just a few yards from my accommodation advertising itself as 'The Coast-to-Coast Support Shop" and assuring "all hiking and outdoor gear". It would be my post-breakfast first port of call.

Back at my accommodation, I took a pew, literally, and filled my face with my oriental cuisine before retiring to my room. It was evident that the occupants of the room at the other end of the small corridor were unaware that they had company as they chatted aloud with their bedroom door wide open, prompting me to noisily unlock my room and enter 'audibly'. Their conversation paused and their door was subsequently closed. Enjoying the luxury of sitting on a proper bed, I took some notes on the day's narrative before phoning Number One for a lengthy catch-up. As was normal evening practice, I got into bed with my guidebook to refresh myself on details of the day ahead tomorrow before completing my Thursday evening catching up on some more of Richard Osman's "Thursday Murder Club".
I didn't manage to listen for more than a few minutes.

February 2017

It was a customarily chilly February morning as I sat at the kitchen table, cup of tea in hand, looking out through the patio doors into the blanket of winter darkness. Normally there wouldn't be time for a cuppa before heading off to work for a 5.30am start but I had soared out of bed just after 4am like a feverish child on Christmas morning. It was comforting and somewhat emotional that my beautiful wife-to-be remained asleep upstairs, having risen to transport me and my bicycle to work on precisely 61 occasions over the past nine months. The car key on the table in front of me induced the pervading air of anticipation and I would have at least half an hour to reflect on the past nine months before getting back into the driver's seat and turning that key.

Our pre-planned criteria for making it through the ban had functioned like clockwork. I worked two dayshifts followed by two nightshifts. Joanne would transport me to work on the first dayshift and I would cycle home with the same procedure followed on the second dayshift.
For the first nightshift, I could either cycle the 20 miles, leaving shortly after 3pm or trains were available to the city centre which would subsequently involve just a mile and a half cycle to work.
I had to wait around after nightshift to catch the first morning train to the 'Shire at 6.15am but as my fitness inevitably began to reach levels not seen for a few years, a 20-mile cycle home post-nightshift began proving elementary. Cycling mileage over the period was calculated to be in excess of 2,000 miles and, having given an undertaking to my management team that the ban wouldn't affect my availability, I took great pride that after nine months, not a single minute of scheduled or additional duty had been lost. At regular intervals throughout the disqualification period, an added jocular distraction arose as the available cycling routes afforded the opportunity to wend past Joanne's parked car at the hospital. This would periodically involve attaching a variety of pre-prepared notes to her windscreen confirming her succumb to the 'phantom cyclist'. On one occasion, the windscreen attachment included a box of 'Milk Tray' chocolates with a note suggesting it was "all because the lady loves Milk Tray," in the exact style of the note left by the James Bond-style character in the TV commercials of a previous era. Some

romantic horseplay to counteract the serious ongoing undertaking at hand couldn't do any harm.

My medical condition had been a major beneficiary of the ban. The stress of the case had been removed, coinciding with the necessity to maintain high levels of physical fitness together with the mental boost of retaining my employment. The combination created a healthy state of mind and body and resulted in my ulcerative colitis enjoying its most controlled period since diagnosis.

The previously mooted 4-day hike on the Affric Kintail Way was comprehensively re-evaluated when Joanne and I undertook a 3-day practice run on the Deeside Way in early June. After a relatively short but heavily laden first day hike ahead of an overnight pitch at a campsite, I awoke in the morning to casually ask Joanne what she would like for breakfast.
"I want a decent sleep, a comfier bed mat, those geese in that pond to shut the fuck up during the night, and I don't want to carry all this stuff around all day coz it's killing my back."
A short pause ensued as I processed her morning meal request, before we both broke into laughter.
"Will you be wanting a piece of toast with that?"
Our plans were duly adjusted with Joanne taking a bus back to pick up the car whilst I packed up camp and neither the Affric Kintail Way nor long-distance unsupported walking were ever mentioned again.

Striving to make the ban as non-disruptive as possible, life carried on as normally as feasible and the 6-man tent was dusted down for a week-long camping trip to the Scottish borders with Numbers Two and Three. Public transport was utilised for trips to Edinburgh to see the band "Simply Red" on the Edinburgh Castle esplanade and the Scotland rugby team narrowly lose to Australia at Murrayfield, the latter a wonderful surprise organised by Joanne.

Jennifer's mother Alison sadly passed away in the late summer and Joanne's assistance with transport arrangements at the funeral was greatly appreciated. Having maintained a good relationship with my ex-mother-in-law through utilising her spare room as my Moray accommodation over a few years, I was asked to write and present her eulogy. My summary of her life and anecdotes did raise some chuckles but the minister's prior introduction of the reader as "Alison's ex-son-in-law" also raised a few.

My Drink-Drive Awareness Course took place at an Aberdeen hotel over three consecutive Thursdays in September. Of the twelve attendees on the course, I would learn that I was the only one to have a breath test between the old and new alcohol limits and it did feel somewhat peculiar being on a rehabilitation course as a result of breaking a law that doesn't apply to over 90% of the UK population. The delinquent dozen represented a real cross-section of society and included a lady who had lost half her spleen as she somersaulted her vehicle into a field and a gentleman who had managed to crash into four other cars whilst under the influence. Over the three days, we interacted with each other and became of our own little "breakfast club" faction, directed by an experienced advanced driving instructor who kept us engaged, informed and educated on how the average body deals with alcohol. The course included an enjoyable and eye-opening section aimed at the sanctimonious and judgemental chunk of our population, listing all the traffic offences they will have committed at some point over the course of their driving experience which, with potential quirks of fate, could've seen them behind bars.

Entering 2017 with its now planned November wedding, my divorce from Jennifer, slightly more protracted than Joanne's on account of children under the age of 16 being involved, was finalised in the opening weeks of the year. It was a formality that had become noticeably very important to Joanne as she persistently enquired on the status of the divorce throughout the process.
"Well at least I've got that sorted. You should never have still been married to her."
Occasionally, I strangely felt that divorcing Jennifer was more important to Joanne than marrying me herself.

We approached the end of the disqualification period and a conversation about getting back behind the wheel led to talk of a driving holiday. The North Coast 500, a 516-mile scenic route around the north coast of Scotland was pencilled in for early summer. It was an incredibly pertinent plan when the official start and end of the route was taken into consideration . . . Inverness Castle.

2017/2018

By the end of 2017, I was reflecting on a very good year, clearly enhanced by that reconciliation with my driving licence following its 9-month sabbatical in Swansea.

It was a year of travel with trips around the country to watch football, Number Two's figure skating competitions, the North Coast 500, a theatre trip to Leeds and a holiday with Joanne and Numbers Two and Three in Blackpool. Joanne also enjoyed a spring trip to the Netherlands to visit a friend and an autumn long weekend in Dublin with her friend Kim.

My football team, St Mirren, despite languishing at the bottom of Scottish football's second tier, enjoyed away cup victories at Dundee and East Fife. Having taken the train to the former in January and with Joanne driving to the latter in February, I was able to drive myself in early March with Number One and Number Three to the east end of Glasgow for the quarter final match at Celtic. St Mirren were ahead at half-time (the only other team to hold a half-time lead at Celtic Park that season were Barcelona in the Champions League) but eventually succumbed to four second half goals but had set a platform to avoid relegation to the third tier. An excellent run of results followed, with the great escape completed in early May as Number One and I travelled to Edinburgh to witness a one-all draw with Hibernian which confirmed our second-tier status. A drop to the third tier would have been disastrous for the club and the celebrations amongst the 2,000 away supporters at the final whistle reiterated that point in what was one of my most memorable days as a St Mirren fan. It wouldn't be the only memorable day of 2017.

Joanne's misconception of my passion for football was highlighted after a match earlier in the spring. With some days off and the novelty and freedom of possessing a driving licence once more, I travelled to Kirkcaldy to watch St Mirren play against Raith Rovers on a Wednesday evening. The evening was memorable as I watched the match sat in the same row, two seats away from one of my favourite authors and fellow Saints fan Christopher Brookmyre. It wasn't memorable for the football on show as St Mirren lost 2-0 and I was disappointed for around five minutes until I returned to the car, got the stereo on, and set off on the two-hour-plus drive home.

Arriving home just after midnight, I was surprised to see Joanne still up waiting for me. She approached me with a grave expression and proceeded to give me a long hug.

"Oh Matt, I'm so sorry. Are you ok?" she enquired in a concerned tone.

Having spent the previous two hours duetting with various artists whilst not answering calls or listening to news bulletins, I was beginning to think I had missed something.

"Is everything ok Joanne?" I felt compelled to ask whilst disengaging from our embrace.

"It's just that I saw the result, you lost two-nil" Joanne explained, before repeating, "Are you ok?"

"Goodness me, sweetie," I smiled in relief whilst resuming our clinch, "We really should speak about the football. My team lost. They do that fairly often. It was disappointing for a minute or two but then I resumed life in the real world."

The pre-planned adventure on the North Coast 500 route in early June materialized accordingly.

We posed for a pre-trip photograph to the front of Inverness Castle under the watchful eye of old friend Flora McDonald and the small obelisk marking the end of the Great Glen Way. These were a poignant reminder that despite the unforeseen hardships that life throws your way, here we were, about to embark on a five-day drive amongst the amazing scenery that Scotland has to offer. The trip was an unmitigated success, travelling clockwise, aided by favourable weather easing overnight camping stops in Applecross, Ullapool, Gairloch, Durness in the far north-west, and a final night stay at a hotel in Helmsdale on the east coast. A subsequent video put together for sharing on the North Coast 500 Facebook page received a remarkable reaction, not least from within the family as we undertook to revisit the trip at a later date with Scott, Angela, Number One and their partners.

A theatre trip later in June to see the musical "The Wedding Singer" inspired a secret romantic idea for incorporation into the planned November nuptials. Unbeknown to me, Joanne was formulating the very same idea and the coming months were going to be befuddling for secret-keeping kids and step-kids.

Another secret in July was between myself and Joanne's Yorkshire-based friend Sarah. From the early days of our relationship, I was aware that the musical "Man of La Mancha" was a favourite of Joanne's and I remained on the look-out for a UK-based production but it was proving an 'impossible dream'. Eventually I found a production in Leeds and as a bonus, it would include a surprise catch-up with her friend as I secured three tickets at the beautifully restored City Varieties Music Hall. My 'quixotic' plans were executed perfectly, although on the big reveal outside the busy theatre, Sarah, myself and our fellow theatre-goers hadn't anticipated Joanne's excitedly loud repeated cries of "fucking hell," a moment I remember with a bittersweet chuckle.

One secret I did divulge to Joanne in the build-up to the wedding was the destination for the second half of our honeymoon, the beautiful Lake Como in northern Italy. As a clue, I revealed that we would be flying to Italy and having some 'Magic Moments', guiding her towards naming the singer of that particular song. My gorgeous geographically-challenged girl excitedly exclaimed, "We're going to Perry," a moment I remember with a bittersweet chuckle.

Things built up steadily to the wedding and the special and memorable day duly arrived in November.
Joanne, looking resplendent in a cream-coloured dress with a flower in her styled blonde hair, escorted by Scott, entered the small room in the Registry Office to join myself at the celebrant's table. "A Thousand Years", the song which played its part in the early stages of our relationship played gently in the background as Angela and Numbers One and Two sat behind as bridesmaids with 12-year-old Number Three acting as best man. Our friend Patricia, who had kindly volunteered her photographic services for the day, completed the small intimate gathering.

Just I had been coercing our kids into participating in my musical ruse at the reception, it was suddenly revealed during the ceremony that over the previous few months, Joanne had been doing her own bit of musical recruitment. To my great surprise, it was the very same song from the movie "The Wedding Singer" I had originally planned to perform before preferring an alternative. Joanne had altered the lyrics and with accompaniment from our offspring, it was an incredibly romantic moment. The penny dropped that all the kids had been required to concentrate on keeping a similar secret from each of us in the lead-up to the wedding. Further humour followed as the envelope on the table, purporting to be a pre-arranged speech

I wanted to make, contained only a piece of paper with the words "Have I Told You Today?" in reference to Joanne's daily musing of the previous four years.

Poignant, significant and emotional moments followed as we exchanged vows and our now matching Celtic silver bands inscribed with "anam charaid."

After dinner at a local Italian restaurant with close friends and family, we were joined by our wider circle of friends and family at a local venue where we danced to a ceilidh band throughout the evening. Thanks to the power of social media, my own orchestrated musical interlude was expected by everyone in the hall . . . except my wife. It involved a re-enactment of a scene from one of her favourite movies involving the Bacharach and David song, "I Say A Little Prayer," and everyone played their part in what was another memorable moment.

The first part of our honeymoon saw us upgraded to the fabulous honeymoon suite for four nights at the Castle Hotel on a hill overlooking the town of Dingwall, just north of Inverness. Our first 'lunch date' as a married couple would of course take place at our old haunt, Las Cuevas in the shadow of Inverness Castle, a citadel now intrinsically woven into the fabric of our relationship. Little Squeak, complete with her tartan jacket, had joined us for this part of the honeymoon but would be dropped back home to Angela as we jetted off for part two on the southern shore of Lake Como in the beautiful and historic city of . . . Perry.

Our long weekend entailed a trip to the hilltop town of Brunate, a riverboat trip on the lake to the wonderful little town of Bellagio and a day trip across the border to Lugano in Switzerland. In a remarkable stroke of luck, my online research would provide our honeymoon 'piece de resistance' or perhaps its 'pezzo di resistenza'. On the Saturday evening, the city's theatre, 'Teatro Sociale di Como' was hosting a national touring production of The Nutcracker or 'Lo Schiaccianoci' to give it its local name and I was delighted to procure two tickets.

Passing over the snow-capped Alps en route from Milan back to the UK, I reflected on an incredibly romantic adventure and looked forward with confidence to continuing that adventure as a married couple.

In a felicitous end to the year, we celebrated exactly one month of marriage with 4,000 others in the company of the wonderfully entertaining Michael Ball and Alfie Boe at the Aberdeen Exhibition Centre. The dashing duo had clearly read the script as they performed Christina Perri's "A Thousand Years" and, to Joanne's delight, Michael performed his version of "The Impossible Dream" from Man of La Mancha. . . Fucking hell!

My fair fiancée had become my winsome wife.

Going into 2018, St Mirren, now flying high at the top of the second tier, would play Aberdeen from the top division in the Scottish Cup in mid-January. Number One and myself lent our support in a 4-1 defeat but there would be more important prizes to pursue in the coming months.

A wedding gift was redeemed at the end of February with a romantic night away at a plush hotel on the outskirts of Aberdeen, which included witnessing a memorable Scotland win over England in the Rugby Union Six Nations Tournament, a match that perhaps would've been less enjoyed by a future acquaintance in the Cumbrian village of Shap. We timed our hotel visit well, just before the country entered March and ten days of disruptive heavy snow in what became known as "The Beast from the East."

The sporting theme continued into April as St Mirren were crowned champions of the second tier and promoted back to the Premier League. Joanne, myself and Numbers One and Three formed part of a sell-out crowd enjoying the post-match celebrations in the Paisley sunshine.

May saw exciting times for Scott and his girlfriend Megan as they purchased a property together and advanced to the next stage of their relationship. May's sporting themes involved Number Two figure skating in competition in Edinburgh, while Number One, on completion of her second year of her medicine degree tackled the West Highland Way with friends. Joanne, Number Three and myself enjoyed a short break back in the Cairngorms, allowing us to greet Number One and her friends at the now very familiar "Man with Sore

Feet." The short break would also involve attending our first ever shinty match in Kingussie.

Joanne and I enjoyed a caravan break in the charming little Borders town of Gatehouse of Fleet in late June before we were back on the North Coast 500, this time accompanied by Scott and Megan, Number One and her partner Jake, and Angela on her own with Squeak for company. Our four vehicles and four tents travelled anti-clockwise around the route, meeting up each evening at pre-arranged camp sites for food and drink. It was a memorable trip, greatly enhanced by the attitude, enthusiasm, humour and camaraderie of our young cohorts.

Joanne was off again with her friend Kim in September for a long weekend to Amsterdam

Several trips to the theatre were interspersed throughout the year with the aforementioned North Coast 500 crew attending "Sunshine on Leith", and some highlights for Joanne and I included "Jersey Boys", "Legally Blonde" on the 5th anniversary of our first date, and an open-air production of "Pride and Prejudice".

A short-notice invite from Gary and Laura to join them in Glasgow to see popular Scottish comedian Kevin Bridges was readily accepted in October and in November, the final travel of the year was to Sheffield where Number Two had qualified at her youth level for the British Figure Skating Championships.

2017 and 2018 had certainly flown by in a flurry of varied activities and no little travel and I was loving life with my loving wife.

2019 would continue in the same vein, perhaps even stepping up a notch.

Day 7 – Kirkby Stephen to Keld

Denise, the proprietor of Kirkby Hostel, had asked if residents could possibly appear for breakfast before 8.30am as she had to attend for jury service in Carlisle. I was happy to oblige after a good night's sleep and with a shorter 14-mile day ahead, Denise was happy for me to stay as long as I wished before letting myself out. Besides, I had an important purchase to arrange nearby.

On venturing outside to make that latest acquisition, George and Ryan were exiting the adjacent grocery store. They had also had an earlier night in real beds and, like myself, planned to leave a bit later this morning.
As I approached "Eden Outdoors", one couldn't help but notice the pole outside this local independent store with several old boots attached, upcycled as flower pots. It was evident that my old faithfuls were the latest in a long line of casualties to succumb to the rigours of the Lake District and the limestone pavement of the Westmoreland plateau.
The store owner was most accommodating, offering practical advice, and after trying on a few pairs of potential replacements, I settled on the most comfortable of his recommendations. I must confess things did instantly feel more solid and comfortable with these substitutes, however I kept those initial thoughts to myself, not wanting to upset my old friends who had loyally supported me for the past six years. Glad to contribute to local business, I settled up with the native retailer, grateful that the predecessors to my latest investment would have a useful existence in their retirement. Who knew, one day our paths could possibly cross again in this charming market town.
Au revoir, mes amis fidèles, mais pas adieu.

Returning to my ecclesiastical dwelling, I organised my rucksack for the day, marked the passing of my old faithfuls on social media, as you do, and set off in earnest, shortly after 10am. Taking a final stroll along the main drag to Market Square, I happened upon a bench with a little white placard attached, indicating that it was a "Happy to Chat" bench, with the additional wording, "Sit here if you don't mind someone stopping to say hello". A nice touch by the local

Women's Institute although I didn't expect to see "Blondie" taking a perch thereon anytime soon.

From the Square, signage directs Coast-to-Coasters down a lane to cross the River Eden on Frank's Bridge, an ornate narrow stone bridge, built in the 17th century as a 'corpse lane' to carry coffins over the river from nearby Hartley. On the south bank there stood a wooden signpost advising that I was now only 108 miles from Robin Hood's Bay and that St Bees was 82 miles in the opposite direction. With the official distance of the trail 192 miles, it appeared a couple of miles had evaporated into the ether. With my involuntary diversions, I would require a few more miles to disappear in order to reduce my mileage to the official distance.

I crossed a couple of fields via the 'corpse lane' to enter the little village of Hartley with its two picturesque lanes of terraced housing and cottages. I didn't meet a single member of the local population which numbered 138 in the last census, however just outside the village, on a road called Birkett Lane, I encountered a father and daughter with their Labrador retrievers Nandi and Jussi (pronounced yoo-si). On ascertaining during our brief chat that they were from the preceding quaint village, I'd now met 1.5% of the population of Hartley.

Birkett Lane continued to gather elevation for some time until a wooden signpost directed hikers off onto a path on the left which continued up through the moor towards Nine Standards Rigg. The weather was a combination of drizzle and warmth, resulting in a decision between sweating or getting wet. Other decisions are taken for environmentally-conscious hikers by informative information boards regarding footpath erosion. With the popularity of the route causing significant erosion, hikers are requested to use particular routes depending on the time of year. Coloured red, blue and green, my small contribution to protect the vulnerable vegetation and deep peat soil would involve following the red route.

The Nine Standards Rigg is the name given to the summit of Hartley Fell at 2,171ft and no-one knows for certain why these nine conical pillars consisting of small boulders were constructed in a line along the summit. One feasible explanation is that they simply delineated the boundary between Westmoreland and Swaledale. The views were extensive in all directions.

I was now entering the Yorkshire Dales National Park and this was to be a watershed moment . . . literally. From this summit onwards, all waters flow eastwards to eventually drain into the North Sea . . . some faster than others . . . but more on that later.

The path after Nine Standards was extremely boggy and steady progress was somewhat hindered by all the wide berths accumulating a fair bit of extra distance, accompanied by lots of frustrated cursing under my breath . . . obviously. The openness of moorland once again reminded me to be glad the drizzle was clearing away as it didn't strike me as a handy place to be in a storm. Thankfully the red route descended to eventually team up with the green route on a wider and drier track and progress was somewhat smoother. Approaching a farm on the left-hand side, the scene was very reminiscent of the opening credits in the TV programme "Emmerdale", so much so that I was instinctively moved to hum the theme tune of the popular long-running rustic soap opera. The irony of this was that whilst Emmerdale is completely fictional, I was in fact approaching the subject of a real-life TV programme.

Ravenseat Farm first appeared on TV screens as part of the ITV series "The Dales" in 2011 and subsequently became the subject of the Channel 5 fly-on-the-wall documentary "Our Yorkshire Farm". Over three million viewers regularly tuned in to follow former model Amanda Owen, a.k.a. The Yorkshire Shepherdess and her husband Clive as they manage the farm whilst raising their nine children. On top of this, the industrious matriarch has penned five popular books on her domestic exploits.
The farm also serves cream teas to passing hikers and visitors but alas, there would be no Friday afternoon treat as the 'closed' signs were on display. Nevertheless, on approaching the attractive-looking homestead over a little stone bridge, the picnic tables spread around the grassy grounds to the front of the farm provided a suitable and brief resting place. As the trail ahead rose to pass two stone barns, I could see George and Ryan, who possibly had enjoyed similar respite at this pretty juncture.

Following my short intermission, I set off once more to follow in my London friends' footsteps, climbing past the barns and along the muddy south-easterly path with Whitsundale Beck flowing briskly far below to my right in its almost gorge-like valley.

At a wooden fence overlooking the beck below, there was my old mucker "Blondie" taking photographs.

"How ye doing?"

I received a nod in reply from the reticent rambler.

"It's a cracking scene," I offered in concurrence of his photographic choice.

"Yes."

"Heading for Keld tonight?" my final stab at a semblance of conversation.

"Yes. Keld tonight," my blonde acquaintance replied, evoking a sense of achievement that I managed to elicit three words strung together from the coy Coast-to-Coaster.

I carried on for a few hundred yards where I caught up with George and Ryan who were taking a water break at a farmhouse ruin. Now just a mile shy of the remote village of Keld, they had decided to push on further than the village for a wild camp as their adventure had six days remaining in comparison with my seven. They were planning to stop for a pint at the Keld Lodge, a small hotel just before the village itself, and invited me to join them as it would be our parting day. I enthusiastically accepted and joined them for the final stretch into Keld, progressing along a path above the north bank of the River Swale, a river I would be tracking for the next couple of days. The River Swale was also the fastest-flowing river in England, a fact I wasn't aware of at this point.

General chat turned to our fellow hiker a short distance behind us.

"That blonde chap behind us. He doesn't say much, does he?" I suggested.

"Em, no, he certainly doesn't," George replied, "We could hardly get a word out of him."

"He hasn't been speaking to you?" Ryan interjected with raised intonation on the word 'you'.

"No, but I did get a three-word reply out of him a little earlier."

I don't know if I was supposed to take the next part of the conversation as a compliment, but I did.

Ryan continued, "We were talking about that chap earlier and we reckoned if anyone could get a conversation out of him, it would be you."

"Are you suggesting I'm a chatterbox?" I laughed.

"Well, we're not and you're about to have a pint with us," George grinned.

We emerged from the path onto Stonesdale Lane for a short descent to a bridge facilitating the Coast-to-Coast's first crossing of the River Swale. After pausing to admire the raucous rush of Wain Wath Force, a distant but visible upstream waterfall, we joined the quiet B6270, the road through Swaledale. Passing the cosy-looking yurts of Keld Bunk Barn and half a mile later, I was sitting on picnic benches outside the Keld Lodge enjoying a pint with my capital-based colleagues. A prominent sign attached to the wall of the Lodge indicated that we were sat at the half-way point of the Coast-to-Coast and duty photographs were surely compulsory.

A passing car slowed down to walking pace and the back windows were wound down. The two men on the back seat greeted George and Ryan.

"Eh up guys, how you doing?"

"How you doing?" my two friends jointly replied.

One of the back seat passengers then directed the driver of the vehicle in a jocular voice, "And onward, driver," turning to George and Ryan with a laugh as the car once more picked up speed and departed eastwards.

George turned to Ryan, "What's that all about? Are they actually walking the trail?" as Ryan shrugged in perplexity.

The guys explained that the back seat passengers were Paul and Matthew, whom I had actually passed on two occasions already on the journey. They weren't sure exactly how Paul and Matthew were tackling the Coast-to-Coast but it appeared they were fairly local and this was not the first time they had been seen in a car.

George had purchased the pints on arrival at Keld Lodge . . . thus I would have to reciprocate . . . and subsequently Ryan wanted to stand his round. George and myself naturally insisted that that wouldn't be necessary . . . but we were somehow persuaded . . .

Invigorated with our three pints apiece, we took the short jovial jaunt down into the centre of this most picturesque small village. Rukin's Farm Camping duly appeared on the left at the bottom of the village just as the path swung to the right to cross a junction with the Pennine Way and head up towards Gunnerside. George and Ryan were heading for the village of Muker on the alternative lower route and this would be farewell. With warm handshakes, my acquaintances parted with my best wishes and gratitude for their fleeting fellowship.

I checked into the farm campsite, gathering my hold-all from an adjacent stable and pitched my tent on the peak of a small hill looking back over the farmyard, a short distance from the showers and toilets. My view extended beyond the farm eastwards down the Swale valley with hills on the left to be traversed tomorrow. It was rations for tea but I was able to pop down to a garden area at reception later in the evening where I could purchase a bottle of Butter Tubs, a local ale from the Yorkshire Dales Brewing Company. Using the available wi-fi within the garden area, I was able to contact the family and update them on my progress.

Retiring on this fairly mild evening, I was aware that the weather for the days ahead was about to markedly change with the word "heatwave" read on several forecasts. It was a time to reflect on the first half of this incredible journey. I prepared a mug of tea and sat outside in front of my tent atop the grassy knoll, the sun having plunged below the western horizon behind me. Half-way was certainly the theme, having posed for my photograph at the Keld Lodge signpost earlier in the day. Seven days down, seven days to go, and 96 miles of 192 officially covered. In an appropriate moment of symmetry, my location on the Coast-to-Coast A-Z atlas was on the middle pages, indicated by the two visible staples. Last Friday night, I was making final preparations in my hotel room in St Bees on the Cumbrian coast. This Friday night, I was sitting by my tent at a farm in the Yorkshire Dales surveying the dusky Swaledale valley. With the exception of my slight sense of humour failure amidst the difficult conditions at Angle Tarn, it had already been an unforgettable experience with a few tales to tell. My body had certainly "tuned in" to the task in hand and overall, I was feeling pretty good. The second week was not expected to be easy however it was fair to say that I anticipated it would be easier than the first. The forecast heatwave conditions would perhaps provide an additional consideration. In terms of acquaintances, George and Ryan were now always going to be a day ahead and the "two ladies" had completed their walk in Kirkby Stephen. "Blondie" was out there somewhere at the lodge or a local bed and breakfast and Paul and Matthew would be around somewhere, when they weren't being ferried by car. Of course, at this point I had no idea of the new acquaintances to be encountered and friendships fostered in the second half of my adventure. I looked forward to the week ahead with a final poignant summing up of the week gone by, recalling the words of wise and friendly 75-year-old John in the Kings Arms pub in Shap.

"Life goes on, young Matt, and you're getting out and creating new experiences."

2019 / 2020

Just as happened to Joanne in that memorable affiancing weekend of late February three years earlier, the February of 2019 would mark my own half-century.

A long celebratory weekend began at a Thursday night production of the musical "Cry Baby' with Number One in the leading role, already a veteran of many stage shows and president of her university's am-dram society.

The local golf club were hosting a Neil Diamond tribute night on the Friday and I was delighted that so many of Joanne's family from around the 'Shire attended to help me celebrate. My wife had sneakily arranged through the tribute act for myself to pay my own tribute to the great Mr Diamond and I think my rendition of "Love on the Rocks" just about passed muster.

St Mirren were rather conveniently in town on the Saturday to play Aberdeen and, joined by friends, including some who had kindly travelled from the Glasgow area, my 'Paisley Buddies' gained a point in an entertaining 2-2 draw. After the match, augmented by more friends and family, we had food at a city centre pub before filing into the theatre to watch "Club Tropicana – The Musical," a riotous 1980s cheese-fest watched by a capacity cacophonous crowd. With the sounds of my teenage years still reverberating in my eardrums, we completed a long day in Club Tropicana, the nightclub, another riotous 1980s cheese-fest.

Following our Sunday hungover return to the 'Shire, we were joined by immediate family and partners for a birthday tea at a local restaurant. Afterwards at home with Number One on vocals, Number Two on vocals and ukulele, and Number Three on guitar, I was beautifully serenaded with the song "Never Enough" from the movie 'Greatest Showman', a touching moment later commemorated on a printed and framed soundwave.

Joanne had kept my main present a secret for months leading up to my birthday and it was time to reveal the secret. She handed me a wrapped gift that was clearly a CD, opened to reveal a compilation album by my old friend, the Dutch violinist Andre Rieu and his Johan Strauss Orchestra.

As I warily looked at the CD thinking something was afoot, she invited me to open it. To my jubilant surprise, inside was a print-out of an itinerary involving flights to Amsterdam and a tickets/hotel package to see one of Andre Rieu's summer concerts in his home town of Maastricht. The 2019 version of the 2013 concert I saw at the cinema. It was a wonderful gift and a wonderful end to a wonderful weekend coordinated by my wonderful wife.

In early March, Number One participated in the 24-hour musical. This entailed the entire cast and crew staging a full production from scratch after a continuous 24-hour period. The musical is only revealed to the participants on arrival who are sworn to secrecy, meaning the audience are only made aware when the show commences. Joanne and I were in the audience and thrilled when the curtain was raised ahead of the opening scene of "The Wedding Singer," evoking reminiscence on our nuptials.

March ended with Number Two participating in her first international figure skating competition in Italy. Catching a flight to Milan for the second time in 16 months evoked yet more nuptial reminiscence. With two other skaters representing Great Britain, their mothers and two coaches, I was the tour guide and driver in our 9-seat sunshine bus along the autostrada and up the spectacular west shore of Lake Garda en route the beautiful little town of Egna Neumarkt in the South Tyrol region. 15-year-old Number Two being announced onto the ice representing Great Britain was a special moment regardless of her performance but finishing in a very respectable 7th place in the "Intermediate Novice" level was an added bonus. At the end of the week, I was once more setting off over those snow-capped Alps reflecting on a fabulous break in the company of my middle child.

As part of my 50th birthday celebrations, Joanne had activated a winter membership of the local golf club and as we entered April, it was extended to full annual membership. I hadn't been a member of a golf club since 2001 but by the end of the month, I was allocated a handicap of 15 and began a busy season of golf, entering competitions when possible.

Over dinner at the previous autumn's Kevin Bridges trip with Gary and Laura, I had mentioned that American superstar Billy Joel was playing at Wembley Stadium in June, his tour's only European date. In an extraordinary act of kindness, Gary procured four tickets for the gig. After shuffling some shifts around, it would require travel by car. It's a lengthy return drive from the north east of Scotland to the iconic north London venue but was worth every mile. The 70-year-old New Yorker performed a catalogue of old favourites, captivating the 70,000 crowd in what was another memorable adventure.

Stepping onto the plane at Aberdeen less than a fortnight later heading for Amsterdam, the highlight birthday present was upon us. Catching a train from Schiphol Airport south to the beautiful city of Maastricht, we checked in for our 2-night stay at our hotel and set off in the July sunshine to explore our locale using Holland's most popular form of transport, our hired bicycles. Crossing one of the many bridges over the River Maas which cuts through the city, we surveyed the many historic medieval-era buildings before recrossing the river to sample a beer at the "Brouwery De Ridder" on the east shore of the river. Purposefully avoiding Vrijthof Square which was hosting the opening night of Andre Rieu's twelve concerts, not that there was much chance of getting anywhere near the place, we remained on the east bank of the river to sample some Dutch hospitality at the Stadsbrouwerij, a local brewery and restaurant, before cycling back to our accommodation.

The plan for concert day was to take breakfast in the hotel, head into the city for lunchtime, recce where we could park our bicycles prior to the concert and take a previously booked one-hour boat trip on the River Maas down to the Belgian border. Afterwards we would return to our hotel and prepare for the big event. Cycling back into the city centre in the late afternoon, I had made a pre-show reservation at an Italian restaurant.

As we enjoyed our Mediterranean fare in a most romantic setting, I reflected on the journey to this point from that failed attempt on social media six years earlier to persuade Joanne to join me at that cinema broadcast from Maastricht. And here we were, as a married couple, physically present in this delightful Dutch district about to attend the annual musical extravaganza in the flesh. For me, it was an incredibly symbolic moment of romantic affirmation. I was a "happy chappy".

The concert itself was a memorable spectacle. Nine thousand patrons on Vrijthof Square and a couple of thousand more around its environs at the many ringfenced al fresco pubs and restaurants

enjoying a varied evening of classical numbers and well-known favourites . . . and an unexpected guest appearance from The Village People . . . yes, really.
We located our two-wheeled transport after the concert and, after a crash-course from a random stranger on the operation of the dynamo bike lights, we cycled back to our hotel to discover that a bus had been available to transport guests to and from the main event. It just meant we were at the back of the queue for a nightcap.

A family holiday to Staffordshire followed towards the end of July, Number One deciding to join Numbers Two and Three as it involved a couple of days at Alton Towers theme park.

Another busy year had involved theatre trips to Beatles' tribute 'Let It Be'; 'Lost at Sea', an excellent local production encapsulating the North-East fishing industry; and Jesus Christ Superstar. Number One's 21st birthday celebrations and our second anniversary arrived with the traditional trip to our favourite local Italian before finishing off the year with free tickets to see Rod Stewart in Aberdeen. Well, I wasn't going to pay to see him . . .

It was my firm opinion that 99% of the time, we had an excellent relationship but of course, as with every relationship there has ever been, there would be occasions, past, present and future where disagreements occurred. With lots of passion involved in our relationship, there was an inevitability that the passion could traverse to our rare disagreements. Joanne would respectfully have her own perspective but from my point of view, she could display condescending mannerisms and make disparaging comments during those passionate exchanges, making me feel unworthy and making sure I knew she could do better. My agitated and antagonized responses accompanied by my involuntary reversion into a strong west of Scotland accent made Joanne uncomfortable. In her own words, she knew how to "push my buttons" and vice-versa. It was a source of some frustration that my financial situation wasn't to Joanne's standard but I was always keen to reiterate throughout our relationship that I had never asked her for a single penny. I certainly took my hat off to Joanne's husband who had been successfully employed in the oil industry and was extensively more financially solvent than myself, and I appreciated that that had become the standard for Joanne. Consequently, it was fair to say that Joanne was on a more solid financial footing than myself. With lots of commitments to my children and Jennifer in Moray, I certainly had enough to get by but perhaps not to the standard that Joanne had become accustomed to over the past twenty years. She took pride on the self-proclaimed sound financial decisions she had made in her life and was keen to point out that I hadn't made such good decisions, and she was undeniably correct. That said, I took great pride on serving my country around the world for 22 years, often in environments and situations that Joanne, who had never left the 'Shire, understandably couldn't begin to comprehend.

As an ex-serviceman, I came from a background where things were said in the heat of a moment but readily put to one side. Being dressed down verbally in the OC's office, or administering the dressing down to a subordinate, with some industrial language thrown in for good measure . . . and a couple of hours later, sharing a beer at the bar with the antagonist and having a laugh about it. It was the nature of the beast and that was occasionally how life and discipline worked in the armed forces.

Consequently, when throw-away comments were made to Joanne in the course of a discussion, it was quickly forgotten on my part, but I would become aware of the potential for any such comments and opinions to be 'banked' and recollected at a later date when it suited her agenda.

Fortunately, these very rare moments of dispute were far outweighed by the countless positive aspects of our relationship. Consequently, I was somewhat surprised when, one day towards the end of the year, after a minor difference of opinion on a matter long since forgotten, Joanne made an unexpected suggestion.

"Why do we do that?" Joanne began.

"Do what?"

"Have little disagreements, every once in a while, that can spiral because neither of us will back down. It's just strange when we have such a good relationship. It would be nice if we didn't have those moments at all," she explained

"Agreed," I nodded in accord.

"Would you consider going to Couple Counselling just to talk about it?" she asked.

"That sounds a bit over the top, sweetie. Yes, on rare occasions we have differences of opinion but do you really think it merits Couple Counselling?"

"It could help us to explore why it happens and help us to prevent it happening," she reasoned.

The word 'explore' was a frequent visitor to my wife's vocabulary, an occupational hazard of being a counsellor. She certainly associated the word with counselling, whereas for me, the word evoked thoughts of Henry Stanley traipsing round 19th century Africa looking for Doctor Livingstone. At this point, I couldn't see the harm in agreeing to Joanne's suggestion concerning the word.

"I don't think there's any guarantee that these things can be completely eradicated, nice as it sounds, but if you want to give it a go," I complied.

Joanne suggested an agency in Aberdeen and later in the week, I contacted them to make initial tentative enquiries. Less than a fortnight later, we were attending our first session and Joanne became spokesperson, making our situation clear to our appointed lady.

"As Matt has explained on the phone, we just want to explore why there are odd occasions when we 'push each other's buttons'. We want to make it clear that our marriage is in absolutely no danger. We love each other very much and we won't be splitting up or anything like that. Just feel I should make that clear from the start."

It was the start of six sessions into the new year, five as a couple and one as individuals, the schedule traversing the festive period into 2020.

I had no previous experience of counselling and Joanne thought it would be better if she purposefully didn't mention to her fellow counsellor that she was also "in the business". This undertaking only lasted until the beginning of the second session with her declaration, "You may have guessed by my use of terminology. I'm also a counsellor."

Inwardly, this created a slightly sceptical feeling within myself towards the two counsellors in the room, and it was only when I reached my individual session that I felt able to open up on the aforementioned occasional condescension by my wife and her pointed reminders of her fiscal superiority which was the top trump in her button-pushing pack of cards. Nevertheless, the aim of her request to attend couple-counselling was to eliminate those rare moments of fleeting discord and it was hoped that she would purposefully try to recognise and avoid these occasions to assist with that goal. To say Joanne couldn't handle any form of criticism, however negligible or inconsequential, was an understatement, and for my part, I would consciously try to avoid being led down that particular path to upsetting her.

As we crossed into the year 2020, my 14-year-old son's New Year request that he would like to tackle the West Highland Way with his dad was heartening, although due to forthcoming unforeseen world events, our adventure would be delayed until much later in the year. The New Year period would also entail my first proper flare-up of Ulcerative Colitis in quite some time and an 8-week course of steroids was duly introduced. The medication always helped and I was glad that on completion of the prescribed period and on weaning off the steroids, things would remain fairly settled.

I felt that the couple-counselling did have its merits and on completion of the final appointment in early February, Joanne outwardly agreed with a warm embrace and emphasized its perceived success and the ongoing solidity of our marriage. If there had been some value in exploring our rare disputes, then all the better. Now in the first leap year since 2016, the conclusion of our counselling was also timeous with the first anniversary of her romantic leap-day proposal four years earlier. Joanne had requested that planning be left to her as we naturally headed westwards for the first time in a while to beautiful Inverness.

Once there, Joanne supplied directions to the 5-star-hotel she had reserved for our night away. Knowing I was very much a fan of two particularly well-known hotel chains where guests know exactly what to consistently expect, my surprised look towards my wife was countered with laughter and reassurance.
"It's ok, I got a good deal. Just fancied going posh."
On approaching the reception desk and attempting to check-in, we were instructed to leave our luggage where we stood and invited to take a seat at one of the tables in the adjacent drawing room.
As I was someone used to simply confirming my name and reservation with reception and given a key card and a room number, this was, well, different.
After a few minutes of waiting, a member of staff approached, holding a tray containing a couple of champagne flutes.
"Hi folks, we'll get you checked in shortly. Would you like a glass of complimentary champagne while you wait?"
"No thanks. My wife has booked us a room for the night in this 5-star establishment and I would rather obtain a room key and spend some time in our 5-star room now that we're here, rather than be sat here wasting time with sycophantic ostentatious bullshit," . . . was

probably what my cynical and cantankerous inner self wanted to say to the helpful and diligent member of staff who was simply doing what was required of them. I sensibly opted for the alternative less controversial reply, "Oh, that would be lovely, thank you very much." As we sipped our bubbly, the slight backwards tilt of my head and glance towards reception was astutely observed by my wife.

"No," she declared with a smirk, verbally elongating the syllable in the way that a mother would chastise a toddler.

"No what?" I appealed.

"Just, no," she replied as we subsequently broke into a brief laugh. She knew me well.

Eventually, we were led through some corridors and shown into our very comfortable-looking room, which was decidedly similar to the rooms in the previously described hotel chains, only this one included a bath robe and some slippers.

Fittingly on this 'leap day' anniversary, there was only one appropriate venue for dinner as we once more sentimentally reacquainted ourselves with the ambience and delicious fare of Las Cuevas.

Joanne had booked tickets to a comedy show commencing after 9pm and advised that we would require to leave the hotel early in the morning for an extra surprise trip. Consequently, outwith sleeping, very little time was actually spent in our 5-star accommodation . . . but we did get a complimentary glass of champagne.

On the Sunday morning, we headed to Loch Ness and enjoyed a short cruise down Scotland's second-largest and second-deepest loch. Our trip included some time ashore at Urquhart Castle, just outside Drumnadrochit, another location with a pertinent connection to our relationship. The weather on the first day of the spring season (and St David's Day for some daffodil-wearing Welsh passengers on board) was fairly dank but didn't dampen the spirits amongst the misty beauty of the loch with its cryptozoological reputation.

Returning to the Clansman Harbour on the north west shore, we headed for home, looking ahead to our next 'leap day' anniversary in 2024.

As the world's nervous attention turned to the developing global Covid-19 pandemic, the country entered lockdown. My job would continue as normal as I was deemed a front-line worker. Like the vast majority of the country, I had never heard of the term "furlough" and became concerned that, with my financial commitments to Jennifer and the kids, things would be tight if I had to fully support Joanne if her income completely ceased. In the event, she obtained a temporary part-time nightshift job for eight weeks in a local supermarket, but with government grants forthcoming, together with continuing on-line counselling appointments, those concerns were never realised and her income actually increased.

Matrimony remained solid throughout the spring and summer as the entire planet negotiated difficult and unprecedented times. Joanne's occasional unpredictability remained a standing joke between us as she continued to tell me she loved me every day in her own long-established way, "Have I told you today?"
I would reply, with my tongue in my cheek, "Yes, today you do."
"No, this hour I do," she would quip, "but that may change in the next hour."

The lengthy period of security underwent some unexpected disruption on a random Monday evening in mid-August, one of those rare disagreements which stemmed from nothing. The velocity with which Joanne's mood could swing was highlighted when a routine conversation very quickly took a dark turn.
With the country partially reopening post-Covid, we had reserved a small cottage in rural Perthshire and we had planned to set off early on the forthcoming Saturday morning, with a trip en route with Squeak to "The Birks of Aberfeldy", a renowned woodland walk.

We were routinely sorting out the washing-up after dinner when Joanne interjected, "Gary and Laura have invited us over on Friday night for drinks before we go on holiday."
Joanne was aware that I had arranged to play golf in the early part of the Friday evening with a friend, which wouldn't affect our planned early rise ahead of the trip south.
"Oh, that would've been good, darling, but we'll be setting off early doors on Saturday. You know if we go, we'll have more than a few drinks and we'll get never get away early on Saturday as planned."
"Yeh, but you're ok to play golf," came her unreasonable and unnecessary reply in a sudden and marked change of tone.
"Joanne, I'm playing golf at five. I'll be home before nine and sober. Slight difference from drinking into the wee small hours."

Her very sudden and needless antagonism continued unabated, "Just face it, Matt. You don't like Gary and you don't want to go." Notwithstanding that her allegation was unfounded and that Gary and Laura were long-term friends of Joanne, the irony wasn't lost on me that since I had met her, she had continually griped about their regular cancellation at short notice of any event or function that had been arranged. Her reactionary phrase, "Well, we're meant to be going, but it's Gary and Laura so there's a fair chance they will cancel," had become commonplace over the years, somewhat ignorantly when Laura's poor health was taken into consideration.

Agitated by her unforeseen antipathy, I reacted, "Where is that coming from, Joanne? We're having a perfectly rational discussion and you're turning it into an argument about nothing. We've arranged to leave early on Saturday morning and late-night drinking on Friday night wouldn't allow that. Surely we can rearrange for some other time soon."
Unfortunately, Joanne had quickly sunk into her condescension mode.
"Nope, it's all because you don't like Gary," she categorically asserted with an arrogant air of certitude that was beginning to 'push the buttons'.
"Why are you suddenly being like this, Joanne? You know that's not true," I replied in exasperated frustration.
"It is," her succinct and contemptuous comeback.
Feeling provoked and pushed towards an aggressive reaction, I snapped, "This is ridiculous behaviour, Joanne. You're making stuff up and just fucking lying," before leaving the room and heading upstairs.
Joanne had successfully pushed those buttons and, for the first time in the year 2020 and the first time since couple counselling, I felt an immediate sense of disappointment that I had allowed her to elicit a snap in my disposition. I took a couple of deep breaths and even before I had reached the summit of the stairs, I immediately realised that I had let myself down.

I sat on the edge of the bed, reflecting on discussions conducted during those couple counselling sessions and felt disappointment on allowing her provocation to tip me over the edge after learning to control any such disparagement in a more constructive way. I allowed things to potentially settle for a few minutes before returning downstairs with contrition at the forefront of my mind.

"I'm sorry Joanne. That was unacceptable. I did feel provoked but I can't speak to you like that and I apologise. You pushed my buttons and I snapped."

Joanne remained in her chair unmoved and declined to comment.

"Can we perhaps talk about it?" I enquired.

With her phone in hand, my wife just stared at the screen and again her silence suggested there was currently little scope for dialogue. Deciding to give her space, I continued, "I'm heading out. Be back soon."

For the next couple of hours, I drove around the 'Shire, including a lengthy stop-off at a drive-through Starbucks.

Arriving home later in the evening, I entered the living room to find Joanne watching TV, hopeful that things had settled.

"Hi. You ok?"

"Yeh, I'm ok," Joanne replied, suggesting that she had returned from wherever she had gone.

General conversation ensued about the TV programme she was watching and I decided I would leave her to it and retire to bed.

As I was leaving the room, Joanne advised, "I'm sorry, Matt. I won't be sleeping with you tonight. I'll sleep in the spare room."

My reaction to her surprising and sudden directive was to stop in my tracks, stunned. Every sinew in my body wanted me to express my extreme disappointment and frustration that such an innocent conversation had deteriorated into such a farce but, aware that any further reaction would only exacerbate the situation and allow more successful 'button-pressing' for her, I went to bed.

The following day, Joanne was busy with clients but cordial words were exchanged in passing throughout the day and I left at tea-time to start a run of three nightshifts. Our usual 11pm call went ahead as normal and Joanne instigated a review of the previous night's disagreement. For my part, I explained that for the first time since couple-counselling, I was disappointed that I had allowed her button-pushing to provoke an angry reaction for which I had quickly apologised. Joanne explained that she simply couldn't get into to bed with someone who had said she was "fucking lying" only a couple of hours before. I felt a mutual conciliatory tone in our exchange, however I was taken aback when the conversation ended with another surprising directive from Joanne.

"I'm back in our bed tonight but when you come home in the morning, if the spare bedroom door is open, then you're sleeping in there."

The rest of the nightshift elapsed uneasily. I loved Joanne and therefore had to hope that normal service would be resumed on getting home or accept anything to the contrary. Sadly, to my disillusionment, on arriving home, the spare bedroom door had been purposefully left open as wide as it possibly could be. It was a clear indication of where I would be sleeping.

On surfacing from my sleep, things remained cordial and admittedly I was on edge and mindful not to broach the subject, hoping my punishment would be complete. However, when conversation related to our impending holiday that weekend, another stunning statement was forthcoming which I knew I couldn't react to.

"I'm not sure I'm still going on holiday. I haven't made my mind up," was Joanne's disinclined declaration before reiterating that the spare room door situation would remain extant for the time being.

To my abject disappointment, Joanne's enforced bedroom impasse would continue for the remaining two nightshifts, returning home in the mornings to find the spare room door wide open. I wasn't naïve enough not to realise that Joanne was exercising control to remind me who was in charge, but I did feel there was nothing I could do about it.

On the Friday afternoon, I began preparing the car for the holiday which would include attaching our bicycles to the roof bars. As Joanne passed in the driveway, and with time moving on, I felt compelled to nervously enquire, "Em, sorry Joanne, I need to know how many bikes I'm putting on."

"Put them both on. I'll probably end up coming. We've paid for it." I took her reply as a promising sign that my castigation may well be nearing completion and had the car ready to go prior to my arranged golf match with friend and work colleague Simon. It was an enjoyable round of golf on a pleasant evening but after four days in the doghouse, poor Simon had to endure a couple of hours of confidential offload regarding a difficult week.

Returning home at 8.30pm and with packing for our holiday complete, I suggested to Joanne we could perhaps watch a movie of her choice and so it was a revisit to the excellent musical treat "Jersey Boys." After the film, I entered the kitchen to put on the kettle, becoming aware that Joanne had followed me. As I turned around, she stood directly in front of me, arms outstretched.

"Give me a hug."
I immediately engaged in a warm embrace with my wife, maintaining the stance for some time. The hug escalated into a passionate kiss as I simultaneously felt the stress of the past four days evaporate. Breaking off from the kiss, Joanne looked at me and spoke softly, "You know you can't speak to me like you did the other night."
"I know," I readily agreed.
With a nodding acknowledgment of my response, she continued, "Let's go to bed."

Not for the first time in our relationship, Joanne's postcoital observation, "I love having make-up sex after a fall-out, it's the best sex" would leave me decidedly reticent to concur. My preference was not to have the fall-out in the first place and my own postcoital thoughts in such circumstances were more centred around relief.

Our week's holiday involved a couple of cycling trips, a boat trip on Loch Lomond, a day trip to Oban and the Isle of Mull and a visit to the excellent Crannog Centre on Loch Tay. Individually for me, a hillwalking day ticked off two Munros and two rounds of golf were tackled at the local course, whilst Joanne maintained her yoga regime in what was an active week. Overall, it was an excellent break, blessed with fine weather and I could never have anticipated that it would be the last holiday I would ever have with my wife.

Things were very quickly back on course following the holiday and more months of solidity followed.

The rearranged West Highland Way trip with Number Three would take place in October. Several practice walks were undertaken on the Speyside Way before eventually heading to Milngavie in mid-October.

Another fabulous week ensued on what was my third foray on the famous trail and we were blessed throughout the week with unseasonably favourable weather. My 15-year-old son ably coped with the demands of the challenge as we powered through our seven days.
On the penultimate day of our adventure, it was Jennifer's birthday and as a special treat for Number Three, we had arranged for his mum and Number Two to meet us in old faithful Kinlochleven. My

son and I had booked some hostel accommodation and Jennifer and Number Two would be staying in a hobbit house nearby.

On that eve of the final day's hiking, a heartening facetime conversation would take place with Joanne on our phones. We had sporadically kept in touch during our expedition ahead of her own travel to Fort William to meet us for the finish and transport us back home.

"Are you on your own?" she injected into the conversation.

"Yes, I'm outside the hobbit house. It's a fairly mild evening for October."

"Ok, can I tell you now since you're nearly finished?"

"Tell me what?"

"I didn't want to intrude on your time with your son," she began, "but this week has been so hard for me because I've missed you so much." Her on-screen emotional appearance complemented the wistful tone of her voice as she added, "I so miss not having you in my bed and can't wait to see you tomorrow."

It was a touching moment and heightened my sense of anticipation on catching up with her in person the following day, blissfully unaware of what sensationally lay ahead less than a month later.

Day 8 – Keld to Reeth

The dawn chorus resounding in the bright morning sunshine heralded Day 8 as I breakfasted on chicken sausages and beans from a small stock of military rations in my holdall.

Today's route was scheduled to be 11 miles to Reeth on the high route via Gunnerside Moor. 11 miles punctuated with ups and downs would remind me of that 10-mile stretch from Kingshouse to Kinlochleven on the West Highland Way with my son just over seven months earlier. There was an alternative lower route to Reeth which was reputedly just as popular, but with clear views and more anticipated breeze on the higher levels, the altitudinous option was favoured.

With the 'Factor 30' liberally applied, my holdall was duly returned to the dedicated stable and I was departing this tranquil secluded Dales village by 10am. Within a few minutes, the route intersects with the Pennine Way, an official national trail running from the Scottish border to the Derbyshire Peak District. The 200 yards of the Coast-to-Coast shared with the 268-mile Pennine Way includes a bridge back onto the north bank of the River Swale and the pretty East Gill Force waterfall. Feeling a sense of accomplishment that I had now completed 0.03% of the Pennine Way, I turned right to join a track above the north bank of the river with pleasant views back towards Keld. Following the wide stony path, with extensive views down Swaledale, I passed the ruin of Crackpot Hall.

This was not a somewhat crude nickname for a former asylum but rather an 18th century farmhouse, abandoned since the 1950s. Formerly used as an office connected to the lead mining of the local area, this was the beginning of a fascinating day immersed in scarred landscapes reflecting the industrial history of this part of Yorkshire.

Just after Crackpot Hall, the track bears left and narrows across fallen rocks along the west bank of a ravine carrying Swinner Gill to the River Swale. At the head of the ravine, I could see another ruin, the Swinner Gill Smelting Mill. As I neared the disused mine, I met a hiker going in the opposite direction. Having completed the Coast-to-Coast twice, west to east, this gentleman was now undertaking his third expedition, this time from east to west. He relayed some interesting information regarding the Swinner Gill Kirk, a cave access further up the ravine involving a scramble off-piste from the Coast-to-Coast. In the 17th century following the Reformation, Catholicism was outlawed and Catholic mine workers would slink upstream to attend secret prayer meetings at the 'kirk'.

The remains of an old bridge afford access over the Gill and past the old lead mine where the path begins to climb sharply, aided by flagstones in the steep boggy sections. After a few hundred yards, Gunnerside Moor is reached where the gradient flattens and joins a wider path by a signpost reminding walkers to stick to the track in order to protect fledgling curlews and lapwings. With an even and dry track, a pervading light breeze and all-round views across the moor, the walking was most pleasant for a while. After passing more evidence of mine workings on either side of the track, a smaller path off to the left is taken. This narrow defined path heads north-east through the heather until reaching a keen descent towards the next abandoned lead mine, Blakethwaite, which sits beside the flowing Gunnerside Beck.

Taking advantage of the agreeable conditions, I decided to stop and make a brew before the climb down, enjoying the view across the valley of Gunnerside Gill to Melbecks Moor beyond. Whilst enjoying my hot drink and the vista around this scenic spot, a fellow hiker approached from behind.
I raised my mug in acknowledgement of "Blondie" as he passed and I almost dropped the mug as he sparked conversation.
"Nice spot you've found there."
"Em, yes, lovely," my reply, somewhat fazed that my low-key colleague had instigated dialogue.
Looking up from what was presumably his hand-held map, he continued, "Heading down to the beck and up the other side before I stop."
"Yes, just a quick brew for me. Hoping to reach Surrender Bridge for a late lunch," I replied in reference to my subsequent plans.
"See you," he concluded as he carried on towards the forthcoming downward incline.
"Yes, catch you later."

As I watched "Blondie" put some distance between us, I felt a sense of accomplishment for the second time that day. The completion of 0.03% of the Pennine Way paled into insignificance when compared to extracting dialogue from my blonde-haired acquaintance. In that moment, I wanted to convey details of the occurrence to George and Ryan, by now several miles further along the trail, that Matt McKay was indeed the "hiker whisperer".

The narrow path down to the ruins of Blakethwaite Lead Mine includes a hairpin on approach to the west bank of Gunnerside Beck. The beck is crossed via a huge concrete slab to the baroque remains of a former peat store before climbing back up the east bank. Reaching a four-way signpost by the next small ruin, I duly followed the guidebook's advice and headed upwards and eastwards. The straight-on option involved an almost 4-mile detour south to rejoin the lower route at the village of Gunnerside. Apparently, there was a popular pub there, the Kings Head, but I had chosen the high route and would resist the temptation . . . and the extra mileage.

After the climb, I joined a wider track and proceeded across the surface of the moon . . . at least if someone had told me it was the surface of the moon, I would've had no reason to doubt them. If I am to believe what I witnessed as a babe-in-arms back in the summer of 1969, there were no tiny patches of vegetation and sporadic remnants of mining buildings on the lunar landscape, but otherwise it was a barren rocky wasteland reaching the horizon. The spectacular nothingness and feeling of remoteness evoked memories of an 8-hour drive across the Arabian Desert back in my RAF days, although that particular journey wasn't regularly interrupted by mountain bikers out on their Saturday jaunt.

On traversing the horizon, I reached a bridge over Hard Level Gill and began tracking this waterway as it streamed south-east towards Surrender Bridge. This 2-mile stretch featured more evidence of the bustling business of the past with several ruins, the most notable being the extensive remains of the Old Gang Smelting Mill, listed as a Scheduled Ancient Monument to help protect its heritage. A large car park on the south side of the gill and the arched stone Surrender Bridge afforded an achievable stroll for most visitors to the Old Gang Mill and consequently caused a little delay as I paused for the occasional short chinwag. On reaching the bridge, I found a spot by the water and utilised the Jetboil to provide spaghetti Bolognese as part of a leisurely lunch break in the pleasant sunshine.

Setting off once again past some more ruins, a short sharp descent leads to the amusingly named Cringley Bottom and is immediately followed by a short sharp ascent. The industrial scars were now replaced by sloping farmland as several sheepfolds are crossed before the route traces the upper edge of some woodland. Passing a farmhouse, I followed the tarmac road down to a T-junction by the village of Healaugh, my problem being that the village of Healaugh . . . was on the low-level route. Consulting my map and guide, it transpired that I'd missed a fork onto a higher path before the tree line and had subsequently joined the low route. Clearly the pronunciation of the village was along the lines of "hee-law" but under the circumstances of adding another unintended detour, I could only literally read "he-a-laugh"! The resultant option was to retrace my steps back uphill to the higher route and complete the final two miles or to carry on for a similar distance on the lower route. I recalled Mr Wainwright's advice to deviate and make one's own route and also recalled that variety is the spice of life. The decision to join the lower route may also have been influenced by the word 'uphill', not the most inviting word towards the end of the day. On passing through the solitary street of another quintessentially Dales village, a signpost directs the low-route hiker due south for a couple of hundred yards to rejoin the north bank of the River Swale, England's fastest flowing river.

On a beautiful Saturday afternoon, the walking was very flat and very pleasant once more, albeit in contrast from this morning's derelict rocky wasteland to this afternoon's fertile green riverside, and I passed many families enjoying an afternoon picnic on the riverbank. These blessed household gatherings were in regular proximity to some permanent ovine residents of the riverside. I sensed the latter's curiousness as to why this idyllic spot wasn't quite as popular in December.

Within an hour, the path deviates slightly north away from the river and joins Back Lane as I entered the village of Reeth. My guidebook and my map both advised that I could reach my accommodation, The Orchard Caravan Park, without visiting the village centre by simply sidestepping to the south. However, the noise and bustle reaching my ears from the village centre above to my left piqued my curiosity and a small detour was in order.

The large open space known as 'The Green' formed the centre of yet another charming and sizeable Dales village. Surrounding hills served as an aesthetically-pleasing rustic backdrop to the carnivalesque scene before me, incorporating marquees, market stalls, bunting and grassy overflow car parks filled with vehicles. The three hotels, in close proximity to each other, had several external tables all filled with locals and visitors enjoying drinks and contributing to the convivial atmosphere. The locals I'd encountered so far on this memorable journey had been friendly and accommodating, but this latest batch had surely gone above and beyond to organise such a fantastic welcome for me. On investigation, my appreciation was overhasty as it transpired that my stopover actually coincided with the Reeth Family Fun Day, an event forming part of the wider two-week Swaledale Festival. It was heartening to see communities come together in an annual tradition that began in the early 1970s, particularly in light of the unforeseen global pandemic.

As I meandered past the throngs on the cobbled hotel frontages to make my way down to the campsite, a couple of giggling women had visibly been enjoying a few afternoon refreshments as one of them pointed her index finger at me.
"You can come and sit here with us," she announced stolidly, her open palm tapping the space next to her.
With thoughts of a particular film involving Julia Roberts in a bookshop in Notting Hill, it was "tempting . . . but no." I offered a friendly smile and continued past to head downhill towards the caravan park on the southern outskirts of the village.

The Orchard Caravan Park is reached via a lane leading to the cottage residence of Ian and Sharon, the proprietors. With the ongoing annual festivities nearby, it was no surprise that a sign at the entrance indicated the site was fully booked and I was relieved that I had made my reservation in advance. I collected my holdall and Ian escorted me to an excellent pitch amongst caravans and awnings in close proximity to the toilet, shower and laundry block. The latter was important as I had planned to make use of the clothes-washing facilities and on sharing those intentions with my genial host, he returned to the house to change my paper money into the requisite coinage. I realised that I didn't have liquid or powder detergent and when Ian returned, he kindly produced a liquid tab to be placed in the machine, his assumption based on previous experience of through-hikers. He also recommended that due to the local festivities, I should book now if I required a table for dinner. It was good advice as the Black Bull was fully booked all evening but on my second call, I successfully reserved a table at the Kings Arms Hotel next door. After my evening in Shap, this would be my second visit of the trip to a hostelry by that name, but with my table for one, this evening surely wouldn't be as sociable . . . or would it?

With my laundry complete and a clean fresh albeit limited wardrobe, I prepared a cup of tea and sat in front of my tent feeling contentment with the agreeable tea-time setting, quiet but for the chatter emitting from the holidaymakers next door.
My peaceful intermission was interrupted by the friendly voice of a lady who appeared a bit older than myself, egressing from within that aforementioned caravan awning to my right.
"Would you like a chair?"
"Oh that's very kind of you," I replied, getting to my feet, "but I'll be heading back up to the village shortly for tea."
"No car with you, I assume you're hiking the Coast-to-Coast. We see a few coming through" she surmised.
"Yes, Day 8 complete, six to go."
"Well done you. Looks like you're getting some great weather for the rest of your trip."
"Yes, looking good. Got the Factor 30 handy in the rucksack."
"It'll be busy up in the village tonight. Have you booked?" she enquired.
"Yes, I've got a table booked at the Kings Arms. They squeezed me in at half six," I advised.
Our brief conversation was interrupted by a male voice coming from the awning behind her.
"You've still got half an hour. Come and have a beer with us before you go, lad."
Within a few minutes of sitting with my cup of tea in solitude, I was now sat in a chair within a caravan awning enjoying a beer and a chat with Sue and her husband Jim and their friends Des and Sandra who were residing in a caravan nearby. They were all from the Middlesbrough area and tried to visit their Reeth holiday home at least one weekend per month.

"So, with that accent, you're from north of the border," Jim asked, a question that had become all too familiar on my journey.

"No, I'm actually from the east end of London. Born and bred. Never lived anywhere else," I replied with a deadpan face in my broad Scottish accent.

My reply was met with a silent pause . . . until a smile slowly developed on my hitherto expressionless face and all four of my latest acquaintances burst into laughter.

"You had us for a moment there," Jim exclaimed.

"Been asked that question a few times on this adventure. Thought I'd mix it up a bit," a reply greeted with more laughter.

"Originally from Paisley but been away over 30 years. Now live in Aberdeen," I confirmed Jim's presumption.

"Yeh, I've been to Paisley a few times," Des interjected before showing his limited knowledge of the town, "So, are you a blue or a green?"

"I'm sorry. I don't follow," I replied, having followed his question perfectly.

"Are you Rangers or Celtic?"

"There's only one team in Paisley and they don't play in blue or green," I explained.

Jim joined the conversation, "A St. Mirren man then."

"Of course. Forgot about them," Des reacted.

"Sadly, a heck of a lot of others in Paisley have forgotten about them too, preferring to be a blue or a green," I conceded before metaphorically placing my tongue in my cheek, "So you're from Middlesbrough, Des. Tell me, are you a Magpie or a Mackem?" I asked in reference to the two larger clubs within the north east area.

"Touche," he replied with a smile.

The time quickly approached to head off for dinner and my new friends generously insisted that I join them for a drink on my return from the village. My resultant enquiry as to the location of any available off-licence in the village was met with some mockery and confirmation that their caravan was 'full of beer'.

It was a pleasant early evening stroll back up to the village hub, my joie de vivre enhanced by the latest kindness and friendliness of my very temporary neighbours. On entering the sizeable Kings Arms Hotel, I was led through variously sized dining areas to a small section towards the rear consisting of four tables. There was a table for six, a table for four and two tables for two. The friendly waitress showed me to a table for two and took my drink order, advising that the table was mine as long as required. I assumed that with many solo hikers passing through, the sight of a lone diner at a restaurant on a Saturday evening wasn't overly unusual. I was perhaps more conscious of the scenario on realising that this was the first time, since setting off from St Bees the previous weekend, that I had formally sat down for an evening meal in a hotel pub/restaurant.

The fun was just starting.

Taking in my surroundings, I had been seated directly beside an ornate stone alcove in the wall, illuminated in warm blue light, shining upon the only contents of the alcove, a small vase containing two fresh red roses. Attached to the wall below the alcove, level with the table top, was a small wooden carved outline of a house with a white love heart centrally attached. Just to the right of the alcove, hanging on a hook six inches from my right elbow, was a small ceramic grey-coloured love heart, an almost exact replica of an ornament which hung in the kitchen at my previously shared home with Joanne in the 'Shire. It appeared I had most definitely been allocated the 'romantic date' table.

To accompany my visual processing, the hi-fi speaker mounted high on the wall on the opposite corner emitted the LeAnn Rimes classic "How Do I Live" at a volume I considered slightly louder than background music. My large swig of the newly-arrived overpriced pint of Italian beer was quaffed through a wry smile, and when the lovely LeAnn was followed on the airwaves by Lady Antebellum's "Need You Now", the smile became more beaming than wry. I was beginning to enjoy my hot date with myself and seeing the funny side of life. The humour was enhanced when another member of staff appeared at my table and placed both her hands on the chair opposite, saying, "Ok if I take this?" and removed it before I got the chance to thank her for reminding me that I was flying solo.

I imagined the conversation.

"We're a chair short at Table 14."

"It's ok. There's a sad bastard at the dating table. Take his spare."

By the time my delicious tempura king prawn starter had arrived, I was ordering the second 'birra' and foot-tapping along to Charlie Rich's classic "Most Beautiful Girl in the World".

The menu had advertised that the Saturday Special was the 'Sausage Sizzler', promising a "different sausage every week". I could safely say, hand on heart, that at no point in my life had I uttered to another human being, "What's the sausage of the week?" and that situation wasn't about to change. Besides, did I really know that much about sausages? Did I really know 'anything' about sausages?

Playing it safe and extending my temporary pescetarianism, I opted for the wholetail scampi which arrived in timely fashion after my starter, in tandem with three gentlemen taking their places at the adjacent table. Adding respective room numbers to their food and drink orders confirmed their residency.

As a lone diner, it can be difficult not to unintentionally eavesdrop on the conversation of others and I was taken aback when the word "Lossie" was heard. The oldest of the three gents, whom I estimated to be in his early 60s, began referring to a tragic air accident at RAF Lossiemouth in Moray some years before, an incident I was familiar with. Subsequent conversation related to details of the base where I served two tours of duty in my service career, and I couldn't resist politely interposing into their conversation. If I thought the world was small back in Ennerdale Bridge on Day 1, it was about to get much smaller.

Colin Webb lived in Moray and was a retired RAF navigator who had operated on Tornado aircraft at the Moray airbase. Together with his two friends from other parts of the UK, they were walking Wainwright's Coast-to-Coast in aid of a veterans' charity. Astonishingly, it transpired that Colin lived less than 200 yards from Jennifer and furthermore, on exchanging details and checking social media, we had mutual ex-RAF friends, one of which had recently donated to both of our respective benefitting charities. Colin contacted our mutual donor to advise that we were remarkably sat together in a pub in the small village of Reeth in the Yorkshire Dales. We both received replies advising to get the drinks in. Their table for three became a table for four as I joined Colin, Rob and Bruce for a drink.

The Champions League Final was taking place in Portugal between Chelsea and Manchester City and with the requisite satellite TV channel unavailable in all three Reeth hostelries, Bruce had an earpiece tuned in to Radio 5 Live and was providing updates. More importantly, Colin and I had RAF careers to reminisce over.

It was approaching 10pm when Cesar Azpilicueta lifted the large trophy for Chelsea following a solitary goal by Guy Havertz for the London team and I figured it was time to head back to the caravan park. Bidding my friends good night, I strolled back in the dusk towards my tent, shaking my head and smirking about some more Coast-to-Coast serendipity, and advised Jennifer of my evening with her nearby neighbour in Upper Swaledale. As I approached my tent and began to hear the chatter of voices next door, I recalled my earlier invite and, having had a few drinks, wondered if I could enter my tent unnoticed.

"Hey, there he is. That was a long meal!" exclaimed Jim from the illuminated adjacent awning.

"It certainly was. I'll only stop for a quick nightcap. You won't believe what happened," I began to explain, going on to furnish brief details of my unforeseen encounter.

It had been an unexpected evening, in a good way, very contrary to the most unexpected evening I had endured six months earlier.

November 2020

The month of November 2020 will live long in the memory as one of the most bizarre and inconceivable months of my life.

The month started in good fettle with Joanne beating me to the "pinch punch" just after midnight on the opening day as I worked a nightshift. Continuing on the midnight theme, we reached our third wedding anniversary early in the month, and as we crossed the witching hour on the previous evening, I had recorded a song for her on a popular mobile phone karaoke app. As I made my excuses to visit the bathroom in order to forward my rendition of Frank Sinatra's "The Way You Look Tonight", I was elated to receive a simultaneous message from my wife. On the same mobile phone app, she had re-recorded a rendition of the song she sang to me at our wedding ceremony exactly three years prior. Receiving this recording was a fabulous surprise and further testament to our kindred spirits. We laughed at our congruity of feelings in a touching moment of consanguinity.

The following evening, we once again celebrated another passing year of marriage at the same local Italian restaurant.

On the next evening, a seminal moment of Scottish sport would occur when the Scottish men's football team qualified for the European Championships after winning on penalties against Serbia in a covid-empty Belgrade stadium. It was Scotland's first qualification for a finals tournament since 1998 and we joined in the nation's euphoria. With the champagne dusted down and drafted in from the garage, the mini-celebration was a welcome distraction from the country's preceding difficult year.

The feel-good factor would endure for a few more days until the very unexpected and unfortunate news that Joanne's son Scott and his partner Megan were going their separate ways. Scott and Megan had been together since before I met Joanne and solid friendships had been built with Megan's parents, who would naturally remain good friends. Scott was going to utilise the downstairs spare room in the interim whilst sorting things out. Advice and support were of course offered by Joanne and myself and I was heartened when Joanne told her son during these exchanges that our marriage was 'solid'.

Later, on my nightshift that night, I received a message after midnight from Joanne.

"Last shift for you. 3 days off. Woohoo! Golf tomorrow . . . yaay!
Angela has an interview tomorrow.
Scott has counselling tomorrow.
Number One settling in to her new place.
Plenty going on at the mo, ta very much xxx"

She followed up her message with a jocular GIF featuring the character Charlie Brown from the Peanuts cartoon strip saying, "Good grief. What else could go wrong?"

The answer to her 'joke' somewhat appallingly lay just ahead.

Just 48 hours on from my wife's endorsement of the strength of our marriage and what began as a routine Friday in late November would go down in my personal history as one the most unpredictable, unfathomable and incomprehensible days of my life. After an early rise and some breakfast, we established that Joanne had no clients until lunchtime, prompting some flirtatious chat about our "free" morning and a return to the bedroom.

I would subsequently and disturbingly reflect on my complete oblivion at this point that the morning intimacy I was enjoying with my wife would be the final time any such relations would take place.

As Joanne prepared for her inaugural clients of the day, I would be undertaking the outstanding pile of ironing but didn't feel compelled to commence the task immediately, rather waiting to merge it with Joanne's belated start to the day. In the meantime, my phone app was providing accompanying music to sing-a-long tracks and I was enjoying some exercising of my vocal cords. The atmosphere certainly felt jovial, therefore I was completely flummoxed when Joanne suddenly appeared in the living room to interrupt my tuneless meddling.

"So will you be doing the ironing then?" she enquired acerbically in an unexpectedly pugnacious tone.

"Yes, of course I am," my somewhat startled reply, taken aback by her sudden and unpredictable change of tone.

Feeling somewhat irked by her unnecessary belligerency, I continued, "Are you ok? I'm planning to do the ironing after you start work. Am I not allowed to do something I enjoy on my day off?" The last part of my comment evoked a look I'd seen before in my wife and I moved swiftly to avoid any unnecessary escalation. "Alright, Joanne. I'm not serious. Just a wee reaction to your sudden change of tone. Didn't mean anything by it.," my reply accompanied by a smile to reassure her that's all it was. "Ok, fine," her reply.

Thankfully, as it was a non-incident, there appeared to be no issues as Joanne sporadically reappeared throughout the day and pleasantries were routinely exchanged.

It was early evening when we sat down after tea that my life was suddenly about to unravel horribly in spectacular fashion, even allowing for Joanne's previously demonstrated incomprehensible capriciousness.

"I want to speak about what happened this morning," she began. "What happened this morning?" my genuine reaction. "Your comment about not doing what you want on your day off." "Oh right. Yeh, it was a throwaway comment like I said." "Well I'm not happy about it," she retorted. "Well I can't take it back, sweetie. Like I said, it was just a comment in reaction to your tone and I believed we sorted it at the time. I apologise if it upset you and I had no idea that it was going to be classed as some sort of incident." There followed a period of silence which was making me uncomfortable and I moved to ascertain where I stood. "Sorry, Joanne. Can I confirm that I'm not in the doghouse over this?" Again, a period of silence resulted. "Am I to assume by the silent treatment that I am in the doghouse or are you still making up your mind?" Joanne eventually breached her silence in the most unimaginable way.

"I think you should look for somewhere else to live."

It was my turn to enter into a stunned silent mode as I attempted to process what I'd just heard.

"What?" my reactionary shocked response, turning to my wife with an involuntary nervous smile, "Is that some sort of sick joke?"
Joanne once more reverted to silent mode.
"Sorry Joanne, you can't be serious. Am I imagining things?" and with a stupefied scoff, I continued, "You're surely not suggesting that our marriage is suddenly in jeopardy over a throwaway comment when pressed about the ironing."
It was possibly the most unintentional and inappropriately timed pun in my lifetime, which neither of us picked up on.
"It's not just about that, Matt. I've been feeling like this for a while."
"For a while?", I immediately enquired, "and you thought you'd bring it up now after a misunderstanding following a throwaway comment this morning?"
"Matt, we just push each other's buttons."
"Yeh, you're right, darling. We can argue on who exactly pushes whose buttons but it happened perhaps on a couple of occasions a year. The other 99 per cent of the time, everything's fine. Fairy tales don't exist, Joanne, but we're not a kick in the arse off it. Since couple counselling at the start of the year, we've had one blip back before our holiday in August. We both agreed how successful the counselling had been at the time. Was that just bullshit?"
As the enigma, sat opposite, once more regressed into her silent mode, I felt the oncoming reaction of my buttons to her pushing was, under the circumstances, more than justified.
"So, when you insist on telling me you love me every day, when you're always telling me that you won the lottery when you met me. Is that bullshit too? When you were practically in tears last month because I wasn't in your bed. Bullshit? When you sat in that very chair just two days ago and told your son our marriage was solid. Bullshit? When you prepared your romantic little musical interlude for our anniversary last week. Bullshit? When you realise that I'm wary of your unpredictability and reassure me I've got nothing to worry about. Bullshit?"
Her silence continued, heightening my baffled exasperation.
"Joanne, we had sex this morning. Today. This day. A few hours ago."
My concluding observation finally elicited a reactionary cruel response.
"Yeah, I know. I guess I was just using you."
I paused, trying to grasp the evilness of her words and the deliberate and unnecessary nasty undertone in her voice. It was clearly

designed to push the necessary buttons but the shock at her vindictiveness helped me to stay calm. I had been led to believe over the years that her mother was capable of such foulness and my mind began to ponder on how far the apple had fallen from the tree.

"Did you really just say that, Joanne?" I questioned, feeling abject disappointment at her malicious provocation.

My reaction was met with further silence and I felt a desperate sinking feeling.

"Joanne, you can't just play games with people's lives. This is my life. I love you. I'm beginning to think you have no idea what the word 'love' means, having used it every day for over seven years. I know you reckon you have some mental issues but this is frightening. For mental issues, read serious psychological problems and you need help. Don't you think you should get some professional help before ruining someone's life on a whim?"

Again, Joanne would put her continued silence down to her self-diagnosed 'dissociation' but I couldn't help thinking it was convenient and timely.

The silence continued for some time whilst I intermittently glanced in disbelief towards my expressionless wife.

"Joanne, you asked me to marry you back then   Why?"

Her uncontrollable 'dissociation' appeared to be strangely under control as another reply was offered.

"Guilt, I suppose."

"Guilt? For what?"

"For the drink driving thing. For everything I put you through."

"Joanne, you must know I never wanted to get married again. I did the right thing by saying yes. And now you're telling me that all that elaborate planning was just to satisfy your own guilt. Can you not see how much worse that makes things? All those wonderful memories we've created are a result of you feeling guilty? It wasn't going to make the 20-year criminal record go away. It wasn't going to change what happened but for some reason, you thought proposing marriage would make you feel better? All about you, sweetie."

Despite my exasperation, I did feel that my wife's responses were in the heat of the moment and hoped there was a whole lot of love involved too. That was perhaps the catalyst for my thoughts turning to darker reasons for her sudden inclination towards our separation, prompting a more subdued tone of question.

"While we're on the subject of saying ugly things, and as this is all incredibly sudden, I suppose I need to ask the horrible question although I'm hoping I know the answer. There isn't someone else involved, is there?

My wife purposefully gazed directly at me, assuredly uttering, "Yes, there is."

It was certainly not the response I was expecting and the shock exacted my own wide-eyed return of her gaze and immediate de-escalation of my impassioned posture.

Feeling rooted to the spot, my helplessly opened mouth mumbled, "Oh . . . right. Em . . . I had no idea. Ok . . . em . . . ok."

I took a moment in an attempt to compose myself before continuing in a softer more coherent tone.

"Em, is it someone I know, actually, sorry, that's a stupid thing to ask. I don't really want to know anything. Sorry, I'm just a bit taken aback. I had absolutely no idea."

Joanne then casually uttered, "Matt, do you really think I'm having an affair? Of course I'm not, there's no-one else involved."

My startled gaze returned, "You what?"

"I'm not having an affair."

"So why did you just say you were?"

"I don't know, I suppose I just wanted to see your reaction."

I paused, took in a deep breath and pursed my lips for an intentionally slow exhalation, bowing my head slightly with a vexed glance upwards to face my clearly disturbed partner.

"I'm sorry, Joanne, but at times, you're an absolute fucking fruit bat and you need to sort out some help. This morning, we were making love, having a laugh and being a happy couple. This evening, you want me to move out. I really don't want to split up, separate, whatever, and you need to have a serious think about things before you potentially destroy my life. Take the weekend. I'm going to bed. What you do is up to you."

It was a long worrisome night and involved no sleep of any quality as my wife never joined me. With Scott back in his own place for the weekend, I sincerely hoped that Joanne would decide over the weekend that there had been a massive overreaction to whatever was going on for her.

I tried to let Saturday pass without incident, pending my return to dayshift at work on the Sunday. Again, Joanne elected to sleep in the spare room and another very anxious night was endured ahead of a 4.30am alarm for work. During the small hours, Joanne had forwarded articles about Borderline Personality Disorder and additional articles about something called 'Rejection Sensitivity'. I hoped it wasn't just self-obsession but rather an explanation for her behaviour ahead of another apology.

Arriving home from work on the Sunday, I received some hope that Joanne had come to her senses.
"Oh, hi Matt," she chirpily greeted as I entered our home, "I'm running a bath for you."
I tried to keep my ever-hopeful emotions in check as I went upstairs and undressed for the bath. As I entered the bathroom, Joanne appeared at the door.
"I'll come in and chat with you," she declared as I climbed into the bath, adding with a giggle, "it's not like I haven't seen you naked."
I lay back in the bath as Joanne perched on the seat-down toilet, a familiar scene in our family bathroom. I felt a nervous but excited sense of anticipation and my inner emotions began to fantasize on the impending possibility of a beautiful moment of make-up and apology. Joanne then matter-of-factly began the chat with one the most deflating and disheartening sentences I would never forget.
"I've been on a few websites today and there's some nice properties in Aberdeen to rent at decent prices."
The hot water engulfing me began to metaphorically chill from the coldness emitted from the mouth of the woman who had asked me to marry her. Whilst simultaneously processing yet more unanticipated thoughtlessness, I spoke softly but wilfully.
"Get out. Get out of the bathroom, please, now," and as she exited, I added, "and can you close the door behind you?"
The sickly feeling of worry and hopelessness was inducing an irreversible tidal wave through my lacrimal glands. It was uncontrolled pain-filled sobbing and I didn't want Joanne to bear witness as it would only enhance her egotistical control of the situation. She'd now had 48 hours to mull things over and appeared determined that I wouldn't be released from the throwaway comment doghouse, and deep down, I really didn't want to lose my wife.

Over the years, a traditional Sunday bedtime routine was to tackle the weekend quiz in a well-known newspaper. Bedtime arrived once more and Joanne advised that she would "of course" not be joining me but would come up and pose the weekly quiz. Under the desperate situation I found myself in, I was in no position to question her actions. Shortly afterwards, I was tucked up under the duvet when my wife appeared. She lay parallel to me on the bed, atop the duvet but with her head on the pillow directly next to me and relayed the 25 questions as per any other Sunday evening. It was incredibly sadistic and controlling of her but I knew I was in an impossible situation and completely at her mercy.

Three more shifts elapsed at work and I was left with no option but to investigate the property rental scene in Aberdeen. By the end of the week, I had carried out a virtual viewing, completed the necessary preliminaries, and agreed to relocate to a small maisonette property on the outskirts of Aberdeen in early December.

It was a most awkward two weeks, effectively living 'together apart', still dining together and sharing a home. One night, we were watching tv together in our usual positions when I extended my hand towards my wife for some 'hand hugs'. Joanne instinctively took hold of my hand and continued to watch the programme whilst I smiled at her. About 30 seconds elapsed before she realised that I was smiling at her and as her eyes met mine, she looked down at our embraced palms and quickly withdrew her hand.
"Did you forget you had dumped me?" I smiled.
Her embarrassed silence emphasized her ambiguous state of mind and lack of rationale.

Following a confirmatory in-person viewing at the Aberdeen apartment the following week, and after spending the weekend packing up my belongings, I moved into my new home just 17 days after that most unforeseen and harrowing Friday evening. Like everyone else, I had been through some lows in my life but there was a personal sense of disbelief and foreboding that I was about to enter an unavoidable and ominous darkness.
Joanne had provided assistance through the day but as the early evening approached, she announced that she would leave me to it and be in touch. She gave me a hug, and looked at me with what appeared to be sincerity.
"I'm sorry, Matt."
I had received countless apologies from Joanne over the years for the various turmoil she had put me through but this time it was desperately different. Those numerous previous apologies had symbolised the end of tumult and a return to the status quo.

As she departed my new abode into the chilly early December blackness, I stood transfixed at the closed door in eerie silence before almost involuntarily adopting a crouching position which in turn became a sitting position with my arms wrapped around the bent knees in front of me. As I gently rocked backwards and forwards, the tears came effortlessly and uncontrollably. Joanne had of course induced tears over the years but I was about to enter new territory.

19 short days prior, my wife was advising her own son that her marriage to his step-dad was 'solid'. 17 short days prior, I was enjoying some Friday morning intimacy with my wife in our matrimonial home.

Now my desperately despondent psyche was consequently trying to process that here I was, suddenly living on my own in a tiny apartment 25 miles away, and it appeared that my wife in fact didn't love me at all.

It was difficult to look ahead to anything or to contemplate any sort of future as I continued to cry for what seemed like a couple of hours.

This was the lowest point. To use boxing parlance, I was lying on the canvas with the referee standing over me, counting, but I had no desire to regain my feet and fight. Forlorn hopelessness and a fear of surviving the immediate future without the woman who, until recently, I believed I would be spending the rest of my life with. During this dark episode, I tried to embolden myself in the knowledge that I had three wonderful children whom I loved very much.

I had just commenced two weeks of annual leave and, through my tears, I resolved to use it as an opportunity to try to make some sense of my predicament. This would prove difficult as I had no work commitments and there were two nearby grocery stores with an off-licence. Despite my obvious awareness that this wasn't a recommended strategy, I would weakly succumb to the use of alcohol to numb the pain.

At this stage, I clearly had no idea of the six months or indeed the Joanne that lay ahead of me.

Day 9 – Reeth to Brompton-on-Swale via Richmond

It was 7.45am and I was sat at the entrance to my tent enjoying the Sunday morning sunshine with my cup of tea, nodding acknowledgement to the periodic passing dog-walkers and their canine companions. It was forecast to be another warm day for my 15 miles to Brompton-On-Swale. Most hikers tend to stop at Richmond, the largest town on the Coast-to-Coast but that leaves a 22-mile Day 10 thus I opted to push on and reduce the following day's mileage. Colin and the boys were only going as far as Richmond where their respective partners had arranged to meet them for a stopover.

My neighbourly nightcap involved a couple of bottles of beer and this morning's slightly groggy head didn't crave anything substantial for breakfast. It occurred to me that I hadn't fully anticipated the social aspect of the journey when I set out on this solo 192-mile hike. The vast majority of my time was of course spent alone with my thoughts and often in conversation with myself, but my "newsy" demeanour combined with the regular kindness of strangers had inevitably led to regular cordial interaction which in turn gave my quest a very personal uniqueness.

By now, the morning pack-up rigmarole was all fairly routine, even allowing for the tender head. However, this morning's heavy dew in the shade of the abutting treeline effected a wet outer tent which I draped over an adjacent fence to receive attention from an unobstructed rising sun.

The daily meticulous nurture of my lower limbs revealed a first small blister on my right heel as my feet continued to break in my new Kirkby Stephen acquisitions. A small Compeed plaster was duly applied in addition to the routine preparation involving the liberal application of Vaseline on my soles and the maintenance of Compeed plasters on known vulnerable areas.

With my kit prepped and a slightly drier tent, I donned my rucksack and wheeled my holdall back along the access road to Ian and Sharon's enchanting cottage, thanking them for their excellent hospitality. Within a couple of hundred yards, I re-joined the B6270 and Day 9 was fully underway. A Coast-to-Coast signpost directed me over some fields and I was soon enjoying a brief pleasant section back on the north bank of the River Swale. Crossing a minor road, a stile provided access into a field which climbed to provide a pretty view through the warm hazy sunshine back to Reeth and its encompassing hills. Continuing across several sheepfolds, a short descent arrived at Marrick Priory, a 12th century Grade 2 Listed Building which acted as a Benedictine nunnery until its dissolution in 1540 when the 17 residents were pensioned off. I glossed over the part concerning the "depredations of marauding Scots" and fast-forwarded 400-odd years when the priory was revamped to its current function, an Outdoor Education Centre providing accommodation and various outdoor activities for youth groups. Opposite the priory, the trail enters Steps Wood which incorporates 375 steps, reputedly shaped by those pensioned-off vestals hundreds of years before. Although a steep climb, the thick wood provided welcome shade before emerging onto a field which in turn reached a tarmac road by a barn. I was now in the small elegant village of Marrick which consisted of several quaint cottages, a phone box and a bench. The signage in the village directed hikers south on a convoluted "long way for a short cut", skirting around some cottages before diverting north behind the same properties. If I lived in this beautiful locale, I wouldn't want pesky marauding Scots taking a shortcut through my drive either.

Still surrounded by hills, the terrain was now wide-open more gently rolling countryside and I stopped to take on some water and get photographs of the appealing all-round sunny panorama. Colin, Rob and Bruce caught up with me at this panoramic spot and after a brief chat, I carried on as they stopped for a breather.

The route headed north east through several of these rolling fields before descending to join a minor road towards the village of Marske. I had been slowly gaining on a couple of walkers for the past mile or so. It was Paul and Matthew, last seen in a motor car outside the pub in Keld two days earlier, and I joined them for a bit on the uphill approach towards Marske. My estimation put them in their late 20s /early 30s. Paul and Matthew hailed from Northallerton, a town that would be a couple miles south of the trail at one point tomorrow. With various family in the local area, they were able to arrange pick-ups and drop-offs to facilitate visits and meals.

"Yeh, I know this area really well," Paul declared, "Did you know that the River Swale is the fastest-flowing river in England?"

"Fucks sake," Matthew quietly reacted to his friend's disclosure.

With a puzzled look and a curious smile, I turned to Matthew, "Ok?"

Matthew returned my smile, "I have to hear that so many times a day. And when he doesn't have hikers to share it with, he just tells me . . . again."

I grinned at his light-hearted exasperation.

Paul, openly unfazed by his friend's vexation, nonchalantly affirmed, "It is, though. It's something I find really interesting."

"Don't I know it," Matthew mumbled, much to my amusement.

On reaching the village of Marske, a left turn uphill at a junction leads over a bridge crossing the Marske Beck which flows into the fastest-flowing river in England and past the Church of St Edmund the Martyr. This beautiful 12th century shrine also advertises drinks and snacks to passing hikers, a fact I was aware of in advance . . . as I had recently acquainted someone who knew the area really well. Paul and Matthew had pre-planned a break here but after acquiring some bottled water, I was pushing on in the warm sunshine.

Shortly after leaving the village, a signpost directs north-east across some fields, descending into a wood to cross Paddy's Bridge. Emerging from the wood, the path climbs towards Applegarth Scar, a limestone cliff but before the summit, the Coast-to-Coast joins a track eastward. Traversing this track afforded extensive views across the rolling countryside, the green lushness of the rolling pastures enhanced by the sun's lustre.

The track soon narrowed to a path meandering past some farms, the shining River Swale visible in the valley below to the south.

Following a section through a wood, the town of Richmond appeared in the distance through the warm haziness and the trail descended to a tarmac road past another farm. It is often noticeable on a hike when one is nearing a town as afternoon strollers from the town become more frequent. This applied to the chatty lady with her two young sons I encountered in the aforementioned wood before I approached a standalone wall with a white sign attached, advising I was within Richmond. From my slightly raised viewpoint, there appeared to be two random hats on the wall as I approached from the west. Attached to the side of this small stone structure was a plaque with a quote from the man himself which I had read before but would take the time to read again:

"There is a thrilling view of Richmond ahead. Richmond is a town unlike others, a place unique, rich in relics of the past, steeped in a long history that still lingers in the ramifications of its castle and the narrow alleys and quaint buildings that huddle in the shelter of the massive Norman keep. The castle, dramatically poised on a cliff high above the Swale, is a dominating feature. It is a town of reminders of times long past. It is too good to be by-passed."
Alfred Wainwright 1907-1991 – A Coast to Coast Walk

The Richmond and District Civic Society had erected the plaque which also reminded hikers they had 76 and a half miles remaining until Robin Hood's Bay. I found it rather touching to be reading a quote from a book that I was actually carrying in my rucksack. Mr Wainwright devised the route in 1973 and in the intervening half-century, the trees had grown. There was no view of Richmond.

"You'll be walking the Coast-to-Coast then?" came a voice from the wall.
For a brief moment, I was rooted to the spot in puzzlement.
Did this wall just speak to me? Was Mr Wainwright conversing from beyond? Did I imagine it?
Tilting my head slightly to my left revealed that the east side of the wall had a small bench attached, whereupon an elderly couple sat, hitherto in silence. The previously viewed random hats from a higher vantage point sat upon their heads.
"So sorry. I didn't see you there," I instinctively replied, "the bench is well tucked in."

The elderly couple's correct assumption of my task in hand sparked a lengthy conversation. The gentleman had completed the route many years before and was happy to reminisce on his experience in an entertaining manner. His wife jokingly reminisced on her gladness to be rid of him for a fortnight. Despite my supposition that she had heard his Coast-to-Coast tales many times, it was a joy to see her apparent keenness to listen in with lovesome glances. It reminded me of my own situation and the possibility that I wouldn't get the opportunity to share my experience. Perhaps I would write about it one day.

Such was the length of our discourse, I was overtaken by Paul and Matthew, and shortly afterwards by the chatty lady and her sons. When Colin, Rob and Bruce passed, they revealed their relief to discover the elderly couple on the obscured bench beside me. It appeared to them as they approached that I was deep in conversation with a wall. To be fair, it wouldn't have been the first time.

With a fond farewell to the devoted duo, I set off on the final short leg to Richmond with something of a spring in my step, heartened by my latest exchange. The affable life-partners, sat in comfortable silence together, enjoying their view of the fields and trees in the early afternoon sunshine. Another episode contributing to the restoration of my faith in humanity.

The descent towards the town gradually joins more and more civilization as I wended my way via quaint Rosemary Lane and the brilliantly named Finkle Street to the large cobbled open town centre eponymous marketplace, bustling with people and activity on the eve of a Spring bank Holiday.
On entering Market Place, originally the keep and walls of the adjacent 11th century Richmond Castle, the 15th century Trinity Church clock tower rose in front of me as a focal point. The church housed the Green Howards Museum, commemorating a light infantry regiment formed in the late 17th century. Around this centrepiece on all sides were shops, restaurants and hotels, all within buildings that helped to retain the town's historic feel. Based on this snapshot, Richmond was a beautiful town.
Strolling around this busy hub with my rucksack and walking poles, I was aware that I still had around five miles to my destination at Brompton-On-Swale thus would find somewhere to eat. On some seating outside a café, I was poignantly reminded of dear Squeak when I met Alfie, a long-lived 16-year-old Bichon Frise whose owners were only too happy to allow me to take a photo.
On the south side of the square, a sizeable white building emblazoned with "Town Hall Pub and Dining" had no free tables externally with patrons enjoying the summer conditions, however signage indicated seating was available inside. After spending a few hours hiking in the sunshine, the idea of some indoor shade was appealing. On entering the spacious establishment, there were indeed plenty of tables available. The 'specials' board advertised a large Sunday roast with all the trimmings. Consequently, there was no need to peruse a menu and an hour later, I felt fully satiated with roast beef, roast potatoes, Yorkshire puddings (of course) and no

end of vegetables, all washed down with a beer and a couple of iced water chasers.

It was shortly after 3pm when I set off once more from Market Place, with plenty of carbs to burn off, for the last leg of the day. My route down to the river included a sharp descent on a narrow lane called 'The Bar', named after an adjoining postern gate in the town walls. Information on a small wall-mounted metal plate advised that it was built in the year 1312 on account of Scottish incursions. Two years later, an incursion in the opposite direction hadn't ended too well for the English at Bannockburn.

Ironically, from both an historic and a personal perspective, from the very same lane, the top of Culloden Tower was visible just a couple of hundred yards away. Now a holiday home, it was built in 1746 to commemorate the Duke of Cumberland's victory over Bonnie Prince Charlie on the Moray Firth that year. It didn't mention my old friend Flora MacDonald's role in assisting the escape of Rome's "Young Pretender" but even here, hiking on the eastern boundary of the Yorkshire Dales, my inextricable link with a particular Inverness landmark was evoked.

Leaving the town, England's fastest-flowing river is crossed once more on a road bridge with impressive views up to Richmond Castle high above the north bank. The imposing Norman fortress would remain visible for some time as the trail leaves the road and joins a path along the south bank and around Richmond Town Football Club. Soon, through the trees, I passed Richmond Falls, a collection of small waterfalls on the River Swale in the shadow of the castle. Being a warm sunny Sunday afternoon on a Bank Holiday weekend, the falls and indeed the river itself were barely visible due to the human mass covering them. Crowds of people clambering over one another to procure their own small bit of the river to dangle their feet in, or even immerse their torsos. Beauty is in the eye of the beholder as the saying goes and I understand we all like different things. "How utterly awful" was my personal thought on the palpable purgatory before me.

The path deviates away from the river and emerges at a row of houses called Priory Villas. The gentleman at No 7 was enjoying some gardening and another ten minutes or so was lost in conversation. Sharing his Scottish roots, Mr McIntosh was also critical of the lack of considerate parking by the aforementioned visitors to the river. Moments after the chinwag with my fellow Scot, his point was illustrated as police vehicles were patrolling in both directions to warn drivers of the bottleneck created by pavement parkers on the A6136, the main Richmond to Catterick road.

The route doesn't stay on this main road for long, turning off left to pass a sewage treatment plant before climbing through some woods, now back beside the Swale's south bank. Signs indicating that I was entering a military training area emphasized my proximity to Catterick Garrison, the largest British Army garrison in the world. Once clear of the woods, I crossed some nondescript fields and reached a fence decorated with "C2C" accompanied by a directional arrow in red spray paint. Flanking a very bright yellow field of oilseed rape, I entered the small town of Colburn. The Coast-to-Coast only fleetingly passes the northern edge of the town in what is effectively a slightly detached village, but does pass directly in front of the local pub, The Hildyard Arms. It was late Sunday afternoon in fine sunshine on the eve of a Monday holiday and as could be expected, the garden to the front of the cream-coloured cottage-type building was very busy. The clientele consisted mainly of groups of men in their late 20s/early 30s of a physically fit appearance. As a serviceman of 22 years, my hunch told me that some denizens from the local garrison were enjoying some down-time . . . quite a lot of down-time.

"Oi mate, you're just in time. It's your round," came the shout as I strode past.

I aimed a large smile in the direction of the inebriated troupe of troops.

My military 'mate' continued, "Seriously though mate. You can camp here round the back. They do food and everything. But it IS your round though."

"Got accommodation booked in Brompton, but thanks for the offer," I grinned back.

"Fair dos mate," his parting remark as I continued on my way.

Carefully adhering to my guidebook, I planned on taking the direct route to Brompton-On-Swale which involved deviating off the trail before St Giles Farm and scrambling down the south bank of the Swale through some trees. I reached a track traversing a rickety old bridge which enabled my final Coast-to-Coast crossing of England's fastest-flowing river. Continuing on the track north for a few hundred yards, I turned right onto the B6271. Despite being prefixed by the letter 'B', this was the main road for returning day visitors from Richmond and the northern Yorkshire Dales to join the A1(M) heading north or south at Catterick. Consequently, it was lively and the final half mile to Brompton-on-Swale was sluggish as I was restricted to the unkempt raised grass verge until reaching sidewalk sanctuary on entering the village.

The Brompton-on-Swale Bunk Barn sits across a yard behind the home of its owners Chris and his wife Rosa. The bunk barn hosts twelve people in three rooms and there is an area of the garden behind set aside for tents. On entering the premises from the main drag through the village, a signpost on the gate read *"Please close the gate. Killer geese on the loose."* A sense of humour was evident and there was a relaxed air as, following a pleasant chat with Rosa about my day and the adventure thus far, she led me through the yard behind her house to the allocated garden area. On the right-hand side of the yard, the long face of a horse peered at me over the open upper half of a stable door. Rosa pointed out an indoor area that included a toilet and shower facility for my exclusive use as I was the sole guest. Within my exclusive garden enclave were some children's toys, a trampoline and a picnic table as my host revealed its shared purpose as her grandchildren's play area when unoccupied. Unlike a more official campsite, the homely welcome and atmosphere of the place felt more akin to friends allowing me to pitch overnight at their home. Whilst erecting the tent, that pervading feeling was further enhanced when Rosa reappeared carrying a tray laden with a pot of tea, cup, milk, sugar and biscuits.
"You'll be needing a brew," she declared, much to my appreciation.

After making use of the excellent facilities and completing some admin, I visited the well-stocked grocery store in the village and picked up some snacks for the evening and tomorrow's scheduled 17 and a half miles, not forgetting a nightcap bottle of beer. On my return via the yard, Rosa, Chris and what appeared to be their adult children and grandchildren were enjoying a barbecue in the evening sunshine.
"Mr McKay, you're very welcome to join us for a beer," Rosa kindly offered.
"Oh, please call me Matt, and that's very kind of you."
Whilst touched by her kind offer, I was aware that a family gathering was in progress and I didn't want to overly impose but neither did I want to appear introverted. The compromise occurred to me.
"I'll have a quick one, thank you. I got into company last night in Reeth and had a little more than anticipated. Perhaps I'll take it easy tonight. Long day to Ingleby Cross tomorrow."

A folding chair was immediately made available for me and there I was, sitting in a back garden enjoying a beer with a welcoming family, once more touched by the kindness of strangers and reminded once more that there are lovely people in this world without agenda. It momentarily brought to mind an incident at an Aberdeen petrol station just before setting off on this adventure, educing a private emotional cognizance.

Our interaction ascertained that Rosa's sons were local to the area and were both benefitting from the Bank Holiday, hence a visit to Mum's for a barbecue. It transpired that I was the first Coast-to-Coaster to pass through, post-lockdown, and I shared details of my exploit thus far. I turned down the offer of a second tin of beer, thanking my hosts for their generosity, and retired back to my private garden, with their reminders of the impending hot weather for the week ahead.

Sat at the aforementioned picnic table, I enjoyed my nightcap in the surrounding peaceful and dusky stillness, completing another amazing day on this extraordinary journey, approximately 125 miles in. The realisation of where my head was at, after nine days of hiking and reflection, now induced some acknowledgement that my lovelorn actions over the previous few months had been cringeworthy to say the least, and I certainly hadn't helped myself.

December 2020

How could she so suddenly stop loving me and stop being attracted to me? In hindsight, I may have quickly reached the 'denial' stage of my grief as I simply refused to believe that I would never be intimate with my wife again. The thought evoked dull pain and I couldn't simply shrug off my feelings for her. I wanted to believe that an alternative type of relationship was possible and an opportunity to probe possibilities would present itself a few days after moving into the new place.

Joanne got in touch, sharing photos of her having her hair done like we were best buddies. She advised that a former work associate had some furniture to give away, and enquired if we could use my car as that had the towing hook for the trailer. There was a free microwave oven involved in the deal, a requirement for my new place.

On the journey, I asked her outright.

"Joanne, are you absolutely sure that any physical relationship between us is beyond any possibility? I know we've separated but I'd rather be used by you than not. You were quick enough to jump back into Dave's bed, despite all the shit you say he put you through."

I realised that recalling her previous promiscuity, for which she claimed to be sorry about, probably wasn't the wisest move and that may have contributed to her cutting retort.

"To be honest, Matt, the sex wasn't that great anyway," Joanne nonchalantly replied in a manner like she was describing how much she hadn't enjoyed her lunch.

I stopped breathing for a few seconds.

"Ouch, sweetie. That was low."

Having listened to Joanne regularly describe her difficult sexual background from the outset of our relationship, her callous comment felt like a kick in the teeth after years of paying sensitive attention and showing awareness and respect to her troubled sexual past.

The irony wasn't lost on me that I was hearing this apathetic sideswipe from the woman who had continually told me how much better than her previous partners I had been.

"I don't think you mean that, Joanne," I asserted before concluding, "Just never say never, Joanne. It's no skin off your nose."

Securing her requested items in the trailer together with my new cooking appliance, I conveyed Joanne back to the 'Shire. My newly-estranged wife had mentioned in earlier conversation that she had been in Forfar earlier in the week. When she later repeated that she had been to the Angus town, some 60 miles south, and then advised of a further forthcoming visit, it was clear what she wanted to happen.

"Ok, Joanne, why are you visiting Forfar?" I enquired in a slightly resigned tone.

"Oh, right. I've been seeing a lady," she began, enthusiastically and completely oblivious to my underlying acquiescence.

"Oh aye. A lady?" I interrupted in a light-hearted tone, momentarily taking my eyes off the road to aim a raised eyebrow at my passenger who smiled in response.

"She's actually a specialist psychologist, Matt. I'm just trying to work out who I am and why I act the way I do."

"In Forfar? No psychologists or psychiatrists in Aberdeen?"

"She comes highly recommended. By the way, she's a psychologist, not a psychiatrist."

"Whatever," I replied, realising that my wife was seeking psychological help AFTER ruining my life, and from within an area well away from home, perhaps for privacy reasons, a bit like her original dating profile.

It was heart-wrenching to drop off Joanne at my home of the previous six years and head back in surreality to the sudden new home I didn't want to be in. Another trip to the off-licence was par for the course.

The support of Jennifer and the kids was appreciated during this distressing period as they kindly kept in regular contact. A couple of days later, Jennifer referred to a telephone conversation from the previous evening that I couldn't remember, and I had to concede I was using alcohol in an attempt to be somewhere else during my period of annual leave.

Another few nights of inebriation elapsed before my beloved St Mirren enjoyed a rare victory over Rangers in the Scottish League Cup with a last-minute winning goal, made even more significant as it was Rangers' first defeat of the season in their 28th game. My elation was slightly tempered as, unbelievably, towards the end of the match, Joanne was sending messages regarding the latest score and cheering on my team. Coming from the woman who had criticised my interest in football, misunderstood my enthusiasm for the sport and had recently ended our marriage on an apparent whim, my head-scratching was becoming routine.

My eldest daughter, having enjoyed some previous memorable moments regarding St Mirren, also phoned to share in the excitement of the result. During the ensuing conversation, we arranged for her to come over in the morning for a catch-up. Using the surprise result as a convenient excuse, my over-indulgence in celebratory drinks would result in my oversleeping for that particular engagement and my frustrated daughter's subsequent pep-talk the following morning concerning a strategy, leading to conversation around the Coast-to-Coast.

The thought of planning and preparation for a long-distance hiking challenge encouraged me to find some appreciation that life would have to go on, with or without Joanne, and following Number One's visit, I perused some online reading material to form a more detailed impression of the Coast-to-Coast than my previous cursory glimpses.

Later in the evening, Joanne would share screenshots from online conversations with her niece Katie who was due to be married the following month. With limited numbers allowed at the wedding due to Covid regulations, Joanne's screenshot displayed her message to Katie, "*So exciting sweetie. If Matt can't come, can I take Angela as a partner?*"

I stared at the message in perplexity, trying to understand why she would share this with me, notwithstanding her ignorance of the fact that I had been looking forward to the wedding of the lovely young couple I had built a friendship with. When pressed by Katie as to when she would know about my attendance, Joanne's further screenshot stung a bit.

"*Let's just say he won't be there ok. He is gutted by the way.*"

My frustration and disappointment at her obtuseness towards the upheaval and upset caused by her actions would continue unabated.

The following day, she telephoned to advise that her mother had passed away. As someone that Joanne hadn't spoken to in over 10 years and whom she openly despised, it was no big deal and she would certainly not be attending the funeral. I would later learn that Joanne expressed surprise during communication with Number Two that I hadn't phoned my daughters to tell them that her hated mother, a woman I had never met, had passed away.

Another day later, Joanne forwarded a screenshot of the 'death notice' in the local newspaper, accompanied by her own deprecating comments on its impassive content. Shortly afterwards, she forwarded a photograph of the newspaper cutting detailing her father's 'death notice' from years before I met her, highlighting the much more affectionate content. However, less than 48 hours later, a further message advised me that she had now destroyed her framed photograph of her father with accompanying disparaging comments about his "enabling" of her mother.

My bald patch was in real danger of accelerated expansion from the perpetual head-scratching, but her apparent compulsion to keep in touch where possible allowed me to hope that an alternative form of relationship would remain a possibility.

A week before Christmas, I awoke to find another message:
"Here's an interesting question for you. Do you see me as having different versions? How many? Which do you like and which are you not fussed with?"

Glossing over the glaring egotism in the first sentence of her message and the inference that there would be nothing I didn't like, rather just be 'not fussed with', I took the time to reply.

"Well, the list isn't exhaustive, but here's a starter for ten. Firstly, there's the unpredictable Joanne who will make snap decisions without any rationale; the Joanne who wants to do everything herself without asking for any assistance; the Joanne who will misinterpret the most innocent comment to the nth degree before placing me in the doghouse; these versions can be frustrating.
The bouncy Joanne who can exude an infectious enthusiasm for fun; the Joanne who expressed her love for me daily; the Joanne who appreciates kindness (and my cooking); the Joanne who has a sharp sense of humour and laughs at my reciprocal humour; I particularly like these versions.
There's also the potential future version of Joanne who could be intriguing."

The last sentence was aimed at inducing thoughts of that potential future relationship.

Her tactless reply arrived a little later.
"Just trying to understand my versions and thanks for your help with that. I appreciate your time as it's not really your bag now."
The latter sentence was fairly cutting, considering she had asked me in the present tense before reminding me that her 'versions' were now nothing to do with me less than a fortnight after I moved out. Her reply included an online link to an article she had found in a psychology magazine regarding Complex Trauma, Borderline Personality Disorder and Structural Dissociation but I refrained from enquiring if she was self-diagnosing herself with all three. The lengthy article included a section on 'Signs of Structural Dissociation', one of which was 'Partial Amnesia', accompanied with the sentence, *"Even if we know something happened, it does not feel real. We lose parts of our memories and so our story of the past does not make sense"*

It did make me ponder an extremely fateful evening back in 2015 near Inverness, the consequences of which remained particularly prevalent.

Communication remained regular over the Christmas period, from discussing the conclusion to a multi-season drama we had been watching prior to our split, to little 13-year-old Squeak being diagnosed with the canine disease 'Cushing's syndrome' and placed on steroids. Small festive gifts were also exchanged and spirits were lifted when Number One and Jake, her partner of the past five years, announced their engagement.

I was working dayshift on Christmas Day and had hoped that Joanne may have kept a low profile under the circumstances. However, a lunchtime scroll through social media disclosed a photo of my estranged wife drinking and enjoying festivities with her friend Kim, who would provide today's company. It reminded me of a previous disparaging declaration by Joanne regarding her former accommodation provider's lack of sociability but I suppose without me, she could simply "use" someone else.

A sombre Christmas, totally unexpected just over a month prior, came and went, and two days later, another message was received from Joanne.

"Hi Matt, hope you are doing fine. Wondering if you want a catch-up? I'm taking Squeak to the vet on Hogmanay so we could maybe meet for a walk?"

Joanne's legitimate travel into the city for veterinary reasons would not contravene the Covid travel regulations re-imposed on Boxing Day as a result of a surge in infections and a liaison was duly arranged for New Year's Eve.

Since splitting up with my wife, one disturbing aspect would be what I referred to as "Joanne dreams". These would generally entail a vivid dream, in which Joanne had apologised for putting me through more heartache, asked me to forgive her and to return to normality. I would accept her apology, breath a huge sigh of relief and revel in the delight that my marriage had been saved. On awakening and realising it was only a dream, those first five minutes of the day proved very difficult, realising that the brief euphoria had in fact just been a dormant delusion.

I felt that the intervening 'Twixmas' week wouldn't pass without online discourse and my instincts were proved correct when I awoke one morning to find another message from Joanne regarding her own overnight subconscious vagaries.

"Got woken again last night with what I believe are called night terrors or parasomnia. All part of my jigsaw."

Whilst reading her message indicating her discovery of a potential new addition to the list of disorders to diagnose herself with, another message would follow almost simultaneously.

"Something evil this way comes."

I wasn't sure if misquoting Macbeth's witches or indeed the title of Ray Bradbury's classic 1960's novel could be added to her list. Her messages were bizarrely accompanied by a screenshot of her Google search page, listing numerous previous online searches ranging from "dissociative identity disorder sleep" to "parasomnia night terrors".

A third message arrived post-screenshot.

"My searching at 4.20am when I was desperately hiding under the covers. Fuck sake I thought to myself. Just how fucked up am I? . . . . rhetorical"

I desisted from sharing details of my own troubling dreams which I figured would be given short shrift in comparison to her self-absorption and I tried unsuccessfully to lighten the mood somewhat, sending her a photo of my black dressing gown hanging on a hook on the bedroom door.

"Try waking up to that in the dark," my message with the photo.

Her concluding and confusing messages arrived.

"You can vouch, mine is a regular occurrence? I think I saved us several times in the past."

Nothing automatically sprang to mind as she continued.

"See, I'm not a fruit loop. Just stuck in high stress arousal, that's all."

'High Stress Arousal' appeared to be yet another addition to the list.

The last day of 2020 duly arrived and we met at a popular wooded area within the city boundary for a stroll and a catch-up, not only with Joanne, but also with my beautiful and poorly Bichon Frisé.

As we walked, general chit-chat regarding family and wee Squeak ensued before she took the opportunity to revisit her previous correspondence regarding her 'versions' and appeared keen to point out that her sessions with her psychologist were progressive.

"So you know I have different versions," Joanne reiterated, before casually asking, "Do you know which version of me you are with just now?"

In response to my shaking head indicating my negative response, she declared, "The version that adores you."

Pausing to make her remark in a friendly manner within my personal space, I wasn't sure if Joanne wanted me to kiss her or wanted me to think she wanted me to kiss her. Either way, there were other pedestrians around and we carried on strolling, changing the subject. Once back at our vehicles, we undertook to meet up in the new year and I was happy to do so, hoping that the version of Joanne that had just openly expressed her adoration for me may still present an opportunity to be in some form of relationship, moving forward.

"Just do me a favour, Joanne. Never say never. If it never happens, at least I can still have hope."

I was aware that Joanne was still wearing her wedding ring and perhaps it was hope combined with the imminent new year that compelled me to ask.

"Are you still going to wear your ring?"

Joanne paused, apparently giving my question a few seconds of thought before replying.

"Tell you what," she commenced, simultaneously removing the "anam charaidh"-inscribed silver band from her wedding finger and handing it to me, "you take this and give me yours."

I didn't give much thought to her spontaneous direction and complied accordingly, consequently questioning on my drive home why I had simply followed her senseless suggestion without question.

On arriving back at my apartment, it felt a little strange not to be wearing my Celtic token of wedlock as I safely placed Joanne's corresponding piece of silver into the rear of a drawer on my bedside cabinet. Shortly afterwards, I received a text message.

"Was nice to catch up but I felt really sad on the way home. Taking part in an online Hogmanay quiz with Scott tonight. You up for helping?"

As it was a 'school night', I agreed to assist in the early part of the evening.

Whilst waiting for the quiz to commence, Joanne again texted.

"So, are we pals?"

After affirming my wishes face-to-face with Joanne earlier in the day, she was well aware that I desired to be more than pals thus I perceived her positive vibe as hopeful.

"Of course we are."

With a 5.30am start on the initial day of 2021, I headed to bed before 10pm, receiving a final text from Joanne.

"Happy New Year, Matt. May all your dreams come true."

With the events of the past month and the conversation earlier that day, I allowed myself an ironic smile at yet more thoughtlessness from the person who at that moment, controlled the outcome to those dreams she referred to. I wondered if she had heard of the word 'schadenfreude'.

It was teatime on New Year's Day when a social media notification advised that I had been tagged in a post by Joanne McKay. On opening the link, Joanne had posted a picture of her feet adorned with the novelty slippers I purchased as a Christmas gift, thanking me for the ace gift. With only a very select few aware of our situation, the post purported that we were still very much a couple with no indication of her ending the relationship over a month earlier. Yet more resultant head-scratching ensued with messages regarding her overt coarseness duly arriving from some of those within that select few.

That opening week of 2021 continued with the now routine bizarreness as she unnecessarily shared a message she had sent to her family.

"Hiya, that's my family know. Here's what I sent them:

(Hi and here's us into the new year. Hope you had a good one. Just to let you know, at the end of November, I split up with Matt. He has been living in Aberdeen for the past month and we're officially separated.
I know this will come as a shock to you and Matt would say it was to him too. But things changed at the end of 2019 when we went to Couple Counselling. Our different personalities just bring out the worst in one another.)

Sent this to people we care about."

Having previously agreed as to the success of the Couple Counselling, I considered Joanne's reference to it in her message to her family as a fairly pathetic attempt to hoodwink them into thinking this had been coming for a while. The line *"and Matt would say it was to him too"* was also egotistically ensuring that her family knew the split was her decision. This deluded show of decisiveness to her family, less than five years after her fateful proposal of marriage, would only serve to enhance her reputation within her family as a fairly imbalanced individual. My instant reaction was to contact members of her family I remained close with, to respectfully reiterate that her message was very much her own perception of things and bore no resemblance whatsoever to my own views.

Throughout the early weeks of the year, contact remained sporadic on general matters and I agreed to uplift a belated Christmas gift for Number One on a mid-month Friday evening whilst returning from Moray. After several knocks at my former front door, it appeared there had been a communication breakdown and I carried on towards Aberdeen. Ten minutes into that resumption of my journey, I received a call from Joanne.

"I'm so sorry Matt. Scott says he heard knocking at the door and he assumed I would get it, but I must have been out in the office."

Unperturbed by this very plausible reason, I acknowledged her call and agreed to uplift the item another time. Joanne's response took me my surprise.

"That wasn't deliberate, Matt."

"What wasn't deliberate?"

"Not answering the door to you," she replied.

"Why would you deliberately not answer the door to me when we had arranged for me to pick stuff up at a specific time? Of course it wasn't deliberate," my perplexed retort.

"Just letting you know. I'll be in touch. See you later."

It felt like Joanne's comment was inadvertent acknowledgement of her egotistical tendency to be pointlessly spiteful towards me.

Following delays due to wintry weather, we arranged for me to pick up the parcel towards the end of January, incorporating a walk and catch-up with Squeak. Prior to the walk, I really didn't want to be bringing up the subject again of being in some form of relationship with Joanne. An idea occurred to me over the festive period which would prevent the subject from recurring and would simultaneously afford the opportunity to inject some humour into the situation, oblivious to the consequent cringing further down the line. I prepared a printed declaration which I would allow Joanne to retain and thus the matter could remain latent.

Joanne, for your retention:

"The Ex-Certificate (see what I did there)

I, Matt McKay, being of questionably sane mind and body, hereby declare the following proclamation from the start of the year of our Lord, 2021. Mrs Joanne McKay is hereby afforded 'carte blanche' to take any sort of advantage of the above Matt McKay in any way she chooses, desires or orders, whether this take place at his home or any other location as designated by Mrs McKay. Mrs McKay will, at all times, have full control of any such liaison and Mr McKay will do as he's told.

Having made this proclamation in writing, Mr McKay acknowledges that it provides irrefutable documentary evidence that any such liaison can in no way be misinterpreted, misconstrued or misunderstood as anything other than what Mrs Mckay deems it to be.

Signed: Matt McKay

On returning to our vehicles following an enjoyable walk and catch-up with Joanne and Squeak involving amiable chit-chat, I retrieved the enveloped 'declaration' from my car and offered it to my estranged wife.
"What's that?" she smiled.
"With reference to you 'never saying never', it's my wee declaration, moving forward, that will save either of us mentioning it again," I explained with a corresponding smile.
Her facial expression suddenly changed, "I don't want it Matt."
"Ok Joanne, it's a bit of humour and nothing you don't know already," I reassured her.
"Nope, don't want it," Joanne insisted and got into her vehicle.
Not for the first time or indeed the twenty-first time in our affiliation, I was slightly taken aback by her unexpected impulsiveness.
"Oh well, whatever you think," I observed.
"I'll see you later," she replied as she started her engine and drove off, leaving me standing with my undelivered envelope and feeling a little foolish.

Despite the innocent intentions, the note didn't transpire to be one of my better decisions and I had to accept that at the time, I was continuing to miss my wife and struggling to accept things. After that disappointing end to what was otherwise such an amicable stroll, I messaged Joanne on returning home.
"Thanks for a lovely walk. Nice to see you. Perhaps I made my note sound more than it was. Only a bit of fun as you're already fully aware of the context of the content."
Her reply was cordial.
"Yes, it was a lovely walk. We do blether away fine. No bother. I do get the gist of your note, but no, it's not what I want."

I knew that it wasn't what she wanted, this week, but had asked her to 'never say never' to allow that little bit of hope. Consequently, there was abject disappointment that this appeared to be exactly what she had just done. With my little bit of hope seemingly eradicated, I took some time out to consider her reply and my precarious situation regarding my own mental health.

An hour later, I was surprised to see my phone screen advise of an incoming voice call from Joanne.

"Hi Matt, I just didn't like the way we went our separate ways this afternoon. Just touching base to make sure we're ok."

"I didn't like it either, sweetie. My note was just a bit of fun so I wasn't expecting that reaction."

"I know that," she replied, "but can we just drop the talk about being in some form of relationship?"

"That's exactly what my little missive was intended to do," I explained, "which you would have understood had you taken a moment to read it."

My gut instinct was sensing a finality about the conversation and I allowed myself the weekend to gather my thoughts.

Hitherto, I had been bowling along in the vain hope that some kind of relationship could be rekindled, imploring Joanne to 'never say never' as my underlying feelings remained despite everything she was putting me through.

A most difficult decision had to be made as I logged into my e-mail account on the Sunday evening.

Hi Sweetie,

I've taken the weekend to confirm my only real option and this is undoubtedly a difficult e-mail for me to send.

After meeting up on Friday and your reply to my message after I got home, I feel backed into a difficult corner. Fed up with pretending to be ok, I'm compelled into making one of the hardest decisions for the sake of my mental health and any potential recovery from a badly broken heart.

On that fateful morning in November, I was a happily married man making love to his partner, not a perfect man as none of us are, but happily looking forward to spending the rest of my life with my beautiful wife. Within a few hours, my wife decided the marriage was over and my world unravelled horribly.

The transition was always going to be easier for you as you simply shipped me out. Your life would continue as normal and disruption would be minimal and that was what you suddenly felt you had to do for Joanne. You have also become wrapped up in your own self-diagnosed conditions and that has unfortunately resulted in your consistent lack of sensitivity to the situation you have created for me. As I've alluded to in person, there is no point going through the numerous incidents as it isn't going to matter anyway, moving forward, as Friday's message was the last straw.

I loved meeting up and spending time in your company but it naturally reaffirmed my attraction to you. Unlike yourself, I can't just automatically switch off that attraction after more than seven years. Clearly I would rather have been in a proper relationship with you but any relationship is infinitely preferable to none. Very sadly however, your message on Friday has killed that little piece of hope stone dead.

Much like the similar situation from the characters in 'Sunshine on Leith', "I canny just be your pal", but take it as the compliment it is. Happy to stay in touch but cosy walks and chats are going to have to cease forthwith as with that little bit of hope removed, they will simply become more counter-productive to my mental health. I trust you'll understand.

If you do ever decide to take life a bit less seriously and make it potentially a bit more 'interesting' before we shuffle off this mortal coil, you know where I am. It's ok though, I won't hold my breath.

Take care

Matt
X

Our lives were inextricably linked through families and dozens of mutual friends and therefore some form of contact would be inevitable. It would come to my attention through some of those mutual contacts that Joanne's reaction to my correspondence was to "restrict" me on social media, whereby I could only view her "public" posts. With the option to just "unfriend" me, I was convinced she wasn't bird-brained enough not to know that with so many mutual friends, her attention-seeking actions would be obvious. I refrained from offering any desired response she clearly sought.

I couldn't deny times were hard as I continued to adjust to single life. So many little things happened during periods of incommunicado that I would instinctively want to share with Joanne. Each time a reminder that I was no longer with her. I missed my friend, missed holding her hand, missed random hugs and kisses in passing around the house, missed watching TV programmes together, missed chats in the bath, missed our amusingly inane routine when leaving for work and the list went on. My 'denial' showed no signs of letting up, however, I had to try to focus on preparation for my late Spring adventure across England, pouring over online maps and forums, procuring new kit as required, and undertaking practice hikes.

On the football front, St Mirren had created a welcome and temporary distraction, reaching the semi-finals of both national cup competitions. Defeats to Livingston and St Johnstone followed, the latter cup final scheduled to coincide with Day One of my Coast-to-Coast.

In early February, Joanne forwarded a photo of some important-looking mail which I asked her to open. As suspected, due to being classed as immuno-suppressed due to my ulcerative colitis, I would receive the newly rolled-out Covid immunisation expeditiously.

Valentine's Day arrived at the end of a particularly cold and snowy period. Social media was to be avoided to prevent the constant reminder that I was missing my sweetheart. We had never acknowledged Valentine's Day in the traditional way but rather rechristened it "Creme Egg Day" and exchanged the well-known chocolate confectionery associated with Easter. That was us.

With my birthday only days after Valentine's, I surfaced on an early Sunday afternoon from nightshift and headed to Moray to spend a couple of days with Numbers Two and Three.

On return from Moray on my birthday, it was a little relief to find a birthday card had arrived in the post as it would have been a disappointing end to an otherwise excellent day.

Her own birthday arrived at the end of the month and I posted a card and a belated Creme Egg. Receipt was duly acknowledged via text message and I took the opportunity in a non-confrontational manner to mention how I would be unable to see her messages on social media due to being blocked. Her instantaneous retort was to absolve herself of any intent and shortly afterwards, she "surprisingly" discovered that I was indeed on her "restricted" list and would therefore be derestricted forthwith. This tiny victory elicited a brief altitude gain on the 2021 rollercoaster, quickly meeting a despairingly rapid descent as I had inadvertently granted myself access to my non-existence.

Eradication was the word in my head. I foolishly continued to scroll through the previous seven years of her social media as my heart simultaneously reached for new nadirs on witnessing the complete eradication of our relationship and my existence in her life. All tagged posts, all tagged photos, meticulously removed. I wasn't naive enough to think that perhaps one day in the future, Joanne may remove romantic links and photos but this, so hurriedly, was debilitating, coupled with the knowledge that all my own previously joint tags were now individual tags. Ultimately my own fault as I had broken my own code and was taking social media seriously.

Just 24 hours later, on the eve of the 5th anniversary of her romantic leap-day proposal, she was haphazardly back in her fluffy non-consequential world, forwarding a 90-second video of 'our' little dog and her daughter's new pup playfully gambolling around 'our' home. Yet again, her callous lack of awareness induced a tear.

Roll on the month of March.

Day 10 – Brompton-on-Swale to Ingleby Cross

"Hey Matt, look at him," Joanne suddenly declared.
Her declaration distracted me from the meal we were enjoying.
"Look at who?" I enquired, glancing around the restaurant.
"That guy at the table just across there. On his own too and he's absolutely gorgeous. Think I'll go across and chat him up."
"You what?"
My reaction was ignored as Joanne changed tables to join the handsome stranger, ensuring she was loud enough for all fellow diners to hear.
"Hi, how are you, I'm Joanne," she opened and nodded back to our table, "That's my estranged husband I'm having a meal with. We're separated and I'm single and you're gorgeous. Can I buy you a drink?"
My shock at her wanton coquettishness caused my eyes to open and I was suddenly looking around the inside of my tent.

I'm no dream interpreter and I don't know of anyone capable of casting an oneirocritical eye on what just occurred prior to waking up that morning, but it was certainly of a different genre to any previously experienced dormant vision regarding Joanne.

It was the final day of May, shortly after 6am when the loud honk of one of the advertised killer geese began to penetrate the birdsong and morning mist in what gradually became more of a dawn cacophony than a dawn chorus. Saving my gas, I made use of the kettle provided at the indoor section and enjoyed my Monday morning brew with a couple of triangular breadcakes known as scufflers. When in Rome, as the saying goes.

I packed away my kit, trying to shake out the dewy dampness on the tent and left my holdall in the allocated shed for pick-up. The clinging mist had certainly reduced the temperature and I would be donning my waterproof jacket for the early part of the day, however the forecast promised another scorcher in due course. I returned back through the yard towards the house under the watchful eyes of those waterfowl non-silent assassins together with Mr Ed's good morning nod from the stable. I settled up with Rosa, insisting she took more than the paltry sum advised, and was soon once more on my way through the village and heading under six thundering lanes of the A1(M), one of four 'motorway' sections of the A1 between Edinburgh and London.

Today's segment of my expedition would involve crossing the Vale of Mowbray, a low-lying section of agricultural land filling the gap between the Yorkshire Dales and the North York Moors. An advertisement on social media seen the previous evening would necessitate a negligible detour off the trail at Danby Wiske to visit Vicky and Steve, the proprietors of the recently opened Church Holme Camping, complete with tuck shop for passing hikers.

Bridge Road in Brompton-on-Swale reached a T-junction at the Farmer's Arms pub where I turned right to very briefly join Gatherley Road before once again joining a path on the north bank of the River Swale on my eastward quest. A lake to my left, about half the size of a football pitch, showed potential to be a lunch-stop for later hikers from Richmond. However, perhaps in recognition of the potential for unwanted guests, the local farmer had delineated the boundary of the lake with a fence and an accompanying signpost indicating that the resident aggressive bull didn't take kindly to human interlopers around his habitat.

My three-day association with England's fastest-flowing river was nearing its end as the path continued east to traverse a quarry, away from the southbound river, and towards the village of Bolton-on-Swale, the last mention of the word 'Swale' on this journey . . . well, in the guidebook anyway. After following a farm track, I re-joined the B6271 momentarily. My research revealed that this road was the main route from Richmond to Northallerton . . . and I knew a couple of folks from there. A couple of folks I certainly didn't know were sat on a bench ahead of me just as the main drag turned left into East View towards the village's focal point, St Mary's Church.
I assumed they were fellow hikers due to their accompanying rucksacks. They appeared to be late 20's /early 30's in age, but looked rather tired, and had stopped for some breakfast.
As I passed in the morning mist, the slightly elder looking gentleman of the two enquired, "Hi there. You walking the Coast-to-Coast?"

"I certainly am," I replied, "Just left Brompton-on-Swale this morning."
"We couldn't get a spot at Reeth the day before yesterday due to
some annual fair so we pushed on and wild-camped. Set off really
early this morning so just want to find a spot with facilities today.
We're tired."
"I saw online just last night that there is a new campsite in Danby
Wiske. Church Holme. They have a social media page advertising
all camping facilities and a tuck shop. I'm planning to stop there for
lunch myself," I explained.
"Ok, thanks. I might give them a phone," my latest acquaintance
replied.
"All the best, good luck with the remainder," I concluded.
I had no idea how regularly these two brothers would feature in the
remainder of my journey.

The beautiful 14th-century St Mary's Church added to the list of
Grade 2 listed buildings on the trail. A welcoming sign on the gate
invited hikers to utilise the facilities provided for making hot drinks
and help themselves to snacks, inserting the requisite fee into the
honesty box of course. Within the churchyard cemetery was an
obelisk dedicated to the memory of one Henry Jenkins, a man who
allegedly lived an unremarkable life of remarkable length. Born in
1501, he passed away in 1670 at the age of 169. So remarkable, in
fact, that it took until 1743, 74 years after his death for the obelisk to
be erected. Subsequent online research revealed that "longevity
claimant" Mr Jenkins stated under oath in 1667 that he was aged
166 years and could remember carrying arrows to the English
archers during the Battle of Flodden in 1513, some 154 years earlier.
I was fairly impressed as I regularly can't remember why I walked
into my kitchen.

A short distance outside the village, signage directed me to cross a
field towards Bolton Beck and I tracked this meandering burn over
more fields until joining a country road. I would be on this quiet and
flat country road for three and a half miles to the small village of
Streetlam, passing the tiny settlement of Whitwell en route. During
this slightly mundane period, the sun began radiating fully and the
suncream was lathered on once more. The sight of a vehicle on this
tranquil section was a rarity and motorised transport was easily
outnumbered by riders of both bicycles and horses.

As the road entered the environs of Streetlam, I noted that the large field to my left had football goalposts spaced an appropriate distance apart. The 'pitch' was dotted with around 22 grazing sheep, or was it 23 and the black one was the referee? I figured they might set up in a 4-4-ewe formation . . .

Before 'moving swiftly on', I ascertained that Streetlam Farmers FC compete in Division Two of the Hambleton Football Combination as featured inside the back pages of the locally circulated Darlington and Stockton Times. Based on previous experience, I guessed the brief match details had been phoned in by the club secretary, otherwise referred to in the local weekly as 'staff reporter'.

Leaving the road once more in the centre of the village, the trail passes around behind a horse enclosure prior to reaching a poorly defined overgrown and muddy section through some trees. Emerging from this less than enjoyable passage, I was met with the even less enjoyable prospect of crossing over two large fields densely populated with friends of a bovine persuasion . . . replete with their unsettling synchronised staring in my direction. The arrow centred on the little circular Coast-to-Coast sign attached to the gate at the field's entrance confirmed that there wasn't really an alternative and it was time to don the big boy hiking trousers and plough on.

Plough was an appropriate word as progress was hindered by the boggy conditions created by the field's occupants and I sped through as best I could. On reaching the far side of the field, feeling a sense of unnecessary embarrassment, I began to breathe again. The mood was lightened as a handwritten sign attached to a wire was emblazoned with "Live and Eletric".

Shocking . . . and that was just the spelling.

Re-joining the road for a brief uphill incline, I entered the village of Danby Wiske. Quickly reaching the centre of this small settlement, the hiker is welcomed by the modest village green comprising of two wooden benches to the front of The White Swan, the village pub which was closed. I already had other plans for lunch and a prominently-positioned laminated sign on the fence surrounding the village green reminded me I was only 200 metres from Church Holme Campsite.

Steve and Vicky had moved to Danby Wiske the previous October and converted an old small brick outhouse into a welcome and well-stocked tuck shop in addition to developing adjoining acreage into a small campsite with facilities. Steve was installing a new gate at the entrance in the now vibrant sunshine whilst Vicky introduced me to the facilities within the tuck shop which included home bakes, sweets, crisps and cold drinks within two fridges. Offering me a selection of sandwich fillings, she disappeared with my order, returning shortly thereafter with a freshly-made sandwich and a welcome mug of tea. Pleasant chat continued with my accommodating hosts, briefly interrupted by a telephone call from two brothers making camping arrangements. When the conversation turned to my precautionary reapplication of Compeed every few days, it was a welcome surprise that they could also provide replenishment of the modern gel-filled plasters.

After extending my visit with another mug of tea, I was complimenting my genial hosts on leaving when the two gentlemen I encountered in Bolton-on-Swale arrived at the freshly-erected gate. Acknowledging the group of recent acquaintances, I was on my way once more.

Passing back through the village green, both of the aforementioned wooden benches were now occupied, Colin, Rob and Bruce on one, Paul and Matthew on the other.

Having only just taken a lengthy lunch break, I was conscious of the nine miles ahead and only stopped to chat briefly with the former. Passing Paul and Matthew, the latter asked what I thought of the facilities at Church Holme and I heartily recommended.

"Really good facility, Matthew. Great tuck shop and Vicky can make you a sandwich. I was able to top up my Compeed supply too." With a mischievous smile, I continued, "Not sure about their knowledge on the local area though. They reckoned the River Swale was the fastest-flowing river in England."

"Yeh, thanks Matt. Are you still here?" my smiling namesake retorted as I marched off with a chuckle.

Following 20 minutes of road-walking, the trail crosses some fields diagonally before reaching the Oaktree Repairs Garage on the busy A167. Joining this bustling road on a well-trodden grass verge for a third of a mile, a sign by a stile directs into a field before the path enters a tree alley. With trees thick with leaves on either side leaving no scope for sunlight and lots of unavoidable mud, this section got my vote for the least enjoyable half-mile of the entire Coast-to-Coast. Emerging with muddy boots from this most banal passage onto a very brief section of a quiet country lane, I was to receive an unexpected pick-me-up. An approaching cyclist, a stocky similarly-aged chap, slowed down as he passed.

"Coast-to-Coast?" he loudly and cheerfully enquired whilst simultaneously raising his thumb.

"Yes", I replied, raising a walking pole.

"Good for you, lad," he exclaimed triumphantly.

A simple moment at a timely juncture which lifted my spirits and induced a smile to replace the slight grimace.

The route zig-zagged past four farms on a mixture of paths and drives. Leaving the last of these farms via a stile at Wray House, several items of fake sinister paraphernalia had been placed in the hiker's midst. A witch's broomstick, a skull, a spider, a stern-faced owl, a skeleton's detached hand hanging over the stile and a prominent sign attached to a post warning to "beware of the witch". My smile in appreciation of the efforts made by the farm to amuse Coast-to-Coasters was unexpectedly disrupted as I stepped onto the stile to trigger a sensor which activated the sound of cackling laughter. I never anticipated being cackled at by an invisible witch when I set out from St Bees, nine days and 130-odd miles ago.

Crossing railway lines and a couple of crop fields, I joined a quiet tarmac road which soon became a rough track for a mile and a half. The Vale of Mowbray crossing is considered by many the least captivating section of the route and combined with the warm sunshine, my limbs were beginning to ache a little, thus before leaving the shade of a treeline, I paused for a break and an afternoon cuppa. As I sat against a tree trunk by the side of the track, Colin, Rob and Bruce came past and stopped briefly. Staying in hotels and B&Bs, they weren't carrying brew-making material and Rob seemed particularly impressed that I could enjoy a cup of tea anywhere en route.

Setting off once more for the final couple of miles, two more farms were edged around before a lane led to Exelby Services on the northbound side of the A19, a major dual-carriageway. At the end of the lane stood a wooden "Coast-to-Coast" sign I was familiar with. Whilst returning north via the A19 from Number Two's participation in the British Figure Skating Championships in Sheffield in 2018 with Joanne and Number One, we stopped at Exelby Services. I had a photo taken by this sign and hoped to pass it again one day on foot.

Three years on and it was poignant that on this occasion, I had walked 140 miles to be reunited with the same piece of etched wood. Before undertaking the most dangerous road-crossing of the entire route, the excellent shop within the service station provided snacks and drinks, a necessity as the next village grocery shop would be in Glaisdale in two and a half days time. Colin, Rob and Bruce were being picked up here by their accommodation host and I bade them cheerio until tomorrow.

"Frogger" was a computer game developed in the early 1980s. In those primitive stages of home computing, the uncomplicated strategy involved trying to get one's frog safely across a busy road and river avoiding several obstacles. Faced with four lanes of busy traffic and two filter lanes of the A19, I found myself transported back to those early teenage years sat in front of my ZX Spectrum. This was reality "Frogger", 2021 style. Waiting for an appropriate gap, I briskly crossed to the relative sanctuary of the small grassed area between the central reservation metal barriers. A lengthy wait was required before safe passage was procured across the south-bound carriageway to join the lane leading to the village of Ingleby Arncliffe and on to the adjoining Ingleby Cross.

On approaching the centre of the village, I passed 'The Joiner's Shop', an old workshop transformed into a café, promising "fully traceable single origin coffees", a phrase I couldn't even pretend to understand but may well have been music to the ears of connoisseurs. Painted neatly across the black wooden lintel above the double doors was wording indicating that the establishment was 140 miles from St Bees and 50 miles from Robin Hood's Bay. Again, two miles appeared to have disappeared into the ether. At the village cross-roads sat The Blue Bell, a large inviting country inn. A sizeable grassed area to the rear provided camping facilities and it transpired that as the lone camper, I once again had my own shower and toilet, a toilet I had used before, passing en route to the production of Man of La Mancha' in Leeds in 2017. Refreshingly, the fact that I had briefly visited The Bluebell Inn with Joanne four years earlier evoked no feelings of despondency. Six months earlier, that lack of gloom would have seemed very improbable.

I set up camp and made use of my exclusive shower facilities before returning to my tent. My daily admin revealed that I had sustained another blister on the right side of my right heel. The cartilage at the back of my right knee was also producing some pain at the beginning and end of the last couple of days but thankfully felt ok whilst hiking. Minor ailments were to be expected after 140 miles and it was hoped that they remained of the minor variety for the remaining 52 miles. Just a few yards from the tent, I occupied one the vacant picnic tables dispersed around the rear of the pub and ordered a pint of Theakston Dark Smooth, brewed just 20 miles away in the town of Masham. Taking my time, I enjoyed the late afternoon sunshine and the ambience of the pub garden setting amidst the muffled chattering of the other clientele.

Early evening arrived and on entering the establishment, there was a homely feel, with its table lamps positioned around the bar and dining area, illuminating the pre-booked table I was shown to. Passing through the bar area, I once again encountered Paul and Matthew from Northallerton, a town now just eight miles away and, unsurprisingly, they appeared to be in the company of friends. My fellow hikers were keen to recommend the 'parmo', a word I was completely unfamiliar with. I was allocated a table for four and with no readily viewable romantic ornamentation and the pub not overly busy on this Monday evening, there was a fair chance that, unlike in Reeth, the chairs wouldn't be required elsewhere. Also notable was that my table was located near the entrance to the kitchen, the door to which was ajar, a somewhat insignificant detail . . . at this point. Perusing the menu which included 'parmo', some brisk online research revealed that this recommended dish originated in nearby Middlesbrough. It consisted of a breaded cutlet of chicken topped with a white béchamel sauce and cheese. The dish also attracted some notoriety for allegedly containing up to 2,500 calories and up to 150 grams of fat. Just the job, I cheekily endorsed, and being the 'fun guy' I could be, I went one step further and ordered the large 'parmo al funghi'.

Whilst waiting for my locally-recommended heart attack on a plate, my audible attention was drawn to the two older ladies sitting nearby and their dissatisfaction with their repast. Their accents suggested they were from the Emerald Isle, somewhere south of the divide. "I'm telling you, Bernadette. My burger isn't great and I'm not sure how fresh this salad is. How's yours?"

"I'm with you on that one, Imogen," Bernadette replied, "I've had better. Shall we just complain and maybe get something else from the menu?"

Drawing the attention of the teenage waitress, the Irish ladies explained that they were not enjoying their imperfect patties and wished to 'send them back' and have something else.

"No problem, I'll speak to the chef," their pubescent attendant replied.

The problem lay in my earlier observation that the kitchen door was ajar and some louder remarks were liable to be heard by patrons. Subsequently, a loud male voice emanated from the direction of that open kitchen door.

"What's their problem? There's fuck all wrong with the burgers. I've got some lasagne going spare but that's it for fuck's sake. It's Monday."

'Awkward' was the word that sprung to my mind as the young lady re-emerged and returned to the table of the Celtic guests, but before she could explain the outcome of her excursion into the kitchen, Bernadette or Imogen had clearly been privy to the same interaction and saved the waitress an explanation.

"We'll try the lasagne, thanks."

I sensed their general attitude lacked the spirit and camaraderie that I had experienced throughout this adventure thus far, and it was safe to assume that these elderly Irish colleens were not part of the Coast-to-Coast community.

I had no such grievance with my fare and thoroughly enjoyed the local indelicate delicacy with added mushrooms, complemented with a side salad (yes, really) and a portion of potato wedges, all washed down with a couple of pints of local ale, naturally.

Stuffed to the gunnels, I returned through to the bar and shared my accord on the deliciousness of a 'parmo' with Paul. Matthew and their friends. My fellow hikers advised that they were walking some 20 miles the following day to The Lion Inn on Blakey Ridge and as my itinerary had me arriving two days hence at the Lion Inn, this was to be farewell to the acquaintances who would forever remain responsible for my knowledge that the River Swale is indeed the fastest-flowing river in England.

I purchased a final pint and returned outside to the rear garden picnic tables as the sun was about to disappear beyond the adjoining village cricket field. Enjoying my fifth drink of the evening in yet another peaceful setting, my train of thought turned to my recently acquired knowledge regarding the River Swale. How does science discover this fact? Why would science want to know this fact? To declare a fastest river, does that mean there are speed statistics for every river in England? Is the speed constant or do they take an average from various parts? Does it involve a huge nationwide game of Poohsticks or something slightly more sophisticated than A.A. Milne's literary whimsy? Do they float an unmanned vessel down the river and point a speed gun at it? Should I have no more drinks and retire for the evening?

Acknowledging that midnight would herald the month of June, I was reminded of a quirky monthly marital custom, a memory somewhat sullied in recent months.

March 2021

Following the gut-wrenching end to February, any upbeat and hopeful expectations that March would be more kind were obliterated, astonishingly less than 30 seconds into the month! As I patrolled around on my nightshift, a message was received on the stroke of midnight from Joanne. It simply contained two emoticons indicating a pinch and a punch for the first of the month. I stared at the screen incredulously. One of 'our' things. An indication of the romantic, fun marriage I was very happy to be in and a stark reminder of what she had ended on a whim. I was trying to comprehend why she was doing this. Was she trying to tell me she was thinking of me? If so, why? Was she just toying with my heartstrings like she was sticking pins into a voodoo doll? Had her ego gone completely off the scale? On a darker note, as these incidents continued to build consistently, I was once again drawn to thoughts of the reputation acquired by her late mother.

At times like this, I hated myself for loving her, trying to convince myself that her continuous digging into my cardiac chambers was albeit thoughtless but ultimately unintentional,
I didn't react until later in the shift. A simple GIF of a man shaking his head in a friendly but exasperated manner. Nothing too reactive but on point, a reaction to her thoughtlessness which consequently heralded a few weeks of incommunicado.

Towards the end of the month, I received a text message from my stepdaughter Angela.
"*Sorry to message you with such shite news but we wanted you to know that Squeak is not doing great. Vet says she doesn't have long. If you're up to it, we can arrange for you to see her. I can get her so you don't have to see Mum but thought you'd want to see her (Squeak) before that happens.*"

I couldn't quite believe the pretentious insinuation that I couldn't face Joanne under such sad circumstances and immediately messaged my estranged wife to commiserate, indicating my hope to see Squeak in early course. Her reply, indicating that if I didn't want to see her in person, she could arrange for me to see the dog with Angela, confirmed my former partner's delusional neurosis and I made it clear that I had no problem in meeting Joanne and Squeak together. A meeting was duly arranged for the Friday of that week as I would be passing on my way to Moray.

Before then, accompanied by yet more perturbed head-scratching, the month of April would see disturbing and insensitive repetition as Joanne once more egotistically forwarded a pinch and a punch on the stroke of midnight. This time, as I was retiring for the evening, I chose to ignore her doltish disregard for my disposition.
I subsequently received a message from her in the morning indicating that Squeak was really struggling and a vet's appointment had been arranged. Sorrowfully, a further message following the appointment advised that our little dog would be taking a terminal journey to the veterinary practice that evening. I was due to visit the following day and therefore rearranged to visit that same afternoon.

I felt an air of apprehension as I approached the threshold of my former home for the first time in over two months.
My knock on the front door was met with Joanne's shout from within. "It's open."
I entered the hallway and continued into the sitting room. The gorgeous Squeak lay in her little dog bed looking sorry for herself as I approached her for an emotional reunion.
After a few minutes of poignant catch-up with my poorly Bichon Frise, Joanne was sat on her sofa with paperwork in her lap.
"Just sorting out my books for March. Couldn't believe it was April already when I sent you that message at midnight."
"Yeh, about the pinch punch, first of the month thing. What's all that about Joanne?"
"Well I knew you were coming over on Friday so I was just having a bit of a laugh"
I averted my attention momentarily from Squeak to Joanne and spoke assertively.
"I found it about as funny as cancer, Joanne. Please stop it."
"You're not still mad at me about everything, are you?" she asked.
I was taken aback by the flippant manner in which she posed the question, suggesting the complete destruction of my life was an elemental triviality, similar to forgetting to put on a lottery ticket that won twenty pounds or a spontaneous throwaway comment when reminded that some ironing was outstanding. Under the

circumstances of why I was there, I purposefully refrained from entering into dialogue with potential to go south, preferring instead to let it slide. I hadn't anticipated how difficult that was going to be.

I strived to maintain cordial conversation as we caught up on life in general. As part of the Covid vaccination programme with my inclusion on the vulnerable list due to ulcerative colitis potentially weakening my immune system, I had received my second dose of vaccine expeditiously. My condition had remained manageable since my last flare-up and the course of steroids a year earlier and I vainly hoped this was on my estranged wife's mind when she commented, "Yeh, check you out with your two doses of vaccine and there's nothing wrong with you."

It was a disappointing moment for me and surely for Joanne too, as someone who had spent so many years in a 'caring' profession. My former life partner had witnessed over the years how the condition affected everything I planned, and her callous indifference evoked feelings of disappointment in the woman she now represented.

I was still reeling from her obtuseness when she began furnishing me with a very detailed account of her regular visits to see her specialist psychologist over the past four months, desperately trying to convince herself that the expensive fees she was paying were seeing dividends. The drink-drive episode was routinely dragged up again and I suppose I was at the stage that when she mentioned or analysed the whole sorry business, I zoned out, due to being the party who ended up with the 20-year criminal record and a meaningless guilt-ridden marriage proposal on the back of it.

A particular highlight of her vainglorious account was that she felt "safe" being on her own. As her partner who had spent the previous six years of co-habitation in regular wariness of her impulsive unpredictability, the irony of her pontifications was laughable. That sense of irony continued as I was forced to witness that the psychological treatment she had been undergoing for those months was paradoxically responsible for the continuing narcissistic monologue unfolding in front of my eyes and ears. She concluded her exclusive sermon with complete oblivion and inconsideration for the fact that I was the one who had a broken heart on account of her spontaneous actions back in the November.

"So, Joanne. Where do I fit into all that? Collateral damage?"
She paused before concurring matter-of-factly, "Yeah, I suppose you were."

I instinctively responded in disbelief, "Collateral damage? To your complete mentalness?"
I could have chosen a real word in the circumstances but nonetheless, Joanne's affirming nod was a solid kick in the teeth. As my mind tried to process being told that the last seven years of my life had been "collateral damage," my estranged wife sat opposite consumed in thoughtlessness, bathed in her lack of emotional intelligence. Joanne had been through a tempestuous previous marriage to Dave and had described the violent physical acts inflicted by her ex-husband. If her allegations were true, then of course there is no place in society for that kind of behaviour, but in that moment as I controlled my emotions regarding her disturbingly malevolent demeanour, I understood how human nature could topple someone over the edge into a physical reaction to such provocation. That nonchalant declaration had to be one of the lowest ebbs, evoking so many mixed feelings of hurt, disbelief and consummate anger. With the imminent demise of little Squeak, I focussed on the reason I was there and the solemnity of the situation about to unfold.

A final very slow walk was undertaken around a local park with Squeak and on returning to my former marital home, Angela had arrived to spend some final company with the family pet and it was good to catch up with her, albeit in unfortunate circumstances. I stayed for approximately an hour before an emotional farewell to my wee faithful friend. At several junctures during that hour, Joanne had positioned herself inside the kitchen door, out of Angela's view, and signalled that she wanted me to join her in the kitchen. As I did so, she retreated out of sight of the living room and her outstretched arms beckoned me to give her a hug. They were extremely difficult moments for me as I warmly hugged the woman who had devastated my life but of course, it was all about our little dog. "I do miss you, you know," she strangely informed me.
"Just not enough though, sweetie, eh?"

On my return to the city, I reflected on a disappointing day in so many ways. My wife appeared to be morphing into an unrecognisable person and the chances of discouraging her transition into complete egotism appeared to be diminishing. The old phrase that sprang to mind was that if she was made of chocolate, she would eat herself. I was beginning to realise she had potentially been exercising that egotistical control for several years through frequent sweet nothings and the threat of instant castigation for anything she didn't like. Her egomania reminded me of her regular self-aggrandizement of her abilities as a counsellor over the years. The many occasions when she triumphantly declared her aptitude following a session, with phrases like "I'm a brilliant counsellor", "I'm great at my job", "That's going to be more brilliant feedback" and so on.

As I contemplated those regular incidences of pretentiousness, it brought to mind all the information Joanne had regularly shared with me regarding her clients, resulting in several breaches of confidentiality and ethical standards. From the distraught young lady grieving over her stillborn children; to a gentleman suffering from Post-Traumatic Stress Disorder following his military experience in the Middle East, including details of her appearance at a tribunal on his behalf. From a Syrian student struggling to cope with the war in his homeland which was preventing any return home; to a gentleman originally from the Shetland Islands who wanted to end his marriage but feared wrestling with the consequences. She liked the latter client's accent and I assured myself that I had almost certainly formed the wrong impression that she had taken a very unprofessional and unethical shine to a vulnerable man who had sought her help.
On another occasion, recommending to an unattached male client that her friend Kim would make a perfect partner for him was more dating agency than professional therapy.

My observations also triggered memories of a social media post from 2018 where Joanne displayed a photo of her 1000th receipt for counselling services rendered. It wasn't lost on many people that she was effectively bragging about how much money she was making from other people's misery and I had to field private comments that no other "professional" would advertise so egotistically. Again, I wouldn't have dared broach the subject with my wife, as any perceived criticism towards her, however slight, would never end well for me. I defended private comments from friends by insisting that her boastfulness was due to her lack of intelligent thought rather than any lack of scruples.

Overall, perhaps Joanne simply wasn't the brilliant counsellor she constantly championed herself as.

Later in the evening, Joanne forwarded a message to sadly advise that our beloved little Squeak had gone and the following day, commemorated our companion with an online comment on that video of our original North Coast 500 adventure, which frequently featured Squeak. She also forwarded a sentimental message. *"Thank you for being there yesterday. I know she loved you to bits, you dog whisperer."*
A few days later, I received a photo of a small precious package received from the vet's practice, to which she attached the message, *"That's our wee dog home."* Squeak had been a loyal companion in the years I knew her and her personality would be missed, however some consolation would be taken that her late-life suffering was now at an end.

Periodic messages from Joanne continued through April and it was beginning to feel somewhat regressive to my chances of accepting things. One particularly lengthy message referred to intimations and was a general update on family and friends. After being told that I had been "collateral damage" just weeks earlier, it felt uncomfortable but at the same time, I had to confess I was lonely and I missed her, something her ego would have surmised. I purposefully took a back seat from interaction with her and within a few days, it was brought to my attention that she had deactivated her Facebook account. I had never really understood anyone deactivating their social media account. If one wants a break, simply stop for a bit without announcing it to the world to get attention. If they really have no intention of using Facebook, they can delete their account completely. Needless to say, Joanne clearly got the desired attention from somewhere as her Facebook account was reactivated and back up and running within 48 hours. At the same time, I received a message advising that our bank required a letter to authorise the closing of our joint account. She requested that I type the letter due to my 'eloquent penmanship'. I expressed my doubts on just how much 'eloquent penmanship' was required for a letter consisting of two sentences but complied with her request respectively.

In the last few days of April, I undertook a 54-mile practice hike on the Cateran Trail, a circular route from the town of Alyth in Perthshire. It involved two nights of wild camping and one night at the recently post-lockdown reopened Kirkton of Glenisla Hotel. Despite sub-zero overnight temperatures, it was a successful trip overall and certainly served as relevant preparation for the forthcoming Coast-to-Coast challenge. I published my Walk Report on the excellent Walk Highlands website, a superb resource for anyone considering a walk of any length around Scotland.

Thankfully, Joanne had registered the message regarding the pinch, punch first of the month and we entered May without the cruelty of the previous two months.
A social media memory appeared on the eighth anniversary of our first date, referring to poetry I had written the previous year with a jocular theme indicating no sign of a seven-year itch. I resisted the temptation towards posting some sardonic revision.

Having made space within the garden shed at my maisonette, I contacted Joanne to request the retrieval of my remaining camping equipment still being stored in the attic at my former matrimonial home. Some of it would be useful for my forthcoming trip. Joanne and Scott had stacked everything in their garage and the weekend prior to my adventure, I combined my final training session, a 30-mile cycle in the 'Shire, with an uplift of kit. This collection would include the karaoke machine which was destined for Number One after Joanne had excitedly told me that Number One would like to have it. She omitted the bit where she had contacted Number One to tell her the machine was originally bought for her and as such, would she like to have it? Number One had far more technical recording media at her disposal but under the circumstances, didn't feel she had a choice in the matter. It reminded me of a certain day in 2016.

The Saturday arrived and I was unable to squeeze everything into my car and undertook to return the following day to gather the remainder.
I was aware that Joanne was looking after Angela's little dog Pippin for the weekend and two o'clock arrived on the Sunday when I received a message from Joanne.
"*Hi Matt, are you coming out today? Just wondered as I haven't walked Pippin yet.*"
I replied, "*Just heading over now if that's ok.*"
"*Yea, of course. I have walked Pippin already and went on a cycle with Patricia so I have tired legs, but if you fancy a walk?*" came her reply in complete contradiction to her previous message.

Half an hour later, I was heading off on what felt like a contrived walk with Joanne, admittedly curious about her keenness to spend time with me.

Conversation was cordial and flowing, ranging from the latest tv programmes to latest musical tastes and, with now only six days until I headed to St Bees, preparation and plans for my impending adventure on the Coast-to-Coast. I was also enjoying my inaugural meeting with Angela's boisterous little dog but, as had become the norm for Joanne, the conversation would take an unpredictable turn. "Patricia was asking me the other day about moving on and dating other men."
Fairly unimpressed with Patricia's line of conversation and Joanne's reference to it, I immediately intervened, "Joanne, I really don't want to know and have no idea why you're sharing this with me."
Joanne stopped in her tracks to look me in the eye.
"No Matt. I need you to know what I told her. I told her I loved you and I wouldn't be looking to date anyone else."
Not for the first time, I was compelled to respond to her declarations of affection, "Just not enough though, sweetie, eh?"
Her standstill to increase the effect of her risible statement that she wasn't looking to date anyone, less than six months after destroying a man's life, was simply pitiful and deserved sympathy rather than ridicule.

On arriving back at my former home, and after loading my car with the last vestiges of my existence at that abode, Joanne offered to make a cup of tea. With none of my personal effects remaining at her home, it was possibly the last time any such invitation would be offered, and after a little hesitation, I agreed and took a seat in the back garden patio. I did get the sense that she wanted to spend more time with me but was wary that it was perhaps more about getting my attention. We enjoyed a cup of tea and routine conversation centred around her plans for reducing her workload, readily contradicted with her plans to obtain new qualifications as well as plans for improving the garden. I discussed my plans for my forthcoming adventure which she undertook to follow on social media.

The time came to depart and I entered the kitchen, placed my cup beside the sink, took out my car keys and approached Joanne for a simple farewell hug. Joanne instantly and unexpectedly raised her arms towards me with palms facing downward, declaring, "No, Matt. No hug."

"What?" my perplexed response.

"Sorry, I just don't want a hug."

"Ok Joanne, as you wish. You couldn't get enough hugs from me when I was here last month. You really are a strange wee woman," I concluded with a wry smile.

"I could slap you for that."

"Whatever you think, sweetie," my reply accompanied with a shake of my head.

Despite her bizarre refusal of a standard parting, Joanne would follow me out to my car to say a hugless farewell and wave me off, pausing to discuss further gardening exploits, like the previous two minutes hadn't just happened. I entered my car and drove off, still baffled by her latest peculiarity.

Akin to my previous visit in April, I took the opportunity to reflect on the day as I drove back to the city in the late afternoon. Her willingness to structure her day around an invite to go for a walk with Angela's dog, her little declaration that she loved me, her inclination to invite me in for tea, her pathetic dramatization of refusing a simple farewell hug. As part of her manipulative and controlling nature, did she want me to think there was an outside chance? Was there an outside chance? By this stage, did I want there to be an outside chance? She knew I couldn't switch my heart on and off in the manner that was second nature to her, and it had become obvious that she enjoyed drawing my attention. Fuel would quickly be added to the flames.

Shortly after arriving back home and consequently only an hour after her latest afternoon of self-absorption, she forwarded a message advising that she had donated to my charity page ahead of my adventure. A further message was received later in the evening stating she had enjoyed reading my report on my practice hike on the Cateran Trail, adding that she hoped all my preparation would pay off on the hike. She seemed to have taken a sudden interest in my life.

Less than 48 hours later on the Tuesday evening, I received an unexpected message from my son-in-law to be, Jake.

"Hi Matt. *Just how much of a fucking fruitcake is your estranged wife?*"

"What you on about?"
"Have a look at her latest post on social media, direct from her own wee planet in the cosmos."

On investigation, Joanne had shared my charity post for my impending hike. Contrary to February's previous obliteration of my existence, I was tagged for all our friends to see and it was accompanied by her own message requesting that people support Matt McKay's efforts for a cause "very close to home", reminding everyone that the man himself suffers from the condition he is supporting. The post was written very much in 'supporting my husband' mode and as neither of us had ever intimated our separation on social media, it didn't offer any suggestion that the hike was a product of her own whimsical destruction of my life the previous November. It was indeed a curious incident, prior to another unconnected, unexpected but seminal incident that lay ahead the following evening.

With only a couple of nightshifts to complete before heading across the border, I was driving to the first of those shifts and, as was a fairly regular occurrence, I stopped by the service station en route to pick up a snack. This particular establishment served up some decidedly overpriced but nonetheless delicious Cornish pasties. At £3.50 each, the frequent "2 for £4" deal was often seized upon, saving the latter for my second nightshift.
On this particular evening, it appeared that the "2 for £4" deal had been temporarily discontinued and I consequently joined the queue for the cashier, armed with a lonely singular pasty.
Once at the counter, I casually enquired to the young man, "I'm assuming the two for four pounds deal isn't on tonight."
"Yes, don't know why it's off this week. Usually quite a permanent deal," the courteous assistant explained.
"No problem at all," I smiled, "Just the one then, thanks."
I duly swiped my card on his machine and headed for the exit, only to be stopped in my tracks by the same young man.
"Excuse me, sir, can you just wait here at the counter?"
"Em, ok," I replied with a quizzical expression, as the attendant briefly disappeared 'through the back' before returning seconds later, holding a small tray with a Cornish pasty and a couple of hot "all-day breakfast" wraps.

"They can only stay on display for a few hours and their time ran out a few minutes ago. Please take them," he requested, holding the tray towards me.

"You didn't have to do that. Are you sure?" I asked, somewhat taken aback, "Do you not want them for yourself?"

"I have my supper with me," he replied with a nod and, hovering the palm of his free hand over the tray, he implored, "Please. Take them all."

I gathered the snacks whilst purposefully expressing myself, "That is so kind of you. Thank you so much."

It's hard to reflect on exactly what was rushing through my mind as I returned across the forecourt towards my car with my smile, my purchased pasty and its three complimentary accompaniments.

If I had really needed two pasties, I could have afforded the £7, however I only regularly purchased a pair because of the deal. Point being, I didn't need two and consequently didn't buy two.

Did the thoughtful employee feel that I needed two but couldn't afford them?

I got into my car and placed my horde onto the passenger seat, placed my key into the ignition and prepared to drive off.

Then it happened . . . inexplicably.

I was unable to drive off due to the sudden eruption of tears clouding my eyes.

And I cried . . . and cried . . . uncontrollably, whilst attempting to rationalise why I was suddenly blubbering over some free snacks.

Perhaps it occurred to me that I hadn't experienced much kindness in my life over the past six months.

Perhaps it was a sharp reminder that there remained kind people in this world more than willing to carry out random acts of kindness.

Perhaps I was releasing a lengthy period of pent-up sadness, all instigated by a free Cornish pasty and a shop assistant who wouldn't know how his very simple act of random kindness touched me so deeply and created such an emotional outpouring.

It took me a few minutes to compose myself before setting off on the short drive to work.

The following afternoon, a young lady, a door-to-door charity worker who I figured wasn't having the best of days, appeared on my doorstep seeking a monthly donation for her charity. She certainly appeared to be asking more in hope than expectation, no doubt for the umpteenth time on her shift.

To this day, I reflect on that altruistic young service station employee every time my monthly direct debit to the Royal National Institute for the Deaf shows up on my bank statement.

Joanne's thoughtless social media pretence, counteracted with my petrol station reminder that kindness still prevailed in this often cruel world, instigated the final catalyst in a thought process that had been evolving within me for a few weeks. It felt like a major moment of epiphany was about to unfold. It was possibly the impending embarkation on a sizeable new adventure that had inspired me to take a step back, investigate my feelings, and create a way to extricate myself from an unacceptable situation.

Six months of my own culpability in allowing her to maintain her manipulation of my feelings for her. Six months of feeding her increasing narcissism and egotism. I had made it clear that I simply couldn't just be her friend but I was allowing her to maintain that contact and friendship, in detriment to my own personal advancement. I realised that for myself to grow, to move forward, to regenerate and to accept my fate, I would require to take control of the situation and remove the nagging uncertainty she was deviously creating. There would be one definitive final opportunity to move forward with Joanne or move forward without her.

The very questionable wisdom of my thoughts and actions would certainly not be fully realised at this point.

Day 11 – Ingleby Cross to Lord Stones Country Park

The A172 is the main link road between the city of Middlesbrough and the A19 and passed the southern end of Ingleby Cross less than a hundred yards from my tent pitch. The noise of traffic, particularly lorries, became discernible from shortly after 4am, waking me up. Any sleep thereafter was fitful due to the steadily increasing rumble of trucks. Suddenly the honking of 'killer geese' didn't seem too bad. My walk to Lord Stones Country Park was the shortest scheduled day of the adventure at eight miles, and subsequently I tried to lie in for a late start only to find myself enjoying a morning brew and a croissant before 7am. By 8am, the temperature had reached 19 degrees Celsius (higher inside the tent) and I was back sat at my favourite picnic table applying sun tan lotion.

There was a sense of excitement that early in today's hike, I would be entering the third and final national park of my adventure with three nights remaining, one of which would be spent in a hotel room with a bath

Returning my holdall for pick up at the Bluebell Inn entrance by 9am, I decided that I would carry my tent with me today in the event of arriving at my destination before the courier. It was around 9.30 when I set off from the village, intending to incorporate several breaks into the day's trek.

Crossing the aforementioned busy A172, a road and track are ascended for ten minutes to reach Arncliffe Wood. Once in the woods, the track continues uphill and climbs past Park House Country Guest House where a fairly new-looking wooden signpost quirkily advised that Robin Hood's Bay is now only 48 miles away, involving 4,586ft of ascent and 111,792 steps. The first several hundred of those steps were uphill, winding southwards to join a hairpin bend where the trail joins the Cleveland Way and heads north east. With the sketched map in the guidebook annotated with the words "relentlessly uphill", the next 20 minutes were tough-going, thankfully in the shade of the trees. The climb was rewarded when a very short offshoot path led to a small clearing, confirming I was now on an escarpment with extensive views westwards over the Vale of Mowbray to the Yorkshire Dales beyond, a reminder of the scale of the hike being undertaken. Also enjoying the view were Colin and Rob, two thirds of the ex-RAF trio who had an earlier start from Exelby Services following drop-off. Enquiries confirmed that Bruce was still very much part of the trio but had disappeared into some nearby bushes with his trowel to do some gardening . . .

Passing through a couple of gates and shifting away from the treeline, the Cleveland Way enters Scarth Wood Moor, open heather-clad moorland with paving stones laid to protect the ground. Thanks to several hikers coming in the opposite direction, I became embroiled in conversations which were conducive with the beautiful weather conditions and there being no need for any urgency. Just under a mile later, I crossed a road to enter woods and was once more climbing up through trees on an excellent firm path which had levelled out by the by the time I veered off onto a narrower path on the left. A stone marker indicated that I was on the Lyke Wake Walk which descended to briefly join a wide track before continuing south-east on another narrow but well-maintained path through pretty conifer woodland for just over half a mile.
Descending through an open field to rejoin woodland, an attractive wooden footbridge spanned the babbling Crook Beck where I took the opportunity to replenish my water supply before emerging onto a country lane for a few minutes to the tiny hamlet of Huthwaite Green. Signage for both the Lyke Wake Walk and Cleveland Way (the Coast-to-Coast didn't appear to merit a mention) directed me into more woods and the beginning of a sustained climb, very steep for a section, up onto Live Moor.
Once onto the high open moorland, paving slabs again helped underfoot and the clear conditions afforded views north to the contiguous metropolises of Stockton-on-Tees and Middlesbrough. Some distance behind, I could make out the profile of the ex-RAF trio emerging from the woods.

On reaching a large cairn and aware that I now had just under two miles to my daily terminus, I elected to take a lengthy lunchtime break and settled down on the east-facing lee-side of the cairn to prepare a mug of tea. The 'Yorkshire Pasty' I had purchased at Exelby Services looked and tasted suspiciously like its Cornish cousin, and I was pleasantly reminded of my emotion-inducing service station 'freebies' just a fortnight earlier. Colin, Rob and

Bruce stopped for a chat on passing. They were heading for Clay Bank Top where their B&B host was picking them up. Consequently, as they were finishing a day ahead of myself, this would be another parting of ways, and after exchanging numbers with Colin, I warmly shook the hands of the three amigos and wished them 'fair winds and following seas'.

A reapplication of sun cream was administered as I laid back against the cairn to relax for a bit.

Around a quarter of an hour elapsed before the next passing hikers appeared and took a seat just a couple of yards away on the cairn. The two older women looked vaguely familiar and when they began conversing in an Irish brogue, I realised I had been joined by Bernadette and Imogen, to be sure.
"Hi ladies, just having an extended lunch break. Only going as far as Lord Stones Country Park. You folks going far?"
"We're being picked up there and taken to Carlton, the Blackwell Ox Inn," Bernadette or Imogen replied.
"Ah, yes, the Blackwell Ox. The chef from there has told me there's fuck all wrong with their burgers," was what I could've replied but I of course desisted.
"Walking the Cleveland Way, ladies?" I enquired.
"No, we're actually walking Wainwright's Coast-to-Coast. That goes across the whole country. We've been going for 15 days now from St Bees in Cumbria. You doing the Cleveland Way?" Bernadette or Imogen responded.
Feeling somewhat guilty regarding my assumption that these ladies who appeared to be in their late 60's with their aversion to undercooked burgers couldn't possibly be walking the Coast-to-Coast, I replied, "Wow, good for you guys. I'm on Wainwright's too. Day 11 of 14 for me."
"19 days for us, retirement has its advantages."
I regained my feet and began sorting out my rucksack for moving on, and now standing close to my Irish acquaintances, Bernadette or Imogen proffered, "Have we met before on the hike?"
Loading my rucksack onto my shoulders and gathering my walking poles, I smiled at my fellow Celts, "Maybe try the chicken tonight. Don't go upsetting the chef."
"Ah yes. You were sat next to us last night in the Blue Bell."
I nodded in acknowledgement, "Enjoy the rest of your adventure, ladies," and was once more on my way.

The well-made path continued along the edge of the scarp, cutting through the heather, dipping down before gradually ascending onto Carlton Moor, passing a weather station and summiting at a trig point painted bright white. From this uppermost vantage point of the moor, the views again extended to the industrial heartland of Teesside with the North Sea vaguely visible in the background. My abstinence from any real sense of excitement on seeing this body of water reflected the fact that my ultimate destination was still in excess of 40 miles away.

A sharp half-mile descent followed to cross Raisdale Road and enter today's objective, Lord Stones Country Park, named after three large stones in the grounds supposedly marking the boundaries between lands belonging to three historical local lords.
Entering a central courtyard with plentiful external seating, the adjacent building consisted of a café, restaurant and an upscale well-stocked shop offering gifts and local produce. Despite my best efforts to prolong today's eight-mile hike, it was only shortly after 2pm when I approached the main counter and enquired about my booking for camping, made online a few weeks earlier. My lofty expectations felt justified as the fee paid for my 'Woodland Retreat' camping pitch was the most expensive of the entire expedition by a considerable distance, almost double that of the youth hostels and triple that of the others. For the first time since leaving St Bees, I was handed a check-in sheet where I had to fill in my personal details, on completion of which I was presented with a leaflet. On the information leaflet, the receptionist referred to a site map and directed me to the camping area where I had been allocated Pitch Number Three. All fairly straightforward . . . so far. My holdall had arrived and after collecting it from the shop's entrance corridor, I was wheeling it back out past the courtyard entrance and across the Cleveland Way. The brown wooden toilet and shower block for campers sat directly on the long-distance path which probably accounted for the Simplex combination locks on the doors.
Continuing on a track which swung left uphill for around 30 yards, I came upon a circular clearing amongst the trees, reminiscent of a cricket field. A sizeable family tent sat immediately to my right and a male occupant, sat outside on a camping chair, nodded as I proceeded left around the sphere in a clockwise direction. Dotted around the circumference were some tents and in an area on the far side, construction works were ongoing to evidently build some

235

timber-framed 'roundhouse' accommodation. Having been allocated a numbered pitch, I expected to see some numerical indication but alas none was to be found. From the map I had been given, Pitch Number Three appeared to be busily occupied by a very large tent accompanied by a smaller pup tent. I guessed the whole family were on that trip. Looking around and just wanting somewhere to pitch my tent, there appeared to be a generous gap next to the construction works on the far side. Shortly after setting up camp, a vehicle pulled up close by and a couple alighted armed with the same leaflet and aimed a few furtive glances in my direction. Explaining the situation, I offered to unpeg and move my tent closer to the construction site to give them more room which they appreciated and subsequently began setting up their tent. All was under control . . . until another vehicle pulled up next to my new neighbours and aimed similar inquisitive glances in their direction.

After a cordial 3-way conflab and aware that my small tent would take up least room, I spied an area back down near the entrance which was next to a pathway and, on consulting the site map, was an unspecified pitch. Any observers were now treated to the through-hiker unpegging his tent . . . again . . . and dragging it across the centre of the 'cricket pitch', hoping to be third-time lucky. As an encore, I doubled back to pick up the rest of my kit and shuffled across once more, looking like a human game of "Buckaroo".

After organising myself, it was time to make use of the toilet and shower facilities, Lord Stones winning another prize for having the least conveniently distanced toilets of my Coast-to-Coast. After the previous two peaceful nights as a sole camper with my own space, this unforeseen clash with busier commercial tourism hadn't enjoyed the most auspicious start. Thanks once more to the kindness of strangers, things were about to improve considerably.

My route to the facilities took me past that first tent I saw on entering the camping area and I nodded once more to the gentleman sat outside.
"Are you having fun moving that tent around?"
I smiled in acknowledgement, "Hi, how you doing? Yeh, I had a booking for Pitch Number 3 but seems to be occupied," tilting my head to the heavily occupied allotted place opposite.

"Tell you what, they arrived last night and were setting up elsewhere but didn't seem to like it so they just switched to there. It's certainly had a knock-on effect."

"I'm just stopping overnight so don't really want to make a fuss," I replied.

"On a hike, I assume since you don't have a car?"

"Yes, I'm doing Wainwright's Coast-to-Coast."

"Coast to coast? What does that entail?"

Describing previous parts of my challenge to my neighbour seemed to prompt a very genuine interest in the magnitude of my journey and the conversation expanded to his own reasons for being there on a midweek break with his wife, two infant kids and border terrier from nearby Middlesbrough. After taking advice on which was the best of the two working showers, I headed off to freshen up, accepting the very kind invitation to stop for a brew with 'Mark' on the way back.

On returning to Mark's tent, I was introduced to his wife, young daughter and son and Remy, his friendly 5-year-old border collie and enjoyed a mug of tea. Mark and his family had regularly gone abroad on holiday but as a result of the pandemic, they were exploring the increasing staycation trend, purchasing camping gear and having a local recce before venturing further afield.

With the site shop closing at 5pm, I was keen to top up my snacks for Day 12 and obtain a bottle of local ale for later. Accepting Mark's very generous invite for a bacon roll in the morning, I returned to the shop, acquired a sandwich for tomorrow's lunch and a bottle of beer, before opting for a further bottle to enjoy on the terrace benches in the late afternoon sunshine.

As I was enjoying my libation, three hikers entered the courtyard, two of which I'd last seen arriving in Church Holme in Danby Wiske the previous day. Joining me at my table, I reminded them that the shop closed at 5pm and to acquire food and drink if required. Beers were duly acquired and lengthy engaging conversation ensued with the hikers I had only fleetingly met on two previous occasions.

Jono and Nick were brothers, originally from Manchester but now both living in central London. Fascinatingly, Jono, a photographer, lived with his wife on a narrowboat which necessitated periodic relocation due to various rates. Younger brother Nick worked in administration within the Houses of Parliament. Nick made the odd comment regarding members of the House but I sensed if he went into any great detail, he would then have to kill me. They had always wanted to tackle the Coast-to-Coast walk with their other brother, but alas, this eldest third sibling, reputedly the keenest hiker of the trio was a school teacher who couldn't get the time off.

Our conversation revealed that I had a holdall being transferred daily and with his tongue in his cheek, Nick questioned if this was cheating. I reminded him of a conversation I had with Ian, the helpful proprietor of the Orchard Caravan Park back in Reeth. Ian had pointed out that a 200-mile walk is a 200-mile walk whether you use hotels, B&B, tents or a baggage transfer facility. The sense of achievement, walking down the final hill at Robin Hood's Bay is exactly the same.

I also countered Nick's remark by reminding him that he had over 20 years on me and an old man was entitled to take advantage of available non-walking assistance whilst simultaneously supporting local business and smelling fresher than my younger fellow hiker. "Fair enough," Nick laughed.

The fourth occupant of our table, Dave, had arrived in Danby Wiske the previous evening. An engineer from South Yorkshire, Dave had completed The Great Outdoors Challenge several times, an organised Coast-to-Coast event, west to east, across Scotland every May where each hiker plots their own route, culminating with celebration dinners in the town of Montrose. Dave highly recommended the Caledonian crusade and it was certainly something I would be looking into.

Almost an hour passed in pleasant prattling as my three new friends had managed to organise camping in an open field within the grounds of the country park with use of the facilities for a fee considerably lower than mine. They also expected further hikers, a married couple, who were due to arrive from Danby Wiske. I bemoaned my over-priced 'holidaymaker' pitch, even if it was less of a hike to the toilets, but wouldn't be moving for a fourth time.

Returning to my tent, I could see through a gap in the trees to the open field where Dave, Jono and Nick were setting up their tents. I was reminded that there were also kind engaging people within my own 'Woodland Retreat' when Mark appeared and stated, "Hi Matt, just to say we're heading out to an Indian restaurant down in Marton, this side of 'Boro. They do takeaway if you want some food bringing back."

"Oh Mark, that is so kind of you to offer. I'm actually spoiling myself with a three-course meal from my rations but I really appreciate the offer."
"No probs. See you for your bacon roll in the morning."
"You certainly will and thanks again."

Feeling a little overwhelmed and emotional, I retired to the privacy of my tent and purposefully tried to avoid shedding any tears as the restoration of my faith in the kindness of fellow human beings continued apace.

After tonight, my two remaining evening meals had been arranged and consequently this would be the last supper involving my ration packs. The banquet began with Thai-style chicken soup followed by chicken curry with potato and rice. Rice pudding with strawberry completed the feast, washed down with a large mug of tea. With three days of hiking remaining, my culinary inventory consisted of a sandwich, some chocolate bars, crisps and a couple of scotch eggs. Replete following my last 'ration pack' supper, I sat afront my canvas dwelling engulfed in the surrounding peace of the woods with my thoughts. Despite having over 40 miles to go, one couldn't help feeling a tingle of excitement in anticipation of completing the longest hike I'd ever undertaken.

Taking a stroll across the open camping field to a viewpoint showcasing the impressive sunset over the Vale of Mowbray, I once again met up with Jono and Nick. Also present were a 30-something couple and I was duly introduced to Dan and his wife Andrea, more Coast-to-Coasters camping in the 'cheap' field who had arrived earlier in the evening from Danby Wiske. After obtaining photos of the impressive sunset reddening the surrounding sky in anticipation of another sunny day ahead, I headed via the ablutions back to my polyester boudoir to retire for the evening.

Inevitably, hiking 200 miles on my own and having these long days and evenings alone enabled a cognizant focus which had afforded the opportunity to not only look back on the last few years, but perhaps a chance to analyse and learn from my failings, and to understand and bring clarity. I would subsequently learn that the official term was "reflective practice". I initially remained oblivious to just how elucidating this "reflective practice" had become over the course of this adventure.

Looking back at my initial contact with Joanne in the spring of 2013, I failed to see a troubled woman residing in the spare room of a friend, creating some necessary space away from ongoing conflict with her estranged husband whilst trying to locate a new home. She had falsified her location to a town 100 miles south of her temporary residence and I hadn't questioned it. Within 48 hours of meeting her, I was receiving continuous texts from a 47-year-old woman explaining she couldn't get me out of her head and was struggling with work, interspersed with messages about Dave's harassment and interference which effectively cancelled our second date. When our second meeting did materialise, she was bragging about her sexual prowess, oblivious to whatever my own sexual background entailed. There had clearly been ongoing tumult in her life created by her extra-marital affairs and her husband's slightly unconventional reaction, but despite that, she had decided to sign up to a dating website behind the back of a supportive and benevolent host. Moreover, I recollected that evening in my flat when she opened up about her past and my perception at that time of a lovely lady courageously recalling her past. My emotional attachment prevented me from seeing someone who was confessing that she had effectively faked her relationship with the father of her kids for over twenty years. Being a fool for those same fake charms would also prevent me from questioning why I should have been any different.

My reluctance to accept all my "dumpings" back in those initial few months, countering with my correspondence via letter or e-mail, had ultimately and undoubtably played to her uncontrollable ego and contributed to my later downfall. Blinded by loving possibilities back then, some embarrassment was now felt regarding my cringeworthy documentary efforts. A harsh lesson had to be learned, a lesson I was undoubtably responsible for.

In between these "dumpings", it was relayed back to me through a mutual friend at work that Joanne had been in her local hairdressing salon telling the stylists, and any other patrons who would listen, that she had just met an ex-RAF guy online, who was "gorgeous and I love him" at a point when she barely knew me.

Her apparent sincerity about getting me to trust her, just moments after revealing her alleged faux-pas between the sheets with Dave, was perhaps not as false a step after translation. And this coming in the same week that she positioned herself outside my flat to maintain a slightly sinister watching brief from her car.

I suppose I was lonely enough to be taken in by her somewhat over-the-top friendliness and allowed myself to gloss over those early setbacks. On the occasions when I sensed a concern about her behaviour, I wanted to believe she could be fixed and retrospectively had to acknowledge my lack of awareness on just who I was becoming involved with. When her mask regularly slipped, I continued to readily accept her continuous apologies and hoped and believed that her incessant impulsiveness would diminish in time. Sitting here years later in a tent in the depths of the North York Moors National Park, I would have to recognize my early part in my later downfall.

Joanne's regular observations that Jennifer didn't maintain the tidiest home in Moray had proved a real bone of contention on any visit to Moray. In complete contradiction to her need for me to curtail my contact with Jennifer, she figured I should be 'having a go' at my former wife about the unkempt state of her home that I continued to pay the mortgage for. My explanation to Joanne that any intervention would be dismissed by Jennifer on account of the fact I didn't live there appeared to fall on deaf ears. Consequently, Joanne would refer to Jennifer as "the fat lazy cow". She would use the phrase sporadically and I always felt it was more of an attempt to get a reaction from myself in order that she could accuse me of siding with my ex-wife over her. I distinctly recalled one particular conversation where she noxiously referred to the "fat lazy cow" and, appearing conscious of my aversion to react, she repeated the distasteful moniker in her next sentence. This purposeful second reference certainly made her intentions clear and justified my silence for the greater good.
Looking back, it was now a source of regret that I was too afraid of the inevitable consequences to mention my uneasiness with her referral to the mother of my children as a "fat lazy cow".
When Joanne was being most pleasant to Jennifer whenever face-to-face meetings occurred, I felt an uncomfortable degree of complicity as I smiled along, knowing that Jennifer would be back to

being "the fat lazy cow" in due course. Ironically, it was now an elementary observation that Joanne's "fat lazy cow" had more humility and integrity in her little finger than Joanne would ever possess.

With my children back in Moray, there would inevitably be regular contact with their mother and I now reflected with a degree of embarrassment on the fact that I mostly telephoned Jennifer from work with the explanation that it was "just easier." My chicken-hearted nature towards Joanne was highlighted as Dave could phone and chat to her whenever he liked and I wouldn't have dared make any comment. In further irony, I hadn't been near Jennifer's bed in over six years prior to meeting Joanne. In complete contrast, Joanne's reality concerning Dave's bed couldn't have been more different.

Expounding on these reflections over the recent past and certainly during the current sustained periods of solitude on the trail, it did occur to me that Joanne's distorted behaviour was by no means exclusive to Jennifer.

As I pondered her friendships, I began to realise that Joanne was prone to an underlying but almost natural unkindness towards almost all of her friends.

I recalled my initial introduction to her older friend Patricia after we had been invited for lunch at Patricia's home nearby. Joanne had described her as "a bit weird", a description my initial impression simply couldn't concur with. Our host had prepared a delicious broth accompanied by homemade bread and I thoroughly enjoyed my introduction to Joanne's down-to-earth and unassuming friend and her friendly little dog. On subsequently sharing my favourable impression of Patricia, Joanne was keen to back up her initial description.

"Wait 'til you hear this, Matt. I asked Patricia what she thought of you. Her reply was to ask what you thought of her. How weird is that?"

How dare someone not prioritise Joanne's question.

Sarah's slight speech impediment always took a battering as soon as her Yorkshire-based friend came into conversation.

Her friend Annabelle lived on a farm with her husband in the 'Shire. Anytime we were scheduled to meet up with them, Joanne seemed to take an unsettling relish in repeating her account of Annabelle's "creepy husband" Rob and that time years ago when he approached Joanne at a function to tell her he was "just popping into the woods for a wank." Joanne appeared to interpret his 'creepy' behaviour as a declaration of his affection for her.

The periodic cancelling of catch-ups by Gary and Laura was also a bone of contention for her. At one point her annoyance escalated to her declaring, "I'm fed up with it. We always have to go and see them. They can never come over here to see us." That statement served to further highlight her vindictiveness regarding my nights in the spare room "doghouse" the previous August over her specious claim that I disliked Gary.

Perhaps the biggest eye-opener on her regular derision of her friends came when she returned from a long weekend city-break in Dublin with her friend Kim.
"So how was it?" I eagerly enquired, expecting a detailed account of the craic in Ireland's 'Fair City'.
"Och, it was ok, Matt. I was with Kim, she's not the most sociable. It would've been much better if you were there with me."
I was taken aback by her pejorative comments regarding a long-standing friend but now, in hindsight, I could see it was actually par for the course.

I recalled my first ever encounter with Kim back in 2013, unaware that Kim had made it clear to Joanne that she had no wish to meet me. Joanne evidently and nonchalantly disregarded that request when I was ushered to join her as she was picked up something from her former temporary home.
Kim's demeanour throughout this inaugural encounter made me feel, to quote the wonderful Billy Connolly, about as welcome as a fart in a spacesuit. In hindsight, Kim's stance was perfectly understandable. Being aware of her friend's previous affairs and having provided accommodation to offer respite from her difficult marital situation whilst her lodger sought a new home, Kim would have been disappointed to discover that Joanne was simultaneously and covertly advertising herself on a dating website from her spare room
"So what do you think of Kim?" Joanne asked, just after that rather awkward first meeting, "Pretty, isn't she?"
"Yes, she's a good-looking woman," I agreed.

"Yes, but she takes two hours to put that face on every morning," Joanne retorted indignantly, taking apparent disdain at my concurrence.

These were also the initial signs of Joanne's underlying green-eyed monster which would make sporadic appearances over the years.

As a more cordial relationship with Kim developed over time, that initial concurrence wasn't forgotten as I was occasionally teased with pointed comments, examples being, "You can collect the dog from Kim's. You'll get to see her then" and "Why didn't you go for someone like Kim? She's more your type." These barbed observations appeared to be based on her arrogant misperception of similarities between Kim and my previous partner Siobhan.

I wasn't aware of quite how obsessed she was with Siobhan until one day she revealed that my former friend had amended the previously incorrect spelling of her name on her social media page.
"How the hell do you know that?" I enquired.
"I just happened to notice as I have an occasional look at her page," she revealed.
It appeared that the fixation hadn't diminished when years later, she randomly asked a most bizarre question.
"Matt, did you and Siobhan ever make love by a set of standing stones?"
"You what?" I exclaimed in headlong puzzlement.
"She's changed her cover picture on her social media and as it's public, she will know that anyone can see it, so I was wondering if she was trying to send you a message."
Engaged to be married to Joanne at this stage, her statement raised many questions concerning her concocted jealousy towards someone I hadn't seen or spoken to in several years, or indeed had never visited any set of standing stones with.

On returning from the annual 'Jolly Boy's Outing' in 2018, my wife put me in the metaphorical dock.
"Where were you when Lamby was making videos?"
She was referring to the fact that my close friend James Lamb had taken several photographs and posted videos of the day's shenanigans on social media and I hadn't appeared in some of them.

"I've no idea, sweetie. Probably standing next to him or at the bar or chatting to one of the other guys," I offered in explanation. "It was just noticeable that you didn't seem to be around and I was just wondering if you were somewhere else, or with someone else." I looked her in the eye with a reassuring smile, "Joanne, why would you even ask that? At our age? Really? I love you, Joanne. My friends know I love you. I haven't been anywhere near any woman since the day I met you. So, rest assured, I'm not interested in any nonsense."

Admittedly, I found it flattering that Joanne could be so jealous over my self-perception of a fairly average-looking man in his 50th year, and I naively allowed her possessiveness to further solidify my perceived strength of our relationship.

Reflecting on the Joanne-led trip to celebrate the leap day anniversary of her marriage proposal, I pondered on how well she actually knew me. Five-star hotels, unless in my military career in far-flung lands at the British taxpayer's expense, really weren't my cup of Earl Grey. I found the grandiosity of such establishments a little forced and perhaps it had been more Joanne's thing all along and she had 'put up' with less expensive and more informal hotel chains. Certainly not a criticism because each to their own but just not really my thing and, acknowledging some balance, the surprise trip down Loch Ness on the same weekend was wet, windy and wonderful.

On the subject of that fateful proposition day in Inverness, I was yet to learn of the derision amongst her own family regarding her shock proposal. Heads metaphorically in hands, asking in exasperation "what is she doing now?" She had garnered a nickname as "Crazy Aunty Joanne" and I observed that she would consistently engage in outlandish and puerile behaviour when in their company to conveniently feed that belief, blissfully unaware of the mockery surrounding her. In retrospect, I realised that her family had known her for almost all of her life whereas I had metaphorically known her for five minutes. Whilst believing her personality was misconstrued by her kith and kin, I should have perhaps been paying more attention to those opinions of people who had known her over a considerably longer period.

It also occurred to me that despite my own 22 years of service in the RAF, Joanne knew virtually nothing about them. Within 10 minutes of knowing her, she enquired about any retention of military uniform in what ironically transpired to be one of the last questions she ever asked about my service career. Several times during our relationship, in my presence, she reiterated to friends and my own family that she would never have been interested in me if I had still been in the Armed Forces. It was only more recently that I reflected on how incredibly unromantic and disparaging that had been, basing one's attraction to someone on what they do for a living. Of course, I should also have remembered from those inaugural online exchanges that standing less than 5'10" tall would have fastidiously ruled me out too.

Intrigued by a fellow hiker's earlier comments about narcissism, combined with all the previous thoughts concerning her narcissistic nature and aided by a decent internet coverage at Lord Stones, I came across an online article on my phone which stopped me in my tracks:

"Narcissists are not capable of love and the reality is that they do not see others any differently than they see any inanimate object like a table lamp or a chair. Malignant Narcissists are damaged in a way that leaves them void of having emotional intelligence and are stuck in a state, similar to that of a toddler. When a toddler is hungry, they are fed, when wet they are changed. Their entire existence revolves around their needs. Toddlers don't comprehend, understand or even care that mummy, daddy or whoever is their caregiver, have feelings and emotions. As far as the toddler is concerned, life and what they know of it, revolves solely around them.
Narcissists are no different and for whatever reason, they are perpetually stuck with that very limited emotional intelligence. Narcissists also lack object constancy and whole object relations, meaning that they don't bond to others nor can they comprehend that you can be angry with a person and still love that person. When a narcissist is upset or angry with a person or a partner, they automatically hate that person. There is no middle ground and you are either all good or all bad. Narcissists are extremely dangerous as they lack the ability to put themselves in another person's shoes so they don't sympathize or empathize with their partner's sorrow or pain. Narcissists are damaged in such a way that they lack introspection and self-awareness, nor do they have the ability to self-actualize.

When you combine these factors together, it isn't difficult to understand why narcissists can move on from relationship to relationship with no care or concern for the pain and anguish they undoubtedly leave in their wake. Narcissists without empathy can never know true love nor can they relate to or truly bond with another person.

If you are in a relationship with a true malignant narcissist, be prepared to be hurt and understand that you are never seen as a person with feelings and emotions as to the narcissist, you are no different to that table lamp or other inanimate object. When the narcissist becomes bored or you fail to fuel their ego, you will be replaced, tossed aside and soon replaced with a new and exciting person that gives the narcissist the supply and fuel they constantly crave and desire.

Relationships with narcissists are simply an exercise in futility as they can't really love you and don't care about any hurt they cause. There is no cure for these types of narcissists, no love great enough to change who and what they are, and no amount of hope, prayer or care will ever change their fixed disordered personality.

Beyond the desire to focus primarily on themselves and be held in high regard by virtually everyone in their lives, people with malignant narcissism tend to have a darker side to their self-absorption. These individuals can be highly manipulative and don't care who they hurt as long as they get their own way.

Although there is only one official diagnosis for narcissism (narcissistic personality disorder), there are different types. Someone with grandiose narcissism, for instance, requires excessive praise and attention; while someone with vulnerable narcissism tends to have a lot of anxiety and needs a lot of supportive attention.

People with this subtype contain the general traits of NPD, including regular egocentricity. They also have antisocial traits and even a sadistic streak, as well as a poor sense of self and lack of empathy. There is often some paranoia involved with narcissism as well."

I stared at the screen, open-mouthed. The article had just summed up Joanne with uncanny and unerring accuracy. I read it over again with several nods of affirmation. All those disorders over the years that my estranged wife had diagnosed herself with, and yet here was the most definitive description. I figured that she was too much of a narcissist to be able to recognize her narcissism. The article went on to list some symptoms:

"Symptoms of narcissistic personality disorder and how severe they are can vary. People with the disorder can:
Have an unreasonably high sense of self-importance and require constant, excessive admiration.
Feel that they deserve privileges and special treatment.
Expect to be recognized as superior even without achievements.
Make achievements and talents seem bigger than they are.
Believe they are superior to others and can only spend time with or be understood by equally special people.
Be critical of and look down on people they feel are not important.
Expect special favours and expect other people to do what they want without questioning them.
Take advantage of others to get what they want.
Have an inability or unwillingness to recognize the needs and feelings of others.
Be envious of others and believe others envy them.
Behave in an arrogant way, brag a lot and come across as conceited.
Insist on having the best of everything — for instance, the best car or office.
At the same time, people with narcissistic personality disorder have trouble handling anything they view as criticism.
People with narcissistic personality disorder may not want to think that anything could be wrong, so they usually don't seek treatment. If they do seek treatment, it's more likely to be for symptoms of another mental health problem. What they view as insults to self-esteem may make it difficult to accept and follow through with treatment."

A very interesting, eye-opening and thought-provoking article indeed.

I settled into my sleeping bag and listened to the end of "The Thursday Murder Club" which concluded with the character Elizabeth slipping a note under the door of the character Joyce in what appeared to be an indicator of the forthcoming sequel. It reminded me of the note I had posted to Joanne 11 days earlier.
"What was I thinking?" I reflected with some exasperation.

Day 12 – Lord Stones Country Park to Blakey Ridge

"Morning Matt. Saw the door unzipped. Assumed you were up. Mug of tea for you, pal. I'll just leave it here. Bacon roll over at ours when you're ready, oh and I found your online page and made a donation."
Mark placed a mug of tea at the entrance.
"Thank you so much, Mark. Really appreciated."

It was 8am and I wasn't long awake. My 4am visit to the toilet was later than usual and also a longer trek due to the more distant facilities. With sunrise and the dawn chorus before 5am, my fragmented sleep was at least more peaceful without lorries thundering down a nearby trunk road. A 13-mile day lay ahead to remote Blakey Ridge and Mark's kindness, added to the pleasant sunshine glinting through the trees had given Day 12 an uplifting beginning. That uplift was enhanced when I popped over to Mark's tent, relaxed in a camping chair and enjoyed a couple of bacon rolls with him and his family. Remy took a particular shine to me as I held a bacon roll in my hand, and as conversation established that my latest canine friend hadn't had his morning walk, we resolved that Mark and his border collie would join me for the early part of today's hike.

The all-too-familiar morning ritual ensued, packing away my bed and sleeping bag and prepping my rucksack and my feet for the day ahead, discarding my small amount of litter and finally disassembling my tent.

Mark and Remy accompanied me back down to the courtyard where I dropped off my holdall and we were off. The Cleveland Way departed east from Lord Stones Country Park, fairly flat at first, before a gradual incline skirted a small enclave of trees.

"I hope you don't mind me asking, Matt, what with you making this journey on your own. Is there another half in the life of Matt?"

"Don't mind at all, Mark. I was married until she ended it very suddenly last November."

"Aw, sorry to hear that, pal."

"Thanks, Mark. Actually, it's the main reason I've ended up on this journey. I took it pretty badly and allowed my world to crash down round about me for a bit. This walk gave me something to focus on and it's been a very enlightening reflection on things. The intense period of time to myself has helped me realise what a fake person she actually is, not just to me but to everyone else in her life. Her constant need to promote herself to the world as some sort of caring 'angel' is very telling. From the outside looking in, as they say, certainly makes things clearer. It's timely that you should ask me about it this morning, as only last night I was reading an article about narcissism. Ironically, over the years, she has diagnosed herself with various disorders after reading about them in books and deciding she fitted the bill. She seems to have avoided the reading materials on narcissism."

Mark nodded in acknowledgement, "It can be very therapeutic taking time on your own. You certainly come across like you are in a good place."

"Cheers, I am in a good place. The North York Moors," I replied with a grin.

"Your patter is rubbish though," my charity's newest contributor joshed.

"Seriously though, Mark, this is the most relaxed I've felt in a long time. I'm realising there's a potential new world out there waiting to be experienced, God willing, without that underlying fear that an unpredictable narcissist of a wife is susceptible to creating havoc on a whim."

"Good for you, Matt. Long may it continue."

The incline became steeper as the trail climbed onto Cringle Moor and we reached the viewpoint at the Alec Falconer Memorial Seat, just under a mile from Lord Stones Country Park, a walk that Mark and Remy had undertaken previously and the point where they would turn around and head back.

A metal view-finder attached to a nearby plinth pointed out many local towns and was lovingly inscribed with the words "*This plate and seat were erected by his many friends in memory of Alec Falconer 1884-1968*". My subsequent research revealed that Alec Falconer was a founder member of the Middlesbrough Rambling Club and had actively campaigned for the opening of the Cleveland Way.

Sadly, he passed away just one year before the trail was officially opened, hence this fitting memorial.

I thanked Mark for his kind hospitality, shaking his hand and Remy's paw, and we parted in opposite directions.

Feeling blessed to have met so many kind and interesting people on this incredible journey, I continued along Kirby Bank until reaching a steep descent on paved stones. It was certainly a morning of ups and downs, literally, as the trail climbed once more past a densely populated sheep fold to reach a summit before quickly meeting another sharp descent. The penultimate climb of the morning led to the impressive 'Wainstones' where I removed my rucksack for a short scramble to the summit. Known locally as 'The Stones', this dramatic rocky outcrop is a prominent feature of the National Park with stunning views, both ahead and south to the heather moorlands, and northwards over the patchwork of fields extending into the yonder from the foot of the steep cliffs on my left.

Reunited with my rucksack, I was departing 'The Stones' when a couple of fell runners approached from the east and stopped for a chat.

"You look like a man on a mission," one of them quipped.

"I am, thanks. Hoping to reach Robin Hood's Bay on Friday."

"Ah, you're on the Coast-to-Coast. Always fancied hiking that. Never got round to it."

"Or you could run it," I replied, adding, "a runner passed me last week in the Lake District on his way to breaking the record for the quickest crossing. Less than 40 hours. I'm taking 14 days."

"Great effort. Well done you. Are you doing it for a charity?"

I shared the details of my charity page and the fact that I suffered from the disease I was supporting.

"We'll get on that and good luck. Nice to meet you," my energetic acquaintances pledged as they cantered off westwards.

The path was paved once more as it flattened out along the ridge of Hasty Bank. With a pleasant breeze piercing the hazy sunshine, the airy panoramic walk along the ridge was simply magical. The end of the ridge met a long descent through the ferny hillside to cross the B1257 at Clay Bank Top before immediately climbing steeply once more on paved steps. Amidst this ascent towards Carr Ridge, a handily placed wooden bench by a gate would provide the perfect lunch stop and an opportunity to top up on the Factor 30. My guidebook promised that on reaching Urra Moor shortly after lunch, it would be a relatively flat seven miles to the Lion Inn at Blakey Ridge. Following my sandwich and cup of tea, an extra spring in my step was also inevitable as I had booked a room and was anticipating the reprieve from tent-pitching and my first 'bed' since Kirkby Stephen Hostel back on Day 6.

The initial climb complete, the excellent paved track cut through the beautiful heather-clad open moorland on a barely noticeable gradient across Urra Moor. Arriving at a crossroads, Bloworth Junction, the large wooden signpost was in pristine condition and looked like it could've been erected yesterday. This intersection would mark a parting from the Cleveland Way as it headed northwards and my route continued eastwards for five miles onto Farndale Moor on the route of the former Rosedale Ironstone Railway, constructed over 150 years ago to ferry iron ore across the moor. Picking up the pace on this isolated wide sandy track, it meandered round the northern edge of Farndale Moor. There were continuous fabulous views down to the lush green valley forming a spectacular contrast between the dominating pinkish brown heather and the floor of verdure below.

The track seemed to go on forever and when a bend on the horizon was reached, the anticipation of seeing something different was short-lived as I was presented with another distant bend on the horizon. Passing some grouse butts, there was a stone marker clearly inscribed with the name "Sykes". My wandering mind pondered if this was the name given to these particular butts or the surname of the person who had ownership of them. Thinking of characters named Sykes, I envisaged Bill, Charles Dickens' angry antagonist from Oliver Twist, shooting a game bird and sending his terrier Bullseye out to collect it. On a more light-hearted notion, we could've had the late great Eric Sykes and Hattie Jacques encountering some grouse-shooting mishaps in an episode of his eponymous long-running 70's sitcom.
Yes, I had perhaps been out in the fresh air of the exposed moor for too long.

The track passed south of the source of the River Esk, a name familiar enough for me to confirm that it was a namesake of other waterways in Scotland and Cumbria and not the same one. Eventually one of those bends on the horizon did provide a different view when the Lion Inn came into view and half a mile later and before 3pm, I was bidding farewell to the former railway line and ascending a boggy path to my accommodation on the Blakey Ridge, the highest point of a 15-mile stretch of road across the moors, a very popular driving route amongst car enthusiasts.

The Lion Inn was built in the 16th century and had functioned as an inn for over four centuries. Located at an elevation of 1,325 feet and referred to as the 4th highest pub in England, the panoramic views over the local valleys were evident as I located the main entrance amongst the several adjoining red-roofed old stone buildings. Camping was officially not allowed, but for a nominal fee was tolerated in the grassed area behind the inn for Coast-to-Coasters only with back door access to a shower and toilet. The 'Coast-to-Coast only' rule allegedly came about as a result of some parsimonious Teessiders enjoying cheap accommodation after a night on the sauce.

The interior of this historic inn was delightful with several inter-connected sections and low beam ceilings, complemented with the pervading aroma of pub grub to add to the authenticity. I was allocated a room on the first floor and after collecting my holdall from a small passageway towards the rear, ascended a very narrow staircase to a small landing with four doors. Unlocking and entering the requisite door, I was presented with two cosy-looking beds, a double and a single and through another door on the left, an en-suite bathroom containing the 'jewel in the crown', a bath. As someone who enjoys a regular bath at home, it was a matter of priority that the hot water tap was turned on and the provided sachets of shower gel were utilised as bubble bath. A short time later with some admin complete, simplified when it doesn't involve setting up camp, my tired body was gratefully enveloped in warm soapy water. I had 'officially' traipsed 163 miles to get excited about reclining in an acrylic receptacle filled with hot water. Heavenly.

Half an hour of blissful suffusion later and I was sat wrapped in a towel on one of my beds, feeling rather indulgent. My room window overlooked the pub garden and almost immediately below my window at a picnic table sat Jono and Nick with beers and I couldn't resist popping my head out of the window.

"Excuse me, commoners, would you mind keeping the noise down in the cheap seats? Some hotel residents are trying to luxuriate in peace up here."

The London-based brothers grinned up at me, "Check you out, snob. Up there with your big holdall. Get your arse down here for a beer."

A few minutes later, I was sat having a beer with Jono, Nick and now also Dave who had joined the table. We shared tales of our day on the moors and I realised that a section of the population had never heard of Eric Sykes. Scandalous.

A gentleman, similar in age to my London-based friends, entered the beer garden, laden with rucksack and walking poles.

"There's Graham," Dave observed, beckoning his acquaintance to the table, "I was chatting with him the other day."

"Hi Graham. Come and join us," invited Dave to our new arrival.

Putting two tables together in a beer garden is a fairly simple act but it was a wonderful moment. Strangers from different walks of life and different parts of the country bonding by a common interest and mission. Sharing our similar experiences on our individual trips making for a great sense of camaraderie, assisted by the sunshine, the beer and some delicious chicken goujons, duly ordered from the snack menu.

The introductions around the table ascertained that Graham, a fellow solo hiker, was a farmer from the Nottingham area and had procured a couple of weeks of leave to tackle the Coast-to-Coast and we reciprocally went round the table introducing ourselves. I didn't know whether to take it as a compliment or not, but our new colleague intervened when the introductions reached myself.

"Hi, I'm Matt."

"On your own from Aberdeen?" Graham immediately enquired.

I paused and looked across at my land-working cohort, "Well, yes."

Graham smiled, "Yep, I've heard of you. You've came up in conversation."

"All good I hope?" I laughed.

"Absolutely," farmer Graham nodded.

Dan and Andrea, like myself, also had a room booked and arrived shortly afterwards and our group now occupied a table for seven. More drinks were ordered in the late afternoon sunshine and conversation turned to our respective itineraries for the remainder of the expedition.

There were 29 miles remaining to Robin Hood's Bay and my pre-walk research revealed that one more long climb remained after leaving the village of Grosmont (pronounced Grow-mont) at the 13-and-a-half-mile point. A road climb, very steep at first, ascending over 800ft in less than two miles.

"Is everyone staying in Grosmont tomorrow night?" Jono enquired, "Only that leaves over 15 miles on Friday and apparently it's an uphill slog to start the day out of Grosmont."

"I'm booked into Intake Farm in Littlebeck," I replied, "It's a farm just over three miles past Grosmont and gets the climb out of the way tomorrow, leaving a final day 12 miles to the Bay. Judith runs the farm's B&B but also has a small camping area and access to a toilet and shower. It's in the middle of nowhere but she does an evening meal too. It's recommended on the forums."

Graham had accommodation already booked at a B&B in Grosmont and as he had to get back to Nottinghamshire for a function on Friday evening, would be setting off around 5am on Friday morning, not really any hardship for a farmer.

"That sounds like a plan, Matt. Do you have her number?" Dave enquired.

Passing the number onto Dave, he was straight on the phone and conversing with Judith, presumably.

"Yeh, that's fine," Dave stated down the phone and it looked like he would be joining me at Intake Farm. Dave continued on the phone, "Yeh, I know. That chap is actually sat here next to me at the Lion Inn."

After ending the call, Dave announced, "Just you and me, Matt," and, turning his glance to the London siblings, "at the moment."

Moments later, Jono was in a call with Judith, "Yes, thanks. For me and my brother, two tents," before concluding, "Yes, we know. They're actually sat here next to us at the Lion Inn."

Following his booking, Jono reminded us that Judith did not run a licensed establishment and of her consequent advice to obtain any alcohol requirements en route in Grosmont.

With the time around 5.30pm, thoughts turned to evening sustenance and a table for five was reserved within the Inn for 7pm, Dan and Andrea having already booked for later. This afforded the opportunity for my dinner dates to organize their camping facilities to the rear of the establishment whilst I retired upstairs to my room to relax before tea . . . on my real bed.

7pm and this lone hiker found himself at a table in the company of four other hikers enjoying a beer and perusing the menu. In continuation of the camaraderie felt in the beer garden, stories of similar experiences on the hike thus far were flowing effortlessly with enthusiastic narration met with knowing nods and laughter.

We were, perhaps, slightly unaware of the volume we were creating amongst fellow diners, when a member of staff, in the midst of compiling the order from an adjacent table, suddenly turned to our table and announced at a fair volume, "Gentlemen, this is a restaurant, not a pub!" before seamlessly returning to the task in hand.

Immediate silence enveloped our table, as five grown men with a combined age of around 200 years looked downwards like chastised school children.

Remaining in that chastised child mode, furtive accusatory glances were exchanged around the table.

"That was your fault," I whispered towards Graham, accompanied with a grin.

"Goodness me, she went from nought to a hundred in no time," Nick observed with a similar whisper, adding, "I think she'll find that as I can come in here and buy beer without ordering food that it's actually a pub that does food, not a restaurant."

Following concurring gestures from around the table, I turned to Nick.

"That's a fair point, Nick, but I think we'll let you take that point up with her on our behalf," eliciting stifled laughter

The same member of staff, who had undoubtedly dealt with excitable Coast-to-Coast hikers nearing the end of their pilgrimage on an almost daily basis, returned to our table shortly afterwards.

"Good evening, gents. How are you? What can we get you this evening?"

Recommending the 'parmo' to my new friends like I was a seasoned local, I ordered my second 'parmo' of the trip, a choice echoed by a couple of others. When in Rome.

On completion of our meal, we retired to the 'Snug Bar' in this most attractive and traditional establishment for a nightcap . . . or two, where we met up once more with Dan and Andrea.

Dan advised that following our earlier discussion regarding Intake Farm, they had also booked a pitch but would possibly be dining later to assist Judith with logistics. A few hours earlier, there was one tent booked into Intake Farm. Now there were five tents and six

people for dinner.
An earlier comment from Nick was proving accurate. The journey was certainly reaching a final night crescendo.

I climbed into my real bed upstairs with a quick perusal of Mr Wainwright's literature ahead of my penultimate day on his epic walk. As I turned out the light, a final thought once more turned to the correspondence forwarded to Joanne on the eve of my adventure, which would surely be inconsequential, I wholeheartedly hoped.

Day 13 – Blakey Ridge to Littlebeck

Back in my early RAF days, I learned that if officers resident in the Officers' Mess required baked beans at breakfast, they would have to acquire and pay for them themselves as baked beans were foodstuff considered to be "unbecoming of an officer." Similar, albeit less draconian dogma applied to my ulcerative colitis as I negotiated a labyrinth of low ceilings to the breakfast dining area and enjoyed my first full English of the entire trip, minus the aforementioned plebeian pulses.

It all felt rather grandiose, being served a hearty hot meal in the morning at my table with a proper little pot of tea, after climbing off a comfy mattress. However, with the previous afternoon's aperitifs, drinks with dinner and nightcaps, I'm sure I would have slept just as comfortably under canvas out back with the guys. The plus-side of sleeping in a real bed was the resultant lack of morning rigmarole involving the packing away of camping gear.

Returning upstairs to sort things out for the day, my holdall was returned to the pick-up area and I was heading out onto the moor for my penultimate day of walking amidst a cool morning breeze. With plenty of fuel on board courtesy of the excellent Lion Inn kitchen brigade, the plan was to pick up some light lunch in the village shop in Glaisdale at the 10-mile point of today's hike.

I headed due north for a mile and a half on the wide verge of the Blakey Ridge Road before turning eastwards onto Knott Road, looking back towards the shrinking Lion Inn on the blurry horizon across the valley. Soon, just a few metres off the road, I encountered a shaped rock known as Fat Betty.

Fat Betty resembled a shorter than usual triangulation point with a wider than usual girth. Atop this four-foot-tall stone was a form of Celtic cross carved into an attached circular stone. The top half of this 1000-year-old Grade 2 listed piece of stone (yes, seriously) was painted white, helping it to stand out amongst the surrounding grass and heather and believed to be a way marker for travellers on the moor. A tradition over hundreds of years has been to leave a food offering and take a food offering to "aid sustenance to travellers in

need", a statement as illogical and mystifying as the reasons why the millennium-old monument came to be named after curvy Elizabeth with her few extra pounds in the first place.
A fairly crushed packet of McCoys (other brands are available) crinkle-cut crisps that had been tucked away in my rucksack for some time would provide my offering. I wasn't too enamoured by the reciprocal and somewhat eclectic choices available in this 1000-year-old version of Multi-Coloured Swap Shop (it was a tv programme on a Saturday morning back in the day . . . . oh, never mind). There was a Viscount chocolate biscuit, readily identifiable by its distinctive green circular foil wrapping. An individually wrapped boiled sweet looked forlorn and detached from its friends and an entire packet of high-protein energy bars suggested that someone was uber-confident about their daily hike . . . or had given up already. My particular favourite was a small wrapped circular bar of soap looking very inedible and uncannily like the soap I had been using in my room at the Lion Inn. Despite the fact that in my military career, I had met many comrades whose industrial terminology may have figuratively benefitted from eating a bar of soap, I was somewhat perplexed as to why a resident at a hotel would plunder the complimentary toiletries, only to pointlessly surrender them a short time later in the name of a centuries-old meaningless tradition. It was time to move on.

Re-joining Knotts Road, a fellow solo hiker was simultaneously passing and we began walking together as I explained the intricacies of millennium-old traditions regarding local obelisks. After a few minutes ascertaining that he was also on the Coast-to-Coast and that we appeared to be of a comparable walking pace, I was unknowingly embarking on the longest section of the entire mission spent in company.
Alan had hiked to the Lion Inn where his farmhouse bed and breakfast provider picked him up and duly dropped him back this morning for his next stage to Grosmont. The next three hours would be spent in the convivial company of the bespectacled gent of a slightly younger age (I guessed) from Leeds as the Wainwright journey traced the River Esk (other River Esks are available). The conversation flowed as easily as the miles whilst we negotiated the stony track across the brilliantly-named Great Fryup Dale before a barely appreciable ascent over Glaisdale High Moor, followed by a gradual descent on Glaisdale Rigg to the village of Glaisdale itself.

Alan's marriage had ended unexpectedly some four years previously and he had struggled for a while but was now in a place where he would "get back out there" and undertake new challenges and experiences and get on with his life. I obviously had complete empathy for his situation, describing my own recent past and jocularly suggesting my timeline was over three years ahead of his.

The weathered 'Welcome to Glaisdale' signpost proudly advertised the settlement's past glory of "Northern Village of the Year – 2002" and now was surely a constant reminder to the locals that for the past 19 years, it wasn't.
The village shop provided a sandwich and a drink for lunch and Alan pushed on as I took a seat on a convenient bench opposite. Now off the moor, the weather was markedly improved as the sunshine became more prevalent. Preparing to set off once more a short time later, Dan and Andrea arrived in the village with similar lunchtime plans and took over my bench.

A back road descends down to the village train station with welcome toilet facilities before a very short detour under a railway bridge leads to the Beggar's Bridge, a 17th century single arched packhorse bridge built by wealthy local merchant Tom Ferris. Legend says that a poor young Tom's proposal to Agnes Richardson was turned down by her father on account of him being a 'beggar'. Tom decided to head to sea to make his fortune and before leaving was unable, due to high water levels, to cross the River Esk to say goodbye to his love. When he returned a rich man years later, he married Agnes and built the bridge in order that future lovers wouldn't be parted. My inquisitive mind failed to see how he couldn't just have waited for the water levels to drop before heading off, or indeed how powerful his love was that he hadn't considered a quick doggy-paddle across the 10-metre span of river Anyway, thankfully on his return to North Yorkshire, he was considered rich enough by Mr Richardson to marry his daughter. How romantic.

Returning under the railway, the trail leaves Glaisdale via a small bridge over a stream and climbs through pretty East Arncliffe Wood on a path, the make-up of which fluctuated between slabs, railway sleepers and mud. Emerging from the trees onto a country lane, this quiet road was followed downhill towards the village of Egton Bridge. On entering the outskirts of the village, some activity was going on to my left in a large garden area to the front of a building, the

Horseshoe Hotel. A fast-food and bar hut had been set up in the grassed area and several picnic tables were occupied with chatting patrons. I was hiking past on the road when I noticed a familiar face at one of the tables waving at me. After spending three hours in Alan's company, it felt almost predestined that we would enjoy a pint together. With only a couple of miles to his daily destination at Grosmont, Alan ordered some food and another drink, but with my destination at Littlebeck a further four miles on, I would push on.

Passing an old mill and shortly after crossing the village's eponymous bridge, an opening through a closed gated entrance afforded a glimpse to the rear of opulent Egton Manor, another addition to the list of Grade 2 listed buildings on the journey. Only 100 yards on, I turned right through an open gate onto Barnard's Road, an old gravel toll road through the Egton Estate to Grosmont. Mounted on the wall was a small signpost, dated August 1948, advising of the applicable toll fees, ranging from four pennies for a horse-drawn two-wheel vehicle to three shillings for a "motor bus". It appeared that pedestrians in the year 2021 received free passage and over a mile later, the track joined a country lane, Front Street, leading into Grosmont via the village cricket club and under a railway bridge.
Dominated by iron ore extraction and ironworks in the mid-1800s, Grosmont was a hive of industry but was now a peaceful attractive village. The village was also the point where the River Esk disconnected from the Coast-to-Coast, flowing north-east on its final few miles to rendezvous with the North Sea at Whitby, some six miles north of my own scheduled appointment with the shoreline the following day.

These days, the focal point of the village was the North Yorkshire Moors Railway crossing the main thoroughfare via a level crossing at the end of the station platform. The adjoining platform on the Esk Valley line was scheduled to be an early port of call on my train from Whitby to Newcastle two days hence. I had previously passed through this station some 13 years earlier on the steam train from Pickering to Whitby on what was Number Three's third birthday during a family holiday near Scarborough.

Occupying a building immediately opposite the train station, Britain's oldest "coapy" has been serving the local community since 1867 and would be supplying the alcohol to accompany my evening meal at

Intake Farm. The charming interior of the shop featured lots of wooden shelving, some standalone, which made effective use of space. Standing at the wooden check-out desk armed with my rucksack and walking poles and clutching a bottle of red wine, the shop assistant smiled.

"Ok, what's going on?" she asked.

"I'm sorry?" I replied, somewhat confused, as I removed my rucksack from my shoulders

"You're the fourth hiker that has come in today and purchased a bottle of red wine. Is there something I should know?" she chuckled.

The penny dropped and I instinctively laughed.

"We're stopping over and having dinner at a farm near Littlebeck tonight. Our host advised us to bring our own drinks for dinner," I explained, "and I assume my three cohorts have already been in."

"Yes, that would certainly explain it," she nodded, as I swiped my debit card on the contactless reader.

With my mischievous tongue in my cheek, I continued, "I can't believe they didn't warn you that an extremely handsome Scotsman would be in later."

She laughed as I replaced the rucksack on my shoulders and made for the exit.

"I'll look forward to that Scotsman arriving."

It was my turn to laugh, adding, "Nope, you took too long to come back with that," and as I opened the door, "Cheers now."

Once across the level crossing, there was a fenced-off gravel garden containing several picnic tables. I recognised farmer Graham sat at one of the tables and joined him for a chat. Graham was staying at a local B&B, aiming for that 5am start to be back in Nottinghamshire in time for a function with his girlfriend. With the possibility that our paths may not cross on the concluding day, we shook hands, vowing to keep in touch.

With the village centre fairly sunken into the surrounding hillsides, departure from this picturesque settlement was, not unexpectedly, relentlessly uphill. Once quickly high above the village, a right turn was taken onto Fair Head Lane and during this seemingly endless ascent, a welcome breather was taken on an inviting wooden bench by the side of the road offering extensive views northwards across the Esk Valley As the road eventually began to even out as it crossed Sleights Moor, I passed the bronze age stone circle known as High Bride Stones, only two of which remained upright. A signposted path led off the road and across the moorland for almost half a mile to the A169 single-carriageway. From this elevated vantage point, the coastal town of Whitby with its hilltop abbey was clearly visible to the north, providing a tingle to my tiring body as it reminded me the end was nigh. Intake Farm was half a mile off the route and as recommended in my guidebook, I would be taking an intentional detour a short distance along the A169. Leaving the Coast-to-Coast before its descent into Littlebeck, I followed a track south-east around High Quebec Farm and Low Quebec Farm before a slight downhill traverse over a boggy field to my pastoral destination.

Knocking on the farmhouse door and introducing myself to jovial Judith, I was led around to a square-shaped level grassed area by the side of the house where three tents were already in place. Jono and Nick were lying on the grass enjoying the late afternoon sunshine and Dave was sat by his tent sorting out some kit.
"You didn't say there would be other people here, Judith," I uttered in a raised voice, "I couldn't possibly share with these riff-raff."
"Just put him over there in the corner, Judith," Nick joked.
"Nobody puts Matt in the corner," my instinctive reply, unsure if my younger colleagues had even heard of Patrick Swayze or Dirty Dancing.
"He'll need space for that big bag that he gets someone else to carry for him, Judith," Nick teased.
"An old man like me needs those little extras," I uttered in defence with a grin.
Sat upon a picnic table in the centre of the allocated camping area were two trays, each containing a tea pot, cups and plates. Whilst erecting my tent, Judith reappeared with a similar third tray, the plate containing a delicious piece of lemon sponge cake.
Subsequently enjoying my tea and cake, Dan and Andrea arrived at Intake Farm and set up in an additional grassed area to the rear of the house. Judith explained that for logistical reasons, there would need to be two sittings for dinner and it was agreed that the four gentlemen would dine first, allowing our married couple a romantic last night private dinner.

After taking our turns to enjoy the excellent showering facilities, the early evening arrived and we were shown through to a homely room within the house where a large dining table had been set up in the centre. The sideboards with their occupied plate display racks, the armchairs, framed old photos on the walls and the views of green through the large window all combined to create a warm feeling that we were having dinner at a friend's countryside home. Looking at her four guests each holding a bottle of wine, Judith laughed, "You'll be needing glasses then," and produced four wine glasses from the lower section of a sideboard.

The home-cooked cottage pie with plentiful accompanying vegetables was simply exquisite, enhanced by the convivial company and welcoming environment. The delicious apple pie and custard dessert was a challenge undertaken determinedly. The volume was maintained at a respectable level and there was no requirement for our host to remind us that we were in a farmhouse, not a pub.
Retiring outside to allow Dan and Andrea to enjoy similar fare before they re-joined us in the garden, a most enjoyable evening was spent reflecting and sharing more anecdotes from our respective adventures, past and present.

The sun began to lower in the sky and our wine was down to the dregs when I suddenly remembered what had remained hidden at the bottom of my holdall for a fortnight, waiting almost poetically for this climactic moment.
"Folks, this Scotsman has remembered that hidden in the bottom of my holdall is a little taste of home. A half-bottle of 10-year-old malt whisky, brought along to warm the cockles on a potential chilly night but never opened. I would love to open it now for us all to toast our adventure."
An immediate consensus was reached and there we were, utilising varying receptacles, enjoying a dram in the garden of a North Yorkshire farmhouse as the sun set on a memorable evening. A fitting last night finale to this elucidating experience on Wainwright's Coast-to-Coast.
Nick smiled, "Hey Matt, what a brilliant idea to have a courier carry those important little extras."
We laughed.

Inspirited with the warm glow of the "Water of Life" and the convivial company, I retired to my familiar dwelling for a final night's rest ahead of an anticipated emotional day.

If my behaviour had been cringeworthy in the early stages of the relationship, it almost paled into insignificance compared to my behaviour since Joanne ended the marriage in such a sudden and perverted manner.

Her unnecessarily vile comments on our sex life, literally just hours after shipping me out of our matrimonial home, only served to highlight her previous pointless and persistent platitudes throughout the years. This was quickly followed by her disturbing compulsion to provide me with a running commentary on her self-obsession as she continually strived to diagnose herself with more and more disorders.

I hadn't fully appreciated the sinister significance of her "pinch, punch, first of the month" text messages in March and April. It was only more recently looking back at the messages that I noted they had both been sent at 00:00 hours, not 23:59 or in the minutes after midnight. She had prepared the messages prior to midnight and hovered to ensure they were sent within the requisite 60-second window, illustrating how nefarious her pre-meditated actions were.

I had to acknowledge my own stupidity over the previous six months, clinging on to a hope that didn't exist. My shock and disbelief at my very sudden change of circumstances psychologically leading to my determined resistance to accept my situation. That lovesick behaviour had inevitably massaged her already over-inflated ego and encouraged her maternally inherited twisted nature to play with my broken state. I had foolishly allowed my blind hope to diminish the awfulness of her many wicked words.

Being told that seven years of my life had been "collateral damage". Being told daily throughout those years that she loved me. Being told that my incurable life-long condition constituted that "nothing was wrong with me". Being told by her that she "does miss me". Being told by her that she "loved me and wouldn't be looking to date anyone else" within six months of the marriage ending, like it was somehow virtuous.

The list went on.

And, to embarrassingly top it all off, my final act of lovelorn fatuity on the eve of this adventure.

Hi Joanne,

As we cross the 6-month threshold since that fateful November day and I cross the start line on my adventure, I've made sure I have enough batteries for my torch. The other torch I'll be carrying doesn't require batteries but it's time to place all my chips on the table and spin the wheel.

Of course, I'm only too well aware it's a daft long shot and I'm really not expecting anything, but as my Banksy picture reminds me every time I leave the house, hope is a good thing. One positive thing I've come to realise amidst this most horrible period of my life is that the only person who can take my hope away . . . is me. Hope is under my control.

Anyway, I won't ramble on (planning on doing enough of that over the next fortnight!) so please find enclosed:

1. *A route and map for a potential drive to Robin Hood's Bay on my final day.*

2. *Booking for Victoria Hotel, nice accommodation booked right next to the village car park overlooking the old village bay (short walk down to the finish).*

3. *My credit card to cover all expenses (PIN attached).*

4. *A stamped-addressed envelope to return my credit card, perhaps once you've stopped laughing at this attempt to woo my lady!*

Obviously I'm not expecting to see you but I would really appreciate it if you desisted from telling me you're not coming. Although I suppose it doesn't actually matter, referring to my comments above regarding hope . . . as I would still hope to see you there anyway! A fanciful pitch to create a most romantic moment and when it fails, I solemnly undertake to leave you be.

I do get terribly sad that you can't just use me for whatever in this short life,

Friend with benefits
Plus One
Lover
Boyfriend
Husband

I know, I know. . . you're looking for the "None of the above" option!

Regardless, I "hope" to see you.

An important and elucidating journey begins . . . .

Yours Aye

Matt
x

At the time of writing the note, my estimated probabilities reckoned there was a less than 1% chance that I would be in some form of relationship on my return and a more than 99% chance that I would be able to completely extinguish any faint hopes and wipe the slate clean in a definitive way.

I hadn't anticipated how I would be affected by this enlightening two-week exploit and how my ethos now viewed that 1% estimation as uncomfortably high.

My unambiguous plans for the completion of the adventure were on course and I remained totally convinced that no-one would be setting off in the morning from the north east of Scotland towards Robin Hood's Bay as a result of that regrettably inane pre-adventure correspondence.

Day 14 – Littlebeck to Robin Hood's Bay

As the crow flies, it was less than six miles from Littlebeck to Robin Hood's Bay but Mr Wainwright had us taking a nine-mile zig-zag scenic route to join the Cleveland Way at the coast followed by a concluding three-mile coastal cliff walk.

I was in no hurry to get away as I brewed up for a morning cup of tea and there was a poignancy about packing away my camping gear for the final time on this incredible journey. A seagull had made a deposit on the front of my tent in what was an auspicious reminder that I was nearing the sea. 180 miles into the walk and my mildly aching body was conveying to my brain that this would be the last day of walking. Sipping my tea in the morning sunshine, I contemplated that even allowing for the documented sense of humour failure on Day 4 at Angle Tarn, the whole thing had been a memorable experience I wouldn't forget.

All set to head off for the last time, I reported to the front door to drop off my holdall and settle up with Judith where I was greeted by a clowder of fetching felines dutifully waiting at the door for breakfast, presumably after another nightshift of striving to ensure the farm was rodent-free.

After a lengthy chat with my excellent host, I headed northwards and downhill for half a mile to rejoin the Coast-to-Coast in the tiny village of Littlebeck. After fording the Little Beck, the road climbs briefly, passing some aesthetically pleasing detached rustic homes complete with their landscaped gardens. A wooden sign advised that 'Falling Foss" was a mile away and directed me into Little Beck Wood Nature Reserve.

A pleasant walk ensued through the woods on wooden boardwalks and steps and small bridges over a couple of streams until a brief climb to The Hermitage. The Hermitage is basically a large boulder that has been hollowed out and made into a cavernous shelter with a doorway and seating ledge within. It reminded me of those occasions with Numbers One, Two and Three when heavy snowfall enabled the building of an igloo by way of hollowing out a huge ball of snow. With the initials "G.C." and "1790" carved conspicuously above the doorway, I fancied it would have taken local builder George Chubb slightly longer to construct with limited late 18th century technology than my snowy igloo in the early 21st century with my plastic shovel.

The path then descended to a bridge over a stream before another climb, during which I met a couple heading on a woodland walk with their two young children to The Hermitage. Another lengthy chat delayed my progress and admittedly there was some gratification when mentioning I was on the final day of a 200-mile walk, although I was pretty sure the kids were unimpressed with my endeavours as they just wanted to explore the woods. Reaching a road, I turned left and crossed a bridge, taking a short detour to visit the Falling Foss Tea Garden, a 21st century redevelopment of Midge Hall which had lain derelict for 50 years. It was a delightful spot in the trees above a 30ft waterfall and a quick cuppa was in order.

Continuing south through Little Beck Wood, the route tracked the east bank of May Beck for three quarters of a mile, reaching the May Beck Car Park before a sharp left turn onto a tarmac lane departed the last forestry of the Coast-to-Coast. A further three quarters of a mile on this road on a gradual uphill gradient reached a wooden finger post sending me onto boggy heather-clad Sneaton Low Moor. Despite the sustained period of dry weather, there was still some soggy ground to negotiate and thankfully a section of boardwalk enabled steady going. With clear views to the North Sea, I crossed the minor B1416 road and joined Graystone Hills, an innocuously named moor which again was very boggy. Some more boardwalk sections assisted progress and before descending down a stony track between high hedges, Whitby Abbey was once more visible on the southern side of its town. The track arrived at a country lane which was followed briefly until a first sign for Robin Hood's Bay sent me onto Back Lane towards the adjacent villages of Low and High Hawkser. The sign advised that my final destination was only three and a half miles away but thankfully, my prior research prevented any unexpected chagrin as this was the distance by road and I knew I had in fact over five miles to walk.

Low Hawkser consisted of a farm and a couple of houses and I continued along Back Lane to the more sizeable High Hawkser with its caravan park, hotel and pub. Trudging along beside a hedge and approaching an open gate on my left, I heard voices from the other side of the hedge.

"That will most probably be Matt," was a decipherable phrase.

Reaching the gate, I saw Dan and Andrea tucked into the corner of the field enjoying a rest and stopped for a very brief chat before moving on. Crossing amidst the Friday lunchtime traffic on the busy A171 Whitby-Scarborough road and skirting the south edge of High Hawkser, I headed uphill on a grassy roadside path. Branching left onto Bottoms Lane and heading towards the visible sea, I passed the private Seaview Holiday Park. The larger Northcliffe Caravan Park was reached minutes later and this less private affair advertised the Coast Café Bar and Shop, open to all. With a Coast-to-Coast sign intimating that only three miles of my quest remained, I took a seat at an inviting picnic table whereupon a waitress took my order for a sandwich. Asked whether my lunch would be accompanied by a hot drink or a beer helped me recognise that I had officially completed 189 miles of a 192-mile trail. There could only be one response to her enquiry and shortly after, I was enjoying my sandwich and my pint in the pleasant sunshine in a contemplative frame of mind as my adventure neared its conclusion.

It seemed a very long time ago that I was sat in the garden of the Fox and Hounds in Ennerdale Bridge on Day One with my first pint on the Coast-to-Coast. My observation back then about a rucksack and walking poles attracting discourse from strangers remained as extant 174 miles later.

"Cleveland Way or Coast-to-Coast?" the similarly-aged gentleman at an adjacent table enquired, with his first-mentioned route about to be re-joined on the clifftops in about 300 yards.

"Coast-to-Coast," I replied, and puffed out my cheeks to slowly exhale a lungful of breath, "Just about done and dusted."

"I did it three years ago and found it quite emotional towards the end. How do you feel?"

"Yeh, it's been quite a journey. I suppose I'll find it very strange, not hiking tomorrow, and not creeping ever closer to Robin Hood's Bay. Perhaps because of the pandemic, I didn't expect to meet and chat so much with so many nice people, both fellow hikers and locals, whether that be on the trail or in a pub . . . or sitting outside a café in a caravan park," I explained with a smile to my latest acquaintance.

I continued, "I've been recording notes on a voice recorder to help me differentiate between the days. One day, it may help me if I decide to write about my experience."

"All I remember is my aching legs, my beer at The Bay Hotel and my desire to start planning the next walk," he laughed as he stood to leave, adding, "Enjoy the last three miles and don't forget to sign the book at the hotel."

I set off downhill through an on-site road between rows of static caravans before joining a grassy path which led to a junction on the cliff-top and a reunion with the Cleveland Way I had parted from at Bloworth Junction two days earlier. The next two and a half miles would be spent enjoying views out to the North Sea as the path swivelled around the headland to meet the first residences of Robin Hood's Bay. En route, I stopped to update my voice recorder, a recording I would later listen to with the authentic and poignant background sound of waves rolling in to meet the shore:
"A beautiful day standing on the cliff tops of the Cleveland Way about a mile and a half from Robin Hood's Bay. Quite busy with families having picnics but still an atmosphere of peacefulness. Watching the North Sea washing the cliffs below me, and having spent the last fortnight getting here from the Irish Sea at St Bees, it's an amazing feeling, although I'm beginning to feel absolutely knackered. Think my brain is telling my body I'm just about finished. Looking forward to seeing the guys at the finish. A finish which I can turn into a beginning."

A few yards on, a gap in the bushes afforded the first glimpse of my destination. I recalled looking back from the cliff-top towards St Bees shortly after departure on that first morning and here my naked eye was looking at Robin Hood's Bay almost 200 miles later. A surge of emotion coursed through my veins. I was reminded of the similar terrain closer to home on the short Aberdeenshire Coastal Path where I undertook my first practice walks, realising I was on the very same coast, just a 200-mile crow flight south.

Passing through a gate, a path was followed along the front of some houses before a further gate accessed Mount Pleasant North, the first residential street encountered in Robin Hood's Bay. Mount Pleasant North led onto Station Road, opposite the Station Car Park but there was no train station in the village. Dr Beeching had decided, way back in 1963, that I would require a bus to catch my train at Whitby the following morning.
The impressive traditional frontage of the Victoria Hotel with its large conservatory and garden overlooking the old village was reached.

This would be tonight's rather salubrious accommodation. Crossing a mini-roundabout, a road sign indicated the end of the line for most vehicles with private parking only beyond that point and limited parking. A triangular warning sign reminded any drivers of the 30% hill ahead. I had no idea of the science employed to reach that figure, however "bloody steep descent ahead" would have sufficed.

This was it.

Busy with Friday afternoon tourists, the emotion was building as I proceeded down the steep and narrow lane on the final 300 yards of Wainwright's Coast-to-Coast. The mostly early 18th century buildings illustrated the historic need to squeeze as many shops and houses as possible in to the steep hillside. Small alleyways off to my left and right contained more tightly packed and variously shaped homes. It was a truly historic and beautiful village providing an exhilarating and fitting end to this epic ramble.

My triumphant traipse was interrupted by a familiar face coming up the hill towards me.
"Matt. You made it. Well done," my Nottinghamshire-based farming friend announced.
"You too, Graham," I reciprocally congratulated, shaking his hand.
"So good to meet you. Have a safe journey back to Scotland and keep in touch online," one of my newest social media friends advised.
"I certainly will, buddy, and enjoy the wedding dance tonight."
"Thanks Matt, the guys are down there waiting for you. Dave left earlier, but he says he'll see you on the TGO challenge next year. The rest of them have the best seat down there at the Bay Hotel, under the finish sign," Graham replied, and a grin came across his face as he added, "also, it doesn't look like there are any random women standing around waiting for someone either."
We laughed and parted on our separate ways.

Passing an ice-cream shop, complete with a large selection of buckets and spades hanging outside, provided a truly authentic seaside ambience amongst the visitors, some of whom were watching a young busker strumming his guitar in the pleasant sunshine and belting out some well-known tunes.

The modest but determinate slipway leading to the North Sea was sandwiched between two whitewashed buildings. These were the last two buildings on the Coast-to-Coast, the Old Coastguard Station Visitor Centre on my right and the Bay Hotel on my left with its sign above the doorway pertinently marking the entrance to Wainwright's Bar. Approaching the slipway to complete those last 20 yards and meet the high tide which was roughly lapping the cobbles, some cheering and applause broke out from one of the many occupied tables to the front of the Bay Hotel. There were the brothers Jono and Nick, together with Dan and Andrea who must have passed me as I was having my sandwich at the caravan park. A wave of my hand acknowledged their appreciated plaudits as I continued on the momentous final few steps to the water's edge, reminding myself that I was about to experience a moment to be treasured.

I slowly inhaled the sea air though my nose and exhaled through my mouth as I stood looking out towards the distant horizon over the great mass of water and felt an immense sense of achievement, tempered only slightly by the realisation that this superb adventure had come to an end.
Nick appeared behind me, "Well done Matt. Give me your phone and we'll do the duty pic thing."
After posing for some photos, I retrieved the small pebble I had garnered at St Bees 14 days earlier and, as Nick took video footage with my phone, hurled it into the North Sea.
Mission accomplished and tradition observed.

It was fortunate that the weather was favourable. Due to the cramped nature of the 18th century interior of the hotel bar, adherence with social distancing guidelines was problematic and only the external seating area was available, with drinks being served via a temporary counter at the entrance. Jono was standing at that entrance under the 'Wainwright's Bar' sign.
"Pint, Matt?"
My facial expression in reply required no words.
Just as Graham had advised, the London brothers, Dan, Andrea and myself were occupying the table immediately in front of the hotel's "finish" sign, a wooden oblong plaque attached to the wall embossed with the wording "Coast to Coast Walk, 192 miles. The end."
Another photograph was deferentially acquired, directly below this milestone marker, complete with celebratory beer in hand.

With the first beer "failing to touch the sides", I was soon making my own way to Wainwright's doorway to replenish the glasses on the table.

"Are you another Coast-to-Coaster with them?" the barman asked, tilting his head towards our table as I paid for the drinks. Following my affirmative reply, he reached to a shelf behind and picked up a large hardback bound book, adding, "You'll all need to be signing this then."

After delivering the drinks, I returned to the "door" and retrieved the Bay Hotel Coast-to-Coast Log Book and returned to the table.

Taking a fresh row on the page, I annotated my name and home town on the requisite columns and penned my comment.

"An amazing experience and a pleasure to meet so many fantastic people"

There was an undeniable emotion felt when affording myself a cursory glance at the previous entries annotated on the columns of the A3-sized hardback book:

George and Ryan from London;

Paul and Matthew from Northallerton;

Dave from Rotherham;

I had also noted the names Colin, Rob and Bruce from Moray and Suffolk, accompanied with the comment, *"A wonderful adventure enjoyed with the very best of friends and a lifetime of memories."*

With astonishing timing, I received a message just minutes later from Colin.

"Hi Matt, I assume you will be finishing sometime this afternoon if you haven't already. Hope you enjoyed the last few days. Don't forget to sign the finishers' book at the Bay Hotel. Was great to meet you. Give me a shout when you're up in Moray and we'll get a pint."

My reply to Colin was accompanied by a photo of the current page of the document showing my own entry below his.

"Great timing, Colin. Just recently finished. Great to meet you guys too. See you in due course."

Celebratory drinks and excitable conversation continued and a short time later, I looked out towards the aforementioned 'bucket and spade' ice-cream shop to see Alan appear through the holiday-makers and day-trippers towards his final triumphant few yards. Echoing the earlier scenes for myself, we broke into cheers and applause, acknowledged by Alan as he completed his adventure.

Just as Nick had done for myself, I joined Alan on the slipway to facilitate his commemorative photographs and he subsequently joined us at the best seat in the house.

My walking companion from the previous day insisted on buying drinks for the table, which I helped him transfer from the bar. As we continued to bask in our sense of achievement, there was a sudden period of incommunicado where my new-found friends collectively appeared to stop their interactions and turn to me.

Nick spoke up, almost like a spokesperson for the group.

"Well?"

"Well what?" I replied, before I scanned round the other apparent inquisitive faces at the table and chuckled on the realisation of the question being asked.

"Don't be ridiculous. She was never going to show. It was a symbolic gesture mainly for my own closure. Besides, I'm going to be half-pissed, fairly shortly," I proffered.

"Bet you still breathed a sigh of relief though," added Alan, before adding, "this adventure ends here, Matt, and a new one will surely begin."

By late afternoon, Dan, Andrea, Nick and Jono were all scheduled to be heading back southwards with Alan heading back towards Leeds. A "one for the road" was duly enjoyed by the Coast-to-Coast 'crew' before we ascended the hill back up to Station Road. After those celebratory drinks, this may well have been one the most difficult ascents of the last two weeks. On reaching my hotel, my friends would be turning left onto Thorpe Lane to catch a scheduled bus to Whitby or Scarborough for onward rail connections. As with Graham earlier, a fond farewell ensued with hugs all round and a concordance to remain in touch through social media.

Suddenly, it was just me, alone in Robin Hood's Bay, standing in front of my hotel. Having spent the previous two weeks alone with my thoughts, there was great comfort to be had on realising I was very much at ease.

The Victoria Hotel was the quintessential British seaside hotel, its prominent hilltop position affording spectacular views out to sea. After a short wait at reception, my necessary little white lie advised that my wife had been delayed and possibly would not be able to join me this evening.

"Not a problem, Mr McKay. I'll assume by your attire and rucksack that you don't require a pass for the car park opposite. If you need one later for your wife, come and see us," the attentive receptionist advised. "Have you stayed with us before, Mr McKay?" My negative reply resulted in being taken on a brief informative tour of the hotel en route to my room, a reminder that I wasn't in any well-known budget chain of hotels. A further reminder occurred when I enquired about my couriered holdall.
"That will be in your room, sir."

Built in 1897, the current proprietors had owned the establishment for 11 years. As I was shown the hotel restaurant, my word for today would be 'orangery'. Hitherto, I would have referred to the airy dining area as an oversized conservatory, but an 'orangery' was historically a building set aside in stylish homes to protect fruit trees in winter. My room was reached by ascending the two floors via the staircase with its ostentatious wooden balustrades. The solid wooden bedframe housing a very comfortable-looking mattress was ever so inviting but the two sets of towels and toiletries thereon reminded me it was time to "sit" in the shower . . . for about an hour.

Taking my table for dinner in the evening, I was looking out through the 'orangery' to the clifftop hotel garden with its plentiful picnic tables and beyond them to the distant village of Ravenscar on the cliffs at the opposite end of the bay. The air was gently filled with the tuneful sound of some well-known romantic hits as the resident pianist tastefully tickled the ivories of the resident piano. The swing-top frosted glass bottle of water on my table, swankily adorned with the hotel's logo, enhanced the gentility of my celebratory supper. Enjoyment of my chicken liver parfait starter, ahead of my steak and ale pie, was temporarily accompanied by the music of Christina Perri's "A Thousand Years".
Rather than inflict metacarpal fractures on the innocent local musician, I afforded myself an ironic grin and shake of my head as the song that played its part at the very beginning was now playing a cathartic almost symmetrical part at the end.

The subsequent music of Bryan Adams' "(Everything I Do), I Do It for You" didn't escape a further ironic grin, considering the name of the village I was in.

Moving outside into the pleasant evening air after my triumphal treat, I would take a rucksack-free saunter around the upper part of the village. The historic railway station buildings survive as bed and breakfast accommodation and my stroll returned via the aforementioned Thorpe Lane, passing the Victorian edifice of St Stephen's Church. The Victoria Hotel Public Bar occupied the north side of the ground floor and once inside, I was able to procure a seat within the ambient surroundings for a nightcap.

As I sat alone in the bar, it felt like an opportunity for a private toast in acknowledgement of just some of the many people who had helped in their diversified ways to make this whole experience unforgettable:
The three 'drunkest men in England' on the eve of the walk;
My England-supporting fellow diner on the first day whose e-mail about blogging I still await;
The many encounters with "two ladies" on the first half of the walk;
The serendipitous evening with the beautiful Natasha at the Borrowdale youth hostel;
My interesting encounters with friends of a bovine persuasion;
The unexpected honour of spending an evening in the company of Mr John Owen, MBE, in Shap;
Those last precious few hours with my old faithful boots before they had to regenerate, Dr Who style in Kirkby Stephen;
My parting pints with George and Ryan at Keld;
The sense of achievement on eliciting conversation from "Blondie" on Gunnerside Moor;
My "entertaining" evening, in many ways, at Reeth;
My lovely 'family' welcome at Brompton-on-Swale;
The super hospitality at Church Holme campsite in Danby Wiske;
My many meetings with the River Swale, knowing it was the fastest-flowing river in England . . . apparently;
That uber-cheerful cyclist near Oaktree Hill, who re-invigorated a tiring day;
The slightly exasperated chef at the Bluebell Inn, Ingleby Cross;
My impromptu game of 'musical tents' at Lord Stones Country Park inadvertently leading to my rapport with Mark and his family;
Dinner and drinks with friends at the Lion Inn on Blakey Ridge;
Walking with Alan to Glaisdale;
A fitting 'Scotch' finale after enjoying Judith's hospitality at Littlebeck.

Other patrons may have wondered why the guy sitting on his own with his pint was emitting random smiles and grins, unaware that he was conducting his private mini-review of the past fortnight.
The same preceding fortnight and associated emotion was taking its toll and, with a comfy-looking bed awaiting, my return upstairs was imminent.

Whilst posting duty pictures on Facebook to mark the completion of my quest, I felt it appropriate to treat social media seriously for all the right reasons as I set up a complete block on my estranged wife on all electronic connections. A purposeful step in a new direction.

The Final "Fling"

Following a surprisingly peaceful sleep, a short Saturday morning bus ride would transport me to Whitby train station where I was catching the noon departure for Newcastle.

Before catching that bus, there remained one final early morning tasking in Robin Hood's Bay.

With a tangible sense of purpose, I retraced my steps down to the famous terminal slipway adjacent to the Bay Hotel and once more liaised directly with the North Sea.
Not laden with a rucksack on this occasion but rather just a few grammes of Celtic silver which had accompanied me all the way from the rear of a drawer on my bedside cabinet to St Bees and then across the north of England. With much less poignancy than anticipated prior to the adventure, I removed the small and formerly precious cargo from my pocket and with one small throw, metaphorically consigned eight years of my life into a watery grave.
I paused briefly, recalling the moment in the movie "Love Actually" when Andrew Lincoln walks away from Keira Knightley's threshold, placards tucked under his arm.
"Enough . . . enough now."

Eight years was the sentence. Eight years of my life I would never get back. A part of me would take a little consolation that it was only eight years, as previous husband Dave had been conned out of over twenty years.
Joanne's ego had been keen to point out on numerous occasions during those eight years that she had made good decisions in her life. Also pointing out openly that I had not, she was of course correct that I had made some less than wise decisions in my life. Failing to heed her endless litany of red flags throughout that inaugural summer of 2013 and throughout the following years was high on the list.
However, at the top of the list of poor decisions were events of the 29th day of February in 2016. The instinctive realisation that

hesitation at that pivotal moment could have potentially ended our relationship. In the most ironic retrospect, it could be argued that being less of a 'nice guy' and not doing the right thing could have saved me five years of that sentence.

My regular misplaced trust and forgiveness of Joanne was also unable to benefit from hindsight.

Love is certainly blind, and I realised that the constant sweet nothings I had enjoyed hearing over the years had ultimately and sadly been manipulative and controlling, and I had to acknowledge my own culpability in allowing this to happen and my ultimately misguided belief that she was genuine and sincere.

Despite her penchant for self-diagnosis of various disorders, I also had to acknowledge her proficiency in passing herself off to all and sundry as a warm and caring person. With her complete dearth of emotional intelligence and awareness, as regularly demonstrated, I was glad she had recognized the need to seek regular specialist psychological help. However, the continued thoughtless and cruel behaviour during these months of therapy had evidently cast doubt on the effectiveness of the treatment she was receiving.

Notwithstanding that, I had genuinely hoped that she would reach a more stable mental disposition by taking the time to grieve for ending another marriage.

Alas, having removed her opportunity to manipulate me through social media posts and private online messages, and with her predilection towards impulsive behaviour combined with the need to feed her incurable narcissism, taking time to grieve would never be on the cards. It was all too obvious that within weeks, she would be rushing into another relationship with the next man she took a shine to, highlighting just how pathetic her statement to Patricia had been concerning potential dating, only weeks earlier.

Whispering the same sweet nothings and manipulating control of the poor man, I could empathise with his susceptiveness, as Joanne had ably demonstrated her prowess at deception over the years. Those years of constantly hearing "I hate not having you in my bed" when, with the benefit of hindsight, the word "you" ultimately meant "anyone".

As a potential added bonus, Joanne would be hoping that a friendly ex-wife was in the background for her paranoia to manufacture another misconceived and unnecessary control over.

Squeak, our dearly departed little Bichon Frise, would sadly be replaced in an even quicker time and her combined behaviours would clearly render all of her psychological therapy an unequivocal waste of time and money.

Equally as disturbing, those same characteristics would also account for her harrowing and outright disregard for the destruction left behind in her wake and any future collateral damage to her new prey. I had no doubts that he would be a most amiable gent who, like myself, would be completely duped by Joanne's consistent fakery and I certainly couldn't fault the man. It was also hoped, for his sake, that he would be in a sound and healthy financial situation, albeit only serving to prolong the charade.

As a supposedly mature woman in her late 50's who had recently ended the relatively short marriage she had so duplicitously proposed, her subsequent desperation to share her latest conquest with the world on social media would inevitably cause much hidden embarrassment to her friends and family. Sadly, Joanne being Joanne, she wouldn't care a jot.

It would also serve to remind me that this particular 'table lamp' had been ultimately blessed with a fortuitous escape and quickly replaced with a new item of furniture which would be dusted, polished and used for as long as it was required.

Moreover, and most significantly for myself moving forward, it was time to take stock.
As any competent counsellor would have helped me to understand, I had plummeted down the 'The Waterfall of Bereavement', and I was ready to finish tackling the 'Whirlpool of Grief', mourn the wasted years, accept my own part in them and, in time, emerge reorganized and hopefully wiser on 'The River of Life'.

Perhaps one day in years ahead, I may even find the courage to trust someone again. In the meantime, I would take the opportunity to seek new solo adventures, to gain a better understanding of who I was, to grow, to continue to appreciate the beauty and genuine kindness in the world and the blessing of having wonderful friends and family.

The noon-departure to Newcastle began to pull away slowly from the platform, initiating a cathartic sense that two eventful journeys of very differing durations had reached their simultaneous conclusions.

I settled down to reflect on my Coast-to-Coast adventure and to ponder on the new phase of my life about to unfold. Taking out my small notepad and pen, I titled a fresh page with two simple words to signify the beginning of another new journey.

"Day One".

Printed in Great Britain
by Amazon